ACCLAIM F

"The awesome power of faith and family over personal desire dominates this beautifully woven masterpiece."

—*PUBLISHERS WEEKLY*, STARRED REVIEW FOR *THE BEEKEEPER'S SON*

"A moving and compelling tale about the power of grace and forgiveness that reminds us how we become strongest in our most broken moments."

—*LIBRARY JOURNAL* FOR *UPON A SPRING BREEZE*

"Irvin has given her audience a continuation of *The Beekeeper's Son* with complicated young characters who must define themselves."

—*RT BOOK REVIEWS*, 4-STAR REVIEW OF *THE BISHOP'S SON*

"*The Beekeeper's Son* is so well crafted. Each character is richly layered. I found myself deeply invested in the lives of both the King and Lantz families. I struggled as they struggled, laughed as they laughed—and even cried as they cried . . . This is one of the best novels I have read in the last six months. It's a refreshing read and worth every penny. *The Beekeeper's Son* is a keeper for your bookshelf!"

—DESTINATION AMISH

"Kelly Irvin's *The Beekeeper's Son* is a beautiful story of faith, hope, and second chances. Her characters are so real that they feel like old friends. Once you open the book, you won't put it down until you've reached the last page."

—AMY CLIPSTON, BESTSELLING AUTHOR OF *A GIFT OF GRACE*

"*The Beekeeper's Son* is a perfect depiction of how God makes all things beautiful in His way. Rich with vivid descriptions and characters you can immediately relate to, Kelly Irvin's book is a must-read for Amish fans."

—RUTH REID, BESTSELLING AUTHOR OF *A MIRACLE OF HOPE*

THE SADDLE MAKER'S SON

OTHER BOOKS BY KELLY IRVIN

The Every Amish Season Novels

Upon a Spring Breeze

Beneath the Summer Sun

Through the Autumn Air (available August 2018)

The Amish of Bee County Novels

The Beekeeper's Son

The Bishop's Son

The Saddle Maker's Son

Novellas by Kelly Irvin

A Christmas Visitor included in *An Amish Christmas Gift*

Sweeter than Honey included in *An Amish Market*

A Christmas Visitor included in *An Amish Winter*

Snow Angels included in *An Amish Christmas Love*

One Sweet Kiss included in *An Amish Summer*

The Midwife's Dream included in *An Amish Heirloom*

The Saddle Maker's Son

KELLY IRVIN

ZONDERVAN

The Saddle Maker's Son

This title is also available as a Zondervan e-book.
Visit www.zondervan.com.

Requests for information should be addressed to:
Zondervan, *Grand Rapids, Michigan 49546*

ISBN 978-0-7852-1711-4 (repack)

Names: Irvin, Kelly, author.
Title: The saddle maker's son / Kelly Irvin.
Description: Grand Rapids, Michigan: Zondervan, [2016] | Series: The Amish of Bee County; 3
Identifiers: LCCN 2015050327 | ISBN 9780310339861 (paperback)
Subjects: LCSH: Amish—Fiction. | GSAFD: Love stories. | Christian fiction.
Classification: LCC PS3609.R82 S23 2016 | DDC 813/.6—dc23 LC record available at http://lccn.loc.gov/2015050327

Interior design: James Phinney

Then people brought little children to Jesus for him to place his hands on them and pray for them. But the disciples rebuked them. Jesus said, "Let the little children come to me, and do not hinder them, for the kingdom of heaven belongs to such as these."

MATTHEW 19:13–14

As a mother comforts her child, so will I comfort you.

ISAIAH 66:13

To Tim, Nicholas and Angelica, Erin and Shawn, and the little ones, Brooklyn and Carson. You are the reason I rise in the morning each day. Love always.

— *DEUTSCH* VOCABULARY* —

aenti: aunt
Ausbund: Amish hymnbook
bopli, boplin: baby, babies
bruder: brother
daed: father
danki: thank you
dawdy haus: grandparents' house
dochder: daughter
doplisch: clumsy
Englischer: English or non-Amish
fraa: wife
Gott: God
groossdaadi: grandpa
groossmammi: grandma
gut: good
hund: dog
jah: yes
kaffi: coffee
kinner: children

lieb: love
mann: husband
meidung: avoidance, shunning
mudder: mother
nee: no
onkel: uncle
Ordnung: written and unwritten rules in an Amish district
rumspringa: period of running around
schtinkich: stink, stinky
schweschder: sister
suh: son
wunderbarr: wonderful

*The German dialect spoken by the Amish is not a written language and varies depending on the location and origin of the settlement. These spellings are approximations. Most Amish children learn English after they start school. They also learn high German, which is used in their Sunday services.

— FEATURED BEE COUNTY — AMISH FAMILIES

Mordecai and Abigail King
Abram (and wife, Theresa)
Phineas (and wife, Deborah; children: Timothy and Melinda)
Samuel
Jacob
Rebekah (Abigail's daughter)
Caleb (Abigail's son)
Hazel (Abigail's daughter)
Susan King (Mordecai's sister)

Leroy and Naomi Glick
Adam (and wife, Esther [Mordecai's daughter])
Jesse (and wife, Leila [Abigail's daughter]; children: Grace and Emmanuel)
Joseph
Simon
Sally
Mary
Elizabeth

Will (minister) (and wife, Isabella [Aaron Shrock's daughter])

Aaron and Jolene Shrock

Matthew
John
James
Molly
Amanda

Stephen and Ruth Anne Stetler
Joseph
Hannah

Levi Byler (widower)
Tobias
David
Martha
Milo
Rueben
Micah
Ida
Nyla
Liam

Jeremiah (bishop) and Lena Hostetler
Vesta
Elijah
Rachel
Susie
Phillip
Noah
Annie
Mary
Henry
Moses

A NOTE TO READERS OF THE AMISH OF BEE COUNTY SERIES

If you wonder whatever happened to the Lantz sisters' cousin Franny, be sure to look for the novella *A Christmas Visitor* in the anthology *An Amish Christmas Gift*. Franny finds true love all her own. Those readers who are feeling a little sorry for Will Glick, who didn't get the girl not once but twice, worry no more. Read the *Sweeter than Honey* novella in the anthology *The Amish Market*. Will finds the woman he's been waiting for all along. Happy reading!

ONE

Alone at last. Rebekah Lantz tugged the creaking shed door shut and leaned against it. The folded piece of paper from her sister Leila weighed heavy as a stone in her hand. When had she managed to tuck it into the two-seater Rebekah drove with Susan to and from the school five days a week? Did she slip in while Rebekah was listening to the younger scholars read aloud? Surely not. Leila had a baby daughter to think about now and a husband. She couldn't be roaming the countryside delivering notes.

The fact that she had done just that made Rebekah's stomach rock. Guilt swirled there, mixing with a swelling ache to see her sister and a baby niece who would see her *aenti* as a stranger. A Plain woman such as herself should forgive. No matter how much Leila's decision to leave hurt. No matter how it left Rebekah with little chance of finding love herself among the young men who looked at her and knew exactly what Leila had done.

Just because Leila had given up everything to follow Jesse into the *Englisch* world didn't mean Rebekah would leave too. She longed to scream out those words at the next singing. Put them to music. Write her own song. Still, it wouldn't change the look on the faces of those boys she'd known her entire life. Deer caught in the headlights of an Englisch truck barreling toward them on the highway.

She had to open the note, read it. Its weight seemed to increase as each second ticked by. The cracks in the weathered boards of the shed allowed afternoon sun to filter through in stripes like bars. The April sun was warm, as if reminding Rebekah Texas didn't wait around for summer like the northern states did. Her eyes adjusted to the dusky interior after a few seconds. The smells of mold, decaying wood, and dirt floated in the air. Old egg crates, a broken desk, a stack of chairs, a wooden door with white peeling paint filled the small room.

She wasn't a coward.

Swallowing against the knot of apprehension that always choked her when she did something of which her *mudder* would not approve, Rebekah unfolded the single sheet of notebook paper and peered at Leila's neat block writing.

> Dear *schweschder*,
>
> Hope you are well. We must meet. I need to talk to you face-to-face. Come to where the school path meets the road Friday at lunch. I'll be driving the green VW Bug. Can you believe I drive? Give Hazel a kiss for me.
>
> Love,
> Leila

Inhaling the ripe scents that reminded her of how everything returned to the earth in the end, Rebekah reread the note a second time. Leila skipped along in life with nary a thought for how her actions affected others. Abdicating her family. Or inviting Rebekah to a meeting that would cause her great trouble if Mudder or Mordecai found out.

Rebekah's job as an aide to Susan King wasn't much, but it was all she had. She would never be allowed to get a job in town. Every day since that Christmas Eve two years ago, Mudder and Mordecai had watched Rebekah, never letting her go far from their sight, as if waiting for her to take flight too.

Mudder blamed Leila's exposure to the Englisch world while working at the day care in town for all her actions. Not love. For surely it was love that made a person do these strange, inexplicable things. Rebekah wouldn't know. How could she when the boys avoided her like poison ivy? At nineteen, Rebekah had no special friend and no chance of having one.

Pressing the note to her chest, she closed eyes that burned with tears she refused to shed. In the two years since Leila had left, Rebekah had never seen her sister or the baby Grace, now ten months old. Why now? And with such short notice? Plenty of time to forgive and forget, as she was called to do. Yet here she stood with pain and anger barricaded together behind the walls of a hardened heart.

She had to see Leila. If for no other reason than to say those words. Saying them was the first step in letting the past go. Leastways, that was what the bishop would say.

A sound, like a muffled sneeze, broke the silence. Rebekah jumped and dropped the note.

The one place she'd thought to be alone.

"Hello?"

Nothing. Apprehension filled her lungs, making it hard to breathe. Her heart pounded. Rebekah scooped up the note and took two steps back. She put her shaking hand on a broken desk that leaned against the wall. "Who's there?"

Something or someone scuttled along the far wall behind the

stack of egg crates. Rebekah took a step toward the door. "I know you're there. I'll go outside and you can come out. I won't hurt you."

Such bravado.

What if a prisoner had escaped from the prison near Beeville again? Memories of her brother-in-law Phineas's bruised face and bloodied arm spun through her mind's eye. Phineas and Deborah had escaped and the prisoner from the McConnell Unit had been captured, but not before damage had been done.

She whirled, jerked open the door, and stumbled into the fresh air and light.

A young girl shot past her, dragging a little boy by the hand. The boy, dressed in faded blue jeans and a gray T-shirt that might have been white at one time, stumbled and fell to his knees. A filthy, bedraggled Mickey Mouse backpack weighed him down. The girl, who looked eleven or twelve, paused and jerked him to his feet. They were both all bones and no flesh, all angles and points. Their faces were dirty, their dark hair matted to their heads. Tears streaked the boy's face.

"Wait, wait, who are you?" Rebekah hurled herself after them. The girl sped up, headed for the stand of live oaks, hackberries, and junipers at the edge of the school yard. "Stop! We have food. *Comida.*"

The girl halted. She swiveled and stared back at Rebekah, the expression on her brown face a mixture of hope and suspicion. Her arm went around the boy, who looked about Rebekah's little sister Hazel's age, maybe five or six. His almond-shaped eyes were huge in his thin face. *"¿Comida?"*

Rebekah had studied Spanish in an old textbook she'd found in a secondhand bookstore for almost three years now, in hopes of one day being allowed to cross into Mexico when the older folks made their trips to Progreso to the dentist or to buy medicines. She knew what the words were but had no idea if she was pronouncing them correctly. "Food. Co . . . mi . . . da. Are you hungry?"

The girl nodded hard. *"Mi hermano tiene hambre."*

They were brother and sister. Who they were and why they were in the district's schoolhouse shed didn't matter as much to Rebekah as the idea that children were going without food. She pointed to them, then the schoolhouse, and put her hand on her chest. "You come inside with me."

The boy began to back away, dragging his backpack with him. He shook his head, fear etched across his elfin features.

"You want me to bring the food to you?"

The girl tugged at her brother. *"Sí."*

"No one will hurt you, I promise. What's your name? *Nombre*?"

The girl cocked her head toward the boy, who pressed his face against her shirt. "Him Diego." She thumped her chest. "Lupe."

"I'm Rebekah." She tapped her chest with her index finger. "Wait here. I'll be back. Don't go anywhere. No one will bother you out here."

She dashed across the yard, hopped over the two steps that led to the small porch, and tugged open the door. Inside, she skidded to a stop. The first graders stood at the front of the room, reading aloud to Susan. The middle grades wrote essays while the older boys and girls graded the younger children's arithmetic tests.

She sidled over to where Susan stood, arms crossed, a patient smile plastered on her plump face. "There you are. You said you were going to get your lunch box from the buggy. I thought maybe you decided teaching wasn't for you and went home."

Susan chuckled and patted Mary on the shoulder. "Good job. Molly, you're next."

"I need to tell you something." Rebekah leaned in and whispered, not wanting to get the entire school riled up. "Over by the stove."

Susan's eyebrows arched. "Caleb, come listen to Molly read for me."

Grinning, Caleb popped up from his seat. Knowing her younger brother as she did, Rebekah assumed he was thrilled to get out of writing his essay, even if only for a few moments.

Susan followed her to the long cabinets that lined one wall, providing storage space for lunch boxes and school supplies. "Something wrong?"

"*Nee.* Well, maybe. I don't know." Rebekah drummed her fingers on the countertop. She had a peanut butter and wild-grape jam sandwich in her cooler. Two oatmeal cookies. Some cold fried potatoes. Not enough for two hungry children. "I found two *kinner* hiding in the shed."

Susan swung around toward the rows of desks. Her hand went up, her chubby finger pointing, and she began to count in a whisper.

"Nee, not ours. I'm not sure where they came from, but—"

"Did you ask them where they came from?" Susan's schoolteacher voice commanded an answer. "What were they doing in the shed?"

"Hiding, I guess—"

"Why?"

"I don't know. They don't speak much English."

"They're from Mexico?"

"I don't think so. They sounded . . . different."

"Why did you leave them out there?"

"They were afraid to come in."

"Why?"

"I don't know."

"What *do* you know?"

"Just that they're scared and dirty and it doesn't look like they have anybody to take care of them and they're hungry."

She closed her mouth and waited. Susan rubbed her upturned nose with one finger, her full lips puckered and forehead wrinkled under a tendril of brown hair that had escaped her *kapp*. "We might need to get Mordecai."

Susan's brother—Rebekah's stepfather—would know what to do. And he was the deacon. Still, it would take thirty minutes round trip in the buggy to get to the farm and back. And then most likely Mordecai would be in the fields tending his beehives. "Can't we feed them first? They look starved."

Susan chewed on her lip for a second. "I can't abide seeing a child go hungry."

"Me neither." Rebekah grabbed her lunch box. "I have one PB&J sandwich."

Susan scooped up the red cooler that had her name written in black marker on both sides. "I have venison sausage on a biscuit."

The reading had stopped sometime during their conversation. Rebekah looked over her shoulder. Their scholars numbered fifteen and every one of them stared at Susan and her.

"Teacher, what's going on?" Of course Caleb, as one of the cheekiest, had the nerve to voice the question written across all their faces. "Is someone out there?"

"We have visitors." Susan made it sound like the typical parent visit. They did come by occasionally, sometimes with a hot meal or dessert, but runaway children who spoke another language, that never happened. "Mind your p's and q's and keep working."

Rebekah scurried to the door, the lunch boxes in her hands. Susan followed. "You're sure they're alone? There's no one waiting in the trees out there?"

"No one I saw. They seem completely alone."

She waited while Susan opened the door for her. Her aunt looked back at the classroom, her expression stern. "Sally, you're in charge. Everyone continues doing exactly what they're doing now."

"Yes, Teacher," the scholars responded in unison.

Rebekah had no doubt they would do as they were told. She couldn't fathom how Susan did it, but her scholars not only obeyed her, they loved her and wanted to please her. Rebekah scurried across the small porch, her gaze on the steps. "Lupe! Diego!"

"Nee, I'm Tobias Byler. Who are you?"

Rebekah craned her head. A man sat in a wagon, his face hidden in the shadow of a straw hat haloed by the midday sun. An older man, cookie cutter in size and lean build, sat ramrod straight next to him, mammoth hands resting on bended knees. Behind them, five children of varying ages filled the back of the wagon.

Rebekah settled the lunch boxes on the ground and raised her hand to her forehead to shield her eyes. "There was a boy and a girl out here. Did you see where they went?"

"The little boy and girl ran away when Tobias yelled at them." A little girl with a lisp, who held two dolls clutched to her chest, volunteered this startling information in a tone that said she didn't approve. She stood and pointed. "They ran into those trees."

"You yelled at them?" Rebekah knew better than to scold

a man, any man, but especially one she didn't know. Still, she couldn't help herself. "They're hungry. They're children."

Tobias lifted his hat, revealing brown hair over green eyes in a tanned face that held a bemused expression. He found her outburst funny somehow. He slapped the hat back on his head as if he had all the time in the world to consider her comment. "I just missed running over the boy when he ran out in front of the wagon. I thought a shout was in order."

"Tobias." The other man had the same deep voice and accent that spoke of somewhere north of the Mason-Dixon Line. "We're newcomers. Let's not get off on the wrong foot."

"But, *Daed*—"

"We brought the kinner by to see where they'll start school tomorrow. I know there's only a couple of weeks left, but they're chomping at the bit to meet some of the other kinner around here." Tobias's daed smiled at Susan, who stood next to Rebekah with her hands on her hips. "I reckon they're not so excited about school itself, sorry to say. I'm Levi Byler, your new neighbor. You must be the teacher."

Why didn't he think Rebekah was the teacher? She opened her mouth. Susan's hand touched her arm. She shut her mouth.

"Pleased to meet you. I'm Susan King and this is Rebekah Lantz." Susan seemed to have lost her schoolteacher voice. The words were soft, almost hesitant. She tilted her head as if looking around Levi. "Five of you? That's a nice addition to our numbers. Y'all are welcome to come in and meet the other scholars."

"What about the boy and the girl—?"

Susan's glare forced Rebekah to stop.

The children tumbled from the wagon and trotted to the door, introducing themselves to Teacher as they tromped by. Rebekah caught the names *Rueben, Micah, Ida, Nyla,* and *Liam* offered in tones that ranged from soft and respectful to downright giggly. Liam, the youngest, barely whispered his name with a cheeky grin before he scampered up the steps. Susan and Levi followed.

Tobias hopped from the wagon and then planted himself next to Rebekah. "I'll help you look."

He towered over her. Up close he looked even more solid and broad through the chest. Tearing her gaze from his beefy arms, Rebekah took a breath. "Why would you do that?"

"Because it's obvious you'll never forgive me if I don't."

"We're called to forgive, no matter what." Her tone sounded tart in her ears. If he only knew how hard it was for her to take her own advice. What a hypocrite she was. She worked to soften her tone. "It would be wrong to hold a grudge."

"Do you always do what's right?"

Her hand went to the spot where she'd tucked Leila's note inside a torn seam on the back side of her apron. He asked too many questions and his green eyes seemed to see too much. "I try."

"Me too."

His shadow made him seem ten feet tall. Rebekah's neck hurt from looking up at him. "I don't think we should go off on our own."

"They're only children. You'll be safe with me."

The faint sarcasm that tinged his words didn't make her feel safe.

Just the opposite.

TWO

Tobias lengthened his stride. Rebekah Lantz might be thinner than his shadow, but she made up for it with a powerful energy that propelled her tall—for a girl—frame across the schoolyard toward a cluster of what passed for trees in South Texas. The exertion, or maybe nerves, brought out the pink along her high cheekbones. She looked neither left nor right and certainly not directly at him. He had a sudden urge to laugh. Not at her, but at the idea that any woman would be nervous around him. Despite having reached the ripe old age of twenty-two, he had little experience with women.

At least not positive experience.

"Are you coming, or what?" Rebekah's gaze darted somewhere in the vicinity of his left shoulder. Her blue eyes were as brilliant as any he'd ever seen under chestnut hair that lined the edge of her kapp. "They can't have gone too far."

"They seemed in an awful big hurry to me." Forcing his gaze from her face, Tobias veered between a live oak and a large sprawling nopales cactus. No little boy hiding there. "Maybe they changed their minds."

"About food? Nee." She sounded aggrieved, as if he personally had starved the poor little ones. "Didn't you see how thin they were?"

Thin and dirty and scared. He let his gaze sweep the carpet of black-eyed Susans just beginning to bloom. Having had a hand in raising his younger brothers and sisters, Tobias knew all about the voracious appetite of a growing child. Worrying about them had become like second nature, like wearing an overcoat year-round. "Lupe! Diego! Come out! I'm sorry I yelled at you."

For the first time Rebekah rewarded him with a smile. It came with a set of dimples that made her look even younger than he first thought. She was too pretty for words. She shook her head. "They don't speak much English. But good try." She cupped her hands around her mouth. "Lupe, Diego. *Por favor. Hay comida.*"

A southern accent gave the jumble of unfamiliar words a strange lilt. "What does that mean?"

"Please. There's food." She ducked her head and studied the overgrown weeds. "At least I think it does."

"You know a lot of Spanish?"

"Nee. And I'm not even sure I'm pronouncing the words right. I got them from a book."

Pretty and smart.

"*Vayan.* Go."

The voice, high and trembling, floated from behind a mesquite tree.

"I'm sorry I scared your little brother." Tobias paused, letting Rebekah move closer first. "I didn't want to hit him with the wagon."

"We go."

The voice shook.

"We go."

"No. Stay." Rebekah seemed so determined to help these two children. Pretty, smart, and kind. She held out a hand as if offering it to the unseen children. "At least eat and then you can decide what to do next. Comida, then go. On the school porch."

"Hombre malo."

Rebekah's glance held something Tobias couldn't read. "What did she say?"

"She says you're a bad man."

"I am not a bad . . ." Tobias clamped his mouth shut.

Rebekah shook her head. "She's probably scared of all strange men. Who knows what has happened to her, running around like this with no one to protect her."

No one to protect her. Tobias's gut twisted at the thought. He saw to it every day that his own brothers and sisters were protected. "I'm not . . . malo." He jerked his head at Rebekah. "How do you say *gut*? Tell her I'm gut."

"Are you?"

She thought he was a bad person because he'd scared off these kinner? "I'm not bad."

The corners of her lips turned up. She was pulling his leg in the middle of this situation apparently of his making. "No malo. *Bueno.* Hombre bueno."

Lupe stuck her head out from behind the tree. She didn't look convinced. "Malo?"

"No. Bueno." Rebekah inched closer. "Come out. Please. Food. Comida."

Diego shot past his sister and scampered across the clearing. "Comida."

"Diego, no!" Lupe followed, one hand outstretched as if to pull him back. *"¡Cuidado!"*

Why was she so afraid? Tobias put both hands in the air to show her he held nothing. Nothing that could hurt her. "I'll go back to the wagon and wait."

He turned and walked away, acutely aware of the sound of Rebekah's soft, sweet murmurs that soothed and cajoled. His own breath eased and the knotted muscles between his shoulders relaxed. No wonder she was a teacher, or teacher's aide. She had a way with children.

A few minutes later the two runaways—they had to be runaways from somewhere down south—were seated on the porch, plowing through sandwiches, pickled okra, and cold fried potatoes. They had gained a modicum of trust in Rebekah, especially after she produced a handful of oatmeal cookies. Her expression grim, Lupe seemed to have one eye on the food and the other on him. He kept his distance for fear she'd take off like a deer trying to escape a hunter.

After a few minutes he reached into the back of the wagon and rummaged in the burlap bag Martha kept there for Liam and the other little ones. They were growing like weeds and always, always hungry. Sure enough. Two beautiful, shiny Granny Smith apples.

With a light step and a careful, neutral expression, he walked toward the porch. Lupe stopped chewing, the sandwich suspended in midair. Fear the likes of which no child should ever feel swirled across her face. He'd seen that kind of fear in the skittish horses his daed trained. As if they were sure their last day on earth had arrived.

"Here." He held out the apples, which fit nicely in his overgrown hand. "Apple." He glanced at Rebekah. "How do you say *apple*?"

She shrugged. "I don't remember that one."

"You give them to her."

Rebekah picked the apples from his hand without touching him. *"Danki."*

"There's more. Martha keeps a supply of snacks in the bag."

"Let's start with this." Rebekah rubbed an apple on her apron and held it out. Lupe took it as if receiving a special gift. She handed it to her brother. "Diego eat, he more hungry."

Tobias doubted that. "Give her the other one."

Rebekah obliged. Lupe took a big bite. The sound of crunching filled the air as she demolished the sweet treat. Juice ran down her chin, leaving a trail in the filth that covered her skin. He itched for a washrag. Martha would have them cleaned up in no time. He could take them to his house, with all the boxes still everywhere waiting to be unpacked. With nine kinner ranging in age from six to twenty-two already crammed into the five-bedroom, ramshackle, wood and Sheetrock structure, what were two more? Everything about their clothes, their dirty faces, and their fearful expressions said they needed protecting.

When it came to children, Tobias made protecting them his business. He couldn't afford to lose any more people he loved. He jerked his head toward the yard. Rebekah followed him a few feet from the picnic feast. "What will you do with them now? You're not really going to let them leave on their own, are you?"

Rebekah shook her head. "We don't know their story yet. I don't want them to leave, but it'll be up to Jeremiah what we should do next. Susan will want to talk to him and Mordecai. Jeremiah is the bishop and Mordecai is—"

"I know. Jeremiah is the one who talked Daed into coming here after Leroy Glick retired. Mordecai came by this morning to welcome us." With a wealth of honey and stories that made even little Nyla, eight, smile, and that girl never smiled. "Let us take them home for now, until it's figured out."

"What makes you think they'll go with you?"

"They're kinner. They'll do as they're told."

"They've found their way to our doorstep from somewhere far away, someplace dangerous. I reckon they have minds of their own."

An impasse. "Let's ask them."

They turned. Lupe had her arm around her little brother. He slumped against her chest, eyes closed, his dirty face relaxed in slumber, his apple still clutched in his dirty hand. He looked so very young. Lupe glanced up at them. She shrugged. *"Mucho sueño."*

Tobias turned to Rebekah. She was smiling at the girl. "Me too. After I eat."

"What did she say?"

"He was sleepy."

"Ah. The beds are already set up at our house—that and the kitchen." He nodded toward the school. "With all those little ones, beds were first, for our peace of mind, and cooking food for theirs."

"I imagine your mudder thinks so."

The knife sliced as deep as ever. Six years of trying to come to terms with God's plan for Daed, for himself, for Martha, who at age ten had taken to carrying around a baby as if he were her own, for all those little ones. It made no sense to Tobias, but Daed frequently reminded him that it didn't have to make sense to them. In those long days working in the saddlery shop in that companionable silence, in those long evenings, legs sprawled on the front porch, contemplating the sheer majesty of an Ohio sky, he'd struggled to absorb his father's stalwart faith, but to no avail. "My mudder passed six years ago."

"Ach." She nodded but offered no meaningless platitudes. Another thing to appreciate. "Your daed has his hands full then."

"We all do. My sister Martha keeps everything running in the house. My brothers David and Milo help. Everyone pitches in, even the little ones."

As was expected in any Plain household, but in particular one missing the cornerstone, the *fraa* and mudder.

"A big job."

Tobias cleared his throat. "Made easy by kinner who know what they're to do."

He turned to look at Diego and Lupe again just as Rebekah did the same. "You should take them." Rebekah's voice was soft. "They'll feel at home with a big brood like yours. Kinner will understand each other."

"But she's afraid of me."

"She saw all the children in your wagon. If they're not afraid of you, why should she be? If they think you're bueno, you must be bueno, right?"

Wise for so young and so pretty.

She slid onto the seat next to Lupe and began to talk softly, almost a whisper. He couldn't make out the words. Lupe kept glancing at him, her expression noncommittal at first, then curious, and finally hesitant.

After a few moments Rebekah stood and brushed her hands together in a definitive gesture. "She says for one night."

"One night. Where are they from? And where are they going?"

"They came from El Salvador. I couldn't understand the

name. I think she says they have family in San Antonio. A daed, maybe. I heard the word for 'family' and 'San Antonio' as the same. Something about eating fish, which makes no sense at all." Her tone combined with her expression suggested she wasn't sure whether to believe much of what the little girl said. "Anyway, it's a start."

Indeed it was. "I'll tell Daed." He clomped up the stairs past her.

"You said Jeremiah talked your daed into coming here."

He looked back. *"Jah."*

"Why did Jeremiah want y'all to come?"

"Because we're saddle makers and we train horses. He figured it was more goods and services to offer to the Englisch folks. To keep the community going, Daed said."

"So you'll work with Leroy's sons breaking horses?"

"They will."

"You don't break horses?"

"I'd rather work the leather." Breaking horses was a dangerous job, one he once had embraced and enjoyed, but now someone had to stand back in order to make sure the kinner were never left alone, never left without someone to protect them. "I'm in charge of keeping the shop, doing the bills, and making the saddles."

Should something happen. Because no one knew better than he did how something could change a man's entire life in the time it took him to inhale the sweet scent of roses in spring and exhale the *schtinkich* of burial plot dirt in fall.

THREE

The bishop managed to arrive before the supper dishes could be cleared. Susan suspected Jeremiah hoped a piece of Abigail's pecan pie might still be on the table should he arrive at the opportune moment. Not tonight. Not with Levi Byler's brood crowding the benches interspersed with Abigail and Mordecai's combined bunch. Susan liked having a full table and a full house. The chatter and the way food disappeared faster than a coyote after a chicken made her feel content. She smiled to herself as she poured *kaffi* in a huge earth-colored mug and added a splash of milk fresh from Mordecai's latest addition, one dairy cow named Buttercup.

All the company would put Mordecai in a good mood too. Her brother liked commotion as much as she did. She needed him on her side to convince Jeremiah to let Lupe and Diego stay until things could be figured out. However long that took. Until that hollow, hunted look disappeared from the little boy's face. He'd polished off two bowls of ham and beans and three pieces of cornbread at supper.

She'd rather they stay here in the King home, not the home of folks she hardly knew, but that would be up to Mordecai. Letting

Levi take them to his house had been a mistake. She hadn't had time or inclination to argue, what with her scholars hanging on every word and Levi standing there looking so . . . so what?

What was it about the man that made her lose her normal gabbiness? She couldn't figure out how Levi, Tobias, and David could look so much alike, yet so different. All three were tall and broad chested, like triplets. They had hair the color of toast well done and eyes that color of green that reminded her of fresh sprouts of grass peeking through the dirt in early spring.

The younger boys, Milo, Micah, and Liam, must look like their mother, with their blond hair and blue eyes. Levi's face had lines around his eyes from squinting in the sun, or laughing, and streaks of gray highlighted his beard. But that wasn't what made him look different from his sons. It was something in the way he carried himself. As if a burden she couldn't see weighed him down. Sadness he attempted to hide cloaked him as surely as if he wore Joseph's coat of many colors.

Though she'd never had to carry that burden herself, Susan had seen it before. In Mordecai after his first fraa died. And then in Abigail when she first arrived from Tennessee, a widow in need of a *mann* for herself and her five kinner. The two had managed to shed their lost air and sadness in a second season of love. Now all seemed right in their world.

Contemplating *Gott's* goodness, Susan picked up a platter of peanut butter cookies—not as good as pecan pie—but they would help soften up Jeremiah. Jeremiah, Mordecai, and Will, the three who would decide little Lupe's and Diego's fate.

She turned and there stood Levi Byler, calloused hands tucked around his suspenders, a bemused look on his face that said he'd been there awhile.

She jumped and dropped the kaffi cup. And the platter of cookies. Hot kaffi splattered in all directions, including on her apron and bare feet. "Ach!"

Levi's eyebrows arched. He strode forward, stopped, and knelt by her mess. "Sorry."

Susan's hands fluttered to her chest and she heaved a breath. "You scared me."

"So I gathered. Hand me a towel." His tone remained soft and distant. "Mordecai asked about kaffi for Jeremiah. Abigail and Rebekah took the kinner outside to organize a game of volleyball, so I came around to see if you might get it."

"There was kaffi." She couldn't contain a chuckle as she knelt across from him. "And cookies."

"That's a shame. Reckon you could make more?" Levi didn't join in her laughter. Contemplating the soft gruffness of his voice, she reached for the platter, which somehow had remained unscathed in its rapid descent. Her hand grazed his fingers. His hand shot back as if he'd touched a skillet on the stove. He stood before she could speak, towering over her, his expression bleak.

"I'll bring in the kaffi in a jiffy." She tried out a smile. He didn't return it. "There are plenty of cookies."

He nodded and turned.

"I wanted to say . . . the children, Lupe and Diego, they should stay here with us. We have room and plenty of food."

Levi pivoted and looked down at her. "That will be for the men to decide."

No equivocation there. "I know, but they're only children, and they're scared and in a country where they don't know anyone."

"You have a heart for children." His gaze rested somewhere beyond her shoulder. His lips twisted as if he were remembering something bitterly sweet. "Naturally as a teacher you would, even though you don't have experience—"

"With my own. Nee." She scooped up the soggy cookies and deposited them on the plate. "That doesn't make me blind to what a little girl and a little boy need."

"That's not what I meant."

"If you call the authorities, they'll send them to one of those holding places and then back to their country."

"They'll get their hearing. It's the law."

From a motherly perspective, that meant little. And Plain folks had their own book of rules. It didn't always jibe with that of the Englischers. "They've come so far. A parent wouldn't send them on such a long, dangerous journey for no reason."

"They can't expect to come into this country without papers and make themselves at home."

"I doubt they expect any such thing. They're children who did what their parents told them to do."

"It's not for you to decide."

She wanted to say it wasn't for him either, but then, he was a man, so he would have more say than she. Men always did. Which was fine, except when it came to kinner. "Since they're here, you could leave them with us. We likely have more room than you do with such a large brood."

"The kinner have adopted them already. They're teaching them English." For the first time he smiled. The years fell away and he became Tobias's twin for a split second. "Martha, Ida, and Nyla are like little mudders. I reckon it comes from taking care of Liam."

The smile fled. Susan caught a glimpse of raw pain before he shuttered it just as quickly. "They may pick up their share of Spanish as well. It might come in handy in this neck of the woods."

"But nine are so many." While she had none. That fact had come to bother her more in recent years. She couldn't say why, nor had she admitted it to another soul. Gott's plan was not to be questioned. "Your beds are surely full."

"Catherine wanted more."

"Your fraa?"

He nodded. "She always said there's room for one more, isn't there? Every time. A house full of kinner is a blessing."

"She was right."

"Nee, sometimes enough is enough." His hands gripped his suspenders so hard his knuckles turned white. "I best get back. They'll think I got lost."

"I'll bring the kaffi."

One quick jerk of his head and he was gone. Yet Susan felt his palpable presence left behind. She shook her head. The man was so still and measured in his movements and his words. But when he opened his mouth and spoke, she felt a storm bearing down on her, the pressure burrowing to her bone and marrow.

"Rubbish." She said the word aloud. It came from one of the many novels she read every night in the endless quiet while the others slept. She checked them out from the library or bought them at garage sales in Beeville when she could. They were stacked in all the corners of her bedroom. *Jane Eyre. The Hounds of the Baskervilles. The Scarlet Letter. The Raven. Little Women. Gone with the Wind. The Oregon Trail.* Stories from across continents and countries she would never see. New words, words no one ever spoke around her, gave her pleasure, a secret pleasure she didn't share with the others. They would think she was daft. This one exactly fit her strange reaction to Levi. "Rubbish, indeed."

FOUR

Men always made the decisions. Even when they weren't the experts. Rebekah pressed her lips together to prevent those words from making a run for it and escaping her mouth. It tended to flap open when it shouldn't. At least that's what Mudder said. She whipped the back door shut behind her and grabbed the plate of cookies from Susan's hands in one fell swoop. Her step-aenti started and shrieked.

"Not you too!" Susan's free hand fluttered to her chest. "Y'all will be the death of me."

"Why? What?"

"Nothing." Susan picked up a tray crowded with five mugs of steaming coffee. "Just people sneaking up on me."

"Like who?" Rebekah squeezed past Susan and dashed to the door. She didn't want to miss this conversation, and any minute Mudder would come flying through the door and tell her to high-tail it back out to the volleyball game. Who could concentrate on volleyball at a time like this? "It looks to me like you're alone in the kitchen. It looks like you could use some help, as a matter of fact."

"It looks to me like you're about to stick your nose into a place where it might get chopped off."

Susan's persnickety tone didn't deceive Rebekah one wit. Her aunt wanted in on this conversation as much as Rebekah did. She could feel her breathing down her neck as they two-stepped into the front room like twins joined at the hip.

Mordecai, Jeremiah, Levi, Tobias, and Will sat on an assortment of rocking chairs and stools gathered in a circle in the front room. They could be visiting like old ladies at a sewing frolic.

Ignoring Mordecai's raised eyebrows, Rebekah passed the cookie plate and stepped into the niche between the wood box and the big, empty fireplace. Maybe they would forget about her presence. That was as likely as she would forget Leila's note in the hem of her apron. Susan bustled about with coffee and napkins. None of the men spoke until she finished. After a few seconds she nodded at her brother and then slipped away. As far as the overstuffed, tattered couch in the corner, where she proceeded to pick up her basket of darning and plop herself down.

Rebekah wasn't the only one determined to hear this conversation.

"It doesn't seem we have much choice." Jeremiah dusted cookie crumbs from his beard with the back of a hand the size of a shovel. He'd taken to his bishop role without a misstep after Leroy's retirement to the *dawdy haus*. "I can call the sheriff's office in the morning. They'll know which authorities to notify."

"Nee—"

Mordecai's glare forced Rebekah to close her mouth once again. He was being kind in letting her stay and she knew it.

"If we do that, the kinner will end up in some warehouse full of little ones just like them." Will might have been the youngest and the newest in his post as minister, but he had proven himself a quick study. He seemed so happy since his marriage to Isabella Shrock, a different man than the one who had pined for Leila. Stronger. More certain of things. "They've traveled a long way. Would it not be kinder to help them find their family members in San Antonio? They can sort out the legalities."

Jah. Jah.

"I'm new here, but I imagine the *Ordnung* is not too different here than up yonder where we come from." Levi's tone was soft and even, yet it commanded attention. "What does that say about us adhering to the laws of the land?"

"Our kind has often chosen to step away from the laws of the land if they endanger our way of life by connecting us too much to the outside world." Mordecai sipped from his cup and then set it on one knee, his calloused hands wrapped around it two-fold. "The Englisch often think they know best for us. From little things like filing blueprints and getting inspections for additions to using companies to remove sewage from our outhouses instead of collecting it for the fields."

"Or sending our kinner to public schools," Will added.

Good job. Good job.

"I don't know that this is the same." Levi straightened in his rocker as if he felt uncomfortable. "This isn't about local laws. This is a federal concern. We might want to consider if we're harboring fugitives."

"They're little kinner." Susan stood and her basket crashed to the floor. Knitting needles rolled under the couch, socks landed on her bare feet, and a red pincushion shaped like a tomato made its home near Mordecai's dusty work boot. "What do they know about laws? They were told to come,so they came."

All five men turned and stared. Rebekah slapped her hand to her lips to keep the chuckle from escaping. Aenti Susan thought her niece had the opinionated big mouth.

"That may be so." Levi stroked his beard with a heavy hand. "Kinner have been known to break the laws, same as adults."

"These aren't our laws."

"We're Americans, aren't we?"

"Our allegiance is first and foremost to the kingdom of God." Mordecai picked up the pincushion and tossed it to Susan, who caught it with both hands. His expression remained as somber as Rebekah had ever seen it. "We're all immigrants and sojourners in this world. Our ancestors were persecuted in other countries. It was only when they came to America as immigrants that they were able to establish the communities they believed were Gott's will for them. And for us."

Silence reigned for several seconds.

Rebekah's stomach felt like it did when the van carrying them to the Gulf roared up a hill and then down the other side in what seemed like a free fall to someone who so rarely moved so fast. "Could I say something, I mean, since I found them? I talked them into staying."

From her spot kneeling on the floor trying to gather up errant spools of thread, Susan employed a vigorous head shake to signal her distress. Mordecai moved his cup from one knee to the other. Jeremiah sighed. "Knowing you as I do, Rebekah, I reckon there's no stopping you now."

Heads swiveled again. This time six pairs of eyes stared at her. She cleared her throat. "It's like Mordecai said. If our kinner were alone and lost in a country where they didn't even speak the same language, what would we want for them?"

"We would never send—"

Rebekah held up a hand, willing Tobias to stop. "I know we wouldn't do it, but what would Jesus do? What would the good Samaritan do? Try to help or send them on their way so they could be someone else's problem?"

Mordecai looked as if he might smile. Will nodded but didn't speak. Rebekah breathed through the trembling that started in her legs and worked its way up through her arms. "There's one thing we could do, though."

Jeremiah took off his black-rimmed glasses and began to polish the lenses on his cobalt-blue shirt. "Go on, finish what you started."

"We could ask Leila and Jesse."

The polishing stopped. Will slapped his coffee cup onto the spindly oak table that separated his chair from Levi's. "Nee—"

"Why would we do that?" Mordecai interrupted, his expression as stern as Rebekah had ever seen on a man given to practical jokes and long-winded tall tales. "They're no longer a part of our community."

The note stuck in the inside hem of her apron would surely fall to the floor and reveal her sin any second. Rebekah smoothed trembling hands across the soft, much-washed cotton folds. "Jesse works with charity groups. They do food banks and help the poor and such." To her relief her voice didn't quiver. "The Englisch churches combine their small offerings together to help others, especially children."

"Why do you know this?" Will's face had turned the color of beets. "Explain that to me."

Six sets of eyes studied her. How, indeed? "Leila writes me letters." Absolutely true. She hadn't written back, a sure sign she'd failed in her bid to forgive. "That's allowed. Mudder knows about it."

"Who are Leila and Jesse?" Tobias broke in. "Why wouldn't we ask the help of Englischers who are like-minded Christians?"

"They're not Englischers." Rebekah hurried to explain before Will could muddy the waters with his version of history. "Leila is my sister. Jesse is her husband."

"They're Englischers now." Will stood and began to pace, his boots thumping against the wood. "They're not involved in our business, not anymore."

"Neither are they shunned. They were never baptized."

"Not in our church."

He was right. Jesse and Leila had been baptized in their new church and little Gracie had been dedicated only a few weeks after her birth. All this Rebekah could rightfully say she'd learned in letters she'd read with a powerful interest she couldn't deny, as much as she wanted to toss them in the trash and never look back. Still, she looked back and longed to change history.

If only it were possible.

"So we cut off our noses to spite our faces?" Susan smacked her basket onto the couch and marched across the room to stand by Rebekah. "Maybe women feel these things more deeply, as mudders. I don't know, but we can't send kinner off to who knows where with who knows whom like they're criminals."

"But you don't have kinner, either of you." Levi looked puzzled. He shook his head. "We have to think of the impact on the district if we're accused of harboring children without papers."

"We have to think of the impact on our eternal souls if we don't help our brethren in need," Susan shot back. Her cheeks were scarlet. She ducked her head. "That's all I'm saying. I'm sure you men will make the proper decision."

"But—"

Susan tucked an arm around Rebekah and propelled her toward the kitchen. "We should get more kaffi and cookies for the men."

"Nee." Jeremiah waved a hand covered on the back side with wiry gray hair. "I think it's best we sleep on it, pray on it for a day or two. Don't you, Mordecai?"

Mordecai nodded, his salt-and-pepper beard bobbing. Will plopped in his chair, arms crossed over his chest.

Rebekah plowed to a stop despite the pressure of Susan's arm on her back. "Then Lupe and Diego can come to school in the morning? They could teach us some Spanish."

Jeremiah stood. "I don't see why not. Levi, you can bring them in with your kinner."

"That's no problem." Levi rose as well. "It's late. Time for chores and bed."

None of the men seemed to be aware of Rebekah's gleeful little two-step as she dutifully followed Susan into the kitchen. She still had time to try to convince them to talk to Jesse and Leila. Or talk to Leila about it herself on Friday. Something good could still come from their decision to leave the community. Good from the hurt. It wouldn't change Rebekah's situation, but if it helped Lupe and Diego, she would learn to live with it.

As much as it hurt to think of facing Leila, Rebekah would talk to her. Just talk. Talking wasn't prohibited by the Ordnung.

FIVE

Tobias leaped and smacked the ball over the net. Caleb and the others groaned when the ball slammed to the ground and careened across the yard toward the barn. Spiking the ball wasn't hard. The ragged net hung almost to the ground in the middle. The ancient gray ball didn't have much bounce left in it—which didn't stop Diego from kicking it. The boy seemed much more interested in kickball than volleyball. He and his sister had declined the offer of clean clothes, despite the dirt and stench of their own jeans and T-shirts. Lupe had, in fact, looked horrified at the offer to cut down one of Martha's dresses for her. Maybe they could find some Goodwill Englisch clothes for them.

"No fair. Weren't you headed home?" Jacob called, forcing Tobias from his thoughts. "Livestock needs watering. This game is more than over."

Indeed, the sun was settling on the horizon. Tobias hadn't intended to stop after the tense meeting in Mordecai's front room, but Liam's determined tug on his hand had changed his mind. That and the fact that Rebekah stood at the back door, watching. Not that it mattered. That she mattered. She had a way of going on about things. The way she'd thrown herself into the men's conversation about Lupe and Diego. She and Susan both. They were two peas in a pod even if they weren't really related and one was rather round and the other more than a little thin. For schoolteachers, they were downright lippy.

Not that he was much different when it came to expressing opinions out of turn.

"We were just leaving." Levi strode across the yard and scooped up Liam, then deposited the six-year-old under one arm like a sack of potatoes. "Let's go. Everyone in the wagon. Chores to do, prayers to say, beds waiting."

Another groan sounded, but Martha, Nyla, and Ida led the charge to the wagon, jockeying for seats on the thick layer of hay laid down for that purpose. David took off on the horse he'd chosen to ride rather than squeeze his lanky frame into the back of the wagon with a bunch of squirmy kinner. Lupe and Diego held back. Tobias motioned with one hand in the universal *let's go* signal. Lupe hopped in unaided, careful to give wide berth to his hand, then turned to tug Diego up and in.

Tobias boosted him from behind. The boy's bony frame weighed nothing. "There you go." He pushed up the wagon's back panel and hooked clasps on both side. "Settle down, all of you. Next stop, your beds."

"We're dirty." Liam held up two very dirty hands. "See?"

"So you are. A quick wipe with a rag might be in order."

"I'll give him a sponge bath." Martha tickled the boy from behind. "Head to toe."

"Nee, nee, not that." Liam threw himself in the hay and did a small somersault to escape his big schweschder.

Tobias climbed in front next to Daed, who shook the reins without any sign of impatience. "Everyone in?"

"Yep." He settled back on the hard seat with a sigh. It had been a long day. "So what's your take on the discussion tonight?"

Daed glanced back at the kinner. "Little pitchers have big ears."

Tobias took his own gander. Martha was braiding Lupe's hair, and Diego looked half asleep.

"They're not listening."

"It's a dilemma."

That was Daed. Short on words, long on meaning.

"If it were up to you?"

No answer. Tobias had learned to let Daed find his own way to a conversation. Sometimes it took days.

Giggles filled the air. He looked back a second time. The girls were rolling around in the hay laughing like little girls did. "Daed, did you know the Spanish word for 'man' is *hombre*?" Nyla hollered. "The Spanish word for 'hunger' is *hambre*."

"So you don't want to get them mixed up, I reckon?"

That observation set off another gale of laughter from the girls. The boys didn't seem to get it. Or they didn't care to be seen laughing like a bunch of hyenas. Daed's smile was worth listening to their silliness.

"You ever think of marrying again?"

Daed's smile faded. "Nee."

"It's been six years."

"I'm well aware."

"Susan seems like she'd make a sturdy fraa."

"Sturdy doesn't have much to do with it."

"What then?"

Daed slapped the reins. Rosie stepped up her pace. "I reckon you got that one figured out."

A not-so-oblique reference to events of the past year. "It doesn't seem that way."

"You hiked off the path, but you righted yourself. That's what's important."

"Seems like these folks have had some hard times with folks who strayed off the path."

"And it's still causing dissension." Daed glanced toward Tobias. "It's good that you figured out where you belong."

Most times he felt the same way. But sometimes Serena's face appeared in his mind's eye—especially late at night—and it was all he could do to bear it. "It's good."

"New beginning here." Daed cleared his throat. "There's that Rebekah. She's a firecracker."

"Does a man want a firecracker for a fraa?"

"Depends on the man."

"Was that why you married Mudder? She had a mind of her own." And no problem expressing it. Not something every Plain man appreciated. She definitely qualified as a firecracker. "She always had a word or two to say."

"Or three or four."

A smile flitted across Daed's face and disappeared. Memories of Mudder and Daed talking, their heads bent and nearly touching in the glow of the lamp's light, their words a soft, quick murmur like the sound of water gurgling in a stream, filled Tobias's mind, warming him. "She had a way about her, didn't she?"

Daed's silence was broken by more giggles in the back of the wagon. "Daed, we fixed Diego's hair."

Tobias hazarded a glance back. The girls had braided the boy's hair while he slept and secured the braids with a rubber band apparently produced by Lupe. Time to give that boy a haircut.

Thinking of haircuts as if Diego would be around for a while. Tobias blew out air. Sometimes decisions were knotty and prickly like the nopales. Like Rebekah Lantz.

"Jah, she did . . . have a way about her." Daed's voice was so soft Tobias had to strain to hear the words. "That's where her daughters get it."

SIX

Bath time didn't usually happen on a weeknight. Nor did it involve so much shouting and carrying on. Tobias wiggled in the hickory rocking chair and tried to focus on the newspaper in his lap. He inhaled the familiar scent of newsprint. The same everywhere. He'd done this hundreds of times in their old house on their old farm back in Ohio. Got his hands black with ink reading about what Plain folks were doing all across the country, how they planted, how they grieved their dead, and how they welcomed their newborn. School picnics and birthdays and loads of folks headed out for visits.

He should be headed to bed himself, but he wanted to see what was going on in his old neighborhood. Edith Byler, a distant cousin, was a faithful scribe. A wave of homesickness flooded him. Serena's face floated in his mind's eye. *Stop it.*

"Get back here!"

Martha's screech filled the room, followed by a streak that turned out to be Diego hurling himself across the front room, his skinny legs and arms pumping. He wore only the dirty pants he'd arrived in and the scruffy Mickey Mouse backpack that never seemed to leave his side.

"Whoa!" Tobias unfolded himself from the chair, sections of the newspaper slipping to the floor. "What's going on here?"

Diego planted himself behind Tobias, one arm around Tobias's leg just above the knee. He peeked out, a frown swallowing up his dark face.

"He won't get in the tub." Sweat dripped from Martha's face. Her cheeks were red with exertion and exasperation soaked her words. She wiped at her face with the threadbare towel in her hands. "He can't get in bed like that. He's filthy and he reeks of garbage. And he won't let go of that backpack. He needs to set it aside for five minutes while I scrub him down."

"Where's Lupe?" Tobias peeled Diego's hands from his leg and knelt. He put an arm around the boy's shoulder. "Maybe he doesn't want to take his clothes off in front of a strange girl."

"I sent her upstairs with Nyla after her bath. Nyla and Ida will try to get the snarls out of her hair. We may have to cut it to comb it. And I'm not strange—"

"A stranger. Someone he doesn't know." Tobias patted the rocking chair. "Diego sit?"

Diego shook his head and hugged his backpack to his chest. His ribs stuck out so far Tobias could count each one. He had a long scar on one arm and chigger bites ringed his waist above the waistband of his sagging pants.

"We won't take your backpack, I promise." Tobias moved toward the kitchen door. Diego moved with him. Progress. "What if I help you take a bath? We'll send Martha upstairs with the girls, where she belongs."

"Hey—"

Tobias shook his head. "The boy needs his privacy."

"Of all the—"

"Humor me."

Martha whirled and stomped up the stairs, her chest heaving with indignation.

Tobias grinned at Diego. "Women."

Diego's smile was tentative. He didn't understand, but then, words weren't the only way to communicate with little boys.

"You like to swim?" Tobias moved his arms in a swimming motion, ducking his head and bringing it up as if breathing between strokes. "I like to play in the water. Splash. Splash."

He marched toward the kitchen, not glancing back to see if Diego followed. Martha had filled the washtub in the laundry room off the kitchen. By now the water she'd warmed from the stove had likely cooled, but on a late-spring evening in South Texas, who needed warm bathwater? Tobias knelt and trailed his hand through the water. "Feels good. I wish it was bath night for me. I'd jump right in."

Diego's lower lip protruded. His dark eyes looked suspicious. He let one hand rest on the edge of the huge tub. He shook his head.

Tobias plunged his arm in the water and splashed Diego.

"Ay!" The boy ducked and staggered back.

"What, are you afraid of a little bit of water?" Tobias laughed and splashed again, making sure to get plenty on himself. "It's only water. I'm thinking you and Lupe crossed some creeks and streams and rivers to get here. At least this is clean water."

Diego laid his backpack next to the pile of clothes that Tobias fully intended to burn when the boy wasn't looking. He splashed with both hands, giving Tobias a good soaking.

"Good job!" Tobias splashed back. Diego giggled, a sweet, sweet sound. Tobias laughed. He plunged both hands in to keep up with Diego's shorter, faster efforts.

In seconds they were both dripping.

"Get in—you're wet now anyway."

Still grinning, Diego cocked his head. He eyed the backpack.

"I won't touch it." Tobias pointed his finger at Mickey. "It belongs to you. I understand."

Diego's command of the English language might not be much, but somehow he understood. Before Tobias could help him, he climbed over the edge of the tub and threw himself in the water, underwear and all.

Good enough. Tobias tossed in an old, yellow rubber duck someone had given to Liam. He insisted on keeping it around for bath time. Diego bobbed in the water, scooping the toy up and tossing it about. He giggled, sounding like Liam or any other little boy his age.

"Now for the soap." Tobias tossed a bar into the water. Diego backed away. "The point is to get clean."

He made scrubbing motions on his face, pantomiming cleaning behind his ears, his face scrunched up as if he really hated it. Diego plunged his face into the water and came up with his hair dripping. "Good job. Now soap."

"Soap." Diego grabbed the floating bar and held it up. "Soap."

"Clean."

"Clean."

"See, you'll speak English before you know it."

Diego lay back on the water in a semifloat, his face blissful. The water had already turned brown without the help of soap and a washrag. He should smell better too. Not that most little boys didn't smell like dirt and sweat anyway.

"What do you think is in the backpack?" Martha peeked around the corner. She kept her voice a whisper as if afraid Diego would run again. “He seems to think we're going to steal whatever it is.”

“I reckon it's all he has left of home.” Tobias sat back on his heels and rubbed his aching knees. “Whatever it is, it's none of our business.”

“He might have clean clothes in there.”

“After traveling thousands of miles from home, I doubt that. It's not like they stopped in at a Laundromat along the way.” Diego began to sing in Spanish, a breathy tuneless song that told Tobias he had relaxed like a little boy taking a bath should. “Besides, he's about Liam's size. He can wear his clothes.”

“That's what I thought. I brought him these. If he doesn't want the nightshirt he can sleep in the clothes.” Martha held out a clean, folded nightshirt, pants, and shirt. “Make him wash that hair. It smells like a Dumpster.”

“I may have to get in there with him to get him to do it.”

Martha smiled. “You'll be a good daed one day. You have the knack.”

Pleasure swept through Tobias at the thought. Followed by a wave of fear. More children to protect. His shoulders ached with the imagined burden. Eight brothers and sisters were enough. More than enough. Too much sometimes. The fear of losing them filled his head late at night, keeping him awake. Why would a man want more of that?

He ducked his head, knowing his face had turned red. “We'll wait to see what Gott's plan is.”

Martha disappeared through the doorway, leaving Tobias with his thoughts and a boy who didn't weigh fifty pounds soaking wet. He scooped the soap from the water and rubbed it in his hands until he had a nice lather. "Here we go. Time to wash that hair."

Diego worked his way to the other side of the tub. Tobias went after him. The boy shrieked with laughter. "Don't laugh so loud—the other kinner will want to take baths every night if it sounds like this much fun!"

Fifteen minutes later Tobias was soaked from head to foot and exhausted, but Diego was squeaky clean. Tobias lifted him from the tub and set him on his feet next to the backpack. He handed him a towel. "Wear the nightshirt. You'll sleep better."

Tobias was the one who would sleep well—at least he hoped so. It had been a long day. The discussion with the elders. Volleyball. Rebekah.

Rebekah. He concentrated on rubbing Diego's hair. No thinking of Rebekah. Tall, slim, full of vinegar. Trouble with a capital *T.* What would she see in a man like him who'd thrown his love away on an Englisch girl? He didn't really want to love anyone. Not if it meant losing her the way Daed lost Mudder. Why did a person put himself through that?

Where was Gott's hand in that?

Gott should smite him with a mighty sword for being so hardheaded. Stiff-necked, as Scripture put it.

I'm sorry, Gott. I can't help myself. I've tried. You know I have.

Diego tugged at his hand, his expression rueful. Tobias eased up with the towel. "What, am I rubbing too hard?"

Diego snatched the backpack from the floor and held it out. "See?"

"See what?" He'd made inroads in Diego's trust. The thought made Tobias smile. He undid the zipper, prepared to find family photos, small toys, keepsakes from another life. "I'm glad you want to share."

A small creature peeked its head from the opening. Brown. Beady eyed, its nose wiggling. It ducked back into the pack.

Tobias stumbled back a step. He stared at the backpack, then at Diego. "That's a mouse."

Diego nodded so hard Tobias thought his head might fall off. He slapped a hand to his chest. "*Mi amigo.* Pedro."

"Your friend?"

Diego had a pet mouse. Had he traveled all the way to America from El Salvador, or had the friendship been struck somewhere along the way?

Diego grabbed Tobias's hand. His grin stretched across his clean face, his eyes nearly hidden by squeaky clean hair that needed to be cut. "Mi amigo *también*."

Tobias's heart flopped. Mouse or not, another child to protect or not, it didn't matter. He'd made a friend. From the look on Diego's face, he was the kind who would be a friend for life.

Tobias heaved a breath, his chest tight with apprehension.

Another person he would have to protect.

Another person poised to leave.

SEVEN

The shriek raised the hair on the nape of Susan's neck. School hadn't even begun for the day and the scholars were up to something unruly. Usually she had thirty minutes or more to prepare while they played kickball in the yard before she rang the bell and classes started. Not today, it seemed. Rebekah had stayed behind at the house to help Abigail move some heavy rugs that needed to be cleaned. She would be in later.

Sighing, Susan dropped the piece of chalk she'd been using to write assignments on the board and strode to the door left open to allow the early morning breeze to clear stuffy air from the classroom. The kinner weren't on the makeshift ball field. They were clustered around the girls' outhouse. Boys and girls.

"What now?" She stepped out onto the porch.

Mary broke away from the crowd, raced across the yard, and hurled herself up the steps. "Teacher, Teacher!"

"What is it? What's wrong?"

"Rattlesnakes. Lots of snakes." Mary gasped for air, breathed, and stumbled to a stop. "Baby snakes."

"Rattlesnakes? Where?" Susan grabbed the hoe the girls had

left on the porch after the last frolic to clear the weeds and create a field that could be used for baseball, kickball, or volleyball, her scholars' three favorite recess activities. Usually she didn't worry much about snakes—except the rattlers, and this was the season when many of God's creatures had their babies. "Did anyone get bit?"

"Nee, not yet, but Hazel wants to take one home. She thinks the babies are cute. I had to wrestle her back. I think Diego wanted to go kill them for us. It's hard to tell, he talks so fast." Mary took Susan's arm and tugged. "There's a whole den of them right outside the girls' outhouse."

Goose bumps raced up Susan's arms. Her entire body wanted to return to the schoolhouse. In fact, her head wanted to run home and go back to bed. Instead, hoe in hand, she trotted after the girl. If she could scatter the babies, maybe mama snake would decide to take up residence in another location. If she didn't decide to make an appearance during Susan's attempt to roust her babies. Chopping off the heads would be like trying to bob for apples with no hands.

The kinner stood in a tight half circle well out of reach of the outhouse. Caleb rushed forward, little Diego on his heels. The boy seemed to have latched onto her nephew. "Want me to chop their heads off? I can do it."

"Nee, stay back and keep Diego with you. I don't know how dangerous the babies are, but the momma snake can't be too far away."

"Babies have a lot of venom and they know how to use it."

Caleb surely got his information from Mordecai. Susan wasn't taking any chances with her sister-in-law's only son. "Just stay back."

Hoe lifted over one shoulder, Susan swallowed her dislike and fear of all snakes but this kind in particular and inched forward until she could peek around the corner of the small white shack. Indeed, a whole mess of them roiled about along the back wall. She swallowed again, closed her eyes, and opened them.

"What's going on?"

She whirled. Levi pulled his wagon to a halt in the yard. "Oh, thanks be to Gott."

His bushy eyebrows pushed up and stayed up, giving him a quizzical look.

"I mean, it's just that we have a mess of baby rattlers right outside the outhouse. I'm afraid—"

"I can see that."

"I was going to say I'm afraid the kinner will be bitten." What was it about this man that made her tongue disconnect from her brain? "I was about to take care of them."

Levi hopped from the wagon, his tall, lean body unfolding with a grace surprising in an older man. He reached from under the seat. Out came a long, slim rifle. "Were you planning to weed them to death?"

Susan couldn't decide if there was even a hint of humor in the question. It was hard to tell with his deep green eyes fastened on her face. She wanted to stand there as long as it took to decide. Even with snakes slithering nearby. What did that say about her state of mind this fine morning? That the teacher better stop mooning around and be the teacher? "Chop their heads off." She took a breath and willed herself to move her gaze from his face to the rifle. "You carry a rifle in your wagon?"

"I just hadn't put it away yet from the trip here. It seemed the safest place to keep it with so many curious kinner running around." He held the rifle close to his chest with both hands. "You chop babies' heads off, you have to bury them or kinner will step on them with their bare feet. The kinner need to back up."

The man wasn't telling her anything she didn't already know, yet he sounded so wise with that deep, gravelly voice and even tone. She took a step back. Now why did she do that? "You can't shoot them all."

"I'll scatter them and look for the mudder. She needs to go. Snakes may be good for getting rid of mice and pests, but we can't have a passel of rattlesnakes so close to the school when we're so far from the closest antivenom."

Again, all things Susan already knew. Levi strode past her. She inhaled the scent of leather and man sweat. He glanced back, his gaze now quizzical. "Can you keep them back?"

Of course she could. He was a bossy sort. But then, most men were. Susan didn't get bossed around much anymore, not with Mordecai married now.

Neither was she used to standing around while others did the work, even if it involved snakes.

"I can help." She shifted the hoe so she carried it the same way he did the rifle. "Be your backup. There's a bunch of them."

He frowned and shook his head. His beard bobbed. "Nee. Stay."

Stay? Like a *hund*? She bit her tongue and held back, counting to ten forward and backward. Not because Levi said so, but because the kinner were her responsibility. If Levi got bit, she would be the adult in charge of getting him help. She eyed the wagon. At least the horse was harnessed and ready to go. It took a long time to get from these parts into Beeville and the medical center.

"What's the matter?" Caleb sidled closer, his tone decidedly grown up for a twelve-year-old. Diego mimicked his moves, sidling up on her other side. "Levi will get them for sure."

"I don't like guns either. Guns or snakes."

"Which is worse?" Mary posed the question from her post in front of the smaller children.

"I'm not sure."

"Do the snakes come from eggs like chickens?"

"Nee, they are born alive, just like regular babies." Only with fangs full of venom and ready to strike. Susan tried not to sound too concerned. "They're not fluffy like baby chicks, you can be sure of that."

A shotgun blast pierced the air. Susan jumped in spite of herself. Diego shrieked and threw himself to the ground, arms over his head. Lupe barreled forward and collapsed on top of him, covering his body with her own.

"It's okay, it's okay, it's only Levi. Levi is taking care of the snakes." Susan knelt next to Lupe and laid her hand on the girl's heaving back. "It's Levi. Levi. You understand? Only Levi."

Lupe raised her head a few inches, her face smudged with dirt. "Gun, pow, pow! Hombres malos."

"No, no. It's only Levi killing snakes."

Lupe swiped at her face, smearing the dirt across her cheek and nose. She nodded and moved a few inches away from Diego. Whatever words she murmured to her brother seemed to help. He curled himself up in a ball close to Lupe, and the two huddled together on the ground.

Susan rose and strode to where Caleb stood, arms on his hips in an unconscious imitation of Mordecai. She threw her arm in front of him. "You stay here. I'll go."

He ducked his head and crossed his arms. "I'm old enough to help."

She glanced at the outhouse. No sign of Levi. She turned to Caleb. "Keep an eye on the kinner. If I don't come back with Levi, go for help. Leave Sally and Joseph in charge."

His expression mutinous, he nodded.

Hoe over her shoulder, Susan marched around the building, fighting the urge to tiptoe. She kept her gaze on the ground, willing her breakfast to stay put. No baby snakes curled around her shoes. Levi might need her help. He might have a rifle, but he could still be taken unaware by a rattler and end up with a bite. He was only a man. A tall, muscled man with eyes that lit up his tanned face. Susan shook her head. She was thinking like a teenage girl in the middle of a crisis.

Levi stood at the fence that separated the school property from the Englisch farmer whose field was turning green with alfalfa. He aimed and fired. Again, she jumped. "What is wrong with me?"

She marched across the field, hoe at the ready.

Levi leaned down, scooped up a snake about five or six feet long. He turned, the snake swinging limp from his hand. "What're you doing out here?"

"Helping."

If she didn't know better, she'd say his eyes rolled the way Caleb's did when she told him he needed to wash his hands before supper. "We covered that already. I told you to stay."

"I'm not a hund."

"Nee, you're not." This time he did smile. The transformation was instantaneous. A young man with eyes the color of a meadow in spring and a smile like the taste of homemade ice cream in summer looked at her for a split second. Then he was gone and Levi

Byler, a widower with a face filled with sadness the color of winter, looked at her. "I would've noticed."

Susan breathed and concentrated on the offering in his huge, calloused hand. "So you got it?"

Levi glanced at his hand as if only now noticing what he held. "Done. For now. If there's one, there's surely more. The kinner shouldn't be running about barefoot."

"The closer it gets to summer, the harder it is to convince them of that." Susan averted her eyes from his prize—and from him. "Should we look for more?"

"We?"

"I'm capable of helping."

"You're capable of teaching the kinner to stay away from this field and to wear their shoes. That's your job." His gravelly tone softened. "But the thought is appreciated."

Put in her place but in such a kindly way she could hardly complain. "What'll you do with it?"

"Make a belt. Or some hatbands. The Englischers like that."

Levi moved past her. She whirled and skedaddled to keep up with his long strides. He slowed as they approached the kinner. They crowded closer, their faces filled with curiosity. Levi held up the snake. "Got it. You kinner stay out of the field and wear your shoes."

He glanced at Susan. "And do what Teacher says."

"We always do." Caleb offered the statement. He was right. They were good kinner. "Susan plays volleyball with us."

"Does she?" Levi tugged down the brim of his straw hat with his free hand. "I didn't see her playing last night."

"I was busy cleaning up spilled cookies because a person snuck up on me. On most nights that doesn't happen."

"I guess I'll have to come back on most nights." He tossed the snake in the back of the wagon and laid the rifle under the seat. "It's good that you've cleared the land where they play. Just be very careful around the wood stack and along the fence lines."

"Thankfully the need for wood has passed."

He nodded. "Then I best get to work. Tobias is waiting for me at the shop."

"What about the babies?" Mary walked backward as she posed the question. "The babies were cute."

"Nee, they were not cute." Sally shook her head. "Ugh."

Levi climbed into the wagon and eased onto the seat. "I disposed of a few of them, but the rest are still out there, so be careful where you step. Stay in the cleared areas."

"Time for school." Long past time. Time to focus on her job, one that had been enough for her for years and years. That had not changed. The appearance of a new, mature, single man in Bee County had not changed things one whit. "Everyone inside. Get yourself ready for prayers and songs. Ida and Nyla are new. They get to pick today's songs."

Groaning, the kinner traipsed past her, still talking and giggling about the morning's adventure. Susan waited until the last one tromped through the door, then turned to Levi. Proper thanks were in order, nothing more. "It's good you came by when you did."

"I reckon so."

"Your help is appreciated."

"A person doesn't stand by under such circumstances."

Of course not. "Then I guess you'll be back by for the kinner later."

Silly thing to say. Of course he would.

"Either me or Tobias. Today. After that they'll know the lay of the land and Rueben can bring them."

"That's a good plan." As if he needed her approval. She crossed her arms over her middle, trying to think of a way to end the conversation that didn't make her sound like a silly goose. "I better get inside. I've asked Lupe to teach the kinner some Spanish words. Simple things like *water* and *apples* and *bread*. It's hard, though, with them not speaking English or German and the smaller kinner not understanding English or Spanish. Otherwise they could talk about geography and the customs in their country too."

She was running at the mouth.

Levi nodded but didn't say a thing. He snapped the reins. The wagon creaked and the horse whinnied in protest as it turned and headed for the road. Apparently he had nothing else to say.

Not to a silly goose, anyway.

EIGHT

Nothing better than the smell of cowhide in the morning. Tobias grinned to himself as he followed David into the new saddle shop—what would soon be the saddle and leather shop. He left the door open, better to get some fresh air into the long, narrow room with its bare Sheetrock walls. Short, high windows sported curtains made from small, rectangular Indian blankets. The scarred wood floor needed sweeping of dust and the detritus of leather shavings.

He stretched his arms over his head, cranked his neck from side to side, and inhaled. The place smelled of dust, leather, and old wood. Lots of work to be done here. He felt at home already. It was good of Leroy and his sons to loan them the building next to the corral where the horses were trained. The Englischers would bring the horses and stop in to check out the saddles and leather goods.

Boxes of tools and leather goods they'd brought from Ohio sat along one wall waiting to be opened. They would go into town in a few weeks to see which stores might be interested in selling the smaller items—wallets, belts, holsters, koozies, hunting canteens, and shaving kits. All had sold well up north. Their meat and potatoes when the more expensive saddles weren't in high demand. Here, the market was as yet unknown. Tobias itched to get started with the leather work. Not the marketing so much. He had to do it. Daed had no use for it and David tended to run at the mouth and get little actual work done.

Morning sun burst through the dirty windows that faced the east. A good place to put the saddle maker's bench. He had a saddletree ready to go for the first custom job that came along. He needed lots of light to do the fancy tooling on the leather the Englischers liked. The shop needed some work, but Gott was good to provide this new start in a place where folks valued their horseflesh and the trappings that came with it.

"This place is a pit." David strode through the door, sniffed, and groaned, his green eyes squinted against the sunlight pouring in around him, creating a halo behind his straw hat. "It stinks."

"What do you care? You'll spend all your time in the corral or the barn, anyway."

His brother grinned. "It's not my fault Gott gave me no patience for busywork and all the tools to make horses follow me around like a pied piper."

"Each to their own. Might as well get to work." Tobias didn't rise to the bait. "Unpack that association saddle I finished before we left. We need to display it in case folks come in. Give them an idea of the work we can do."

"Who do you think will buy custom saddles around here?" Instead of heading for the boxes, David propped himself against a wall and dusted dirt from his boots with the back of his hand. "Not a lot of money in these parts from the looks of the place."

"There's plenty of ranches around here with working cowboys."

Tobias had explained this to his brother more than once on the long ride to Texas. "They understand that a custom-made saddle will last them far longer than a factory job. It's worth the investment to know they can ride it hard and long every day for five years or more."

"I hope you're right. Otherwise we moved for nothing."

"Regardless, Jeremiah says there's a man in town who creates websites. We can take orders from all over the country if we have a website."

"You think Daed will go for that?"

"I already talked to him about it. He said as long as I don't bring the computer into the shop, he's happy."

"Times, they are a-changing." David snorted. "I forgot the cooler in the buggy. I'll be back."

Anything to get out of the boring work. Tobias turned his back on his brother and surveyed the boxes. The saddle he'd labored over for three weeks, giving it an elaborate design of leaves and a basket stamp, should be in one of the bigger boxes. Cobwebs decorated the beams of the ceiling over them. He breathed, coughed, and sneezed.

"God bless you."

He looked back at the high voice with a Texas twang. A woman in her early to midtwenties stood in the open door. She wore a red checkered western-style shirt, faded blue jeans, black cowboy boots, and a belt with a silver buckle as big as Tobias's fist. Her blonde hair hung in a braid down her back. Her face was fresh and clean, devoid of makeup. "Sorry, didn't mean to startle you."

"You didn't." He tugged open a box of cleaning supplies and rags on top of a spindly, old oak table in the middle of the room.

They would need to clean up before they started setting up the equipment. They needed to build some counters too. And hang the horseshoes they used to hold all their leather string, twines, threads, and such. "We're not open yet. As you can see."

"But we could be, depending on what you need." David sauntered into the room, cooler in hand, and halted next to Tobias. His gaze lingered on the woman. "I'm David Byler. This is my brother Tobias. He's a saddle maker. I train horses."

Making as if to pick up another box, Tobias smacked his brother on the arm. "We're just unpacking. We're not open."

"Actually, I was looking for Adam Glick." The woman slid her hat from her head, giving Tobias a better look at her blue eyes. "He was supposed to meet me in the corral this morning."

"He's probably running a little late."

"I reckon."

"You're welcome to wait." David threw out the invitation before Tobias could suggest she put her horse in the corral while she waited.

"Thanks. I'm Bobbie McGregor."

"Bobbie?"

"Short for Roberta. My daddy calls me Roberta Sue, but he's the only one who gets away with it."

Turning his back on their visitor, Tobias picked up a handful of rags and a bottle of window cleaner. No matter what his daed wanted, Tobias couldn't lose the manners his mudder had instilled in him. Bobbie was a new acquaintance. "Are you interested in a saddle?"

She strode into the room and stopped by a cowhide stretched over a chair abandoned along one wall. Her hand smoothed the leather in quick, soft strokes. "I might be. Adam showed me a catalog from up north that had some of your work in it. The saddles were nice."

The catalog had been the tip of the iceberg that had gotten Tobias in trouble. They had worked with an Englisch horse farmer to expand their business when farming hadn't been enough to take care of the family. The Englischer had a daughter. Serena. Serena with blonde hair, white skin, and brilliant emerald-green eyes. Serena who favored pink lipstick, white lacy blouses, and long swirling skirts and never went anywhere without a thick book stuck in a big bag slung over her shoulder.

That was all in the past. "If you want to leave a note, we can let Adam know you stopped by."

"I have Cracker Jack in the trailer out there. I'll wait."

"Cracker Jack?"

"The horse I need trained."

"Right."

"So how do you like South Texas?"

"I like it fine."

"Man of few words. Like my dad." She slipped past him, leaving a cloud of scent like roses behind, moving toward the single open chair in the room. She planted a boot on it and propped her elbow on her knee, her chin on her hand. "How come you don't train horses like your brother and your dad?"

"I prefer to work with leather."

"So you're the artistic one in the family. How much do you charge for your saddles?"

"Depends on what you want. Basic working saddle starts at four thousand."

"I already have a basic saddle. Three of them, in fact. A person could never have too many saddles." She pulled a folded piece of glossy paper from her back pocket and held it out. Her fingernails were clipped short, her hands the calloused hands of someone who did work on a regular basis. "It's a barrel-racing saddle with crystal trim. Do you do the fancy stuff?"

They did the fancy stuff because some Englischers who could afford custom-made saddles wanted it. The working cowboys didn't care about it. They were more interested in solid construction that meant the riggings would never slip and the horn would stay put when they were cutting cattle day in and day out. Tobias accepted her offering and studied the photo and description taken from a catalog.

David moved to look over his shoulder. He let out a long, low whistle. "Wow."

Oversized silver conchos, oiled leather carved in floral and basket-weave tooling with little crystals finishing the inside of each flower. Intricate work. Beautiful. The cantle had rawhide and silver lace trim and the seat was a black padded suede with a fleece underside. "Nice."

"Nice? It's awesome. Can you do that kind of work?"

"If you've already found one, why do you want me to make it for you?"

"Custom made is better. It's a tad more ornate than I like. I'd want oak leaves and acorns."

He'd have to order the conchos, the crystals, and the suede. It would be expensive, but she seemed willing and able to pay. Their first customer in Texas. "We can do it, but it takes time and we have to set up the shop first."

"Any idea how much it will cost me?"

Aside from two sides of cowhide and the fleece of an entire sheep? "I won't know until I research the materials we'll have to special order. You'll have to give us a deposit up front."

"You don't have a price list?"

"Not yet." Daed strode through the door, a frown stretched across his face, a long, dead rattler swinging from one hand. "We're not open yet."

"So Tobias said. You must be the dad. You three look like triplets." Bobbie nodded in greeting. "Been doing a little hunting?"

"We may look alike, but I'm older and wiser." Levi slapped the snake on the table next to the boxes. "Adam just pulled up. He said he was waiting on a customer. I reckon that must be you."

"What'll you do with the rattlesnake skin?" Bobbie edged closer to the table. She didn't seem in any hurry to talk to Adam now that Levi had arrived. "That one would make a nice band for the black hat I wear when I barrel race."

"That we can do—once the shop is open." Levi waved a hand toward the stacks of boxes. "I imagine my sons told you we have a lot of unpacking to do first. When you come back to order your saddle, we'll talk about the hatband."

"The name's Bobbie with an *i-e,* not *y,* McGregor. Don't be selling it to someone else." Bobbie turned and tipped her hat to Tobias and David. "Nice meeting you. I'll be back."

"We should be open for business in a few days."

She stopped at the door and looked back. "Good. Consider the saddle your first sale here. Welcome to Texas."

Tobias didn't answer. He knew better. Storm clouds rolled across Levi's usually taciturn face. Better to let his daed deal with the customers. Tobias would simply do the work and keep his mouth shut. A practice that had held him in good stead. Until

Serena. Bobbie disappeared into the bright sunlight of a South Texas spring day.

"I'm gonna go see how Adam does business with the Englisch folks around here." David dashed out the door before Tobias or Daed could respond.

Best to find a new subject quick. Tobias opened the closest box. Wool. Lots of wool. "What's with the snake?"

"Had a mess of babies outside the girls' outhouse at the school."

"You want me to clean it?"

"Jah." Levi sniffed. He wasn't done talking yet, that was certain, but as usual, he appeared to be mulling over his words as if they had to be translated from some ancient, difficult, dead language. "I thought you'd learned something."

Here we go. "She's a potential customer. We need those if we're going to make this store work. Besides, David is the one following after her like a puppy dog."

"He's looking for business. He knows how much we need it."

"I have no plans to repeat my mistakes." *Or to let David do the same.*

"That's gut."

"But you'll have to trust me on that. I have to talk to customers, whether they be men or women." He sprayed the dirty window and began to wipe with more vigor than necessary. "In case you haven't noticed, this place is out in the middle of nowhere. Customers will have to hear good things about us and be willing to drive a piece in order to give us work. We'll need that website I talked to you about."

"I'm well aware. I leave that sort of thing to you as long as you understand the rules."

"I do. Are you also aware that we have to be nice to folks in order to get their business?"

"I'm aware." Levi heaved another box onto the table and pulled back the panels to reveal Tobias's favorite tools of the trade. The skiving knife, lacing awl, bull-nose pliers, leather hole punches, rivet setter, copper and silver rivets, a cobbler's hammer, his beveling tool. They needed to set up the wooden holders he'd built special for keeping all these small pieces organized.

His hands itched to get to work. It had been too long. The work occupied his hands and left his mind to wander over peaks and valleys of thoughts that meandered on a road to nowhere or to understanding, he was never sure which it would be.

"Hey." Adam stuck his head in the door. "David says Bobbie talked to y'all about training her quarter horse. She might be a good one for you to start with. You could handle the training. The saddle is a separate deal, for her barrel racing. You'd be doing that anyway. Make it a package deal."

"I don't want to take food off your table." Levi's words trailed off. He laid the awl on an old towel with the other tools. Thankfulness warred with unwillingness on his face. When Levi took a dislike to a situation, he could be as stubborn as an old *groossmammi*. "We're thankful for your generosity. We could use the business."

"Nee, nee. Just being neighborly." Adam jerked his head. "Come on, you need to negotiate the terms of the deal, or whatever you Northerners call it. Day's not getting any younger."

Tobias turned his back and smiled to himself. Served Levi right for being so distrusting. A man had to take what was given as if it were a gift from God. Because it always was, no matter how unlikely it seemed and whether the gift wore faded blue jeans and a silver buckle.

Levi's tread to the door was slow. "Stop by the school at noon on your way home to eat."

Once the shop was open they would bring their noon meal. Not today. Leftover hamburger-cabbage casserole awaited them at the house. Martha was a good cook. She did a lot with a little and made it go a long way. "Why?"

"That dead snake was the mudder. Bunch of babies out there. Whole area around the outhouse is infested."

"Ach."

"Take a look around. I scattered the babies, but there may be more of the bigger ones. They like to den together in the winter. It's time for them to come out now that the cold has passed."

As if the weather here could be described as cold. Lukewarm, maybe. Tobias nodded. He could check on Lupe and Diego while he was at it.

Rebekah would be there. As good a reason as any to stop.

Rebekah with her dark hair and blue eyes. So different from Serena's blonde hair, green eyes, and deliberate way of telling a story that drove him crazy. No one could draw out a story like Serena. She always had a point. She just liked taking her time getting there.

"Say hey to Rebekah and make sure she's not putting silly ideas in Lupe's and Diego's heads about staying here. Susan already has them teaching lessons and learning English."

If mind reading were possible, Levi would be first in line to provide the service. "Or you could do it when you pick up the kinner after school. You could give Susan a good talking-to for being such a teacher with a heart for lost children."

Levi stalked away without an answer.

Tobias chuckled. Tit for tat. His daed didn't like that, but sometimes a person got what he deserved.

NINE

The snore gave Caleb away. Sometimes teaching was fun. Rebekah grinned at Susan and tiptoed down the aisle to the boys' side where her brother's head bobbed and his open mouth emitted a sound somewhat like a train rumbling on the tracks. A bit of drool teetered on his chin. Any minute and his lolling head would bob forward and collide with his scarred wooden desk. It was a wonder he didn't wake himself up with all that ruckus. It certainly made it hard to hear the little ones practice reading in English. It wasn't very polite either.

She leaned in close, snapped her fingers by his ear, and yelled, "Boo."

Caleb bolted upright, his gaze wild as he whirled around. "What? What?"

"You were sleeping in class." Rebekah didn't bother to keep accusation from her tone. Sleeping set a bad example for the rest of the scholars. Even if it was funny. "You get to lead the class in a song."

Caleb hung his head. "I didn't mean to fall asleep. History is so boring." His face brightened. "Is it time for arithmetic yet? I'm good at numbers."

"If you don't know history, you might end up doing the same thing over. That gets humans into trouble all the time." Susan shook a finger at him. It made her look like such a teacher. "It might not seem important now, but when you're older, you'll understand."

"How about science?" Caleb read all the books about plants and animals. He knew almost as much as Mordecai about the sky and stars and birds. "I do good with bugs and stuff."

"Well. You do well." Susan shook her head, frowning. "A person should be well rounded."

"Why do I have to know this stuff to plant onions and broccoli?" Caleb rolled his eyes, his disgust plain in his freckled face. "It's more important to know about weather and irrigation and how to make things grow in a drought. Families can't eat history."

"You can learn those things, but first you will learn how to do as you're told. Okay, students. It's time for a Spanish lesson. Spanish is practical. We can all use it when we go to the border." Susan clapped her hands together. "Lupe, come up front and be the teacher."

Rebekah inhaled the scent of sweaty feet, chalk, and the taco casserole Susan had heated for her noonday meal. She would never tell Susan, but she agreed with Caleb. She longed to be outside. She could see the sunshine through the windows that lined one side of the schoolroom. A breeze was blowing, making tree branches rustle against the glass. The sound called to her. *Come out and play.*

Which was why she should never be the teacher. So what did that leave her? She couldn't get a job in town. Mudder wouldn't allow it. She touched her hand to her apron as if she could touch Leila's note, still tucked in the hem. At noon she would see her sister and find out what was so urgent that Leila felt it necessary to see a sister she'd abandoned without so much as a good-bye. Maybe she wanted to say she was sorry. After all this time it seemed unlikely. What difference would that make now, anyway? Rebekah had to forgive Leila, one way or another.

The Bible said so. The bishop said so. Mordecai said so.

Only Rebekah couldn't wrap her heart around the words and say them so she meant them. Leila would know that.

Rebekah batted the thoughts away. They were an endless cycle she couldn't stop. Better to focus on Lupe, who had trudged on bare feet to the front of the room, her head down, her cheeks pink. Lupe and Diego needed help. Leila and Jesse might be able to provide that help. Maybe something good would come from their decision to leave the community. To leave Rebekah with a bunch of boys who figured she would go next. Never in her life had she thought of leaving the district. And she never did anything because her sisters did it. More likely, she would do the opposite. Anyone who knew her, knew that.

Stop thinking. Focus on Lupe here and now. The girl stopped in front of the black chalkboard, shifting from one foot to the other on the wooden floor. She didn't like being the center of attention, that was apparent.

Susan pointed to herself. "Teacher."

Lupe tucked her dark, straight hair behind her ear and ducked her head. *"Maestra."*

This was knowledge Rebekah could use. She might still get to go to Mexico one day. That she could look forward to doing. But Lupe looked as if she wished she were anywhere else in the world at that moment. Rebekah edged to the front of the room. "I'll help. You say the word and I'll repeat it."

Lupe squinted as if that would help her understand.

"Maestra."

"You have to speak up, honey. I can't hear you, and if I can't hear you, neither can they." Susan waved her hand at the other scholars. "It's okay, they won't bite."

"Ma-es-tra." Lupe stretched the word out in three long syllables. "Teacher."

"Everyone." Rebekah flung her hands in the air. "Ma-es-tra."

The sounds coming from the scholars varied from close to nowhere in the same county.

"Again."

And again until they more or less had it.

"What about this?" Liam held up his pencil. "What do you call this?"

"Jah, and what about me? What am I?" Nyla pointed to herself. "And my desk, what do you call that?"

Diego popped up from his spot next to Liam. *"Lápiz."*

"Pencil?" Liam waggled his pencil back and forth, his face scrunched up as he tried to work his tongue and lips around the Spanish word. "La-peas?"

Diego raised his hands and did a little dance. "Lápiz, lápiz, lápiz."

"Everyone!" Rebekah matched her dance step to his. "La-peas, la-peas, la-peas."

Caleb burst into a belly laugh that made Rebekah giggle. The scholars popped up from their desks and did the same jig, giggling so hard the words were unintelligible.

Breathless, she stopped dancing. "What? Is there something wrong with my steps?"

"Nee, but your pronunciation is awful." Caleb guffawed and plopped back in his seat. "Even I can do better than that."

"Fine, how do you say it?"

"La-pees."

"That's what I said."

"Nee, it's not. You said la-peas."

"That's enough!" Susan wiped tears of laughter from her cheek with a white handkerchief. "Close enough, right, Lupe?"

A big grin stretched across her thin face, Lupe shrugged. *"Me gusta reir."*

"What does that mean?"

Lupe giggled, hand to her mouth. She smiled big and put her fingers at both ends of her lips. "Ha, ha, ha."

"You like to laugh?"

She nodded. Rebekah put an arm around the girl. Seeing her laugh brought light to a cloudy day. "Me too. Laughing is one of the best things to do, isn't it?"

"Oh no, oh no!" Diego's small face scrunched up in a frown, and he shot from his seat and raced down the aisle to the back of the room. "Pedro! Pedro!"

"What is it?" Rebekah squeezed Lupe's arm and let go. "What's he doing?"

Lupe scrambled after her brother. She glanced back. "Mouse."

"What?"

"Tobias say it is mouse."

"What is mouse?"

"Pedro."

"There it is." Hazel hopped from her seat and shrieked. "Mouse, mouse, Teacher, there's a mouse in the school!"

"It's just a mouse." Susan bustled down the aisle after Diego. "Nothing to get excited about."

A mouse wasn't Rebekah's favorite kind of pet, but Caleb had

had worse. Like a green garter snake. And a hamster. Hamsters were similar to mice. He'd even befriended some beetles. The turtles weren't so bad, though.

Lupe stuck her head under a desk, then another. "He is amigo. Diego sad if he lost."

Rebekah followed her and began to look as well. Anything to make Diego feel better. "Friend?" A little boy who'd left his home, his family, his country, would indeed want to hang on to whatever friends he found along the way on this terrible journey to a new country and new life. "Let's help him look for Pedro."

The scholars needed no prompting. They scattered, peering in corners and under desks and behind the stove.

"Got him!" Caleb held up the wiggling brown creature with long whiskers and a longer tail. "He's cute."

Cute? He was wrinkled and had beady eyes.

"Pedro. Pedro!" Diego hurled himself across the room. *"Ratoncito."*

"Ratoncito." All the scholars joined in. "Ratoncito."

Rebekah slipped up next to Susan. "Ratoncito, Teacher?"

"A friend is a friend." Susan clapped her hands. The scholars dropped into their seats. Diego slipped Pedro back in his little home. Susan's attempt to look stern failed. She smiled. "Everyone sit. Let's learn a few more words, but without the show-and-tell."

Rebekah sidled closer. "The live show-and-tell?"

"Sí."

Rebekah laughed. "Sí." Show-and-tell had never been so much fun. "They're learning from each other, though. That's gut, isn't it?"

"It is gut. We can all learn from each other." Susan cocked her head, her expression pensive. "See, teaching can be fun."

"I know that." Rebekah slipped past her and picked up a piece of chalk. Time to put the algebra assignment up. "I think teaching is fun."

"You tell fibs and your nose will grow."

"I'm not."

Susan patted her shoulder. "It's okay. It doesn't hurt my feelings. I never thought I'd be a teacher either."

"But you like to read and write. You read books all the time and you write letters to your brother and sister every week. I'd rather be doing something."

"Reading and writing are doing something."

"I know. I just thought I would be doing something different."

"Don't give up. Say your prayers and wait on Gott's timing." Susan's expression turned stern. "I noticed you've stopped going to the singings."

"No point in it." Unless Tobias Byler decided to go. Would he? Someone who didn't know all about the Lantz sisters and how one of them had abandoned the community. He had been so kind to the children, giving them the apples, taking them home. He was a nice man. And not bad to look at.

Here she stood weaving a future from thin air. From hopes that were no more than rays of sun that dissipated as if clouds deliberately covered her patch of sky. Tobias had seen her as bossy and wayward, not fraa material. She'd seen it in his eyes. If only she could be more like her big sister Deborah. A mother bird who gathered chickadees under her wings as naturally as breathing.

"Go. Boys have a short memory." Susan touched Rebekah's cheek, something in her face suggesting she, too, experienced cloudy skies on sunny days. "They'll look at you and forget all about what happened with Leila."

"They haven't yet."

"You'll make a fine fraa. Patience is a virtue."

"Is that what you're doing?"

Susan dusted chalk from her fingers. "I am." Her smile faded. "Every day."

Rebekah picked up a stack of papers. "Then I guess I'll start grading these papers, Teacher. We can wait together."

Until she couldn't wait anymore.

TEN

Rebekah glanced over her shoulder. What if one of the scholars decided to follow her? The rutted dirt path that cut through knee-high weeds and meandered between stands of mesquite, live oak, and knobby green nopales was empty. A grasshopper skittered across her apron and somersaulted out of sight in the grass. The steamy air smelled of fresh-cut hay and dirt. Sweat trickled from under her kapp, tickling her neck. She had no way of knowing how long it had taken her to scurry from the schoolhouse to this secluded spot on a farm road. Any minute Susan would ring the bell and classes would resume for the afternoon.

She felt like a traitor. She was Susan's helper. Susan counted on her. Susan expected her to do the right thing. Rebekah was trying to do the right thing. More thoughts running around in circles. She was doing this for the kinner's sake. They were so sweet and so innocent. Lupe and Diego should be allowed to stay. Rebekah would take care of them herself, if necessary. Susan wanted them to stay too. She would understand.

Mudder and Mordecai would not see it that way. Nor would Jeremiah. It didn't make sense. They didn't understand. They hadn't been talking to Leila about Jesse's work in the church. Jesse did all kinds of what Leila called outreach. Rebekah didn't exactly know what that meant, but Leila could ask Jesse if he had any ideas about what they could do for Lupe and Diego. The churches were helping the immigrant children through the legal hurdles that awaited them in this land of opportunity. She'd seen articles about it in the *Beeville Times-Picayune* that Mordecai read in the evenings after he finished the *Budget*.

Diego's tear-streaked face filled her mind. What if they decided to call the sheriff from the store phone today after sleeping on the situation? What if the kinner were sent home? El Salvador must be a hard place if a mother sent her children on such a long, scary journey across entire countries alone.

Rebekah pushed the thought away and trudged forward, her sneakers crunching on cockleburs and weeds already dry in the South Texas sun. She would see Leila and Grace for a few minutes. She would ask her questions. It hurt nothing and she could offer Leila the chance to come home.

Leila might be waiting to be offered a chance to return home. God might soften her heart and help Rebekah bring home the prodigal daughter.

The path dead-ended at an equally rutted dirt road, the only difference being its width. The farm road cut across the property now owned by Levi Byler. Daed of Tobias Byler. Tobias was bossy and way too sure of himself. But then, he was a man doing what men were expected to do. Still, something about his green eyes and towering massive body gave her pause. She didn't want to examine why.

Not now. Rebekah cupped her hand against her forehead to block the brilliant midday sun. A plume of dust in the distance told her a car approached. An engine droned, then sputtered.

Leila's note had said she would be in a green Volkswagen. Rebekah wasn't sure what a Volkswagen looked like, but a car was a car. The fact that Leila drove at all astounded her. She edged along the road, waiting, her damp palms clutching at her skirt. Why the meeting now?

Why now, Leila? Why now?

The green car, dusty and bug splattered, pulled alongside her, its engine making a *putt-putt* sound that even Rebekah knew didn't bode well. Leila stuck her head through the open window and waved. "Schweschder! You came."

Rebekah raised her hand in a quick return salute. Her heart squeezed in a painful hiccup. Leila's face was round, her cheeks chunky, and she'd pulled her wheat-colored hair back in a waist-length ponytail. No prayer kapp for her.

Leila disappeared into the interior again. The car moved to the side of the road and then onto the grassy shoulder just beyond the dirt path, bouncing and jolting over the ruts and rocks. The engine died. The door opened and Leila emerged, her face crinkled in a wide smile. Her long shirt and cotton skirt could not hide an enormous belly. Leila was expecting a baby who would surely arrive during the summer.

Was that what she wanted to tell Rebekah? Nee. She could have written that in a letter. But why hadn't she? She was well on her way to a new baby, not just starting out. Rebekah bit her lip, determined not to ask questions. Why make it easy for Leila? Let her explain. Let her help Rebekah make sense of all this.

"Girl, you are a sight for sore eyes." She enveloped Rebekah in a soft, warm hug. It seemed churlish not to return it. Despite herself, Rebekah leaned into it and inhaled. Leila smelled of baby wipes. "You're thinner. Have you gotten taller?"

Nee, not taller. Her appetite had waned in the weeks and months after Leila fled their tiny district in order to be with a man who'd chosen to leave the Amish faith. Somehow the weight she lost had never returned. "I'm fine. You look . . . healthy."

"Chubby, you mean." Leila's grin widened. She wore an oversized, short-sleeved white blouse untucked and a long beige skirt covered with a tiny lilac-flowered print. It reached her ankles and white sneakers. "I reckon you can guess my secret."

As if she could miss it. "A blessing indeed."

"Indeed. I'm due at the end of July, early August."

More reason she and Jesse should come home. Babies needed family. "Jesse must be happy."

"He is."

Children who would have no grandparents in their lives. No aunts and uncles. No cousins. "Surely you'll come home now."

Leila tugged open the passenger door, still smiling back at Rebekah. "I know what you must think, but our babies will have plenty of family. Our church is our family. Maybe not blood relatives, but people we love who love us."

Not the same.

"What do you think of the car? Jesse bought it from his friend Colton Wise. He sold it dirt cheap, and he's letting us make payments."

It sounded as if it were on its last leg. Rebekah had no opinion on cars, only that Plain folks didn't drive them. "I can't believe you drive."

Couldn't believe that Leila had chosen another way of life.

"I have to drive. I have to get myself to work and this little Bug lets me do it." Leila made a *tut-tut* sound. "Gracie fell asleep. She's been a cranky bear. She's teething. I take her to the day care with me, but they let me visit her on my breaks and at lunch, which is nice."

Another thing Plain women didn't do. Keep working when they were raising their babies. "If you came home, you wouldn't have to work."

"We are home. In our little duplex in Beeville. And we need the money." Her matter-of-fact tone held no shame. "Jesse is taking the last of his classes at the community college to get his associate's degree. His jobs at the church as a lay pastor and maintenance man don't pay much. He's still doing carpentry work with Matthew on the side. We make do."

Rebekah understood about making do. She didn't understand about leaving family and faith to live in a duplex. Still, she couldn't help herself. She inched forward and peeked over her sister's shoulder for a glimpse as Leila undid the straps and lifted the sleeping baby from her car seat. She turned, the little girl nestled in her arms. "She's big."

Dressed only in a pink onesie that read DADDY'S GIRL and featured a huge sunflower, Grace displayed the thunder thighs and chunky cheeks of a ten-month-old. Thick brown curls framed her face—Jesse's curls. She had fair skin and rosebud lips that curved in a smile as if she frolicked in a sweet dream. "She's walking now." Leila held the baby out. "Take her, will you, I'm feeling a little queasy today."

Rebekah did want to hold her niece. Almost as much as she wanted a baby of her own to hold. That might never happen. Not with Mudder and Mordecai watching her every move—thanks to Leila.

"I need to get back. Why did you want to see me?" She took Grace and held her close, inhaling the sweet scent of *bopli*. Babies smelled of innocence and hope and the future, a heady aroma she longed to surround herself with every day. "If it's not to tell me you want to come home, what else could you possibly need to tell me that you can't put in a letter?"

Leila shut the door with a clunk, leaned against the car, and patted her shiny face with a pink bandanna. "You are as persistent as a mosquito on a summer night, aren't you?" She sighed. "I am home. Someday you'll understand that. Home is where Jesse is. We are so happy. I wouldn't change a thing."

"If you're so happy, why are you here?" Bile burned the back of Rebekah's throat. She swallowed and breathed in the warm, humid April air until she could form the next sentence. "Your note said it was important."

"Change is coming, and I felt like I should tell you about it in person." Despite her words, Leila's smile faded, replaced with an expression Rebekah couldn't read. "I know it's hard for you to understand, but Jesse believes he has a calling, and everything that's happened since I left tells me he's right. But there's more, more to come. Gott's plan is still unfolding."

It seemed Leila had forgotten everything she learned growing up about humility and obedience. How could she and Jesse think they knew what Gott's plan was? She sounded so prideful. Rebekah swallowed a retort bitter on her tongue and forced herself to speak softly. "What about you? What about Gott's plan for you?"

"This is it." Leila waved her hand toward Grace and then patted her belly. "This summer Jesse will finish his degree and Grace will have a brother or sister." Her smile faltered.

"What is it? There's more, isn't there?"

"I miss you, all of you, so much." Leila ducked her head and studied the dust that coated her sneakers. A grasshopper somersaulted over her toes and disappeared into the weeds. "Rory and Tiffany and our other friends are so sweet and kind to us."

But they weren't family. "Englisch friends aren't the same as family, are they?"

"They're good friends. They help us all they can." Leila crossed her arms over her swollen belly as if suddenly cold. "But you're right, it's not the same. I miss Mudder and Deborah and I can only imagine how Timothy has grown, and now she and Phineas have a new baby. It hurts my heart—"

"Hurts *your* heart? You didn't see the look on Mudder's face when she realized you were never coming home. You didn't hear her crying at night when she thought everyone was asleep." Rebekah's voice climbed. Pent-up emotions billowed from her. She stopped, letting the *curr-curr* sound of crickets harmonizing soothe her for a second. "I can't even go into Beeville by myself. I'll never be able to get a job in town. I'm barely allowed to go to the singings."

For two years, she'd kept these feelings to herself, feeling guilty about her inability to forgive. Rebekah gulped back sobs. "I'm sorry. It's not for me to judge."

Leila sighed. "But it's only human. I'm so sorry I've made it hard for you."

"It's just that I'm . . . so . . ."

"Lonely?"

"Jah."

"Gott has a plan for you. I promise." Leila squeezed Rebekah's arm. "You'll find your special friend. I know it in my heart."

She wanted to believe it so she wouldn't have to feel guilty. Reality looked much different from Rebekah's vantage point. No buggy rides had materialized from the singings. She was nineteen and had no prospects in sight.

As if hearing the tension in their voices, Grace opened her eyes. They were a stunning ocean blue, brilliant against her fair skin. "Ma-ma-ma-ma." She frowned as she babbled, arms and tiny fists flailing. Rebekah might look familiar, but she wasn't Mama. "Ma-ma-ma."

Rebekah allowed herself to forget for one brief second the circumstances of this secret visit. She patted the baby's dimpled cheek. "Smart girl, says 'Mama' first."

"Really it's just babble most of the time. I don't think she knows what she's saying yet." Leila's eyes, as blue as her baby's, were bright with tears. "Please forgive me."

"I forgive you." Rebekah said the words automatically. Saying it was one thing. Doing it, quite another. "It's just been hard since you left."

"I had to go."

"For Jesse?" She would never know that kind of love. "Why did he have to leave?"

"I didn't leave just for Jesse. I left because I needed to worship in a different way."

The words made no sense. Rebekah stared at the road beyond her sister. Wind rustled the leaves in the trees overhead. Dust rippled and danced in the air. "You can always come home."

"We're not coming home. We're moving."

"Moving?"

"Leaving Bee County. For Dallas."

More words that didn't make sense.

Leila plucked at a loose thread on Gracie's onesie. Her gaze didn't meet Rebekah's. "That's what I came to tell you. Jesse has applied to college. In Dallas. He wants to get his bachelor's and then go to seminary."

"Dallas."

Leila nodded. Tears darkened her blonde eyelashes. "If he gets in, we'll move by the end of summer."

"How long?"

"Two years to finish the bachelor's. Another two to three for the master's. He'll have to work so it'll take longer."

Forever.

"But you'll come back after he's done."

Leila cocked her head, her smile tight, eyes downcast. "It depends."

"Depends?"

"On where he's appointed to pastor. The church."

Anywhere, in other words.

The ache in Rebekah's throat made it impossible for her to answer. They would leave Bee County, and any chance she had of seeing them would disappear on the same hard, cold wind that had taken Leila from them on Christmas Eve two years ago.

"I want to find a way to spend some time with you and the others before we go. So Grace can have a chance to know you. All of you. Her real family."

"It's not possible."

"We're not shunned. We've stayed away out of respect."

"I know, but it would—"

"Hurt too much?"

"Mudder says it's best this way."

"So you don't become infected with our disease?" Leila's gaze didn't meet Rebekah's. "So you won't do what I did and end up going to hell too?"

That's what Mudder couldn't seem to understand. Rebekah had no desire to leave her community. In fact, she only wanted to stay and be a fraa and mudder.

"I'm sorry."

Leila could say that a hundred times and it wouldn't make things better. "It's all right. You and Jesse need to go. Do what you have to do."

"I wish there was something I could do to make it up to you."

"There is." She couldn't send Leila away without asking for her help. It was selfish to think of only herself and how it would be easier not to be reminded of all they had lost when Leila and Jesse made their decisions. "There is one thing. I found these two kinner in the shed at the school earlier this week. From El Salvador."

"You found children in the shed?" Leila took Gracie into her arms and snuggled her against her chest as if thinking what it would be like to have her child off in some distant foreign country. "How did they get there? What did they do? What did *you* do?"

"Convinced them to stay. Bribed them with food." Rebekah wrapped her arms around her midsection, wishing she had Gracie back for a minute more. "They were starving and dirty and scared."

"It's good that you were there to help them, then. Others might not have been as kind."

"We took them in, but Mordecai, Jeremiah, and Will are meditating on what to do with them now. I'm afraid they'll decide to call the sheriff."

Gracie began to wiggle, her round face wrinkling in a grimace. Leila shushed her and rocked her in her arms in a silent lullaby. "Jesse is working with a coalition of faith-based organizations trying to find homes for as many of the immigrant children as they can. Maybe he can help you place them."

Leila used many words now that Rebekah didn't understand, but it didn't matter. Jesse had the means to help Diego and Lupe. "Can you take them to your house?"

"Now?"

"They're up at the school."

"How would you explain their disappearance?"

Rebekah leaned closer to her sister and kissed Grace's cheek. The baby's skin was so soft and warm. Tears threatened to choke her. She breathed. "I would tell the truth. I asked you to help."

"Then they'll really come down on you. They'll never let you out of the house—"

The *thud-thud* of horse's hooves against packed, sun-hardened dirt made them both spin toward the path. *Gott, please don't let it be Mordecai. Or worse, Jeremiah.*

A palomino the color of honey emerged from the stand of live oaks pulling a buggy. Tobias held the reins, his cobalt-blue shirt shimmering in the sun. He pulled up and muttered, "Whoa, whoa."

The horse slowed, then stopped in a prance that spoke of a desire to head for the open road. Tobias's gaze traveled from Rebekah to Leila and back. "You again."

ELEVEN

Rebekah stepped between her sister and Tobias's buggy. He leaned back in the seat, but every part of him seemed tense and poised for action. She stood straighter and introduced Tobias to Leila. "This is my schweschder. We're just having a quick visit."

His unrelenting gaze, filled with a mix of curiosity and what seemed like suspicion, studied her. She fought the urge to pat her hair back under her kapp and smooth her wrinkled apron. He moved on to Leila and then the car. "Strange place for visiting." He shoved his hat back, revealing those green eyes flecked with gold. Eyes that would mesmerize under other circumstances. Now they were cool and brilliant as cut glass in the sun. "Usually people visit in their homes where they can offer their guests a glass of tea or a cup of kaffi. They don't do it on someone else's property on a back road so no one can see them."

Rebekah crossed her arms. Who cared about his eyes? Not her. Or his opinion. The horse pranced and shimmied to one side, but he handled it with ease. It was no concern of his why she and Leila met here. "What are you doing out here?"

"This is my daed's property. He asked me to stop at the school on my way home for lunch—something about rattlesnakes." Tobias glanced at Leila, at the car, and then back at Rebekah, his expression seeming to indicate that he wondered why he was explaining himself. He did have a right to be on his daed's property. "You must be the Leila mentioned at Mordecai's house the other night."

Her confusion apparent in her face, Leila glanced at Rebekah. "Y'all were talking about me?"

"You and Jesse. About you helping the kinner." Rebekah sidled closer to Leila. "Mordecai didn't want you involved—"

"Of course he didn't—"

"Why don't you bring your sister up to the house? My sister Martha made biscuits for breakfast." Tobias's tone wasn't all that inviting despite his offer. "There's honey. Mordecai brought us a batch this morning. Neighborly of him. He didn't mention a visit from a daughter."

"Leila's not his daughter." Rebekah wanted to snatch the words back. Mordecai wasn't their father, but he'd been a good stepfather from the day he exchanged vows with Mudder. He didn't deserve disrespect. "We're his stepdaughters. Leila was just leaving. She'll take the car off your daed's property."

"The proper thing to do would be to welcome a new neighbor."

He was right, but she couldn't trust a stranger to understand. "Leila has to get back. The baby will be hungry soon, and her husband will be waiting for her."

"Best they go, then." Apparently the man excelled at reading between the lines. "I reckon school is back in session after lunches were eaten. Susan must be wondering where you are. Or does she know you're talking to Leila after Jeremiah and the others said not to do it?"

She didn't owe him an explanation. Not at all. "Nee."

"Welcome to Bee County." Leila brushed past Rebekah and offered her hand to Tobias. Such an Englisch thing for a woman to do. Tobias's countenance didn't change. He leaned down and grasped her hand in a quick shake. Leila smiled up at him. "Don't blame my sister for any of this. I wanted to . . . see her. It was my idea and it was a bad one. Since I'm here, she told me about the children from El Salvador. Jesse might be able to help. I'll ask him as soon as I get home."

"I don't think the bishop wants your husband's help."

"He might decide to put his feelings aside about keeping us separate for the sake of the children." Leila spoke in a deliberate tone Rebekah hadn't heard from her sister before. Like she knew what she was talking about and had a right to talk. "In the meantime, I hope you can see that it wouldn't do any good to tell the others about our visit until we know more about the options out there for those two little ones."

"I haven't been in my new district a week and you want me to keep secret a visit you know the bishop would not approve of?" He lifted his hat and settled it on his fine, straight brown hair. "I don't know about you, but where I come from, that's not the way we do things."

"Rebekah has had a hard row to hoe, and it's my fault. I don't want to make it worse." Leila's earnest tone seemed to have no effect on Tobias. "Coming here might have been a mistake, but Rebekah's heart is in the right place. We might be able to help two kids who are a long way from home. That's what's really important."

"Are you shunned?"

"Nee."

Tobias's gaze lifted to the horizon. He said nothing for

seconds that seemed to last years. "Are you thinking of returning to the fold?"

"No."

He cocked his head. "Then you should go now."

Who did he think he was? A stranger telling her sister what to do. Heat rushed to Rebekah's face. Her heart pounded in her throat. She fought off an absurd desire to stamp her foot. "You don't get to tell her what to do—"

"Hush." Gracie cooed, her arms flailing in the air. Leila hugged her to her chest. "He's right. Give the baby a kiss. I love you. I'm sorry for the pain I've caused you. All of you."

Rebekah did as she was told, then straightened. "You'll talk to Jesse?"

"As soon as I get home."

"You won't leave without looking into it?"

You won't leave me without saying good-bye?

"We'll not go until after the baby is born."

That time would come too soon. Three months, four at the most. "Write me."

"I will."

Three minutes later Leila was gone, one arm stuck through the open window, waving as she drove away into the bright, hot light, leaving Rebekah with empty arms and a heart with a hole the size of the state of Texas. She ducked her head and trudged past the man who sat on his high horse—and buggy—with such judgment. "I better get moving. Susan will be missing me."

"I'm sorry about your sister."

The rough compassion in his voice only served to cause the lump in her throat to expand until she found it hard to swallow, let alone speak. Rebekah nodded and kept walking.

"This place sure is dry and dusty."

Rebekah had no trouble remembering her first impressions of Bee County. His words were kind in comparison. Dirty. Ugly. Not fit for humans. Leaving the only home she'd ever known in Tennessee—lush by comparison—had been the hardest thing she'd ever done. Until now.

"It's not so bad." She paused and turned back. "You get used to it."

"I'm not sure I want—"

Caleb came storming through the brush, stumbled over a rock, and fell to his knees. "Rebekah, I've been looking all over for you. Susan is worried." Her brother righted himself. His bewildered gaze flew from Tobias to Rebekah. "Oh."

Oh was right.

TWELVE

For a rutted, sunbaked, dirt back road, this one sure got plenty of traffic. Tobias tugged on the reins and tried to calm Honey. She didn't like surprises, which didn't make her great for buggy pulling on the road. Tobias didn't much like surprises, either. Caleb had the same blue eyes and fair skin as his sisters. Rebekah's cheeks turned strawberry red. She had a beautiful face, high cheekbones, eyes the color of the ocean, dark-brown hair that peeked from under her kapp. Curves filled out her dress nicely.

He shook his head as if he could shake off those thoughts. Embarrassment heated his already warm face even though he hadn't said a word. She'd left her post at the school in the middle of the day to meet a sister who'd left the faith. He should help her see the error of her ways, nothing more.

He cleared his throat. "Anyone else coming? You could have class here, in the great outdoors, if more people show up."

"You're the one who kept spiking the volleyball the other night. What are you doing out here with my schweschder?" The boy popped to his feet and dusted off his hands on dirty pants. He sidled toward Rebekah, his gaze whipping back and forth. "Susan sent me to look for you. She was worried when you didn't come in from recess after lunch, what with the rattlesnakes and all—"

"Whoa, whoa." Rebekah held up her hands as if to stem the flow of words. "I'm right here. I took a walk and lost track of time and I ran into Tobias. He's on his way to the school to check if the snakes have regrouped at the outhouse."

Her gaze begged him to let it go. He shook his head. He wouldn't be party to a lie, not even to a young boy. It was wrong. "I was cutting across to reach the school quicker. I need to get home for lunch and back to the shop. I heard a car."

Let her explain the car. She still had a chance to redeem herself.

"A car. Out here?" Caleb patted Honey's forehead. "This horse is a beaut. A palomino, right? We have to get back before Susan sends out a whole posse to look for us."

Rebekah remained silent, her face miserable. How could someone look so sad and yet so beautiful? It didn't matter. A woman bent on breaking the rules of the Ordnung could not be considered fraa material.

What a hypocrite he was. If she only knew.

Tobias drew back from that white-hot, throbbing place where the memory of Serena resided, careful not to touch it directly. With time, perhaps, but for now, even the periphery of the memory hurt too much.

Daed insisted the move here would erase those feelings.

Feelings for a woman unsuitable for a Plain man.

He'd come to Bee County, Texas, half a country away from his heartache, so he could do just that. He had to establish himself here. Set up the leather shop, get some customers, start working on the custom-made saddles. Three weeks of intensive work to make one saddle. That would keep his mind and his heart occupied until he could trust himself to risk his heart again. It wouldn't be to a woman who broke the rules.

That didn't mean he couldn't be kind. "I'm headed to the school, anyway. Let me give you a ride." He scooted to one side in the buggy. "There's room and it'll be faster than walking."

She shook her head, her brilliant blue eyes cold as snow on a winter day up north. She most likely debated how much he would tell Susan. "We'll walk. It's not that far."

"Get in. We're headed the same direction."

If she shook her head any harder, her kapp would fall off. He wouldn't mind seeing the rest of her chestnut hair. *Behave.*

"We don't need a ride. We're fine."

"Nee, schweschder. I'm missing the spelling test." Caleb ended the disagreement by climbing into the buggy without so much as a by-your-leave. "Because of you. Let's go. I don't want to stay after school to finish. Susan will make me, you know she will."

Rebekah paused, hands on her hips, her expression grim. "Fine." She climbed into the buggy but squeezed herself against the far edge of the seat. "Can you hurry? I'm supposed to be helping the little ones with their numbers."

It was silent for several minutes as the buggy shook and shimmied over thick ridges and ruts in the road. Tobias glanced at her from the corners of his eyes. She seemed to be studying the ruts, her full lips turned down in a pout. "So what did your sister say about helping Lupe and Diego?"

"You saw Leila?" Caleb's voice shot up an octave and then back down in the typical boy-on-the-edge-of-growing-into-a-teenager way. "She was here? Did she bring the baby? What did she—?"

Rebekah's hand shot up in a stop position. Her glare, like a spotlight on a dark night, spoke volumes. "Jah, I saw her." Her voice quivered and broke. She turned in her seat so Tobias mostly saw her back and shoulders. A hard sniff followed. "She'll ask Jesse what he thinks."

"Why are you crying?" Caleb raised one hand as if to pat his sister's back. The hand dropped. Probably afraid she'd bite it off if he got too close. "That's good, right? We want them to stay, don't we?"

"I'm not crying. I never cry." She pivoted on the seat again. Her eyes were red but her mouth set. "I asked about them because they're only children and they're in a strange land and they have no one to help them."

They had no one to protect them. All children should have protectors. "Agreed."

"But . . ." Her mouth dropped open. She didn't appear to have a single filling in her even, white teeth. "You agree."

He shrugged. "Jah, but it doesn't matter. It's not up to you or me. It's up to the bishop and he told you not to talk to Leila and Jesse. You disobeyed. What's more, you know it. You have guilt written across your forehead in big red letters."

Caleb inched closer to his sister. "She probably meant well. That's what Mudder says. Rebekah always means well."

A good *bruder*, this boy, who defended his sister. Still, it was all well and good to agree with Rebekah regarding those poor kinner, but a person still had to do the right thing. Going against the bishop's wishes—and her stepfather's wishes—would only result in difficulties for Rebekah. Tobias had had enough of that sort of thing back in Ohio.

Silence reigned for the remaining few minutes it took to

reach the school. Susan stuck her head out the door as he pulled the buggy to a stop by the front steps. "There you are. I was about to organize a search party." She lifted her hand to her forehead and squinted against the sun. "Tobias, what are you doing here? Your little schweschders and bruders are doing fine."

"Daed wanted me to make sure no more rattlers are hanging around here." Tobias hopped from the buggy. He glanced back at Rebekah. She didn't move to get down. As much as he knew it was the right thing to do, he found himself hesitating. She looked so penitent. "I came upon Rebekah here visiting with her sister Leila out by the road on the back side of our property. Then Caleb showed up looking for Rebekah."

The smile slid from Susan's face. She sighed. "Danki for bringing them back. I would've made them walk, myself."

"What with the snakes and all, I wanted to see how the little ones have settled in." He glanced at Rebekah. Her gaze was glued to the ground as if she found sticks and stones fascinating. "Daed will want to know that his kinner are behaving and that they're in good hands."

"Much better than some folks around here." Susan's frown deepened. "Rest in the assurance that what you saw today is not the norm around here. We follow the Ordnung. Please let your daed know."

Rebekah's face was stained beet red. She raised her head and met his gaze head-on. Something there told him she would offer no apology for her actions. So be it.

"I will. He's very careful, what with my mudder having passed six years ago. He feels a lot of responsibility." Just as Tobias did. Every minute of every day. "He wants what's best for Lupe and Diego as well."

A course of action to be decided by Jeremiah, Mordecai, and Will. Not a girl who decided to interfere even after she'd been specifically told not to do so.

"Come on up and have a peek." Susan cocked her head toward the door. "The little ones are doing addition and subtraction right now."

Rebekah slipped past him without a backward glance. He quelled the urge to say he was sorry. He'd done what he had to do. Still, he was certain at least one person would not be happy to see him at the school.

Or anywhere else.

THIRTEEN

Rebekah stood at the bedroom's only window, staring out, her hand kneading the tattered white curtain. Seeing nothing. Waiting. Dusk had fallen hard and the sun had lain itself to rest behind a flat, barren horizon, its rays fading into oblivion as they did each night with reassuring regularity. Still, the room sweltered with heat and humidity that spoke of the impending arrival of summer. Sweat beaded on her face and traced a route from her temples down her cheeks and onto her neck.

Whatever she'd done, she'd done it for the right reason. Mordecai, at least, would see it that way. Unlike Will, who had deep scars on his heart because of Leila, Mordecai would have the capacity to be fair about this, as he was fair in all things.

With each year that passed, Rebekah remembered less about her own father. When she tried to picture his face, Mordecai's black, curly hair and skin-stretching grin appeared in her mind along with a million jokes, short stories, and pieces of useless information. Mordecai would urge Jeremiah to let him speak to her, counsel her for her disobedience, and he would prevail. If not, it didn't matter. She wasn't sorry. The situation with Lupe and Diego had made it much more important that she do it. Even if it meant going against Mudder and Mordecai's wishes.

Gott, forgive me for my rebellious heart.

And Tobias. How dare he? How dare he pass judgment? She wanted to say that. Rebekah wanted to be mad at him, but she couldn't. He'd done what was right and honorable. On the other hand, she'd asked him to lie for her. Almost a complete stranger. What he must think of her. Shame coursed through her, leaving an ugly, bitter taste in her mouth.

She should leave here. Start fresh. Where would she go? Missouri? She could stay with Frannie and Rocky in Jamesport. She ached to tell her cousin of her latest misstep. Frannie, always in trouble herself until she married her Englisch-man-turned-Plain-man, would understand. Jamesport had several Plain districts. Lots of Plain men. Not like Bee County. Maybe she could stay with them.

Nee, Mudder would never allow it.

"How is she?"

Rebekah closed her eyes for a brief moment and let her dreams of escaping seep away. She could never leave Mudder and Hazel and Caleb and Deborah. She wasn't like Leila. She took a quick swipe at her face with the back of her sleeve, then turned and faced her mudder. "Good. She's good. Gracie, your granddaughter, is a sweet baby. And there's another on the way this summer."

A faint smile appeared. As quickly, it fled. "How long have you been meeting her?"

"It's the only time. I wouldn't lie about that. What she did has caused me nothing but trouble." Rebekah wrapped damp fingers around her apron, willing them to cease trembling. "Still, I couldn't say no to the chance to see the bopli. Leila would like you to see her, too, and Deborah and Hazel and Caleb. The whole family."

"I can't. Neither can you and you know it."

"They were never baptized in our church. We can see them and talk to them. It's not wrong."

"You needn't remind me. I pray for them every night and every day." Mudder eased onto the bed Rebekah shared with Hazel, the box springs squeaking under her slight weight. "And seeing them and having them go away would be too hard. It's too hard. We have to keep our distance until they understand the error of their ways."

"They never will. That's the thing. They'll never see what they're doing as wrong. They were baptized, and Jesse is a lay preacher. He brings folks to the church through his preaching. He brings people closer to Gott."

"Stop." Mudder picked up a book—a prairie mail-bride story that had made Rebekah smile until now—from atop the thin blanket. She ran a hand over it, but her expression said she didn't really see it. "They belong here in their community. Not out there in the world. Jesse could've waited. He could've drawn the lot. If it was Gott's will, he could be speaking the Word to his own people."

"I know, but is it so wrong—?"

Mudder pointed her index finger at Rebekah. "It's wrong. Trust me."

"You don't trust me."

"How can we when you're having secret visits with a sister who has abandoned her family and her faith?"

"One visit. Only one. I did it because I wanted to help Lupe and Diego. Besides, Leila hasn't abandoned Gott. He hasn't abandoned her. She's happy and she has her mann and her bopli." Rebekah hated the tone of her own voice. Like a little girl who didn't get her way. She hated feeling this way. "Much more than I have. How can that be punishment for her for going against Gott's will?"

"It's a slippery slope."

Not for Rebekah. "They can help Lupe and Diego get placed in homes. They work with a group." She struggled to translate the words Leila had spoken into something Mudder would understand. "The Englisch churches are working together."

"You're sticking your nose in where it doesn't belong. It's for the men to decide."

"I found them. I feel responsible for them."

"You're a girl."

"I'm not. I'm a woman."

"Who should remember her place."

"How can I forget? You remind me every day. I'm not Leila, but you're so afraid I'll do what she did, you're driving me away. I might as well go. In your mind, I will. Sooner or later."

There. She'd said it.

How could she be so mean, so ugly, so hurtful? She swallowed against tears, wanting the words back before they left her tongue.

"Don't say that." Mudder's stricken face broke Rebekah's heart. "I'm not trying to drive you away. I couldn't bear it. I know Gott's will is Gott's will, but I can't stand to lose another of my girls."

"Then trust me. Let me live my life so I can find the happiness you have found here. Don't hold me back."

"How can I when you have secret meetings with your sister? What else are you doing?"

"Nothing. That's the whole point. No one . . ." Courting was private. She couldn't tell her mother how she longed for that man to come into her life who would share his innermost heart's desire with her and her with him. She turned back to the window, longing for a breath of cool, fresh air where none existed. "There's no one here to do anything with."

"In Gott's time there will be." Mudder came to stand next to Rebekah at the window. She smelled of homemade dish soap and the onions she'd fried with potatoes for supper. "Patience, child."

"I'm not a child anymore."

"I know."

"Gracie has my eyes."

Mudder sighed, a soft sound so sad it made unshed tears ache in Rebekah's throat. "She has Jesse's hair, but Leila's smile."

The second sigh was even softer, sadder.

"They're moving to Dallas by the end of summer. Jesse is going to college there. And seminary."

Mudder made a sound like she'd bitten her tongue. She turned and trudged across the room. At the door she paused, her back to Rebekah. "Mordecai will want a word with you now. He's at the kitchen table. He'll tell you that there'll be no more visits. It's best."

So he had convinced Jeremiah not to punish her. "He spoke to Jeremiah."

"He did. You're blessed to be so forgiven. Remember that."

Rebekah cleared her throat. "What about Diego and Lupe?"

"Jeremiah has decided to call another bishop he trusts. A friend in Jamesport. For his opinion. He's a wise man. You best remember that. You're only a young girl. Remember who you are and what you are."

How could she? They never let her. "Jah, Mudder."

Mudder paused again, one hand on the door. "Do you really think Mordecai and Jeremiah and Will are so hard-hearted they would send two small children away with little or no thought? Do you think that of Mordecai?"

Shame coursed through Rebekah. She was far too prideful. She thought she knew better than someone like Mordecai. "Nee. I'm sorry. I'm so sorry."

"Tell Mordecai, not me. It's his heart you hurt."

"And yours because you never want to see him hurt."

"Or you. Understand that, child."

"I do."

"Lesson learned, then."

Some lessons were far harder to learn than others.

FOURTEEN

Nothing like hard work to make food smell good. Tobias's stomach rumbled. He'd spent all day unloading boxes and arranging his tools in the shop. It was beginning to look like his home away from home. He'd been so busy he'd forgotten to eat his sack lunch. Being busy was a good thing. It helped him forget about homesickness. And wrong roads taken. Not to mention a certain wayward woman who lived down the road here in Bee County who might never forgive him for doing the right thing.

He *had* done the right thing, so why did he feel so guilty for telling Susan about Rebekah's secret? She'd only been trying to help Diego and Lupe. He understood the desire to do that. But a person couldn't ignore the rules. They existed for a reason.

He sounded like his father. Sighing, he tossed his hat on the counter. So much for not thinking about things. *Shake it off.* That's what Daed would say. He did the right thing and now he had to stand by it.

If Tobias's big snout was correct, Martha had made his favorite spaghetti casserole for supper. It was his sister's sixteenth birthday and she'd spent it working hard. And without saying a word. Likely she thought they'd forgotten. It was an important milestone for a Plain boy or girl. The beginning of *rumspringa*.

He poured more water in the tub and stuck his dirty hands in it, thinking of his own time. Up north he'd grown up with a pack of friends, mostly the same age. They'd done their share of exploring the Englisch ways, pasture parties, kegs of beer, cars. He'd experimented but then had come home at night, glad to be there. What he hadn't done was find a special friend.

Until Serena.

He shook his head. He must look addled, shaking his head for no apparent reason. He dried his hands, focusing on the rough feel of the towel on his fingers. Looking back again. It was a habit that needed to be broken. No need to look backward, only forward. The plot for the vegetable garden was ready for planting. All the boxes had been unpacked. The furniture at the house arranged with much discussion from the girls about where the sofa and rocking chairs belonged. A man could lose a lot of time in the field waiting for them to make up their minds.

"La ce-na." Diego trotted into the kitchen, Nyla at his side. "Ce-na."

"Ce-na," Nyla repeated. "Supper."

"Su-per."

Nyla giggled and shook her head. "Nee. Supper."

"Sa-purr." Diego grinned and squeezed into the space next to Tobias. "Nee? No?"

"Nee is a German word." Tobias tousled the boy's long locks. "Talk about getting confusing. Two languages are surely enough. And you need a haircut."

Diego cocked his head, his expression perplexed. *"¿Cómo?"*

Tobias grabbed a handful of his dark hair and made chopping motions with the fingers on his other hand. "Haircut. Chop, chop."

"Nee. Nee." Diego scampered away, dirty hands flopping. *"Pelo mío."*

Tobias had no idea what that meant, but he swiped a pair of scissors from the prep table and stomped after his guest. "Sí, sí." *Yes* was a Spanish word he did know.

Shrieking with laughter, Diego ducked under the table, Nyla right behind him. "Hide, hide," Nyla yelled. "My bruder is terrible with the scissors. You'll look like Rueben did."

She told the truth. Tobias had once taken it upon himself to cut the boys' hair. Never again. It was, apparently, a job more suited to women. The more Tobias had tried to fix his handiwork, the more hair ended up on the floor below his brother's bare feet. Poor Rueben had looked like a shorn sheep for a few months until it grew out.

Laughing, he knelt and stuck his head under the table. "Fine. I'll let Martha do the honors." He leaned closer to Nyla and dropped his voice. "Did you wrap Martha's present for me?"

"Jah." Nyla's delight at being in on the secret shone on her thin face. She looked like a miniature of their mudder. They were blessed to have a living memory. "I hid it under my bed with Ida and me's presents."

She patted Diego's arm. "Show Tobias what you made for Martha."

"Diego made a present for Martha?" Intrigued, Tobias settled down cross-legged, his head ducked so it didn't bang on the table. "Let me see."

"Birt-day?" Diego plopped down, knees spread, legs and feet behind him, in that loose-hipped way kinner had. "For Marta."

He dug through the pockets of his dirty pants and produced

a small barrel-shaped piece of wood with the bottom hollowed out and connected by a string to a wooden handle that looked like a stick they'd found on the ground by the trees out front. He'd painted it in red and blue stripes. He held it in the palm of a hand that needed a good washing. *"Capirotada."*

Glancing at Nyla, Tobias let Diego place the gift in his hand. "What is it?"

A flood of Spanish words spewed from Diego's mouth.

"Whoa, whoa!"

"It's like a top. Rueben helped us carve it out." Nyla snatched it from Tobias and began to twirl the toy in her hand. After a few expert twists, the ball landed on the stick. "See, easy peasy! All the kinner in El Salvador have them. Now Martha will have one too. And Diego says he can make more for us. It's fun doing what they do in another country."

Indeed it was. International relations right here in Nowhere, Bee County, USA. "Let me try." He gave it a whirl. The ball knocked against his fingers and dangled from the stick. "I might need to practice. What other games do you play in El Salvador?"

Diego cocked his head and frowned. *"Fútbol."*

That one Tobias recognized and he didn't do a half bad job in his younger days. "Maybe we'll play some soccer after the birthday celebration." He touched the wooden toy in Nyla's hand. "Can you make me one?"

Diego grinned and nodded his head so hard it was a wonder it didn't fall off.

"Martha will love it." Tobias unfolded his legs, knees popping and cracking, and edged his way out from under the table. "You better go get the other presents and put them by her plate at the table."

Nyla crawled from under the table and turned to tug on Diego's arm. "Come. We don't want Martha to see her present yet."

Diego followed her, taking a wide berth around Tobias as if still worried about the haircut. "Birt-day!"

Nyla began to sing the birthday song.

They raced from the room, still chattering in the universal way kinner had. Language barriers seemed to fall away at that age. Too bad the same couldn't be said of adults who hung on to differences as if they were badges of honor.

"What are you doing on the floor?"

He looked up. Martha stood in the doorway, a basket of towels in her arms. His little sister was growing up. Sixteen. On the cusp of adulthood. She had the deep-blue eyes of their mother but the tall, thin build of their father. He dragged himself upright. "Happy birthday, schweschder."

"It is happy." She set the basket on the table and began to fold the towels. "New house, new place, new friends. They're all like birthday presents."

"That's a good way of looking at it."

She held up a towel with a big hole in the middle. "I guess this one can become a rag."

"They have singings here, just like we did back home, only smaller, I reckon."

She kept folding, her expression noncommittal. "I'm sure they do, but there's too much work to be done right now. Maybe later."

He'd suspected as much. "This is your time."

"For what?"

"To start thinking ahead."

"I don't have time to think ahead. We have to plant the garden. We're already behind. Liam is shooting up like a weed. He needs new pants and his shirts are stained. The boy doesn't know how to hit his mouth with a spoon. Nyla's dresses are too short. We need to get some canning done or we won't—"

"You're not their mudder."

She dropped an unfolded towel back into the basket and frowned. "That's a mean thing to say."

"It's not intended to be mean."

"You're not my daed."

"Nee, but I know better than anyone around here how you must feel."

"You have Daed."

"So do you."

"It's different." She shook out another towel and began to fold it. "For girls, I mean."

Tobias gripped the back of a chair with both hands, letting his gaze flit to the floor and back to her. He was the last one on earth to talk about feelings with a little sister. "You wish you had someone to talk to and ask questions."

She nodded, her cheeks suddenly bright pink. "There are things . . ."

"Things a girl can't ask her daed."

"Jah."

"I'm sorry it's hard. No one ever says much in appreciation."

"They shouldn't. I only do what any girl would do. It's expected." She picked up another towel and folded it with expert, economical motions, her expression pained. "No appreciation needed or wanted."

"I know. But the kinner will grow up and where will you be? You'll want to have your own bopli one day."

"One thing at a time."

Plain folks didn't talk much about such things, less a brother to his sister. Tobias shifted his boots and searched for words in the wooden planks below the chair in front of him.

"It's okay. I know what you mean." A trace of humor colored her words. "I'm happy doing what I'm doing right now."

"Playing mudder to your schweschders and bruders?" Like Tobias played daed in those long, dark days when Daed disappeared into the shop and stayed until late at night, his expression forbidding questions. "Don't let Mudder's death keep you from having your life."

"I'm doing what needs to be done—for now."

"I don't want you to wake up one day and find you've missed out."

"You, either."

"I messed up my chance." If he hadn't, Martha most likely wouldn't be here in Texas instead of back home with her childhood friends. He'd never given thought to whether she'd had her sights on someone there, just waiting to be old enough. "And you all have paid the price."

"Gott gives many second chances, from what I've heard."

A wise girl, his sister. "I hope you're right."

"Right about what?" Daed tromped into the kitchen, a pan protruding from a brown paper bag in his hands. "Don't you know women think they're always right?"

"Because we are always right. What is that?" Martha reached for the sack. "Is it for me?"

Daed pushed her hand away. "A surprise for supper."

Looking pleased and obviously trying hard not to be, Martha scooped up her basket and slipped from the room. "Supper is about ready," she called over her shoulder. "Wash your hands."

Tobias tugged at the sack and unveiled a pan of chocolate-frosted brownies. "That looks mighty fine."

"Rebekah Lantz made them. She said a girl should have cake on her birthday and she shouldn't have to make it herself."

"How did she know it was Martha's birthday?"

"A little birdie told her, I guess." Daed sounded smug as he lowered the pan on the counter next to a basket of sweet rolls. "What did you get her?"

"Three of those Janette Oke books she likes to read. I saw them at a garage sale before we left home—Ohio."

"Good idea. I don't know when she reads."

"At night, after Liam stops getting out of bed every five minutes for a glass of water or to go to the bathroom."

"Your mudder would say she turned out all right, I think." Daed's face turned pensive. "She was a puny baby. Sickly. Your mudder nursed her every two hours or more those first few weeks, all night long, trying to get her strong. She was so afraid . . ." His voice trailed away and his Adam's apple bobbed.

"She turned out fine. Strong as an ox." Tobias had to clear his throat. He couldn't remember the last time Daed had shown such emotion. Not even at the funeral. His stoicism had been the rock to which his children clung in those dark, uncertain days. "She's a stubborn one though. Says she doesn't have time for singings."

Daed plunged his hands in the water and washed them. "She needs to make time."

"That's what I told her."

"You're one to give advice." Daed didn't often resort to sarcasm, but Tobias heard a tinge of it in the words. "The blind leading the blind."

"I tried—"

"We won't talk about how that turned out." Daed splashed water on his face. It ran down his neck and darkened the blue of his shirt. Patting his skin with a ratty dish towel, he turned and faced Tobias. "I hope you'll take your own advice."

"I'm too old for singings."

"But not for finding yourself a fraa and settling down to make a proper family for yourself."

"It's not that easy."

"Nee, it's not."

His daed should know. Six years had passed and he hadn't found his own way to a second chance. Tobias leaned against the wall and crossed his arms over his chest. "You could think of it yourself."

"Don't start with me now." Daed dipped a finger in the dark chocolate frosting and lifted it to his lips, and a satisfied smile spread across his face. "That Rebekah makes a fine frosting. I reckon the brownies are good too. All her cooking, for that matter. Fraas should be able to cook. And clean. Among other things."

With that he stalked from the room, leaving Tobias to wonder exactly how his daed had managed to turn the conversation around on him with such ease and agility.

He scooped a tiny thimble's worth of frosting onto his index finger. Just a little. No one would notice. He tasted it and licked his finger.

Rebekah did indeed make a fine frosting. If she ever gave him the time of day again, he would tell her so.

FIFTEEN

Buying Englisch clothes made Rebekah's head hurt. She rubbed her temple, inhaling the scent of clothes soap, bleach, and dust. The Goodwill store had too many choices. She glanced out the long plate-glass window. Mordecai and the buggy had disappeared. Surprising, since Mudder had insisted he bring Lupe and Rebekah into town. Mudder surely didn't want her going anywhere on her own right now. Not after the visit with Leila.

What did she expect? At least she'd been allowed to come after much conversation between Mudder and Mordecai. Martha had her hands full setting up the Byler household, and Rebekah spoke the most Spanish.

Besides, Lupe seemed to trust her more. She had been reluctant to leave the house, murmuring about hombres malos. The entire ride into town she'd cast anxious glances behind them and hid her face every time a car passed them. In the store she ducked her face behind Rebekah whenever another customer wandered too close.

Mordecai probably slipped off to the library, knowing him. He'd be back in two shakes. She fingered the pants. Boy's or girl's?

The fancy embroidery on the pockets said girl. She held them up to Lupe, trying to see if the legs would be long enough. The girl was so skinny and her legs extra long. Lupe shook her head and backed away.

"What? Why not?" They'd been through half the clothes on the sales table. Lupe seemed determined to hang on to the stained green pants and dark-blue blouse she'd worn since bolting from the shed at the school. Martha couldn't keep washing them over and over again. "Would you rather have a dress? *Vestido*?"

A vigorous shake of the head answered that question.

So far Jeremiah hadn't said a word about what the other bishops thought of their situation. Not a word. So here Rebekah was, finding Englisch clothes for a little girl from El Salvador who spoke only a smattering of English, flinched every time Tobias or Mordecai or any man came within touching distance, and cried herself to sleep at night.

Stop it. Gott's will. Gott's plan.

The Goodwill only sold clean, gently worn clothes and the prices were affordable, but Lupe really needed to try them on. "What's the matter? No one will notice you."

No one noticed the Plain folks anymore. For that Rebekah was grateful to God. Mordecai said the novelty had worn off when people in Beeville realized their neighbors weren't interested in making a big to-do about their honey, produce, and baked goods. Just selling them like anyone would. Occasionally people from farther north stopped at the store, like the man writing a cookbook who made a video outside the store, but that was the exception to the rule. Even Mordecai's buggy parked on the lot next door would draw only a cursory glance or two. A little girl with brown skin and hair wouldn't stand out in this part of the country where many folks were descendants of people born in Mexico.

"*Esta*. This." Lupe's face broke into a beautiful smile. She held up a boy's green T-shirt. It sported a large picture of Mickey Mouse on the front. "Diego like."

"Yes, Diego would like very much. Doesn't look much like Pedro, though." Rebekah grinned back. She examined the T-shirt for stains or tears. None. Seventy-five cents. They could swing that. And the size looked right. A little big, but Diego would grow, God willing. She added it to the small stack of pants, shoes, and socks she'd amassed for him. "Now something for Lupe."

"No."

"Sí." She pointed to Lupe's stained shirt. "You can't keep wearing the same clothes day after day."

"I no need."

Rebekah held up a pink blouse with strawberries embroidered on the collar. "This is nice. It would look nice on you."

Lupe's cheeks turned the same pink color. "No *dinero*."

"We have money for the clothes. Mordecai gave it to me. You saw him."

"No take money from you."

"Gift. Present. Friend to friend." Rebekah patted her chest and then Lupe's arm. "*Amigas*."

A shy smile spread across the girl's face. "Amigas?"

"*Wunderbarr*."

"Wunderbarr."

The Deutch word sounded so funny coming from Lupe's lips, Rebekah chortled. The saleslady, who looked like she ate one piece of pie too many at lunchtime, looked up. So did a bald elderly man with a pipe stuck in his mouth, examining an old lamp shade. Rebekah slapped a hand to her mouth. "Sorry, Lupe. You are a smart girl. You'll speak three languages before you know it."

Lupe giggled. She draped the blouse and a pair of tan pants over her arm, covering its fine dark hair. *"Gracías."*

"You're welcome. We'll find a couple more. It's either that or I make you dresses like this one." She pointed to her own long skirt. "You want?"

Lupe shook her head so hard her long braid flopped, her lips drawn down in a mock frown. "No like vestidos."

"Fine." In short order Rebekah found three pairs of pants that looked about the right size, along with two more blouses, and dispatched the girl to the dressing room. She took a seat on a spindly chair with wobbly legs in the small, dimly lit hallway and waited. Each time Lupe sauntered from the dressing room, her cheeks now cherry red with embarrassment, Rebekah examined the clothes with a critical eye for stains, rips, or other defects and then pronounced them "wunderbarr," just to hear Lupe giggle and respond with her own garbled version of the word before she scurried back into the dressing room.

The girl had a sweet sense of humor and she was smart. How many more words would she pick up before she had to go to the immigration detention center or on to family in San Antonio? Rebekah wanted to know more about El Salvador and Mexico before Lupe and Diego left. She paid for their purchases, still thinking of how she'd like to know three languages. For what? She'd never been farther than the Rio Grande. She'd never even been to Dallas.

Dallas with its seminary. Where Gracie would grow older and speak English, not Deutsch. Go to school with girls who didn't like to wear dresses and aprons. Maybe even play sports or be a cheerleader in a skimpy skirt that showed her legs from thigh to ankle. Life would be different for Gracie Glick. And Rebekah would not be there to see it.

She sighed.

"Bekah sad?" Lupe tugged on her arm, her face reflecting the emotions welling in Rebekah. "Too much dinero?"

"Nee. No. It's not about the money." Rebekah summoned a smile. "I'll miss you when you go to be with your family in San Antonio."

Frowning, Lupe ducked her head and studied her bare feet, the earlier light of laughter extinguished. "I hope."

"You hope to find your family?"

The girl shrugged. "No *familia*. Only *Papi*."

Papi. "Daddy?"

"Sí. Papi. No see in long time. Mi *abuela* say he's here. No *aquí*." She waved her hands around. "But in San Antonio, *Tejas*."

That would be a start. They could help find Lupe and Diego's father in San Antonio. The city was only two hours away by car. "Do you know where to find him? Address?"

Lupe shook her head. "*Muchos años* no more letters."

No letters for many years. "Then we'll just have to look hard for him." If the bishop would only let them. Mordecai was smart. He would figure out something, if they had to walk the streets of San Antonio until their shoes were worn out. "That reminds me. We didn't look at shoes!"

"No need *zapatos*."

"Yes, zapatos." She patted Lupe's shoulder. "If you're going to a big city like San Antonio to look for your daddy, you'll need shoes. Right?"

Lupe smiled. "Daddy will like. We go fish."

Fish? Lupe didn't understand about San Antonio. It had a lot of big buildings and long streets and honking cars. Not a lot of fish. No need to burst her bubble. "Let's find shoes first."

Another ten minutes and they had a pair of red Converse sneakers in the bag along with a pair of flip-flops Lupe referred to as *chanclas*. Her face seemed a little less haunted by worry. The way it should be. Rebekah plastered a smile on her face. Lupe couldn't know how impossible it seemed to find one man in a big city like San Antonio. Somehow, they would help her find her family.

Outside, Mordecai sat slouched in the buggy, his straw hat tugged down over his eyes. Snoozing. The man could sleep anywhere.

"We're done."

He popped up and slid the hat back. "Gut. I got the groceries we needed so we can hightail it home before supper gets cold."

Lupe climbed into the backseat as far from Mordecai as possible. Rebekah took the spot next to Mordecai. A book separated them. A book about El Salvador. "You've been to the library."

"You're a sharp one, you are."

"Did you learn anything?" She opened the book and perused the pages. History, customs, traditions, current political turmoil. El Salvador was pretty, but like most places, it had its problems. "Besides how to be a smarty-pants."

"I already knew about that." He snapped the reins and Brownie took off at a smart trot. "I found some recipes you might like to try."

"Recipes?"

"Wouldn't it be nice to feed our guests some of their favorite foods from back home?"

"You are such a wise man."

He grinned. "So I'm told."

Slapping away a cloud of gnats, she let the breeze cool her warm face for a few minutes.

"Whatever it is, just ask."

"What?"

"You're chewing on something that's about to choke you, child. Just ask."

Rebekah glanced at the backseat. Lupe's gaze seemed fastened to the horizon. Probably wondering what her family was doing, if they were all right, where she would live now, and when she would be truly home. "Haven't you ever wanted to see the world? Don't you want to know what's going on around the next bend or on the other side of the ocean?"

"Most of the time I'm satisfied to get as far as the kitchen and my next cup of kaffi." Mordecai guffawed in that way that reminded Rebekah of her daed. "I like to stay close to my own kind."

"Then why did you check out this book?" Rebekah held it up. "Reading about it is enough for you?"

"I like to know things." He slapped away a horsefly. "I like to make people feel at home. Especially kinner. I like to understand why things are the way they are."

"Can you explain to me why things are the way they are?"

"Because we're only human and we make a lot of mistakes." Mordecai's tone was so kind, Rebekah wanted to hug the man. He was the one man she knew who would understand such an overt offer of affection. "But we can do so much to help each other get past those mistakes."

"So it was a mistake for Lupe and Diego to come here to the

United States, but we're helping them because they need help getting past their mistake."

"I don't claim to understand the whys and wherefores of their situation or the world." Mordecai glanced back at Lupe, who'd curled up on the seat and closed her eyes. "But wouldn't it be nice if they remembered us as those kind people Gott put in their path to help them on their way? Shelter in the storm. A safe harbor. Good Samaritans who didn't walk on by and ignore their suffering."

"It would. What about Leila? Did she make a mistake when she followed her heart and went with Jesse? Is Gracie a mistake?"

"*Boplin* are never a mistake." Mordecai's fierce gaze flicked to Rebekah's face, then back to the street, filled with cars that slowed then stopped in the wake of the slow-moving buggy. No one honked. One guy waved. Mordecai waved back, but his gaze returned to Rebekah. "Gott will judge us all. Leila and Jesse did as they saw fit, not only for reasons of the heart, but reasons of faith that I cannot, will not, judge."

"How does a person know when to follow her heart?"

"You'll know. But I can tell you this: You're not missing anything. Everything important is right here at home. The things you were meant to do. They're here."

"How do you know?"

"My heart tells me so."

"Or Mudder."

"Jah, my fraa is a force to be reckoned with." Mordecai chuckled, the ferocity gone, his good-natured smile back. "But I am right. You have things to do here. Now."

"Like what?"

"Like read up on Salvadoran food. You know what a *pupusa* is?"

His pronunciation of the word made Rebekah think of Lupe and *wunderbarr*. She stifled a giggle. "Nee."

"Me neither, but I reckon you're gonna learn and I'm going to eat one and like it."

Rebekah shuffled through the pages, looking for the section on food. "So that's what the cabbage is for?"

"Nee, it's for something else that I can't pronounce."

"You're a gut person, Mordecai."

"Average to middlin'."

Far better than that. He set the bar high when it came to following the example of their Lord Jesus Christ. Rebekah picked up the book and began to read.

SIXTEEN

The Byler kitchen smelled like home. With Mordecai's library book and a tattered paperback English-Spanish dictionary stuck under her arm and the bag of groceries in the other, Rebekah peeked into the kitchen. Martha had Lupe peeling potatoes. She wore her new T-shirt with a kitty on the front of it and pale-blue jeans only a little worn in the knees. Flip-flops had been abandoned under the prep table. She seemed at home in the kitchen. Maybe she'd helped her mother with cooking in El Salvador. Maybe she missed cooking.

Rebekah always felt safe in the kitchen with a pot of stew on the stove and bread in the oven. The smells alone gave a person comfort. Lupe hadn't said much more about San Antonio and her father, but Rebekah often saw her watching as if waiting for something. As if ready to run at the drop of a stranger's hat. How much longer would she wait before slipping away to find a father she hadn't seen in years?

Rebekah would like to be content as well. Instead she paced about the schoolroom all day until Susan told her to go outside and run around until she burned off the excess energy. As if that were possible. At least it was Saturday. Another week gone. She had to stop living for the weekends. If she were to be a schoolteacher, she needed to embrace it.

She glanced back. Deborah grinned at her and hoisted little Melinda on her hip. Timothy toddled behind, gnawing on one fist, no doubt trying to assuage gum pain from teething. Susan was on her way with Mudder and Hazel in tow. They were bringing fresh tomatoes, cilantro, and jalapeños from the garden. Naomi had a tortilla press she'd used to make tortillas from scratch. Esther had two heads of cabbage to go with the one Mordecai had provided on the trip into town to the Goodwill store. Tonight, the menfolk would come in from the fields and the apiaries and eat food from a land far away prepared by the womenfolk who knew how to make children feel welcome in a strange new land.

A group effort as all frolics should be. Lupe would experience the true meaning of extended family here in Bee County, far from her own family. The girl handled a paring knife with ease, but worry creased her brow and made her look older than she was. Someone—probably her mother—had taught her to peel potatoes, it seemed. If only language weren't a barrier, Rebekah could reach across the divide and make the girl feel more at ease somehow. She slipped into the kitchen and took a whiff of the peanut butter cookies still on the sheet, fresh from the oven. "Mmmm."

Martha grinned and wiped her hands on a dish towel. "You're here! Lupe and I are making fried potatoes for supper. I figure they go with everything—even things we can't pronounce. I didn't tell her you were coming. I reckoned it would be a good surprise."

"Where is Diego?" What she really wanted to know was the whereabouts of Tobias. She hadn't run into him since that day with Leila. For which she was eternally grateful. He had done what he *thought* was right. What was right? She'd been in the wrong and she asked him to lie about it. It couldn't be undone now. "I thought he might like the food too."

"Daed and Tobias took Liam and Diego to the shop this morning. They can help clean and sweep the floor. Muck out the stalls in the barn. Daed will put them to good work. They should be back for the noon meal, though."

Which meant there would be no avoiding Tobias. It was a small district. She would run into him sooner or later. She squared her shoulders and lifted her chin as if he might walk in the door any minute. "They're in for a big surprise then."

Lupe paused, the knife in the air. Her long, almost-black hair was pulled back in a ponytail, and she had a patch of flour on her forehead just above a big mosquito bite. "Surprise?"

"Sorpresa." Rebekah waved a hand toward Deborah and the kinner. "Mi *hermana* Deborah and her babies, Melinda and Timothy."

Lupe nodded and held out her wet hand. Looking very serious, Deborah shook it. "Pleased to meet you, Lupe."

"Igualmente."

"I think that means the same." At Deborah's puzzled look, Rebekah shrugged. It would be a long afternoon at this rate. "It doesn't matter, though. We can communicate through food. That's the universal language."

Rebekah laid the books on the counter and slipped two cookies from the sheet, careful not to singe her fingertips. She gave one to Timothy, who plopped down on the floor and crowed before taking a bite. She held out the other one to Lupe. "For you."

Lupe dropped the knife and accepted the gift. "Mmmm." She nibbled at the edge. *"Caliente."*

"Jah. Yes, hot. Do you cook in El Salvador?" Rebekah pantomimed stirring with a ladle. "Comida?"

Lupe gave a vigorous nod. She touched the large head of cabbage sticking from the top of the bag on the table. "We make *curtido* with *repollo*."

The other word from the book that Mordecai couldn't pronounce. "Cabbage?"

"Cabbage." Lupe pronounced the word with care. "For curtido. *Ensalada*."

"Salad?" Salad made with cabbage. Rebekah wasn't a big fan of salad, but she generally preferred lettuce to cabbage when she did eat it. She grabbed the dictionary and slid into the chair at the prep table. "What else?"

Lupe took another bite, chewed, and swallowed. A blissful look spread across her face. She closed her eyes and smiled a beautiful smile. *"Me gustan las galletas."*

"Galletas." Rebekah thumbed through the dictionary. This would take years. "Cookies, crackers. I like them too."

Lupe squeezed into a chair across from Rebekah. She rolled the cabbage around in front of her as if contemplating tossing it to Rebekah. *"Pupusas."*

Bingo. Just as Mordecai had said. The book explained that pupusas were a Salvadoran dish like corn tortillas, only thicker and stuffed with cheese, beans, or meat. Sold hot at small restaurants called *pupuserías*. They always came with a cabbage salad called curtido and a spicy tomato sauce called *salsa roja*.

What fun it would be to visit a faraway place like El Salvador and eat food with strange names in restaurants with even stranger names. With red sauce that burned the tongue. She sighed.

"Sad?"

"Jah, schweschder, sad?" Deborah's eyes narrowed. She picked up a cookie and held it out. "One for you too. Cookies make everything better."

Rebekah took the cookie and tasted it. Delicious. Life was good when a person had family and hot cookies from the oven. No sense in being a spoiled brat about it. "Life is gut. Gott is good."

She had to learn to curb her discontent. Mordecai was right. She had work to do here. For whatever reason, God had planted her in this place at this time and she had to be a good friend to Lupe and Diego. That was her job right now. Tomorrow night she would go to a singing. She would rest in the assurance that Gott would bring her a mann in His time. She would believe.

Melinda began to fuss, her loud squall blotting out any attempt at conversation. "She's hungry." Deborah swayed back and forth, rubbing the baby's back. "Keep an eye on Timothy for me? I'll sit in the rocking chair and feed her. Maybe she'll go down for a nap afterward."

"Come back when she's down." Rebekah cocked her head toward Timothy. "He's happy with his cookie now, but he'll be looking for you any second."

She studied the recipe. Mordecai's bag held a bag of *masa* that looked like flour only coarser. "You made pupusas from scratch?"

Lupe looked perplexed. "With hands." She slapped her palms back and forth. *"Así, así."*

Rebekah rummaged in the sack and produced the package of masa. "We'll make them. Pupusas and curtido. And salsa roja." She pointed to Susan who bustled into the room, a basket with tomatoes, green peppers, and onions in her plump arms, followed by Mudder and Hazel. Esther trailed behind them. "We cook."

Lupe understood. Her wide grin said so. She popped from

the chair and enveloped Rebekah in a quick, hard hug that ended before she could reciprocate. "Gracías. Diego, he like too."

"No big deal."

"Yes, big deal." Lupe enunciated each word carefully. She patted the dictionary. "You nice."

"I try." The knot in Rebekah's throat grew, making it hard to form the words. "You deserve nice."

She opened the book to the recipe and began to arrange the ingredients on the prep table. *Masa de harina.* They'd used it before to make tortillas from scratch. Tasty. Carrots, tomatoes, cabbage. Garlic. Onion. Cilantro. Serranos. Not a typical Plain recipe.

All the better. Seeing the world through the kitchen. That's what Mordecai had meant. He saw it through books. She could see it that way too. And live it. Smell and taste it. "I'll start the masa if you and Deborah want to work on the fillings. I think Ruth Anne might come, too, but she has been feeling poorly since she lost the baby."

"Ach, poor thing. We'll take her some food tomorrow if she doesn't make it." Martha studied the recipe. She was a sweet girl. She didn't even know Ruth Anne Stetler—yet. "We have the venison sausage we can use for the filling. And we have beans we can mash to make refried beans. There's some white cheese left from the enchiladas I made last night. Let's make a lot so you can take some home to Mordecai since it was his idea."

Lupe knew what to do, and once she had the ingredients in front of her, there was no stopping her. She grinned and giggled and talked, although neither Rebekah nor the other women could understand her. She mixed the masa with water, rolled the dough into a long roll, then cut it into eight pieces. By then Naomi had arrived with her tortilla press. The women gathered around and watched as the little girl pressed an indentation in each ball of dough, added the mixture of sausage, grated cheese, and refried beans that Martha and Esther had made, and enclosed the dough around it.

Lupe pressed the ball into the palm of her hand, forming a disc that trapped the filling. "Así, así." She grinned, looking like the little girl she was. "¡Me gusta!"

"Now what?" Naomi pushed black-rimmed glasses up her wrinkled nose and crossed her arms over her skinny chest. "What's the tortilla press for?"

Her smile wide, Lupe slipped some plastic wrap over the metal press and added the ball of dough and filling. She pressed the two sides together, lifted the press, and displayed the neatly pressed dough. "Pupusa *revuelta*. Me like."

"Me like too." Hazel crowded between Esther and Mudder. "Me try."

"You try." Lupe presented her with a ball of dough. "You make pupusa."

Hazel patted the dough with her chubby hands and plopped a pile of filling into it. The meat teetered on the edge and fell to the floor, where Dolly, the Bylers' crotchety old hund, always at the ready, ate it in one quick gulp. "Look, Dolly likes Salvadoran food too." Hazel patted the dog's head, chortling with glee. "She probably speaks Spanish too."

The women all laughed, talking at once. "Let me try." Rebekah took a turn. Her pupusa was crooked. Bits of sausage and grated cheese stuck out on one side. She squeezed the dough together with her fingers, trying to capture it. "There must be a knack to this." She held it up. "Help me, Lupe."

A superior smile stretched across her face, Lupe took the poor pupusa and doctored it. "Is good?"

"Is good."

A few minutes later a skillet greased with lard was set on a low flame and the pupusas were frying. The kitchen smelled heavenly of fresh tortilla and onion. The grease sputtered and the dough turned a golden brown with tiny blisters. Lupe handled the spatula with ease, flipping the pupusas and then turning them onto a plate. "Is done."

"Looks like we got here at exactly the right time." Tobias stalked into the room, his mud-caked boots thumping on the wood, Diego and Liam on his heels. Levi and Mordecai brought up the rear. "Something smells gut. We heard something special was being cooked up here today."

He stood so tall. His eyes were so green. Rebekah edged toward the counter. His gaze landed on her. She forced herself not to look away. "It is special. Pupusas. Lupe showed us how." To her everlasting delight, her voice didn't quiver. "Wash up. We're putting them on the table. Now."

Lupe flung the spatula on the counter and dodged past Tobias. Her rapid-fire string of Spanish left Rebekah in the dust. Diego nodded. His cherubic cheeks split in a grin and he threw himself at Rebekah. "Gracías. Gracías."

Those were the only two words she understood, but they were enough. She accepted his hug and returned it, her hands tight on his skinny back, feeling every bony rib. "You're welcome. Now wash your hands and sit. We're having a feast."

"Looks like they're happy with you." Tobias brushed past her, headed to the tub of water in the sink. "They know who their friends are."

What was that supposed to mean? "I try."

"You're a good friend."

"Wait until you get to eat the cabbage salad." Martha picked up the big bowl of curtido. "Yum, yum."

Relieved at the change in subject, Rebekah took the bowl from her. "It has to sit and ferment at room temperature for a few hours."

"Ach no, I was looking forward to it." Tobias wiped his hands with a towel, his grin as wide as Diego's. "Mordecai told us all about it. Sounds like sauerkraut. I like sauerkraut."

"Probably because it's sour like you," Martha teased. "Go on, sit. You're in the way in the kitchen."

Rebekah waited until he was seated on the other side of the room to sink onto the bench on the women's side. She was sure she wouldn't be able to eat a bite with him so close. All the same, the salsa roja, which Esther and Martha had handled, was delicious. The tangy, tomatoey taste with the fresh bite of cilantro was just the right flavor to complement the pupusa.

After swallowing the last savory piece, she stood, wiped her hands, and picked up the pitcher of water. The men had been working hard planting onions and okra to sell to the grocery chain. They would be thirsty. At least that's what she told herself.

"I was going to do that." Susan stood next to her, hand still in the air. "You can finish eating. I'll pour the water."

"I'm finished. I've got it."

"Nee, you should eat another one."

"I'll full. I'm done."

Susan looked as if she might grab the pitcher from Rebekah's hand. Her gaze skittered to the men's table.

Levi glanced up. He smiled. At Susan.

Well. Well, indeed.

"Why don't you see if anyone wants more potatoes? There's still some in the skillet. I reckon the men will want some more."

Her face the color of beets, Susan nodded, whirled, and marched into the kitchen without looking back.

Who knew?

Smiling to herself, Rebekah traipsed up and down the men's table, pouring more water into every glass, just not Tobias's. If he wanted water, he could get his own.

Tobias had added two heaping spoons of the red sauce to his three pupusas. The sauce dripped down his hand and landed on his pants. He didn't seem the least bit worried about it. "I'll take some of that water." He smiled up at her as if there had never been a cross word between them. "This sauce has some kick to it."

She managed to pour water into his glass without spilling it. "You like it?"

He nodded and took a big bite. "Hmmm."

Rebekah handed him a napkin. "I can see that, I guess."

He swallowed and wiped at his face with the napkin. "I like to try new things."

"Me too."

"Gut."

What did that mean? "A person has to be open to new ideas."

"Agreed."

At least they agreed on something.

"I heard there's more pupusas in the skillet."

His pronunciation of the word had to be worse than Mordecai's.

Rebekah took his plate. "I'll bring you some more."

Her fingers brushed his. His eyebrows rose and fell. A smile danced across his rugged face. "Danki."

The way to a man's heart is through his stomach. The words of the old axiom fluttered in Rebekah's head like butterflies released from a net.

And to a woman's heart?

SEVENTEEN

School's out. School's out. The shout rang in Susan's ears even though it had long faded away. After the graduation ceremony for Sally Glick and Rachel Hostetler, the kinner had burst from the schoolhouse door like foals set free to frolic in a pasture after a long winter cooped up in a barn. Similarities did exist.

Susan raised her face to the warmth of a late-April breeze as she plopped down in a rickety folding chair that creaked under her weight. One of the many things Plain kinner had over their Englisch kinner, school was out at the end of April instead of late May or early June. And they only went to school until the eighth grade. Plenty of Englisch kinner would like that.

Diego's fútbol game was about to get under way. The older girls were setting out the food on the picnic tables built by the men years ago when the school was constructed. Mordecai's dog Butch—or was he Deborah's dog now?—curled up under one table asleep. Wrens and sparrows wrestled, their chatter fierce, over bread crumbs that fell to the ground as sandwiches were prepared. It was a perfect day.

Yet a strange, bittersweet restlessness overcame her. The

summer stretched endlessly ahead, another school year behind. Another year as teacher. Another year without her own kinner and mann. Most days, she felt content. This one day out of the year she couldn't find a yardstick that measured her emotions.

She tried to remember what it was like to run instead of walk, to hop and skip instead of trudge. Her scholars were in such a hurry to escape, to live other lives, lives they thought would be more fun and more interesting than what came from books. Truth be told they would spend their lives working. That's what Plain folks did. She had no quarrel with that.

Still, she loved school. What was not to love? Reading, writing, arithmetic, singing, praying, playing together. Those were good days. Ones she had the opportunity to relive every year. Teaching didn't feel like work. It felt like joy.

"Teacher, my finger hurts."

Startled from her reverie, Susan swiveled to find Liam trotting toward her. He held out his small, dirty hand. "I fell."

Indeed he had. Dirt smudged his cheek and a new rip allowed his knee to show through one pant leg. The pants were too short, revealing bony ankles. Martha had some sewing to do, it seemed. Maybe Susan could help with that. "Come here, let me see that." She patted her lap and the boy climbed on, smelling of little-boy sweat and peanut butter cookie. "How did you manage this?"

"I wanted a cookie from the table and Ida shooed me away." His tone was mournful. "She said I had to eat a sandwich first. I'd rather have a cookie. Two cookies or maybe three."

"What does that have to do with your finger?"

"I ran away." He sniffed. "I was eating the cookie and running and I fell."

"That's what happens when you steal cookies."

"I didn't steal it. I borrowed it."

She brushed off the finger, which looked red but not much worse for wear, and kissed it. "There, all better. Were you planning to give the cookie back?"

"Nee, it's in my tummy." Grinning, he patted his flat belly. "It has to stay there now."

"Then I guess that makes you a cookie thief."

"And you know what they do with cookie thieves." Levi towered over them, his face hidden by the dark shadow of his hat's brim. "They make them eat lima beans and cabbage for dinner three nights—nee, four nights—in a row."

"Nee!" Liam slid from Susan's lap. "Danki, Teacher."

He ducked away from Levi's playful swipe and raced away, his giggle trailing behind him.

"He's a sweet little boy." Susan forced herself to sit still, despite the urge to smooth her kapp and brush the remnants of little boy from her apron. "And smart as a whip. He did well the short time I had him in class."

To her surprise, Levi eased into the lawn chair to her right. It creaked under his weight, the crisscrosses of faded nylon material sagging under him. "He takes after his mother." His gaze remained on the makeshift soccer field where the majority of his kinner were racing about, their laughter shrill as they chased after the ball. "He has her face and her eyes. He even sounds like her when he talks. I don't know how that's possible."

"I suppose it's from the older children who had more time with her."

"Any time at all. She died giving birth to Liam."

"I'd heard that."

His gaze shifted to her for the first time. "You're good with kinner."

"A teacher has to be."

"Nee, I didn't mean in that way." He plucked at strings hanging from the chair's arm. "You were . . . motherly."

"Teachers can be motherly."

"I'm trying to say something nice."

And she was being overly prickly about her single status. "I know."

They were silent for a few minutes. Susan sought another less thorny topic. "How are things at your new shop?"

"We have our first customer. An Englischer who wants a custom saddle and her horse trained."

"Gut."

"It is gut."

This man was not one for small talk, that was apparent. Neither was she. Life was too short for small talk. Mordecai and Abigail knew that. They'd lost their first loves. Susan had let time pass. Too much time. She did want her own kinner. She was motherly, and she wanted someone to see that. Life was short and the mother of Levi's kinner no longer mothered them. "You've done right by your kinner. It's obvious to see."

"I'm blessed. Tobias and Martha, they've been like second parents since the beginning." His head bent so she could only see the top of his worn straw hat. He seemed to study a scar that ran in a red ridge along his thumb. No doubt the result of an occupational hazard of a saddle maker who worked with awls and skiving knives and sharp tools of the trade. "David, too, but not like them. I spent my time in the shop, working, making a living for them. Which needed to be done. And they did what had to be done at home."

"Kinner adapt. They manage to blossom even when it's cold and dark." Over the years many children had worn their hearts on their sleeves in her classroom yet managed to pull practical jokes, steal cookies, and smile even when tears brightened their eyes. "It's one of the things I most cherish about them."

"Martha, my oldest girl, has blossomed." He looked up and cleared his throat. "She's been mother to the younger ones for so many years, I think she's forgotten that they're not hers."

"I doubt that. She'll make a good fraa one day."

"That's the thing." He shifted in his chair. "She turned sixteen last week."

"Time for her to spread her wings a bit."

"It would seem she doesn't know how."

Most fathers wanted to keep their daughters from deviating from the path too much during rumspringa. Levi seemed anxious to push his daughter out of the fold. "The singing is at Mordecai's this week. She should go."

"I mentioned it."

"Mentioned it or told her to go?"

"I wouldn't interfere."

Plain parents were expected to give their kinner leeway. That didn't mean they had to like it. At least Susan suspected as much. Neither Mordecai nor Abigail had uttered a word to her, even after Leila left the fold with Jesse. "She said no?"

"She said she had too much to do to mess with such foolishness." His gaze dropped to his hand again. "Especially now that we have two more kinner in the mix. She didn't even come to the picnic today—said she had to finish making the boys' pants. If they go around much longer in what they've got, they'll be shorts."

It would be funny if it weren't sad. "I'm sure it's hard."

"For a man, it's especially hard. She's my first girl. I don't want her to lose her way because of life's circumstances."

His life circumstances. He lost his fraa. Martha had become a substitute mudder to her little brothers and sisters. Susan had experience with that life story. Now Martha stood to lose her chance at the life to which most Plain women aspired. Susan also knew about this.

Levi was asking her for something. In a very roundabout way. Susan's heart gave an odd little *ker-plunk*. Levi wanted her help with his firstborn daughter. That said something about what he thought of her. At least it seemed that way. "I can talk to her at the next frolic."

He sat forward in his chair, his hands gripping his knees. "If it doesn't put you out."

"How would it put me out?" She waved her hand toward the building. "I'm on vacation for the summer."

Hardly. She would cook and clean and can and garden with the rest of the women, but Levi would know that. He leaned back again. "Much appreciated." He ducked his head but not before Susan caught his relieved smile. "Teacher."

Said in his gruff northern accent, the word took on a sheen much like it did when her scholars employed it. She liked the sound of it and the sound of his voice.

Another *ker-plunk* and her heart settled into a rhythm she hadn't felt in a very long time.

EIGHTEEN

"Canta y no llores . . ."

The sound of Lupe's high, sweet voice singing somewhere beyond the school building made Rebekah smile. A child should be carefree and not worrying about where she would lay her head at night or if she would be sent home to a country full of bloodshed.

Rebekah paused at the corner of the school building and looked back, surveying the remnants of the end-of-school-year picnic. Caleb and his friends were burning the last of the hot dogs on sticks over a fire in a rusted barrel. Little Diego had instigated a game of soccer—which he insisted on calling fútbol. In his black pants and blue shirt, feet bare, he looked just like one of the other kinner. Until he opened his mouth and a string of Spanish came out so fast there was no figuring out what he jabbered about. The younger kids screamed and laughed as they chased a dirty, faded basketball up and down the makeshift field, two trash cans at each end serving as goals.

They could do without her. She rounded the corner and trudged toward the sound of Lupe's voice. She wouldn't miss being cooped up in the school now that summer bore down on them full tilt. They would have plenty of gardening, canning, and baking to do. They would sell goods in town a few days a week and showcase the rest in the Combination Store, famous for fresh-baked goods on Fridays. Surely Mudder would let her go into town with the others.

Or not.

She raised a hand to her forehead and shielded her eyes from the sun. Lupe sat cross-legged in the grass, a patch of black-eyed Susans and dandelions all around her. She looked so different than she had that first day when she'd been dirty, hungry, and dressed in ragged, filthy clothes. Her long, dark hair had a bright sheen and her cheeks were pink from the sun. The blouse with the strawberries on the collar made her look like any other twelve-year-old girl. Not Plain, but presentable. And healthy. That hollow, hungry look had disappeared after a few good homegrown, home-made meals.

Her head bent, Lupe stared intently at the flowers she'd picked with their stems still long. She braided the stems, making a belt or a headband of flowers.

Tears trickled down her cheeks.

Rebekah stopped. Should she interrupt a private moment? A crying child couldn't be ignored. "Lupe? *Estás bien*?"

Lupe's lessons each day at the school had resulted in a fair vocabulary for the Plain kinner of Bee County as well. It would hold them in good stead when they made their treks to Progreso in the future. The kinner took turns teaching Lupe and Diego simple English words. German was too much for them. Both sides soaked up the new words with greater glee than others might think they warranted. That, Rebekah would miss. Maybe Lupe would still give lessons while they hoed and weeded the garden or canned the tomatoes at the frolics that would soon come. "Lupe?"

The girl started and dropped her creation. "I am good."

"That was a pretty song you were singing. Me gusta."

Lupe shrugged and picked up her flowers, her face hidden behind a wall of dark, straight hair.

"Why are you sad?" Rebekah plopped onto the ground next to her, then crossed her legs under the long folds of her dress. "You can tell me. You won't hurt my feelings if it's because you don't like it here. I would be homesick too."

"No, no." Lupe raised her head and flung her hair over her shoulder. "I like. I cry because I like."

"Why does it make you cry?"

"They won't let me stay."

"Who won't?"

"La migra."

Rebekah shook her head. "I don't understand."

Lupe clasped her hands together and pointed her index fingers as if she pointed a gun. "Bang-bang, like *policía*, on *frontera*."

Police. Border. Rebekah sighed. "We don't know yet. Jeremiah has been talking to other bishops about it. To wise men. They'll know what to do. Don't worry."

"I worry."

"Why? You're safe here. We'll take care of you. We'll get you to your father in San Antonio." She prayed she wasn't making promises Jeremiah, Mordecai, and Will wouldn't allow her to keep. "Jeremiah is fair and he's kind. So is Mordecai."

Will, too, when he forgot the past and embraced his new life with his fraa.

More tears rolled down Lupe's face. "How? And why he no

write no more? Why he leave and never send money for us like he told us? What if la migra find us first? Or the bad men who brought us over the river?"

Hombres malos. Bad men. So much pent-up worry in such a little girl. Lupe's small, slim fingers covered her eyes. Her sobs were so mournful Rebekah had to swallow a lump in her own throat. She scooted closer and put her arm around the girl's shaking body. Lupe leaned against her chest and gave another shuddering sob. "You haven't mentioned your mother. Where is she? Did she send you to be with your daddy?"

"Mama is dead. Long time. *Mi padre* came to *los Estados Unidos* when I was young. He sent money. Then money stop. We only have abuela. She send us here." Lupe tugged something from her pocket and held it out. Two crumpled, faded photos. "She think it better for us. She think we find Papi."

Abuela. Grandma.

Rebekah took the photo and studied it. A short, buxom woman with gray hair wrapped in a braid around her head stared at the camera, her full lips turned up in a faint smile. She wore a yellow dress that made her look like a sunflower opening to the sky. One hand rested on a much younger Lupe wearing a long braid down her back, the other on Diego, who sat on her lap, wearing only a diaper and a big smile. She looked proud yet somehow sad. Rebekah turned it over. The photo was five years old. Someone had written in a spidery script next to the date: *Ana, Guadalupe y Diego.* "Guadalupe?"

Lupe touched her chest at the base of her throat with two slender fingers. "Me. Guadalupe. Lupe."

Rebekah smoothed the second photo. A young man with enormous solemn eyes, dark hair that curled around his ears, and a beard. Something in his eyes reminded her of Diego. He leaned against the side of a building, one foot propped against the wall, arms crossed against his skinny chest. He was too young to be a daddy. But then, the photo was yellowed with age. "Your daddy?"

"Sí."

"Why did your daddy come here?"

"To escape *soldados.* They thought he was bad man."

"Soldados?"

Lupe scrambled to her feet and stood, her shoulders straight, head back, arms at her side. Then she saluted. "Soldado."

"Soldier."

"Sí."

"What is his name?"

"Carlos."

"Carlos." Carl. "And your mama?"

"Lidia."

"Pretty."

"Sí. No picture of her."

"I'm sorry."

The girl plopped down next to Rebekah and picked up her flowers. "Nice here."

It was nice here. Rebekah hadn't always thought so. When she first arrived in Bee County, she'd thought of it as a barren desert. Now it was home. The people made it home. That and believing God had a reason for sending her here. Now this little girl and her brother were here too. A long way from home. Growing up without a mother. Not knowing where their father was. Dead or alive. It was no wonder Lupe felt so torn. She was safe here. People cared about her. She had no way of knowing what she would find in San Antonio. If anything. Or anybody. "Do you pray?"

Lupe cocked her head, her expression puzzled. Rebekah bowed her head and pressed her palms together in front of her, fingers pointed toward the cloudless blue sky. "Pray?"

The girl crossed herself, forehead, chest, then arm to arm, bowed her head, and pressed her hands together.

She believed in a different way, but she believed. "We'll pray then that we figure out what Gott's plan is for you and Diego. We'll pray we find your father."

"I no know him. He gone long time ago." Lupe shrugged. She plucked a dandelion and handed it to Rebekah. Smiling, she took it and held it close to her face. A universal rite of spring. "You first."

Lupe tugged another dandelion from the multitude that surrounded them. Together, they blew. The soft thistles lifted and floated in the air, tossed and turned by the humid breeze that blew them skyward, then waned as if it were too much trouble. The delicate seeds landed on the photo in Rebekah's lap, covering it like a lacy blanket.

Rebekah sighed. She wouldn't mind sitting here forever. Lupe's sigh joined hers, lifting to the heavens, a prayer all their own on the same breeze that blew the dandelion thistles. *Gott, thank You for this scant moment of peace. Show me what the future holds. Tell me what to do. How to help Lupe and Diego. They need their daed. Help us find him so they can stay.*

He had stopped sending money. Maybe he had none to send. Or maybe he was dead. Rebekah suppressed a shudder. How would they even begin to look for a man in the country illegally? *Help us, Lord. They need our help. Show us what to do.*

Lupe's lips trembled. Shimmering tears kept each other company on her smooth brown cheeks.

"What is it? Don't you think Gott will help?"

"Bad men looking for us."

Bad men. That first day Lupe had been so afraid of Tobias. Even Mordecai's genial smile and simple ways had not dissolved the hard knot of anxiety so apparent in Lupe's face every time he approached her. There had to be more to her story. "You can tell me anything."

Lupe ran her hand across the black-eyed Susans, making them ripple, back and forth, before settling back into formation. "Abuela paid to get us to *Mejico. Más* dinero for us to get over border." She waved her arm to encompass the field. "Aquí."

"You had money to cross the border to America."

She nodded. "It not enough. Men wanted more."

Despite the warm South Texas sun, a shiver scurried up the backs of Rebekah's arms, raising goose bumps usually reserved for the dead of winter. "But they brought you across anyway."

Lupe nodded. Fear made her eyes huge. She swiped at her face with the back of her hand. "They tell me after we cross Rio Grande, they sell me."

Nausea swelled in Rebekah's stomach. The hot dog she'd eaten at the picnic heaved in her throat. Men who sell little girls existed in the same world as sweet Lupe and Diego. Rebekah didn't want to imagine the purpose of such a sale. As nannies? As maids? Or worse. Hombres malos indeed. Rebekah wanted to draw a breath but found she couldn't. She swallowed, her throat dry. "But they let you go?"

"We ran away. Hide."

"In the shed."

"Sí."

"That's why you didn't want to go to the store to buy clothes."

"They find us."

"But they didn't. You're safe with us." It had been days. Those men would never think to look for two Salvadoran children in an Amish community. Thousands of children crossed the border monthly. They'd moved on to other little girls. The thought made Rebekah queasy again. She couldn't save them all, but she could do whatever possible for Lupe. "Mordecai and Tobias and Levi and all the others will keep you safe."

What could they do? Call the sheriff? He would take Lupe and Diego away. Would Tobias and Levi and the other men go to jail for harboring these children who came into the country illegally?

Could they take that chance? Should they be willing to pay that price to keep kinner safe from the evil in the world? Rebekah's head ached, each question like an arrow that burrowed in her flesh, the reverberation bringing fresh pain with each shudder.

"There you are."

As if thinking the name could bring him to them. The deep voice with that unmistakably northern accent—or maybe it was the lack of a southern accent that gave him away—sent a wave of warmth flowing through Rebekah. The pain eased and disappeared. Why Tobias affected her that way, she couldn't say, and it kept her awake at night. Something about the look in his eyes as if he protected everyone and everything that mattered to him. Whatever the cost. She needed him now. Lupe and Diego needed him. She slung her arm around Lupe's shoulder and glanced back. "Here we are. Why? Are you looking for us?"

"Mordecai was." He held his hat in one hand and ran the fingers of his other hand through damp hair. A sheen of sweat glistened on his chiseled face. His shirt was wet and dirt smudged his pant knees. Like a child who'd been running and had fallen.

He'd been playing with the kinner, no doubt. "He wants to talk to you and Lupe. Him and Jeremiah. Will too. They're in the school."

This was it. A decision had been made.

Her hands shaking, legs weak, Rebekah rose to her feet. Her childlike smile fleeing, Lupe snatched up her photos and stashed them in her pocket. Rebekah wanted the little girl back. She tucked her arm around her skinny shoulders. "Why did they ask for me?"

He shrugged. "He didn't say."

Rebekah chewed on her lip until it hurt. Lupe's secret couldn't be a secret anymore. It might cause problems—even danger—for the community. "Wait a minute, Lupe, okay?"

A look of relief on her face, the girl sank to the ground cross-legged again. Rebekah inched closer to Tobias, careful to keep her back to Lupe. Her English was getting better every day. "There is more to their story than she has been telling us."

Tobias rubbed his forehead, his expression perturbed. "What?"

"She didn't tell us everything about how she and Diego ended up in the shed."

"We know they came here from El Salvador and entered the country illegally." Tobias's dark eyebrows rose and fell. "Weren't they hiding from immigration in the shed?"

"Their daed is somewhere here in the States, but he stopped sending money a while back and they have no idea where he is now. Her groossmammi sent them here, thinking it wouldn't be so hard to find him."

Tobias planted his feet and crossed his arms, his full lips turned down in a frown. "And her mudder?"

"Dead."

"And the shed?"

Rebekah told the rest of the story quickly, to stem the flow of questions.

"I can't imagine the kind of human beings who sell little girls." His gaze went to Lupe, his tone soft yet somehow fierce at the same time. "Gott have mercy on their souls."

"If we could find her daed, we could get her away from here. Away from the border. Her and Diego both."

Or they could stay here. With Rebekah and her family. No one would look for them here.

Tobias tugged at his suspenders, his eyes squinted against the sun, making it hard to read his thoughts. "We have to do something, you're right, but how would we even go about finding a man like that in a big state like Texas, especially a man who doesn't want to be found?"

"We could use the computer at the library."

"Do you know how? Or would we have to ask the librarian for help?"

Which would draw attention. "Mordecai does." Rebekah glanced back at Lupe. She had picked another dandelion, seemingly mesmerized by the way the seeds floated in the air. "Or they could stay with us. If she wore clothes more like ours and covered her hair with a prayer kapp, she would fit in more. Diego already does."

"You mean your family or us?" Tobias scooped up his own dandelion and plucked at the seeds, sending them wafting into the air. He glanced at her. "All of us?"

"Same thing, isn't it?" What was he getting at? Or was she reading too much into his tone? "Do you think the immigration people will let them?"

"I don't know about that sort of thing." He let go of the

dandelion. It disappeared into the grass. "If not, we have to find her daed."

This time the *we* sounded much firmer. A *we* that included Rebekah. She nodded. Tobias's gaze caught hers. It held a promise. A vow. He would protect these kinner. Together, they would protect them.

She turned and waved. "Let's go, Lupe. They're waiting."

She shook her head. She ducked her head and crossed her arms over her flat chest. *"No entiendo."*

She did understand and it scared her. "It's okay. I'll be with you." Rebekah wiggled her fingers. "Take my hand. We'll be fine."

"She's right." One arm extended, Tobias moved closer to Lupe. "Take my hand too. Between the two of us, we'll take care of you."

The little girl rose. She took Tobias's hand first. Rebekah found no disrespect in that. He had won Lupe over. He was an hombre bueno. She glanced up at Tobias. He had eyes only for the young girl. He looked like a father comforting his child. With all his little brothers and sisters and no mother, he had experience with this. More than Rebekah had.

It was a good look for him.

Holding hands with Lupe, with Rebekah on the other side, was almost like holding hands with Rebekah. Heat scurried across Tobias's face. He ducked his head, hoping his straw hat's brim would hide the telltale signs of his embarrassment. Something had passed between them in the last few seconds. A mutual commitment to help two children navigate a tumultuous future. Finding their daed seemed an impossible task, but they had to try. Kinner needed family, needed their daeds. Keeping them here and safe and protected in the meantime would be the plan.

Rebekah had no idea how his heart and mind battled. He wanted a fraa, he wanted a family, but he never wanted to feel again the way he felt when his mudder died. Or how he'd felt when he realized his love for Serena had been a terrible mistake, How could he risk loss again? How could he risk his heart again?

He sneaked a peek at Rebekah. If she read anything deeper into their conversation, it didn't show. She looked as young and innocent and pretty as the girl she wanted to help. He knew better. She had a determined streak. A backbone of steel. Rebekah would do whatever necessary to help these children. Her secret visit with Leila had proven that. He'd seen it in action at the meeting with Jeremiah. And she'd never looked prettier than today, frowning up at him, the sun a halo around her head only minutes earlier.

Serena had been a pretty girl with her lipstick, dangling earrings, and flowing skirts, but it was her unerring way of getting to the heart of things that kept him coming back for one more conversation. And then another and another. She had a brain and wasn't afraid to use it.

So many Plain women chose to hide behind their aprons and oven mitts. Not Rebekah Lantz. In her, Tobias had found another woman who spoke her mind. The lack of makeup, the simple clothes, the clear skin and big, blue eyes, the sharp, smart words—those were the package that made Rebekah beautiful. She had all the traits he sought in a woman. All he had to do was have faith in himself and in her.

Why was that so hard for him to do? Daed said Gott used these circumstances to hone character. His should be honed to an edge as sharp as his skiving knife by now. He had a sudden image of God shaving away the rough edges of his character until the smooth, shaped leather appeared. Piles of shavings on the floor around massive feet. His back must be tired by now.

Lupe's soft fingers tightened in his as they approached the school's door.

Tobias stopped and turned to her. "It's okay. They are nice men who want only the best for everyone."

Her expression troubled, the girl turned to Rebekah, who put an arm around her. "Hombres buenos. Like Tobias."

"Sí?" Lupe's gaze swung back to him. "Gracías."

Tobias looked over her head at Rebekah. She shrugged. "She's thanking you."

"I haven't done anything."

"You've been nice to her. I reckon she's not used to that."

The thought caused Tobias's heart to wrench. His sisters Nyla and Ida raced past, intent on a game of tag, their faces red with exertion, mouths open, high-pitched laughter floating on the air. They hadn't always been so carefree. But they had Daed and Tobias and Martha to help them get over their grief and understand that Gott's plan would be revealed to them in time.

Lupe had no one and she had to care for her six-year-old brother while pursued by men whose only goal was to make money from the desire of these people to better themselves, to escape suffering and misery for a life with a future.

"We will get you help." Tobias stopped short of making a promise. He understood how promises made in haste, then broken, served to shatter hearts. "We'll do everything we can."

Lupe might not understand his words, but her face said she understood his feelings. "Thank you."

The words came out *tank you*.

He also understood. He cleared his throat and opened the door. Jeremiah, Mordecai, and Will had dragged chairs into a semicircle at the front of the single, small classroom. Mordecai smiled and waved. Will nodded. Jeremiah simply waited.

With reluctance Tobias let go of her hand and gave her a gentle push. "Go on." He turned to Rebekah. "You too. You're the closest thing we have to a translator."

"Come on down." Jeremiah patted an empty chair beside him. "We won't bite."

Maybe not, but to Lupe they must look like a tribunal of old men. Tobias offered her an encouraging smile. "Buenos, remember?"

She nodded and plopped into the chair. Rebekah squeezed in next to her. Tobias remained standing, not sure they would want or need him for this discussion.

"Have a seat, have a seat." Mordecai waved him over. "We're all family here."

Jeremiah leaned back in his seat and crossed his arms over his ample belly. "You know why we are here?"

Lupe looked at Rebekah as if for permission. Rebekah nodded. "She knows."

"She understands me?"

"She understands a lot. She doesn't have the words to answer." Rebekah glanced at Tobias. He nodded encouragement. "I have to tell y'all something first. Something Lupe just told me right now."

She poured out the story. Jeremiah's face darkened. Will tugged at his beard. Mordecai's woolly eyebrows did push-ups. "We have to help. It's even more important now."

"We can't put the whole community in danger." Will shook his head. "We need to turn them over to the authorities. They'll be able to help them."

"Nee. Nee. Nobody has come after them in the two weeks they've been here."

"She should've told us sooner." Jeremiah frowned, deep furrows like a plowed field on his forehead. "We have to think of the other kinner here in the district."

"Rebekah's right, though. No one has come for them." Mordecai leaned back in his chair. "I say we continue with our plan."

"What about finding their father?"

"Maybe Jesse can help with that too."

This Jesse may have left the community, but he commanded respect, it seemed. Tobias worked to keep his mouth shut. He was the newest member of the community. He wanted to find Lupe's father. He also wanted to protect her. He might not be able to do both.

"I've called three bishops from other communities. None live down here. We're the only Plain district in these parts." Jeremiah broke off, his long nose wrinkled. "I don't suppose you know what any of that means, Lupe?"

Rebekah patted the girl's hand. "It doesn't matter. She knows we're different. She understands we follow Gott's plan for us. I've explained as best I can."

He smoothed his beard. "Then tell her we've decided to go talk to a former member of the community who is involved in a church in town. He does charitable work. He may have the wherewithal to look into her father's whereabouts. We'll take this one step at a time."

"Is that safe?" Will clamped his mouth shut, red creeping up his neck and across his cheeks. "I mean, I have my fraa and the bopli to think about."

"We don't abandon the innocent because of possible

repercussions." Mordecai nodded at Lupe. "Tell her we'll help as best we can."

Rebekah said a few words. Lupe cocked her head, then shook it. Rebekah talked some more. Lupe shrugged and whispered something in the woman's ear. "She wants to know where they'll stay in the meantime."

"Right here."

"Don't give her false hope, though." Will's tone softened. "Those groups will follow the law, which most likely means these children will have to go to the detention center to be processed by the immigration authorities. The likelihood of finding her father is slim to none."

Rebekah nodded. "You voted to talk to Jesse about getting them help?"

Will nodded. "He'll know what to do."

Rebekah smiled at him. Tobias wanted to throw himself in the path of that smile. It suffused her face and made her blue eyes huge and bright. Will simply nodded.

"Then it is settled. Mordecai will take you to Beeville tomorrow to talk to Jesse. As deacon it is his place to determine a course of action for these children in need. Tobias and Rebekah, you'll go with him."

"Me?" Tobias straightened. "You want me to go?"

"Your family has been caring for the children up to this point," Jeremiah said. "I've spoken with Levi. He's deferred to you."

"Me?" Rebekah's voice squeaked as she popped up from the chair. "I'm going too?"

"Mordecai feels you best understand the children's situation." Jeremiah shook his head. "You understand that you're only going because Mordecai is going and he will keep an eye on you. You're not being rewarded for your behavior."

"She's been forgiven for that behavior." Mordecai's tone was mild. "She understands better than anyone what these children have been through. If anyone can make their case, she can."

Jeremiah inclined his head, but his expression remained dubious.

"I'm not anxious to speak to . . . them . . . but I want to do this to help Lupe and Diego." Rebekah ducked her head. "I'll be quiet, speaking by Mordecai's leave."

Mordecai snorted. Jeremiah smiled.

"You'll do your best to behave, I'm sure." Jeremiah's smile disappeared. "Jesse isn't banned, but he is no longer a member of our community. Nor is your sister. You must treat this situation as such."

Rebekah nodded. She might do as she was told, but she would never concede to agreeing with it. Most likely she was already plotting how to find the father.

Tobias turned away before one of them read his face. They would surely see his admiration there. And his uncertainty as to what exactly he should do with it.

NINETEEN

Wonders never ceased. Rebekah skipped and increased her speed to keep up with Mordecai and Tobias's long strides as they approached Jesse's church. She'd long curbed her curiosity about the place of worship that so enchanted her sister and brother-in-law. The place where they'd married, been baptized, and had little Gracie dedicated. The place for which they'd left family and friends. She might see what they saw in it, or she might be aghast at how they chose to worship.

It was indeed a momentous day, even if it wasn't about her. It was about Lupe and Diego. She kept telling herself that, but the up-and-down of her stomach, like a newborn foal trying to stand on long, unsteady legs, made it hard to think. Tobias glanced back at her, smiled, and slowed. She forced a smile in return and tripped over her own feet.

His huge hand grabbed hers. "Steady."

"Danki." Sure her dress would burst into flames, such was the heat that raced through her, Rebekah ducked her head and focused on the building. "I've never been in an Englisch church before."

Mordecai looked back, his expression inscrutable. "Just a building."

He had been quiet on the trip to town. Unusual for Mordecai. Rebekah suspected it was because Mudder hadn't been happy about this trip. Even with Mordecai along, she didn't want Rebekah close to Jesse and Leila. She could only speak her piece and then bow to Mordecai's decision. Mordecai didn't like disagreeing with his fraa. And Rebekah didn't like being responsible for any rift between them. Plus it left her with the task of making small talk with Tobias. He'd seemed ill at ease too. Whether because of her or their mission itself.

Tobias held one of the double doors for her. She followed Mordecai inside and down a long hallway. He seemed to know where he was going. How, she had no idea. Who knew what Mordecai did in his spare time? He kept his own counsel.

The third door opened up into a large room. Rebekah drank it in, curiosity fueling her gaze. One wall featured a stained-glass window with a dove fluttering over a flame. The air smelled of candle wax and a flowery air freshener. Chairs with padded seats were arranged in neat lines on threadbare tan carpet. A wooden pulpit sat at the front of the room. This was where Jesse spoke his messages some Sundays.

She would keep this memory close so she could imagine him up there, his dark curls bouncing as he lifted his hands to make an important point. And Leila sitting in the first row with little Gracie on her lap. Now Rebekah would be able to see it in her mind's eye. Until they moved to Dallas. She tried not to think about that. Not right now. Later.

One thing at a time.

Jesse wasn't in the sanctuary. Mordecai reversed course and brushed past her.

"What now?" she called after him. He kept going. "Maybe he's at home."

Which meant she would have to talk to Leila again. Leila who left her. Leila who was leaving her all over again.

This was about Lupe and Diego. Not Rebekah. *Lord, help me forgive.*

"His blue minivan is out front."

"How do you know what his car looks like?"

Mordecai shrugged. The man knew many things.

Tobias once again held the door for her. It was such a simple gesture, but it made her feel special somehow. Plain men weren't much for ceremony. She picked up her pace and scurried after her stepfather.

Leila had said Jesse also did maintenance work at the church and he worked for Matthew Plank, another who had left the Plain way of life. He did carpentry and restored old houses. "Maybe he only comes here on Sundays."

"Pastors work at the church during the week, or so I've read." Mordecai stopped outside the only other door in the hallway. "It's possible he left with one of the members of the church. Or Matthew Plank picked him up. If that's the case we'll stop by his house. Leila will know where he is."

Would Mordecai paint a picture of that house for his fraa? Would he repeat his conversation with Leila for Mudder? "I could ask Leila. Y'all can stay in the van with Mr. Cramer. It wouldn't take more than a minute or two."

"You're getting ahead of yourself." Mordecai rapped on the door. "Besides, it's for me to handle."

"Come in, come in!"

Jesse's voice.

Mordecai opened the door and strode in, leaving Tobias and Rebekah to follow. Tobias smiled at her and shrugged. He had such a nice smile.

Ach. Behave yourself.

Jesse sat behind an oak desk covered with books and papers stacked so haphazardly it was a wonder they didn't slide onto the threadbare beige carpet under his feet. He looked up, his mouth dropped open, and he stood, knocking two thick tomes to the floor in his haste. "Whoops, sorry!" He squatted and disappeared behind the desk, then reappeared, dark-rimmed glasses askew on his nose.

When did Jesse start wearing glasses? They made him look even more like his daed, Leroy.

"Mordecai! Rebekah!" He whipped around the desk and charged toward them. "I can't believe you're here. This is a surprise. A great surprise."

"We needed to talk to you." Mordecai extended a hand. Jesse halted what looked like a headlong rush for a hug and held out his own hand. Mordecai smiled and shook as if he shook hands with former Plain men who were his stepsons-in-law all the time. "It won't take long."

"Absolutely. I like talking. I talk a lot. Have a seat!" Jesse turned to Tobias. "I'm Jesse Glick. Who are you?"

"Tobias Byler. New to the district."

"I gathered that part." Jesse shook Tobias's hand and moved on to Rebekah. "You're all grown up, girl."

A lump in her throat threatened to explode, and Rebekah forced herself to submit to the hug. If it weren't for Jesse, Leila would still be back at home. She'd probably be married to Will. Gott's plan? How could it be? She stepped back and wrapped her arms around her middle. "How's Gracie?"

"Real good. Grace got another tooth last night. Leila is even bigger this time than last. We think it'll be a boy." Jesse glanced at the two men and back at Rebekah. "Maybe while you're in town, you can stop by the house and see for yourself. She would love to see you."

Mordecai didn't answer. He seemed absorbed in the posters on the walls. They featured Christian rock bands from the looks of them.

Jesse cleared his throat and returned to his side of the desk. He nodded toward mismatched wooden chairs arranged in a line facing the desk. "Grab a seat. What can I do for you? It must be something big if Jeremiah let you come to me."

"In a way." Mordecai relaxed in the chair, his hands clasped in front of him. "Rebekah found two Salvadoran children in our shed at the school. We've been taking care of them for a couple of weeks."

She sank into the last chair after Tobias took the middle one. "We just—"

Mordecai held up a hand. Rebekah closed her mouth. If she wouldn't be allowed to speak, she wasn't sure why she'd been allowed to come.

"Leila told me. Thanks be to God you did." Jesse swiveled back and forth in his chair. Bits of yellow stuffing from the ripped vinyl seat fell on the floor with each turn. "Not everyone is kind."

"Our question is, can you help them?" Tobias leaned back in his chair, looking as if he had conversations with ex-Amish ministers all the time. "They're children, six and twelve. They're in a strange country with no family, no money. They've come a long way to be tossed back over the border."

The emotion in his voice sent a tremor through Rebekah. Tobias had feelings for these kinner, same as she did. She'd known that, but to see him so determined, so fierce about it, warmed her down to her toes.

"Don't believe everything you read in the papers." Jesse leaned forward and steepled his fingers, elbows propped on the desk. "The authorities are trying to do right by the children flooding the border, but they're being overwhelmed."

"So what do we do?"

"Do they have family here?"

Rebekah recounted what Lupe had told her. "I thought maybe we could try to find her father."

"I can ask around." Jesse blew out air. He leaned back in his chair. "I can't do anything directly. Families are being aided by one central church organization. The rest of us help by providing clothing, toiletries, things they need. The kinner who come through Border Patrol unescorted by adults have to be processed within forty-eight hours. They're protected by the Office of Refugee Resettlement. They're sent to what they're calling Respite Centers where they get—"

"Warehouses," Tobias broke in. "Then back over the border."

"No. They receive food, clothing, medical care, and a place to sleep until they have their immigration hearing."

"We can give them all that." Rebekah tried to keep her voice calm. "We are doing that now. I mean, Tobias's family is doing most of it, but we're helping."

Tobias shot her another smile. He needed to stop doing that.

It made it hard for her to keep track of her thoughts and speak in complete sentences.

Jesse nodded. "I understand the desire to help, believe me I do. It breaks my heart. Let me talk to the folks at Catholic Charities, get their advice. Ideally they would help them get processed, a hearing date scheduled, and then release them to you until the hearing."

"Is that possible?" Rebekah sat up straighter, hope buoying her for the first time. "We're willing to keep them as long as need be. I mean, we can take turns if it gets to be too much for Tobias's family—"

"It's not too much for us." Tobias shook his head, the smile turning to a fierce frown. "Diego eats plenty, but Lupe doesn't eat more than a hummingbird. What's two more kinner when you have as many as we do?"

"It's nice that they're so well received." Jesse glanced from Tobias to Rebekah and back, his forehead wrinkled in a frown, his expression odd. "Don't get your hopes up. What I'm describing is what happens with families that come through. They release them on their own recognizance and let them go to their final destination—whatever that is—and then they have to show up for their hearing when the time comes. There are so many it can take a while."

"But it's not the same with children?"

"Nee, the authorities don't release children on their own recognizance. It would be cruel and inhumane."

Tobias snorted. "Like sending them on a journey through Central America on their own, exposing them to evil men who prey on them and all those dangers of the world?"

"It makes you think about just how awful the situation is

in their own countries that they would be sent by their parents on that journey." Jesse shook his head. "It's not our place to pass judgment on them. I can only imagine what pain and anguish those left behind must suffer and how much they must believe in the great American dream. They want something better for their children and they're willing to sacrifice to get it."

"You're right." Tobias's disdain melted. "What do we need to do, then?"

"I'll dig into it, I promise." Jesse's smile was diffident. "Do you want to come back tomorrow, or shall I come find you?"

"Nee. Call Will at the store. He'll get the message to Jeremiah and me." Mordecai stood, his expression kind. "Your cousin will be glad to hear from you. He runs the store now, you know."

Where Jesse had once worked. In his father's store. If the thought brought pain or shame to him, he didn't show it. "I'll call as soon as I have a plan of action."

"We appreciate your help." Tobias slapped his hat on his head. "In the meantime, we'll take care of Lupe and Diego. All of us."

"Gut." Jesse slipped around the desk. He stopped just short of Rebekah's chair. "It's almost lunchtime. You're welcome to come to the house. Leila always fixes plenty. It's hard for her to cook for just three." His gaze slid toward Mordecai. "She'd love to see you. All of you."

"We have to get back." Mordecai's tone was kind but firm. "Remember, you are always welcome to come home. Your mudder and daed pray for it every day. As do we all."

"I'm doing the Lord's work." Jesse's tone was equally firm. "So is Leila."

That decision had cost so much. Hurt so much. Still, the only recourse was forgiveness. Rebekah stepped in front of Jesse and held out her arms. He walked into her hug with no hesitation. "Give her my love," she whispered in his ear. "We miss you."

He leaned in closer, his breath tickling her ear. "I'll tell her you found someone. She'll be so happy."

"Nee, I—"

"Take care." He squeezed her arm and backed away. His gaze went to the two men. "Thank you for coming to me with this. I appreciate that."

Tobias edged toward the door. "Rebekah said you know about these things."

"If you minister in this part of the country, you can't help but know about it. That's the sad, sad truth."

They were silent for a few seconds. Mordecai cleared his throat. "We'll go, then."

Her checks still burning at Jesse's observation, Rebekah went first. What had made him say such a thing? Did something show on her face? Tobias's face? If he felt anything, he hadn't revealed it to her.

Once again she skipped to keep up. Mordecai's long, swinging stride picked up the pace. He might be afraid she would be affected by Jesse's fervor and his commitment to his mission. That would never happen, but somehow, they couldn't seem to trust her.

She glanced back. Jesse had followed them down the hallway. He gave her a small half wave. "Talk to you soon."

That seemed unlikely.

Tobias stepped into her line of sight. Had he heard what Jesse said in her ear? Surely not. "Let's go."

"I'm going."

"We have to get home."

His emphasis on the word *home* wasn't lost on her. "I know that."

"Just making sure."

What did he know about any of this? She picked up her pace. So did he. "What's wrong with you?"

"I have experience with how green the grass can be on the other side of the fence."

"I don't. I'm perfectly happy with the grass on my side of the fence." She slipped through the door he held for her—somehow it didn't seem as nice now. More of his effort to put space between her and the church. "Besides, since Leila left, I've been given no opportunity whatsoever to walk barefoot in the grass that's growing beyond that fence you're talking about."

"Which is as it should be."

"What does it matter to you?"

Red scurried across Tobias's face. His mouth opened. It closed. He let the door slam shut. "You're right. Sorry."

A man had said she was right. And said he was sorry.

Again, wonders never ceased.

TWENTY

Heat melted away knots of uncertainty. Tobias leaned against the corral fence, the early May sun beating on his face. No matter what others said, he liked a heat that seeped into a body and warmed from head to foot. No more snow. No more ice. No more icy void inside.

He heaved a breath and enjoyed the scent of dirt and manure and the way his daed handled Bobbie McGregor's horse. Over a week's time they'd graduated from the blanket on his back to a saddle. Today was the day that the toffee-colored quarter horse with a deep-black mane and tail would learn the art of carrying a rider. So far he'd been fairly eager to please but was on the flighty side. Whoever had begun his training had left him with a few bad habits. He seemed shy and uncertain, unusual for the normally even-tempered quarter horse.

Daed exuded patience with horses, just as he did with kinner. He was a patient man in most regards. Tobias had tried his patience on numerous occasions, but he'd never seen the man raise his voice or his hand in anger. Horses responded to his hand and his voice, infinitely soft and warm.

Soft and warm. Two words that made him think of Rebekah. He leaned his forehead against the fence post for a second and groaned. Since the meeting with Jesse, he hadn't been able to get her out of his head. The girl didn't understand a woman's place, of that he had no doubt. She talked when she shouldn't. She hugged a man who'd left the community and taken her sister with him. The man was her brother-in-law, so why did it bother Tobias? He couldn't say why. Maybe because she'd looked so longingly at the man. Because she'd been so transparently interested in the church and everything about it. As if she might be considering what it might be like to go there on a regular basis.

He had already shown he was not a good judge of women when it came to relationships. He needed to watch himself. Yet when he closed his eyes that night after their return home, she'd been there, messing with his mind. Her smile. The way she looked at him with those bright blue eyes as if she knew something he didn't. She had gotten under his skin somehow. No doubt about it.

"What you are doing?" Bobbie's scent of roses arrived before she did. She slid in next to Tobias, a frosty can of Dr Pepper in one hand. She wore jeans so faded they were almost white in the knees and behind, along with a blue T-shirt that read COWGIRLS DRIVE TRUCKS and well-worn cowboy boots. "You look like you have a headache. Better get over it quick. Your dad is going to need your help with Cracker Jack."

"What kind of name is Cracker Jack for a horse?"

"My kind of horse, my kind of name." She sipped from the soda and grinned. "What? You think his name should be Toffee or something?"

"It should be whatever you want it to be, I reckon."

"You should see Ariel, my thoroughbred, the one I do barrel

racing with. Now, there's a piece of horseflesh. Cracker Jack is different. I saw him and I knew he needed some loving. He needed an owner who would whip him into shape and turn him into a working horse." She threw her free hand into the air like a bronco rider attempting to keep his seat during a buck. "Love at first sight."

Tobias couldn't help but laugh. "Horses are easy to love."

Much easier than people.

"That they are. I'm an animal person myself. They love you no matter what and they don't talk back. They sure never break your heart."

Who had broken her heart? She didn't look like the type to wear it on her sleeve. "I suppose that's true."

"I don't suppose you do any barrel racing?"

"Nope."

"You should come watch me race when the county fair comes to Beeville." She leaned closer, her eyes bright with humor and something else. Curiosity. He'd seen that look before. Something about Plain men presented a challenge for certain Englisch girls. He'd fallen for that once, but never again.

Serena would say never say never. Or some such silly thing. Then she'd smile that smile and have him hooked all over again.

"Not something I have time for, but thank you for the invitation." He sidestepped, putting more space between them. "Cracker Jack has a nice structure. His body should take the pounding for cutting the herd well."

"Yep. I won't be riding him when he's working, but Dad's ranch hands are good with horses. They appreciate a good working horse."

"They need any saddles? We do the basic cutting saddle." He would keep his mind on business. Period. "Give you a good price."

"I'll spread the word to them. You know how it is. They go through them fast, but it's a big investment to replace one." She pulled herself up the fence, flung one leg over, and balanced herself on the top rung. "Cracker Jack had a rough start. The people that sold him said they rescued him from some guy who didn't take care of him. But that's okay. He'll rebound fast. What's next?"

"Next Daed rides him." David strode across the yard from the shop. He tugged the brim of his straw hat down against the sun and grinned at Bobbie. Tobias might as well have been in another state. "I didn't miss anything, did I?"

"Nope."

"Just talking horseflesh and barrel riding." Bobbie slapped at a fly the size of her finger. "There's an exhibition at the fairgrounds this weekend. Y'all should go. It's fun and the horses are beautiful."

David flushed beet red. "I—"

"He has work to do." Tobias would draw his last breath before he would let his younger brother experience the pain he'd dragged himself through with bad decisions and worse judgment. Bobbie seemed like a nice woman, but she was Englisch and David didn't need to get tangled up in that. "Let's get in there and help Daed."

Tobias pushed through the gate, David on his heels, his face still mottled red. They made their way to where Daed had the horse tethered. Tobias's breath quickened as it did every time. A twelve-hundred pound horse could do some damage when spooked or downright angry. "You ready?"

Daed nodded. As he had done every day for the last week, he laid the red saddle blanket over the horse's back. The horse nickered, an anxious sound, and shook his head. "Easy, boy, easy, hush, big guy."

Daed's murmurings reminded Tobias of the nights when he'd listened to him rock Liam to sleep as a fussy newborn baby missing his mama's milk. Whispered lullabies in a gruff voice tight with unshed tears. Always unshed within earshot of the eight other kinner in that house who all cried their own tears many nights, their sobs muffled in pillows, after Mudder's passing.

The saddle went next. Tobias stroked Cracker Jack's forehead and whispered his own sweet nothings. The horse's glance was watchful, worried. His breath quivered and his lips spread apart, revealing a set of teeth ready to nip.

Now the cinching part. Cracker Jack two-stepped backward and tossed his head up and down.

"You sure he's ready for this?" Tobias tightened his grip on the reins and held steady. David stayed close, his expression watchful. "He's awful skittish."

Daed's gaze never wavered from the horse. "He's a little nervous, but he's ready. He has to learn to trust us."

Still murmuring sweet nothings, Daed eased his boot into the stirrup and put his weight into it. His right leg swung over the horse's body and he landed softly in the saddle.

Cracker Jack snorted and reared. His back arched. His long neck and head lowered in a second arch.

The force of his determination knocked Tobias back half a dozen steps. He hung on to the reins for dear life, but it didn't matter. The horse bucked and swiveled and bucked again, screaming in fear all the while.

Daed gripped the horn with one hand, his other flung in the air like a bronco rider. It did no good. A second mighty buck by the enormous, powerful creature sent him flying.

The sickening crunch of bone against sun-hardened earth

echoed in Tobias's ears. He fought to control the animal. The reins jerked from his grasp as Cracker Jack fought with every ounce of strength to remove that alien weight from his back. His front hooves battled air. He reared on his back legs, front hooves flailing.

Tobias scrambled back and back until he found himself wedged against the fence.

David flapped his arms and yelled. "Haw, haw, come on, back off, haw!"

The horse whirled. His hooves trampled Daed.

Daed didn't move. He didn't cry out. His straw hat lay crumpled just beyond the reach of his outstretched, motionless hand.

"Daed? Daed!"

Nothing.

Choked with apprehension, Tobias stumbled forward, flapping both arms. "Move on, move on, haw."

Cracker Jack ducked his head and whinnied, a fierce, high sound. He raced away, circling the corral fence.

Aware of Bobbie shoving through the gate and racing across the dirt, Tobias dashed to his father and dropped to his knees. "Daed?"

Blood seeped from a cut across his cheek. One leg twisted at an unnatural, painful-looking angle. His eyes were closed, his features flaccid. "Wake up. We have to get you up. You're okay, we just need to get you up."

"Is he dead?" David's voice cracked. He dropped to his knees, his anguish etched across a face exactly like his father's. "He can't be dead. We have to get him help. Help me lift him."

He shoved his arms under Daed's limp body and tried to lift. "Come on, help me."

"We need an ambulance." Tobias put a hand on his brother's shoulders. "We have to wait."

"Don't move him. It could make it worse." Bobbie had a cell phone to her ear. She crouched next to Tobias. "Don't touch him. I'm getting help."

"It'll take too long for an ambulance to get here." David jerked away from Tobias's touch. "We can put him in your truck and drive him to Beeville."

"Bobbie's right. If the horse stepped on his back, we can't chance moving him." Tobias kept his voice soft, his own desire to do something, anything, welling inside him, making it hard to breathe. "We'll make it worse."

Bobbie talked into the phone for a few seconds and muttered, "Yup." She slapped it into her front pocket. "They're on their way. Stay with him. I'll deal with Cracker Jack."

Cracker Jack stood at the far end of the corral, reins dragging the ground, his flanks wet with lather. Within seconds, she had sweet-talked him into letting her remove the saddle and tie him to a fence post. The raging animal of a few minutes earlier had disappeared, leaving behind a docile creature who searched his owner's pockets for apples or carrots.

"He's not a bad horse." She knelt next to Tobias. Her hands shook. "He's been badly treated in the past."

"I know."

It would take time, too much time, for the ambulance to arrive. Tobias wanted to holler. He wanted to throw Daed over his shoulder and carry him to help. Instead, he bowed his head and breathed. He leaned closer, squeezed his father's unresponsive hand, and whispered, "Wake up, Daed, please wake up."

TWENTY-ONE

The jars of freshly canned tomatoes glistened in the sunlight that glowed through the kitchen window. The aroma reminded Susan of homemade spaghetti sauce. Of suppers spent around the table as kinner when Mordecai had been on a practical joke streak a mile long and Mudder and Daed pretended to bicker over her cooking or his dirty clothes. It smelled like contentment. Steam billowed from the mammoth pans of tomatoes and green beans on the stove, alongside the wet bath filled with sterilized jars ready to receive their bounty. Sweat dripped down her temples and tickled her cheeks. She wiped the edges of the jar mouth with care not to let the towel touch the contents. "This one is ready for a lid."

"That's the last of the tomatoes." Rebekah bustled along behind Susan, adding flats and rings to the steaming jars. "How are the green beans coming?"

"Everything is snapped." Abigail wiped her hands on a ragged dish towel, her face flushed with the heat of the propane stove mixed with humid May air. Summer had arrived on the first day of the month with a ferocity usually reserved for July in South

Texas. As if Gott knew a canning frolic was afoot. "The girls are chopping cucumbers for the pickles now."

Hazel stuck a cucumber slice in her mouth and crunched. "I'd rather eat them." She giggled, further mashing her words through a full mouth. "Pickles are a lot of work."

"But they're mighty good with a hamburger." Abigail patted the little girl's kapp-covered head. "So stop eating them and start chopping. You'll be glad you did next winter."

Despite the heat and the sweat, Susan loved canning frolics. Having all her favorite women in the same room—crowded though it was—meant lots of chatter and laughter. Different from school where quiet was priceless. Plus, she had a chance to let someone else be in charge. She could relax and not worry about being responsible for the kinner. Canning vegetables was much easier.

"Sorry we're late." Martha Byler stuck her head in the door. The girl looked like Tobias in the face, but without the five-o'clock shadow. The hair peeking from the back of her kapp was dark blonde and her eyes blue. "Nyla was running a fever this morning. I made some chicken soup and left her with Ida reading *Little House on the Prairie* to her."

"I love those books. *The Long Winter* is my favorite." Susan's opportunity to keep her commitment to talk to Levi's oldest daughter had arrived, right on time, and she was talking about books. She couldn't help herself, it seemed.

"I like them all." Martha didn't seem to mind. "And the girls love for me to read to them."

Susan couldn't help but smile at that. Her teacher heart was happy to hear it. She trotted across the room to the table, picked up a knife, and held it out. "Last woman in has to chop the onions."

Accepting the offer, Martha smiled and shooed Lupe and little Liam into the room. "I don't mind onions, especially when that means pickles later on."

"Where's Diego?" Susan patted Lupe's shoulders. The girl settled into a chair next to Hazel. "Working with the men?"

"With Milo, tilling the space we'll use for the garden," Martha answered for Lupe, who ducked her head, a shy grin on her brown face. "He likes playing in dirt and we're way behind in our planting."

"I like playing in the dirt too." Susan liked gardening. Gott was good. She handed a small paring knife to Lupe. "Cut the cucumbers in chunks before Hazel eats them all."

Lupe looked puzzled, but she took the knife.

"Have you ever seen anyone can before?"

The girl shrugged, her eyebrows lifted.

"We cook the tomatoes, put them in jars, and seal them so we can eat them in the winter."

Lupe nodded, but Susan could tell she didn't understand. It didn't matter. She probably would be long gone before winter. The thought made her heart squeeze. Jesse hadn't gotten back to Will yet, but he surely would any day now. "How do you say hot in Spanish?" She pointed to the stove. When all else fails, do what comes naturally. Teach. "Hot."

"Caliente." Lupe obliged. *"Estufa está caliente."*

"Estufa está caliente," Susan repeated. "Everyone now."

The ladies repeated the phrase in chorus, Hazel trailing behind by a word or two. Liam yelled, "Caliente!" after everyone had finished, only it sounded like "cold tea." They all laughed.

Susan squeezed into a chair next to Martha and picked up a huge onion. The greenhouse vegetables had done well this year.

She plopped it on the cutting board and picked up another knife. "How are you settling in here in Bee County?"

Martha wiped a tear from her cheek with the back of her hand. "These are some strong onions." She giggled. "Good. We're doing fine. The house needs some work, but Daed and the boys are busy setting up the shop. That's more important right now."

"Do you need any help? We could organize a frolic. Help clean the place up, plant the garden."

Martha flashed a smile. Susan got a glimpse of what Levi's wife must've looked like. "That would be nice. Ida and Nyla help as much as they can, but they're still small. Between the laundry and the cooking and the baking . . ." Her cheeks turned red. "I don't mean to complain. I love taking care of them."

"I didn't think you were complaining." Susan got to work on her own onion, careful to keep her voice light. "It's a lot of work for any of us. Everyone needs a little help now and then."

She separated the onion into nice rings. "In fact, I was thinking I could make dinner for your family Sunday night at your house and you could come to the singing here at our house. My treat."

Martha frowned, her nose wrinkled. "Did Daed put you up to this?"

"He just wants you to have the same fun other girls your age have."

"Why's he in such a hurry to marry me off?" She smacked the onion with more force than necessary. "Who does he think will take care of Liam and Nyla—"

"He's not in a hurry." Susan touched her arm. "Believe me, he's not. The fact that he wants you to have this time in your life speaks to how much affection he has for you. He wants what's best for you. What's meant to be for you as Gott's child."

Tears brightened the girl's eyes. She sniffed. "I think maybe Gott intended for me to take care of my schweschders and bruders."

"For a while, but not forever. They're getting old enough to take care of themselves and each other. To help you too."

Martha sighed. The knife hung in the air as if she'd forgotten it in her contemplation of her future, surely an uncertain and scary proposition for a sixteen-year-old.

The sound of someone banging on the door startled them into silence. Simon stumbled through the back door. He looked so much like his brother Jesse, but his face would never lose its childlike innocence. Gott had given Leroy and Naomi the gift of a special child. His hat flopped and hit the floor. "There you are, Martha. I looked for you at your house. Levi got thrown from a horse. He's headed to the hospital. Tobias sent me to tell you."

"Is he hurt? Is it bad?" Susan stood. The knife dropped to the table with a clatter. "We need to—"

"Where is he?" Martha's face had turned as white as the onion in her hand. She dropped it and it rolled across the floor and disappeared under the stove. "Is he dead?"

"He's not dead. We don't know how bad he is, though. He wasn't talking and his eyes were closed." Simon's inability to find words was worse when he was under stress. He scooped up his hat and slapped it on his head with more force than necessary. "An ambulance took him to Beeville. Mr. Carson is out front with his van to take y'all."

"Is Tobias all right? Was he there?" Rebekah took Liam's hand. "Was he hurt?"

"Tobias is fine. So is David. They're on their way to the hospital." Simon turned as if to lead the way. He'd been given a job to do and he was trying very hard to do it to the best of his ability. "Hurry up. Let's go, then."

Susan turned to Abigail, who was staring at Rebekah with a bemused look on her face. Susan touched her sleeve. "We'll all go."

"I'll stay with the canning. We can't have all this food spoil." Abigail gave Martha a swift hug. "I'll pray."

Praying would be their job, in the van and at the hospital. That's what the community did when trouble visited. She'd barely had a chance to begin to know Levi. The force of her desire to know him more stunned her. Susan took a breath. This wasn't about her. His kinner had lost a mother. They couldn't lose their father too. She put an arm around Martha. "We'll go together."

TWENTY-TWO

The doctors weren't saying much. Tobias fought the urge to pound his fist against the waiting room wall. An hour they'd been waiting and still nothing. He rubbed his fingers over his fisted hand and forced himself to relax it. The kinner were watching. They would take his lead. They'd lost so much already. They needed Daed. He needed Daed. He swallowed the pain in his throat and forced a breath. Whatever came, Martha, Micah, Rueben, David, Milo, Nyla, Ida, and Liam would look to him for how to handle it. His job was to rely on Gott in all things.

Mordecai strode into the room, his face etched with concern. He eased into the chair next to Tobias. "Any word from the doctors?"

"Nee."

"Waiting is hard."

"It is."

"I understand, having lived through something similar."

"I've heard bits and pieces of it."

Mordecai shoved his hat back and leaned his head against the wall behind them. "The van accident that took my fraa's life and left Phineas hanging by a thread. The younger kinner had scrapes and little wounds, but nothing so bad I couldn't take them home at the end of the day. We weren't in this hospital. We were down in Corpus, but they're all the same. They smell the same. They sound the same."

Tobias knew those sounds, the ticking of the clock, the wheels of the gurneys clacking down tiled hallways, the beep of monitors. He knew the smells. The acrid smell of cleansers. The smell of sickness. The smell of despair. They were branded on his memory. He needed only to close his eyes to be reminded of the sights. Daed leaning over Mudder's still form, his hand on her limp body. His eyes red with tears. "When Mudder died we spent a few hours in the hospital up north, but she was gone so sudden it wasn't much."

"I waited hours while they worked on Phineas, trying to keep him alive." Mordecai's voice roughened. His Adam's apple bobbed. "I know how it feels."

"Daed is fine. He'll be fine."

"Gott's will be done."

The heat of a painful flush scurried across Tobias's face and neck. He hadn't thought to pray in the moments between the horse's reaction to the saddle and the arrival of the ambulance, paramedics putting a brace around Daed's neck and strapping him to a board, the long trip into town while they poked and prodded his daed, hooking him up to IVs, checking his vital signs, assessing his injuries in words Tobias couldn't begin to understand. All he knew for sure was that Daed never opened his eyes. He never moved a limb of his own accord. Tobias bowed his head and tried to summon the words. *Help. Don't take him. I need him.* The words were sparse and selfish, but they were the only words that came. *Forgive me. I was right there, yet I couldn't protect him. The kinner need him. I can't take care of them without him. Please.*

"I'm so sorry."

He opened his eyes and raised his head. Bobbie stood before them. Her face was tearstained and her hands and knees were dirty. He shook his head. "It's not your fault."

He'd been right there and yet couldn't save his own father. If it was anyone's fault, it was his.

"I feel responsible. He's my horse."

"My father trains horses for a living. He's broken hundreds of them. He knows the risk and accepts it." Words he should be saying to himself. "It's no one's fault."

"I can't understand why Cracker Jack reacted that way. He's a good horse."

"Like you said, something in his past. Something his old owner did. Who knows? But it's not your fault. My dad wouldn't want you stewing about it."

"You're nice to say that." She plopped down in the chair next to Tobias and squeezed his hand. Tobias could feel Mordecai's tension next to him. The older man's entire body stiffened. "If you need anything at all, you let me know. My father can get the best doctors, the best surgeons. He'll pay. Don't you worry. This is workers' comp. It was an on-the-job injury."

Plain folks didn't have insurance, but they took care of their own. "That's nice of you, but not necessary."

Bobbie tucked a piece of pink paper in his hand and folded his fingers around it. Her fingers were warm and damp. "My phone number if you need me."

Mordecai cleared his throat, his expression stern.

A flurry of activity at the door cut him off, to Tobias's relief. Susan, Rebekah, and Martha trotted into the room in quick succession, their faces etched with worry. Jeremiah followed, along with Will and Simon. Word spread quickly in the small community. Everyone would gather. Prayers would be offered. Rebekah put an arm around Martha and whispered something in her ear. Susan picked up Liam and marched toward them, her face red with heat and exertion. Rebekah followed, her arm still around Martha.

He had no one who could offer him that comfort. He closed his eyes and opened them. The women stood in front of him. "How is he? Where is he?" Susan beat Martha to the questions by a hairsbreadth from the look on his schweschder's face. "What do the doctors say?"

"We don't know much." Tobias searched for words. They seemed mired in emotion he didn't want to reveal. "The doctor is looking at him now."

Rebekah moved forward. She opened her mouth, then glanced at Bobbie.

Tobias stood. "This is Bobbie McGregor. She's a customer."

"Levi was breaking my horse when he got hurt." Bobbie's voice quavered. She pulled herself up from the chair. "I'll let y'all talk. I know this is a family thing. Especially with y'all."

Her head bent, she brushed past Rebekah, who swiveled and watched her disappear through the door before turning back to Tobias. "Is she all right?"

"Feeling bad about what happened, I reckon that's all."

"You sound . . . parched. Can I get you some water?"

"I'm fine."

"Y'all best have a seat." Mordecai's voice held a warning tone that seemed to be directed at Susan. "It'll be a while, I reckon. Spend the time in prayer."

Susan's face flushed a darker red. She turned away with Liam still in her arms. "I'll take care of the little ones."

"I'll help her." Martha, her face a startling white in comparison, followed Susan. She looked as if she were sleepwalking. "I'll pray."

She needed comfort. He should be the one to give it. He started after her, but his legs felt heavy. His boots stumbled on the thick carpet.

"No sense in getting worked up. Gott will hear our prayers."

Mordecai's voice pulled him back into his chair. Prayer. That was the most important thing right now.

Mordecai closed his eyes, pulled his hat down over his face, and leaned his head against the wall, the picture of a man who left everything in God's hands.

Rebekah plopped into the chair next to Tobias, her fresh, clean scent welcome after the stench of hospital. "We prayed all the way over here. Gott is good. You don't need to worry about a thing. We'll help. School's out now and Susan wants to do the cooking. I can help the girls with the garden. Caleb will help. All of us."

"We appreciate that. My daed will rest easy knowing everyone is pitching in."

"Gott provides."

"He does." The words stuck in his throat. Why did Gott let this happen? It was the same question he'd asked when Mudder passed in the midst of the life-affirming act of giving birth. It made no sense to him. What if Gott's will was to take his father and leave him in charge of eight kinner? What kind of Gott did that? "I'm just . . ." His throat tightened. "Maybe I do need that water."

She popped up. "I'll get it."

His head filled with the sickening sound of hoof crunching bone. Rebekah's hand touched his sleeve. "Maybe you should walk with me. You look like you need air."

He glanced at Mordecai. The older man nodded. "It'll do you good to stretch your legs." His gaze went to Rebekah. "Fresh air does a body good as well."

Tobias stood. His legs felt weak. He lurched. Rebekah's hand came out again. "You have blood on your sleeve. We'll have to wash that soon."

We. The image of Rebekah sorting laundry and tossing shirts into the wringer wash machine filled his mind's eye. The thought, as far-fetched as it might be at this moment, comforted him. "Jah. Martha will fix it."

"Come on. I saw the water fountain as I came in." She cocked her head toward the hallway. "We'll come right back."

He might not want to come back to bad news. He could stay away. He wouldn't be alone. He'd be with Rebekah Lantz.

A person might think *he'd* been conked in the head by a horse, not Daed.

Susan forced herself to settle into the last chair. The one farthest from Mordecai. Her brother read too much in her face. He always had. He didn't need to know how she felt about Levi. She didn't even know how she felt. Only that the idea that he was badly hurt brought a strange terror that caused her heart to pummel her rib cage and her eyesight to dim. Both were terrifying symptoms of something she couldn't begin to explain.

"You look like you're feeling poorly."

Martha squeezed into the chair next to her and pulled Liam into her lap. The boy curled around her and leaned his head on her shoulder as if he'd been there a million times before and knew exactly where his small head would find the most comfortable spot. Martha was the closest he'd ever had to a mother. It hurt Susan's heart to think that, but yet, Gott had provided. He'd provided Liam with the closest substitute for a mother. The boy had a loving older sister who thought nothing of giving up her own happiness for that of a little brother.

"I'm fine. You will make a good fraa and mudder one day." Levi would want her to finish this conversation. No matter how this day turned out. He'd entrusted Susan with this one task. "You have a knack for it."

"My bruders and schweschders need me." Martha's tone said now more than ever. Her voice cracked. "No matter what happens, they'll need me. One way or another."

"The day will come when they won't. They'll have their own lives."

"That seems a selfish way of looking at it." Martha smoothed Liam's ruffled blond hair. He burrowed closer and closed his eyes. "Until that time comes, it's my job to take care of them."

"I just know it to be true. My mudder went first too." Susan let her gaze travel to Mordecai. He leaned his head against the wall, his eyes closed. Whether he dozed or prayed, she couldn't say. He had their mother's dark curls and their father's blue eyes. "She had cancer. Since I was the oldest girl, I took over the cooking, cleaning, canning, sewing, and gardening. There were only four of us kinner. Eventually my sister, Lilly, married and moved back to Tennessee. Our brother Thomas is up north in Missouri.

A few years after he moved, Daed died of a heart attack. Only Mordecai was left. He married and started his own family. I thought I would do the same."

"But you didn't."

"Nee. I had a special friend. For a time."

"What happened?"

"I kept putting him off because I was busy taking care of my family. I figured he'd wait."

"But he didn't?"

"Nee. He married a woman named Sadie. They live in Missouri now."

"I'm sorry."

"Gott's will. Gott's plan. Besides, it was a long time ago." She paused, remembering those days when she'd still had certainty and the nights when she'd admitted her fear and dwindling hope in long-winded prayers. "And then Mordecai's first fraa was killed in an accident and Phineas hurt so badly. They needed me. Again. Between teaching and taking care of my bruder's family, my life was full. More than full."

"But not anymore, now that he has married again."

"Exactly. I love teaching, though. It isn't a consolation prize. It's a calling. Teachers help prepare young folks to live Plain lives." She didn't mean to be bigheaded. Parents did the same. Everyone in the Plain community worked toward that same aim. "I remind myself of that every morning. I pray about it every night."

"But it's not like having your own kinner."

"Nee." A familiar tightening in her chest forced Susan to fumble in her canvas bag for a tissue. "I never will regret the years I've spent teaching. We should pray now for your daed."

Martha nodded, her eyes wide and wet with tears, her face white. "Jah, we should."

Susan closed her eyes. The same strange sensation that haunted her sleep at night, like the sensation of a baby's soft skin brushing against her cheek, caused her to catch her breath. The longing could be kept at bay most of the time. Occasionally, though, it caught her unaware and her entire body ached, filled with the enormous absence of her own flesh and blood held in arms meant to rock a child, hands meant to soothe a feverish forehead, lips meant to kiss a boo-boo on a tiny finger. "A woman has to embrace the blessing of whatever life Gott chooses for her," she whispered without opening her eyes. "We can never know better than Gott what is best for us."

"I don't understand how Gott's plan could be for Mudder to die giving birth to a little baby boy who was so sweet and so smiley and who slept through the night after only a few weeks," Martha answered in the same hushed tones. "He was such an easy baby. It baffles a person."

Susan opened her eyes. Liam had fallen asleep in his sister's arms, blissfully certain the adults around him would take care of him and whatever problems arose in this strange place. She put her arm around Martha. "We don't have to understand. We only have to trust." She patted Liam's soft cheek with her free hand. "The book of Psalms says, 'I will not be shaken.' That's us. We will not be shaken. No matter what happens."

Martha sniffed and nodded, tears trickling down a face that looked like a miniature of her father. "No matter what."

"The doctor."

Susan looked up. Mordecai rose to his feet to greet the

Englisch doctor. Tobias stood at his side. And Rebekah. How Rebekah ended up in the middle of things never ceased to amaze Susan. She helped Martha stand and took Liam from her arms. "Go, be with your big bruder. Right now, he needs you."

Her face pale, eyes red, she nodded and scurried across the room. Susan remained where she stood, bile bitter in the back of her throat. *Gott, Thy will be done.*

"Mr. Byler is a tough bird." The doctor removed dark-rimmed glasses and rubbed already red eyes. "He has a ruptured spleen, one leg is fractured, half a dozen fractured ribs, and a concussion."

"But he'll be fine?" Martha's legs gave way. Tobias's arm swept out and caught her against his towering frame. "He'll make it?"

"We're not equipped for the surgery he needs here. I've contacted an orthopedic surgeon in Corpus." The doctor gave a sympathetic smile under silver locks that looked as if he'd run his hands through them repeatedly, making him look more like a grandfather than a physician. "We'll airlift him down there in a few minutes. The helicopter is standing by."

Airlift. Helicopter. Susan couldn't help herself. She moved closer, Liam's weight barely noticeable in her arms. "But he'll be all right?"

Mordecai's bushy eyebrows did a push-up. He frowned at her. "Let the doctor talk."

"With good medical care and his strong constitution, he should pull through fine." The doctor surveyed the growing cluster of folks surrounding him. "Two at most will be able to go with him. The rest of y'all should go home. You'll be able to visit him in Corpus in a day or two."

His tone said he wondered exactly how they would do it.

"I'll go." David edged between Martha and Tobias. The three

looked so much like each other and so much like Levi. And so very young and scared. David's shirt had blood on it. His hands and face were smeared with dirt, sweat, and tears. "Let me go with him." His voice broke. "I want to be the one to go."

Mordecai cocked his head. "I'll go. As deacon it's my duty to deal with the questions about payment and such. It's up to you, Tobias, how you want to do this. You're the oldest, but consider that it may be many days away. Your family will need attention, your shop and your farm, in your daed's absence."

Mordecai was right. Tobias would want to go, but he should stay. Susan took another step forward, her arms tight around Liam. "We'll help. All of us will help. Rebekah and I will be there for whatever the kinner need."

Tobias cleared his throat. Pain etched lines around his mouth. His Adam's apple bobbed. "David will go. Martha will take care of the kinner and the house and the garden. I'll deal with the shop and the farm." He nodded at Mordecai. "You'll call the store when the surgery's over? Let us know how it goes?"

"I'll call every day until we bring him back."

Tobias turned to Martha. "Take the kinner home. Susan and Rebekah will help you. I'll see Daed before they take him away." He swept her into a hug, his gaze landing on Susan. "He'll be fine. We'll be fine."

From his lips to Gott's ears.

TWENTY-THREE

Maybe school wasn't so bad after all. Rebekah dumped another load of pants into the wringer wash machine and inhaled the fresh scent of clothes soap and bleach. Her back ached and sweat soaked her dress. Mudder handled all this on her own when Rebekah worked at the school. It was nice to give her a break.

She stretched and rolled her shoulders. Thinking of school made her think of Tobias. Everything made her think of him. She hadn't seen hide nor hair of him in the two days that had passed since his daed's accident. He surely had his hands full. The messages from Mordecai at the store had been good ones. The surgery went well. Levi was in recovery. He had his own room. Still, Tobias had to chafe at the thought that he couldn't be there.

She wanted to help. Susan said to be patient. To stay out of his way until the shock passed. They would take food later today. Cold fried chicken, coleslaw, biscuits, and pecan pie Rebekah had baked herself. Susan had taken Hazel into town for sewing supplies, flour, and more sugar. When they returned, they'd all go together. They would offer to help Martha with the laundry and the cleaning and their garden. Caleb could help in the fields. The thought spurred her to move faster. She headed to the door that led to the kitchen. An engine coughed and belched. The foreign sounds brought her up short. She turned and peeked out the one tiny window in the workroom.

A blue minivan covered in dust and bird droppings rolled to a stop by the back door. Dark fumes billowed from behind, dissipating in the halfhearted breeze.

"Jesse!"

He'd come about the kinner. Her breath gone for a second, Rebekah wiped her wet hands on her apron and shot out the door. Mudder beat her down the steps. She glanced back. "You wait here."

"Mudder."

"Wait."

Steely resolve in her mother's tone told Rebekah this would not be the time to test her mudder's mettle. Her stomach knotted, hands sweaty, eyes blinded by the May afternoon sun, she forced herself to plant both bare feet on the small wooden porch. Waiting went against every muscle and every drop of blood in her body, down to the marrow in her bones. *Wait.*

Mudder planted herself in front of the squat minivan shaped like a big bug. The passenger door opened. Leila exited. Mudder's hands fluttered and collapsed in the vicinity of her heart. Neither woman said a word for several seconds. Leila smoothed the long white blouse that draped her baby belly and smiled. "Hey. It's good to see you."

Mudder gave a jerky nod. "What are you doing here?"

"I brought someone I want you to meet." Her smile diminished like a light hidden behind a lamp shade, Leila turned and scurried around the van.

In the meantime Jesse hauled himself out the driver's side. He looked as if he might hurl, but he managed a weak smile. "Abigail."

Mudder nodded. "Jesse. What brings you to these parts?"

"We came to talk to Mordecai. I called the store, but no one answered."

"Mordecai is in Corpus Christi with Levi Byler. He was thrown by a horse, hurt. Will was helping Tobias this morning. I reckon he's back at the store now." Mudder's tone was even, not unfriendly, but neither was it friendly. "You could drive by there."

The faint emphasis on *drive* was unmistakable.

"We could."

"Wait. Wait, it's about Lupe and Diego, isn't it?" Rebekah hopped over the last step and landed next to Mudder. She ignored her withering glance. She would mend that fence later. It was time for Mudder to treat her as an adult, not simply a daughter. "What did you find out?"

"Dochder." Mudder crossed her arms, her frown deepening the lines around her mouth and eyes. "He'll share that news with Tobias, who'll talk to Jeremiah."

Rebekah was to stay in her place, in other words. "But I went with them—"

"Go back in the house."

Her heart beating like a drum in her chest, Rebekah shook her head. Mudder's expression gave her no room to rally. *Gott, when will she see me for who I am? I'm not the prodigal daughter. I'm not the one who sinned. I'm not the one who fled. When will she stop punishing me?*

She retreated once again to the porch. One hand on the screen door, she swiveled to watch her mudder. Surely the emotions must be a storm in her head. No mother could bear to turn away a prodigal daughter once again at her doorstep, even if it was only for a few minutes. Mudder was only human. At least, she appeared so. At the very least she could take a peek at her granddaughter. The gates of hell wouldn't open up over such a grandmotherly thing, would they?

Leila reappeared with Gracie in her arms. The baby's cheeks were rosy with sleep. She yawned, stretched, and cooed. "She looks like you, Mudder." Leila held her out.

Gracie smiled sleepily and waved with one chunky fist. "Hi."

Rebekah held her breath. No one could resist such a beautiful face. Not even Mudder. After a long moment Mudder sighed and took the little girl in her arms. "Ach, you are a sweet thing." She touched Gracie's mass of dark ringlets. "Such a lot of hair for such a little girl."

"That she got from her daddy." Leila grinned. "But her spirit is like Rebekah. Always hopping around and getting into things."

"I do not." Rebekah clamped her mouth shut. Better to keep it shut before Mudder noticed she'd disobeyed again. She itched to hold Gracie, but it was better to let Mudder get her fill.

"It's good to have lots of energy if you channel it right." Jesse leaned against the front of the van, apparently oblivious to its dusty state. "This little girl thinks she should stay up half the night playing with her dollies."

Rebekah dared to take the two steps back to the grass. Mudder was too engrossed in tickling Gracie's cheeks and making her laugh to notice. "What did you find out about Lupe and Diego?"

Jesse straightened and slapped at the dirt on his faded blue jeans. "We need to take them with us."

"What do you mean?"

"We promised the person at the Office of Refugee Resettlement we would bring them in so they could interview them and start the search for their father. They need to be in the system so they can be protected from those predators who brought them over."

A fury rose in Rebekah. It must be what mothers felt when their children were threatened. Rebekah ached for the day when she would have her own, but for now, Lupe and Diego were her charges. They had been since that day in the shed when she'd first seen their dirty, hungry faces. "How does turning them in protect them?"

His face darkening to a dusky rose color, Jesse shoved his fists into his pockets. "It allows the authorities to start looking for their daed. That's what they really need. The authorities have all that data in computers, but it starts with getting the children in there and getting a date set for their hearing."

"What will happen to them in the meantime?"

Gracie began to fuss. Mudder shushed her. "She needs a cookie. I'll be right back."

Rebekah's mouth dropped open. She glanced at Jesse. He shrugged, his smile back, full force this time. Mudder turned and marched into the house, little Gracie on her hip.

Jesse put an arm around Leila, who leaned against his broad chest. "We're hoping they'll let them stay with us, at least until we can figure out something else."

Until they left for Dallas. "You're hoping?" Rebekah felt like a rabbit about to be cut down by a hunter. "While they're in the States? You think they'll have to go back to El Salvador?"

"We don't know." Leila tugged away from her husband. She

wrapped her arms around Rebekah in a tight, warm hug. She smelled like soap. "We're trying to help. That's all we can do."

"I know that." Rebekah swallowed the lump that threatened to choke her. "Lupe's scared. I don't want her to be scared anymore, and I don't want her to have to go home."

"We understand that. The first step is for us to get them started in the process." Jesse tossed his car keys in the air and let them land in his hand. A fat silver cross swung on the key chain. "We thought you could go with us to Tobias's place to pick them up. It might be easier for them."

Rebekah pictured Lupe's tear-streaked face at the school picnic. "It will be terrible. They'll think we've betrayed them."

"We'll explain. They'll be safe with us."

"They're already upset." Rebekah recounted what had happened to Levi. "They're all worried even though they try not to be. They pray and lean on Gott. We all do, but they're only kinner."

"All the more reason you should go with us to talk to them."

"Mudder won't let—"

"She will. You'll convince her. You have a way with her." Leila squeezed Rebekah's arm. "I prayed and prayed that Gracie would meet her grandmother. It took something like this to make it happen. God has a plan and it's bigger than anything we can see. He has a plan for Lupe and Diego."

Rebekah wanted to hold on to Leila's hand and her touch. Why did the plan have to include Jesse, Leila, little Gracie, and the new bopli living far, far away? That's what she wanted to know. Where was the provision in that? She didn't dare voice that question aloud.

"We need to go now." Jesse cocked his head toward the door. "Bring Gracie back out. Come with us to fetch Lupe and Diego."

"We intended to go this afternoon, anyway, to help with chores and take them a meal." They would still do that. "We'll feed them before you take them."

"That's a good idea."

Sighing, Rebekah trudged back up the steps to the screen door. She paused. The sound of sobs so mournful they seemed wrenched from the depths of the very soul wafted from the inside. Rebekah bowed her head. Mudder's invincible front had been broken by a little girl with masses of dark curls.

She slipped through the door and followed the sound into the kitchen. Mudder sat at the prep table, Gracie on her lap. The little girl, her chubby face smeared with cookie crumbs and spit, offered a cookie to the crying woman. Mudder gave a shuddering sigh and accepted it with a watery smile. "Danki."

"Mudder, it's time for us to go."

Mudder looked up. She shook her face, tears running down her cheek and onto her neck. "I know it's Gott's will. I know my brain isn't capable of knowing or understanding the big picture He sees."

"Yet you can't help but wonder how this can be right?"

Mudder nodded and hiccupped another sob. She wiped at her face with the back of her hand. "Ach, this is ridiculous. I just had a weak moment."

"You are human."

"Gott's will be done."

"I feel the same way."

"You shouldn't."

"Ever since Leila left, everyone has looked at me funny as if they're waiting for me to bolt."

"Nee."

"Jah. You most of all."

"I couldn't bear to lose another daughter."

"That's not going to happen. Not with me. Not with Hazel."

Mudder shifted Gracie to her other knee and handed the girl a piece of broken cookie. "I'm more certain of that now than I was before."

"Why is that?"

"Tobias Byler."

"Mudder!"

"You don't have to talk about it. I'm just saying I have eyes in my head and I can see."

"Nothing has happened."

"But you would like for it to happen."

It was a statement, not a question. Rebekah held out her hands. "Come on, pumpkin. We have to go find your mudder and daed."

Gracie would never need to know those German words. They weren't used in her world. In Dallas she would grow up without wood-burning stoves and canning frolics and church services in High German. She wouldn't know her aentis and *onkels* and groossmammis and *groossdaadis*. Rebekah buried her face in the girl's yellow cotton sundress to hide the tears that threatened. Her mudder's touch on her shoulder forced her to look up. "It will be as Gott intended. Her life and yours."

Mudder's tearstained face and the way she held on to Gracie's chubby body a few seconds longer served as a testament to the strength it took to accept such a world as that. Rebekah prayed she had the fortitude to do the same.

TWENTY-FOUR

The shop or the farm? Tobias felt split in two. Without Daed and David, chores at home were piling up, as much as Rueben, Micah, Liam, and even the girls tried to help. The air was heavy with heat and humidity, making his shirt stick to his back. He smoothed the sorrel's leg and lifted it to examine the hoof. The horse needed a new shoe. Teeth gritted, Tobias straightened and patted the poor creature's long neck.

The sky glowered overhead, matching his mood. They needed rain, but rain would keep them out of the fields. They were already behind planting the onions and broccoli that the grocery-store chain bought from the others. And Button could not continue to pull the plow with his shoe about to come off. Tobias would have to ask Jeremiah where the closest farrier was. Unless the Glicks did their own shoeing. Which was possible. He'd never done it, and now wasn't the time for trial and error.

The sound of an engine drowned out the shrill conversation of two wrens roosting in the nearby live oak tree. He wiped sweat from his face with the back of his sleeve and turned to look.

A blue minivan like the one that had been parked outside the church last week putted along the road that led to the house. Jesse. The time of reckoning had come. Martha had Lupe in the kitchen, teaching her how to make bread. Diego had taken to following Rueben around, mimicking his every move. At the moment they should be mending the fence around the chicken coop. The coyotes were making off with more than their share of the hens that provided the Byler family with an important part of their breakfast.

In a short time Lupe and Diego had become part of the family. Keeping a distance from kinner simply wasn't possible. Maybe for others, but not Tobias. His heart didn't have an Off button, it seemed. Teeth gritted once again, he strode from the corral and made his way to the road.

The minivan slowed, stopped, belching fumes and smoke near the hitching post. Seconds later Jesse emerged along with Leila. Thunder rumbled in the distance as the back door slid open. Rebekah popped out, Gracie in her arms. Tobias forgot to look at Jesse and Leila. All he could see was this young woman with a baby on her hip. She looked exactly as a fraa should look. As a mudder should look. The baby had Jesse's dark, curly hair, but Leila's fair complexion and blue eyes.

What would Tobias's bopli look like, his and Rebekah's? The thought sent a wave of heat through him. Such a thought. He hadn't even asked her to take a ride with him. Doing so would mean he had one more person to protect. A person who might leave him.

His heart intended to ask her to take a ride. His brain didn't have the wherewithal to stop it. How could he be thinking of himself at a time like this? He had no time for mushy stuff. He took a breath and turned to Jesse. "You have something to tell us?"

"This is my wife, Leila." Jesse took Leila's hand. "Rebekah has my daughter, Gracie."

"We've met." Tobias tried to keep his gaze on Jesse, but it kept wandering to Rebekah. "What did you find out?"

"That's right. I forgot. At their secret meeting." Jesse shook his head as if to say, *Women*. "We need to take Lupe and Diego in to be processed so they can set up their hearing. That way the government can start looking for their father. He could be in the system. They could be reunited that way."

"What if he's not?"

"Then we'll ask for custody until their case goes to court. That could be months or years."

"We could go to San Antonio, try to find their father on our own. Then they could stay here."

"San Antonio is too big. Where would we start?" Leila stepped between Jesse and Tobias. "We have to have faith in the system. The kinner will be safe with us until their hearing. No one will come looking for them at our house."

Rain plopped on his nose. Up north, rain cooled the air. Here, it didn't seem to do much but create more steam and humidity. Did Rebekah like this plan? Tobias glanced at her. She looked so motherly. So like a fraa. More drops splatted in the dirt, leaving wet blotches that looked like a child's drawings. "What do you think?"

Emotions flitted across her face. Fear mixed with sadness. Determination. "I want what's best for them. I don't know what that is, but I trust Jesse."

Jesse, but not Leila? An interesting omission. If she trusted her brother-in-law, he would have to do so as well. He studied his shoes, not wanting to see the pain on her face. "Lupe is in the kitchen. Diego's working on the chicken-coop fence or getting in the way more likely."

"We'll tell them together." Her dirty sneakers appeared in his view of the ground. "Tobias?"

He looked into her face. Her lips trembled with the effort to control her tears. She didn't want Lupe and Diego to go either. He straightened. "They'll be okay with your sister and brother-in-law. I trust them."

Rebekah nodded but sniffed. "I don't want them to go."

"Me neither. But they'll be in good hands."

"Lead the way."

He tromped toward the house, paused to knock dirt from his boots by the front door, and then led them to the kitchen, all the while listening to Gracie's high-pitched babble and Rebekah's amused responses, a sort of music that soothed the soul of any family man.

He stuck his head in the doorway. "Lupe."

Martha turned, her cheeks red from the heat, a bread pan in one hand. The heavenly scent of fresh-baked bread wafted on the air. "She went to see who's out front. We heard a car."

"We were out front." Tobias jerked his head toward their guests. "They've come about Lupe and Diego."

"She said something in Spanish I didn't understand. Like hombre malo." Martha shrugged. "Then she went out the back door. She let the screen door slam, which wasn't like her at all, but I figured she was excited about visitors."

"We didn't see her."

She plopped the pan on the counter. "I have peanut butter cookies and tea, if anyone is interested."

"Maybe later." He brushed past Jesse and the others. "Let me see if we missed her out front."

No sign of Lupe by the front porch. He surveyed the yard. No little girl who insisted on wearing a red, white, and blue T-shirt with faded jeans every other day. "Lupe? Lupe!" He cupped his hands to his mouth to make his shout carry. "Lupe, we have company here to talk to you."

No answer.

Tobias plodded down the stairs and headed for the backyard and the chicken coop. The baby chatter behind him told him the others followed.

Rueben looked up as they approached, a little ragtag group. "I'm almost done. Good thing too. It looks like the sky is about to open up. Again. It seems the drought is over."

"Where are Lupe and Diego?"

"Lupe came by a few minutes ago and said she wanted to talk to Diego." Rueben pointed with his hammer. "Then she started talking a mile a minute in Spanish. They went off yonder."

Hombre malo. On the day he'd first met Lupe, she'd thought he was an hombre malo. Bad man. She had seen Jesse and been afraid of the bad man. Tobias turned to the others. "She may have seen you drive up and taken off."

"I told you she was scared." Rebekah hitched Gracie up on her hip. "She doesn't trust men she doesn't know."

"I'll go after them." Tobias glanced at the sky. Thunder rumbled in the distance. Lightning crackled across threatening clouds that hung so low it seemed he could reach out and touch them. "We need to find them before the storm hits."

Rebekah handed Gracie to Leila. "I'll go with you."

"Nee, not necessary. It's about to storm."

"A little water won't hurt me."

"I should go." Frowning, Jesse looked from Rebekah to Tobias. "It would be more proper."

That he should be the one to worry about what was proper made Tobias want to snort, but he didn't. "Whatever you think."

"Nee. That's the whole point. She's scared of men. Hombre malo. That's you." Rebekah pointed at Jesse with an accusing finger. "She'll come to me."

Her obstinate tone told him it was useless to argue. "Fine. Jesse, come or not come, it's up to you."

Leila put a hand on her husband's arm. "Let them go."

"Fine."

"Y'all wait inside. Keep Gracie dry." Rebekah headed toward the dirt road that meandered deeper into Byler property. "We'll be back."

It only took a minute or two for him to outpace her. She didn't say anything, her breathing soft, her dress swishing around her legs as she skipped to keep up. He took pity on her and slowed.

"Are you mad about something?" She sounded breathless. He slowed some more. "Did I do something?"

"Nee. What makes you say that?"

"You keep frowning and you look like you have a headache. You're grumpy."

He had reason to be grumpy. He found himself caring about her, when he hadn't wanted to care about a woman again. "I'm worried about Lupe and Diego."

"You looked that way before you knew they'd run off—"

"We don't know they ran off."

"She knew. Lupe's a smart girl."

"She couldn't know."

Rebekah pressed her lips together and flounced ahead.

"Where are you going?"

"They couldn't have gotten far. Their legs are short."

"Not much shorter than yours."

"My legs aren't short. I'm tall for a girl." She whirled and glared, dirt making tiny plumes around her black sneakers. "Are you anxious to argue?"

"Nee. I . . ." He stopped. "I'm short on patience these days."

Her glare melted. "I imagine so. Sorry for making it worse."

Her tone was soft, her face anxious. She had such a good heart and he was making her miserable. "You didn't." He shrugged, struggling for words. "We have a lot of work to do."

"Without your daed, you feel lost."

"Nee. We're capable of taking care of things." He was a full-grown man. He could handle it. "With the farm and the shop and the kinner, I just want to make sure everything goes well."

"Your daed knows that."

"I want him home." Was it wrong to admit such a thing? "I want him well."

"Any *suh* would."

"You lost your daed."

"It seems a long time ago, but jah, I still remember. Your daed's coming back, though."

"I know." He did know, so why did he let it worry him? Worry showed a lack of faith. "Lupe! Diego! Come out. We want to talk to you. It's okay."

"Lupe, come on, it's me, Rebekah."

As if they wouldn't recognize her voice. "It's about to storm. Come on, you'll get wet."

The kinner probably suffered much worse during their sojourn from Central America. The rain went from a mist to big drops that splatted on his hat and face.

Rebekah wiped at her face as rain soaked her dress and apron. "Here we go."

"Lupe, por favor, let us talk to you."

Rebekah grinned. "You learned a Spanish word."

"Several words. She taught us all at the supper table."

"That's gut."

The scattered raindrops turned into a deluge. Rebekah laughed. Her apron was soaked, her kapp hung low on the back of her head, and mud sullied the hem of her dress. Yet she laughed.

"What's so funny?"

"We're always wanting rain. Now, when we have it, it's inconvenient."

Mud sucked at the soles of his boots, making it hard to lift his feet. "I don't mind getting wet."

"Me neither."

Lightning crackled overhead. Thunder boomed. Rebekah ducked. Giggling, she clapped a hand over her mouth.

"Are you still laughing?"

"I'm so silly. Like ducking will help."

This time the lightning sizzled. A tree branch buckled and smashed to the ground.

"Ach, that is a little too close." Tobias grabbed her arm and steered her toward a shack on the tree line. He hadn't had a chance to investigate its purpose yet. It looked as if it might crash to the ground in a heap at any moment, but it had to be drier—and safer—than out in the middle of the elements. "Let's get inside until it lets up a little."

Rebekah tugged away. "Lupe and Diego are out there."

"They're not addled. They'll find shelter too."

Thunder boomed again. Rebekah's hands went to her head. "Fine."

"Fine."

The shed smelled of rotted wood, but it was dry. Tobias longed for a kerosene lamp. Even a candle would do. He held the door open long enough to survey the interior. A wagon wheel, empty egg crates, a broken chair. Junk. The floor was dirt but dry. "Have a seat."

"I'll stand. There might be mice in here." Her teeth chattered. He hadn't been south long enough to find a summer rain cold. "Or snakes."

He opened the door and took another quick look in the dim light of a stormy exterior. Nothing scurried or slithered. "I think we're safe."

"I suppose."

"Are you always so contrary?"

"Depends on who you ask."

Her light breathing was the only sound besides the patter of rain against the roof. He inhaled and tried to let the air out quietly. Rustling told him she'd decided to take his advice and sit. He started to lean against the wall, but thought better of it. The whole shack might tumble down under his weight. His eyes began to adjust to the dark. She sat scrunched up in one corner, her knees up, arms around them. "I reckon that's true of everyone. Daed would say I have a stubborn streak a mile long and a tendency to get myself into trouble."

"Really? I wouldn't have thought you were the trouble type."

"I hope I've grown up a little and learned from my mistakes. You?"

"What mistakes?"

He chuckled. To his surprise, she joined him.

He crossed his arms over his chest and tried to imagine what was going through her mind. She was stuck in a shack with a man with whom she spent most of her time arguing. She disliked him for telling Susan about her secret meeting with Leila. They'd gotten off on the wrong foot.

He didn't want her to be mad. It bothered him. The fact that it bothered him served to irritate him even more. He cleared his throat. She was just a girl. He didn't need girl trouble. He'd had that kind of trouble.

She would be another person about whom he would have to worry.

Someone to lose.

"Maybe we should start again."

He startled despite himself. Her voice sounded high and breathless. As if she'd been running. "What?"

"I'm Rebekah Lantz. I was new around here about three years ago, so I know how it feels. To be new, I mean. So welcome to Bee County."

He breathed in and out. A peace offering. A white flag. He couldn't be so mean as to reject her attempt at patching up the rift between them. After all, he'd tattled on her, not the other way around. "I'm Tobias Byler, your new neighbor. Pleased to meet you."

"Hello, Tobias." She giggled. A sweet sound in the darkness. "We have lots of mosquitoes, huge horseflies, rattlesnakes, wild pigs, chiggers, many bees, and oh, don't forget the alligators up at Choke Canyon Lake. If you like interesting pets, there are plenty to choose from."

Her sense of humor was showing. He liked it. Gott help him, he liked it. "Can you forgive me?"

"Forgive you for what?"

"For being a stickler for the rules and telling Susan about your meeting with Leila."

"You shouldn't apologize for doing what's right." Her tart tone said he should know better. "It's a sign of weakness."

"I didn't apologize. I only asked to be forgiven."

"So you're not sorry?"

"Nee."

Her sigh was exaggerated. "A fine new beginning this is."

"It's gut."

"What's gut about it?"

"I wondered if you'd come out for a ride with me one night—after my daed is better."

Her breathing quickened. Seconds ticked by. Tobias's chest tightened and his own breathing seemed to stop.

"I reckon I might. I'd give it some thought."

He exhaled.

She giggled.

"What?"

"You were holding your breath."

"Nee."

"You were."

"The rain needs to stop." He opened the door a crack. Thunder boomed. He closed it. "I hope Lupe and Diego found a dry spot to wait this out."

"You said they would." She sounded wistful somehow. "Besides, they made it here all the way from El Salvador."

"A long journey."

"How long did it take you to get here from Ohio?"

"A couple of days. We took it slow."

"Did you stop in Dallas?"

Where was she going with this? "Nee. We drove around it. Too much traffic."

She sighed, a sad sound after her earlier giggles.

"Why do you ask?"

"Leila and Jesse are moving to Dallas so he can finish college and go to seminary."

"And that makes you sad?"

"Would you like Martha to move away?"

"Bruders and schweschders do that sometimes."

"Jah, but when they're Plain, you get to see them at weddings and on holidays. When Leila goes, we'll never see her again."

"You don't know that."

"Don't tell me Gott has a plan."

"You don't think He does?"

"I reckon He does. I just don't like it."

Tobias waited a beat or two. Not really expecting a bolt of lightning to hit the shed, but giving it time should Gott deem it necessary. "You think you know better than Gott how your life should go?"

She sniffed, her expression hidden in the dark. "I'm being punished for something I didn't do. It's not fair."

His mudder dying before she could see her kinner grow up. That was unfair. Life was unfair. "With each new trial, Gott teaches us something new. We learn to see the blessings in what we have. We learn to be content in what we have. We learn to step out in faith, knowing He has our best interests at heart."

"I try to be content."

"Try harder." He was one to talk. "I'll do the same."

"Why?"

The plaintive note in her voice said she really did want to know. Yet he couldn't tell her. He wasn't ready. Not yet. "Because it's the right thing to do. You know it is.

"No matter what happens, you have work to do. Leila is gone. You're here. You're committed to your faith. Wait on Gott's timing."

Wait on me. That's what he really meant. Wait on him to have the courage to let another person into his heart. A person he would have to protect. Who might be ripped from him in a single second.

Rain battered the shed roof. Thunder rumbled like a grumpy old man clearing his throat. Her sigh was nearly lost in the cacophony. "Do you have your picture ID card?"

He shook his head, a silly thing to do in the dusk. "Nee, but I will get one if you will."

Step out in faith, Tobias; step out.

"We'll see how it goes then."

See how it goes. Was that an admission that their journeys might take the same path? "You sound uncertain. Like you're sitting on the fence."

"I'm not sitting on the fence." Her voice was small in the dark. "I'm just trying to find my way to the path."

"Me too." For now, that would be enough. He took a breath. Then he took a chance. "Maybe we can find it together."

TWENTY-FIVE

It never rained in South Texas. Except this summer, the pattern seemed to have finally broken. The sky had been cloudy for three days, the air laden with humidity, when Susan set out for town, but that was typical Bee County weather. Maybe the drought was over. Finally. She wiped rain from her eyes and squinted. The driving rain and wind made it hard to see the road in front of her. The wagon swayed and creaked as the horse strained against the gale.

The Byler farmhouse couldn't be much farther. Hazel squirmed in the seat next to her. The little girl tried so hard to be brave, but every time thunder boomed she shrieked and clutched Susan's arm. That made it hard to keep the slippery reins in her hands.

"Child, it's okay. We're fine." She patted Hazel's head for one quick second. The clouds were so dark, the day had turned to night. The ruts filled with water. Lightning split the sky, then receded. "Only a mile or two more."

"I don't like this."

"It's just water." Susan searched for comforting words. "Look at it this way. You've had your bath for the week. You know how you hate taking a bath."

"For two weeks." Hazel sounded only slightly mollified. "You tell Mudder."

"I'll tell your mudder."

Abigail would be tickled. By the time a mother got to her fifth child, baths didn't rise to the level of an argument so much anymore. As long as the child didn't stink or make the sheets muddy.

Thunder boomed so close, Brownie shook his long neck and whinnied.

"Aenti!"

"It's okay, sweet pea. Why don't you sing? Pick a song, any song."

The grip on Susan's arm eased. *"La cucaracha, la cucaracha—"*

"The what?"

Another voice, as young and sweet as Hazel's, joined in. Susan craned her head and peered at the road. Right there, in the middle of the road. Two figures. Short, thin, little. Kinner. "What . . . who is that?"

"Diego!" The taller child—Lupe—tugged at the shorter one and headed for the side of the road. "Come."

Diego apparently had other ideas. He bolted toward the wagon. Lupe whirled to follow. She slipped and fell in the mud. Diego cackled with glee and kept coming.

Susan tugged on the reins. "Whoa, whoa!"

They came to a halt and she hopped down. "Diego? Lupe? What are you doing out here in this storm?"

"Running away." His face streaked with rain and mud, Diego grinned. "We go to San Antonio."

"Diego." Lupe had mud from the tip of her nose to the end of her bare toes. "Stop telling her."

"Lupe, why are you running away?" Hazel scrambled from

the wagon and stomped through the mud with a *splat-splat*. "You can't leave. We haven't finished our baby quilt."

"Hombre malo. Have to go." Lupe grabbed her brother's arm and jerked him away from Hazel's reach. "We go now."

"Why?"

"Man in van come to take us away. Hombre malo."

"In a blue van?"

"Sí."

"That's the people Rebekah and Tobias told you about. Rebekah's sister and brother-in-law. He's a good man. Very good man. He used to live here with us. Tobias and Rebekah went to talk to them, remember?"

Lupe's face remained woebegone. "I don't want to leave."

"We don't want you to leave." Susan smoothed the girl's wet bangs from her eyes with gentle fingers. She looked like a half-drowned kitten. "But we also want to do things the right way. Can you understand that?"

Lupe ducked her head. "What if right way is back to frontera?"

"Doing the right thing isn't always easy."

"Nothing easy."

The rain chose that moment to stop. A sliver of sun peeked through clouds that collided, then parted. "You're right. Life isn't easy, but nobody promised it would be."

To her utter surprise, Lupe leaned her face into Susan's apron. One sob, then another escaped. "I tired."

"Me too." She hugged Lupe's cold, wet body against her. "We have to go back so Jesse and Leila can help you figure out what to do so you can stay. Running away isn't the answer."

"We could go fishing."

Susan turned to look at Hazel. The little girl squatted in the middle of the road, mud squeezing between her bare, plump toes. "See, the night crawlers are out." She held out a fat worm pinched between two muddy fingers. The brownish-gray worm dangled and wiggled as if trying to get its footing to no avail. "Mordecai says these are the best for catching fish."

Lupe slipped from her grasp and knelt next to Hazel. "My papi is going to take us to California. We're going to go fishing. Mi abuela said so."

Hazel grinned. "Do you want to take some worms? Is California far? They could be like Pedro, your pets. Until the fish eat them."

Of all things to be talking about now. "Hazel, put the worm down. This is no time for—"

"Hey! Hey, Susan!"

Susan pivoted in time to see Tobias emerge from a shack tucked along the other side of the fence that separated the road from Byler property. Right behind him came Rebekah. No one followed. Just Rebekah and Tobias.

"Well." She couldn't think of a thing to say. "Well."

"We were looking for the kinner." Rebekah's clothes were wet, wrinkled, and muddy. When she turned to look at Tobias, who was equally bedraggled, she revealed a huge muddy blotch on the back of her dress where her behind would be. "Then it stormed."

Lupe hopped up, grabbed Diego's hand, and took off running. "No, no," Diego yelled, but Lupe didn't stop. They careened across the road. Lupe shoved her brother through a gap in the fence and they disappeared into a dense thicket of juniper, live oak, mesquite, and nopales.

"Lupe, stop." Tobias raced after them, his long stride eating up ground. "Stop, we only want to help."

Rebekah scampered past him, thrust herself through the same gap, and disappeared after them.

Susan looked at Hazel, who stared back, her tiny face perplexed. "Should we go too?"

"Maybe. Maybe they'll come back for you."

Hazel grinned. "Diego likes me."

"Child!"

She shrugged. "I like him, too, but not like that. He's not Plain."

"That's right." The sooner Hazel learned these things, the better. "Your poor mudder has been through enough."

She took Hazel's hand and together they squeezed through the gap and tried to follow the path left by the others. A shriek made her stop in her tracks. Hazel smacked into her from behind. "Hey."

"What was that?"

Susan picked up speed, moving in the direction of the distinct sound of a child crying. Still holding Hazel's hand, she burst through the stand of trees where she found Rebekah on the ground in a gully filling with rainwater. She clutched at her ankle, her face etched with pain. Tobias knelt next to her, his hand outstretched as if he would touch her. He looked back. His hand dropped. "Gut, you're still here. We'll need your wagon."

"The kinner?"

"They got away."

TWENTY-SIX

Horses were like people. Some were stubborn, others docile. Some, like children, had wills that had to be bent before they could become hardworking members of society. Tobias contemplated Cracker Jack from his seat on the split-wood fence that comprised the corral outside the saddle shop. The horse stood in the corner, grazing on a tiny patch of weeds that had sprung up in the hard, cracked dirt.

A blazing, late June sun beat down on Tobias's straw hat. Sweat trickled down his temples and tickled his ears. Why was he standing at the corral fence instead of inside working on the cutting saddle? Because all he could think about when he picked up the skiving knife was Daed. And Rebekah. And Lupe and Diego.

He needed a distraction. If Rebekah hadn't turned her ankle, maybe they would've caught up with Lupe and Diego. Maybe they wouldn't have been gone a week now. He blew out air and wiped sweat from his forehead with his sleeve. Or maybe they would've run faster and farther.

He needed to work. No animal was beyond saving. He slid off the fence and let his knees bend when his boots hit the dirt in a soft *plunk* that sent a grasshopper flying across the dandelions and crabgrass.

Adopting an amble, he began the trek across the expanse of dirt and weeds that separated him from the animal that had almost killed his father. Cracker Jack's head came up. He tossed his long, graceful neck and nickered.

"Hey, friend. Nothing to worry about here."

Cracker Jack shook his head in a startling response that looked very much like a "no."

"You have to learn." He kept his voice soft and singsongy the way Daed always did. "We all have to be broken to the will of another."

The horse whinnied and trotted toward the farthest corner.

He had a long memory, no doubt.

Tobias whistled, a tuneless collection of notes that came from nowhere and trailed away to nothing. Cracker Jack's ears perked up. He snorted and pranced. "Are you dancing for me? I'd like nothing more than for you and me to get to be friends before Daed comes home from the hospital. To get you in shape would do us all good."

Tobias returned to his whistling as he held out one hand. Cracker Jack's ears went back. Not a good sign.

The rumbling of a vehicle engine sounded in the distance, getting louder and closer with the velocity of someone who knew the road well. Cracker Jack whirled and trotted back to his original feeding spot. Without turning his back on the animal, Tobias glanced toward the road. Mr. Cramer's dust-covered, once-white van rolled into the parking lot in front of the Glicks' building. It lurched to a stop by the corral gate. David emerged, his scruffy black duffel bag in one hand. Mr. Cramer raised a massive hand in a wave, made a wide circle, and left, a cloud of dust hanging in the air behind him.

What was David doing back? Tobias back-stepped toward the gate, putting some space between himself and the horse. He turned and strode to the fence. "What happened? How's Daed?"

"Ornery and a terrible patient." David dropped his bag on the ground, climbed up onto the fence, and wrapped his long, skinny legs around the top railing. "He sent me home. Mordecai refused to be cowed into submission. He's still there. Daed said it was crazy to spend all that money on a hotel room for no reason."

"When can he come home?"

"They've got him up, doing physical therapy like a hundred times a day. He doesn't like it much. I think he has a lot of pain, but he won't admit it."

"So no time soon?"

David shrugged. "If he has his way, he'll be home in a few days. Less if he throws a big enough fit." His gaze flitted over Tobias's shoulders. "What are you doing in there?"

"I'm working with the horse. He still has to be broken."

"That's my job."

"I can do it too."

"You never have."

"Things change." He would do this. Tobias would step into Daed's place. It was time. "You can have the next one."

More engine noise. A customer maybe. That would be good. Nary a single one had graced the door of their saddle shop since the day of Daed's accident. A sign on the road and another on the turnoff to the highway hadn't helped. A huge, shiny black pickup truck with chrome wheel covers that glinted in the sun pulled into the lot. Not a new customer. Bobbie.

"She came to the hospital. Did you know that?" David swiveled and heaved himself from the fence. "In Corpus, I mean. She drove all the way down there to make sure Daed was okay. Her father insisted on paying the bill."

"Mordecai let him?"

"He said a person who wants to make something right should be allowed to do so, especially when it's in the best interest of our meager emergency fund. Jeremiah and Will agreed."

"Did she see Daed?"

"She did. Stayed a couple of days."

Something in his tone sent prickles up Tobias's arms. A hint of something familiar rode the words. A lingering hint of longing. It felt like Serena. "Where did she stay?"

"She and her father got rooms at the same hotel where Mordecai and I stayed. In fact, we ate supper together a couple of times before they had to come back home."

"Sounds cozy."

"It was." David's sharp, chiseled chin lifted. His green eyes held a challenge. "She's kind—they're kind folks. They felt real bad about what happened."

"I'm sure they are and they did. Just be careful."

"I'm not you, bruder."

No, he wasn't, but he was a man now, like any other man, with human frailties that Tobias knew all too well. He bit his tongue to keep from saying more. It was David's rumspringa, his time for making mistakes and learning from them. And deciding his own future. Tobias would have to approach with care or he'd drive David right into Bobbie's welcoming arms.

Bobbie hopped down from the truck cab dressed in a simple blue sundress that flowed below her knees. Her feet were clad in the usual black cowboy boots, and she wore a black cowboy hat to match. No jewelry. No makeup. The same scrubbed-fresh look his sisters had. "Howdy, boys." Her smile was tentative as if she wasn't sure what kind of reception she would receive from Tobias. "I was hoping I'd find you here."

"David was just telling me how your father paid the hospital bill. Thank you."

She shrugged and nodded. "It was the least we could do. It was only right."

"Did you come to order your saddle?" Tobias swung himself over the fence with the ease of much practice. "I have the paperwork with the cost estimate in the shop."

"Sure, we can do that." Her gaze remained on David. His face flushed a deep scarlet. She ducked her head and began to make crosses in the dirt with the tip of her boot. "I wanted to take a look at Cracker Jack. Dad's thinking of selling him."

"I wish he wouldn't do that." The words were out of Tobias's mouth before he could stop them. What did he care if they sold the horse? "I mean, don't sell him on our account. Daed will recover."

"Your dad said the same thing." Bobbie snapped her gum as if to punctuate the thought. "I reckon the only thing that will keep my dad from selling him is if we can show he can be rehabilitated. What do you think, David?"

It was David's turn to duck his head, looking like a little boy on the first day of school. "Sounds like a fine idea to me." The words came out in a stutter. David hadn't stuttered since first grade. "Want me to give it a whirl?"

"Nee." Tobias slid into the space between his brother and the gate. "If anybody gets on that horse, it will be me."

"You don't break horses." David's face went from red to a

shade of purple that reminded Tobias of eggplant. "You're the saddle maker and the bookkeeper."

"I'm in charge while Daed is away." Away. A fancy way of saying hurt and unable to take care of his family. "The decision is mine. I won't have you hurt too."

He couldn't take it. Daed in the hospital was more than enough. He wouldn't risk David too.

"It's just a horse." David crossed his arms over his chest, the words full of bluster. Not the little bruder Tobias knew. "I can handle it."

"Not this time." Tobias turned to Bobbie. "Come up to the shop with me. I'll give you the estimate on the saddle. Ask your dad to give me a few weeks with the horse. Give him time to get to know me. We'll get it done for you."

Bobbie seemed to have trouble dragging her gaze from David to Tobias. "I'll talk to him. He feels real bad about what happened to your dad, though. He won't want anyone else to get hurt."

The look that traveled between David and her crackled with unspoken words. Tobias cleared his throat. "David, you should head home. The kinner have missed you and there's work to be done."

David's glare could've singed Tobias's hair. "How do I get home?"

"Take the buggy and come back for me later—"

"I can give him a ride." Bobbie sounded like a little girl begging for a puppy. "It's no problem. Really. It's on the way."

Tobias gritted his teeth. He'd walked right into that one. "Nice of you to offer, but I think David better stay and muck the stalls first. That way I can work on your saddle, soon as you make a deposit."

She glanced back, not bothering to hide her disappointment. Tobias walked faster. Sometimes a person couldn't move fast enough to avoid temptation. It came at a man like a semitruck out of control on a highway.

Or a girl in a sundress and cowboy boots.

TWENTY-SEVEN

The smell of bleach and soap blossomed in the air, fresh as flowers. Susan liked the aroma of clean. She stuck the woolly-headed mop in the yellow plastic bucket and stretched her arms over her head. Her shoulders and arms ached, but the ache spoke of a job well done so she didn't mind. Letting her arms relax, she surveyed her work. The Byler kitchen fairly sparkled. The vinyl was old and cracked but clean. The counters were scrubbed, all the dishes washed and stacked neatly in their places. The prep table was clear and ready for making supper. Martha and the little girls tried, but they didn't seem to get that putting something away as soon as a person finished using it saved work later.

Martha had changed the sheets and pillowcases on Levi's bed first, while Susan dusted and cleaned the front room. It didn't seem right that she should see Levi's room. None of her business how he stacked his pants or hung his shirts. Or didn't.

Everyone was relieved that Levi was coming home. Because they missed him and needed him back, but also because it took their minds off Lupe and Diego. Gone almost two weeks now. Probably in San Antonio by now. With their father, Gott willing.

Or captured by Immigration and returned across the border. Or corralled by the awful men who'd brought them here in the first place with ill intent.

Gott's will? She couldn't be sure. *They're only kinner, Gott; protect them. Keep them safe from the bad men out there who would take advantage of them. If You're willing, bring them back to us. We'll take care of them.*

She had no children of her own. She could take care of them. No problem. *Gott, can You hear me?*

She was too proud, thinking she could do it. Or anything on her own. Gott made those decisions, not a simple woman like herself. Shaking her head at her own thoughts, Susan opened the back door and carried the bucket outside. She emptied it and put both items away. Time to start supper. She'd suggested chicken and dumplings and pecan pie for Levi's homecoming dinner and Martha had agreed, especially after she realized Susan was offering to cook.

The dark circles around her eyes and dispirited efforts with a sponge had clearly indicated the girl was worn out. Maybe now that Levi was headed home, she'd be willing to let Susan and Rebekah help out more.

"They're here, they're here!" Liam streaked through the back door and zipped past her toward the front room. "Daed's here. He's here."

Despite the sudden, painful lurch in her own heart, Susan chuckled. The child tickled her fancy in every way. She dried her hands, pretending to herself that they weren't shaking, and followed him out to the front porch. Sure enough, Mr. Cramer's van, covered with dust and the splatter of bugs on the windshield, was parked just behind the horse posts. The middle door opened and Mordecai hopped out, his hand on his hat to keep it from blowing away in a hot July wind that kicked up dust bunnies and tumbleweeds across the barren landscape.

Liam hurled himself into the van and into his father's lap with a resounding *smack*. Levi's arms wrapped around the boy, whose squeals drowned out any words his father might have said.

Mordecai laughed, that deep belly laugh that made Susan smile. "Easy, suh, your daed's a little sore. You don't want to break any more of his bones."

"He's fine." Levi's voice was muffled, his face buried in Liam's shaggy blond hair. "He's a jumping bean and a wiggle worm all rolled into one."

"We have strawberries, Daed, big ones, you want to see? I picked a bunch of them." Liam hopped from the van, tumbled to his knees, and rocketed to his feet, seemingly unaware of the dirt that clung to his pants. "We can have some for supper. How about that? I'll clean them myself. You like strawberries, right?"

"I do, suh." Levi's voice had an odd tremble. "Why don't you go get them ready? I'll be along in a minute."

Mordecai swatted Liam on the behind. "Go on, you heard your daed. Skedaddle. He'll be at the house when you have the berries ready."

An eager grin plastered across his face, Liam darted away. Mordecai watched him go, then turned to Susan. "Howdy, schweschder. We're home."

"Indeed you are. It's good to see you." It was. The King household had been far too quiet without his steady commentary on the events outlined by scribes in the *Budget* or the silly tall tales he liked to weave for spellbound Hazel and Caleb those long summer nights sitting in sagging lawn chairs in the front yard, watching the sun go down and swatting mosquitoes. "Abigail has missed you."

"Unlike you, who would prefer I not mess up the kitchen with my honey, beeswax, and candles?"

"If you're fishing for a compliment, you'll find none here." All the same, she allowed herself a small pat on her brother's shoulder. Never a better brother had existed. "How is the patient?"

"The patient isn't patient and he's not a patient anymore." Levi pulled himself so that his legs, encased in dark-navy orthopedic boots up to his knees, dangled from the edge of the van seat. His tan had faded, leaving his skin pale. Pain deepened the lines around his eyes and mouth. "He's ready to be in his own home."

Mordecai tugged a set of gray metal crutches from the backseat and held them out. "Have at it."

Levi frowned. A growl much like that of Butch when a cat intruded on his territory told Susan exactly what the man thought of the crutches. He thrust out his hand and grabbed Mordecai's offering. "For now."

Now Susan understood. Levi didn't want his son to watch him struggle to use crutches and extricate himself from the van.

"I'll get your bag and pay Ralph."

Mordecai disappeared behind the van, leaving Susan to watch Levi as he struggled to heave himself from the van and onto the crutches without toppling over in the dirt. She didn't dare ask if he needed help. His expression made that obvious.

A second later he thumped his way up the steps, shoulders hunched, grunting with each step. He paused long enough for Susan to open the screen door before plunging through the doorway with a determined air.

"Sit here." She scurried past him and scooped up a basket of sewing from the couch. "You can stretch out your legs and it'll be easiest for you to get back up."

He kept walking, his crutches smacking against the wood in an angry staccato.

"Or not."

He glanced back. "Going to my room."

To search for his pleasing disposition, perhaps. "I'm making chicken and dumplings for supper."

The thumping stopped. Levi pivoted, his face a study in conflicting emotion. "Did Martha forget how to cook?"

"Nee, I offered." She smoothed her apron with both hands, hoping he couldn't see how they trembled. No one made her feel this way. Ever. Not even John, her long-ago suitor who'd tired of waiting and taken another as his fraa. "Your dochder has worked hard while you've been gone. There's a singing tonight. I thought maybe she should go."

"And she'd like to go?" He sounded aggrieved. His first night home and his daughter wanted to go out. He wasn't a child, after all. "She should, then."

"I would like for her to go." Susan crossed her arms. No need to be snippy, even if he was uncomfortable and tired. "As you should. We talked about this, remember? You brought it to me."

The grumpiness in his face disappeared. "Indeed we did." He turned and began his slow step-and-swing progress toward the hallway. "Danki for all you've done."

"Haven't done much of anything."

"Chicken and dumplings are my favorite." Some of the pique had faded from his tone. He slowed, then turned once again, this time all the irritation gone. He smiled. He had a smile that made her think of Christmas morning and her birthday all rolled into one big, happy, family holiday. "I reckon it would hit the spot after all that hospital food."

After a few seconds she remembered to close her mouth. Then speak. "I best get started on the dumplings." The slight stutter made heat rise on her neck and ascend into her cheeks. "I have a pecan pie in the oven."

The smile widened over a beard just starting to go silver. "Another favorite. I guess Martha told you that."

"Martha and I had a chance to talk about a lot of things."

"She's a good girl." He tapped his way around to face the hall once again. "I'll be out to wash up in a bit."

She doubted that. Fatigue rounded his shoulders and made each step slower. "It'll be a while. Rest a spell. I'll call you when supper is ready."

His head bobbed. The shoulders rounded more. It took a few moments, but eventually he disappeared into the hallway that led to his bedroom.

Mordecai's deep, sandpaper-rough chuckle wafted in the air behind her. Susan whirled and faced her brother. "What's so funny? A man in pain who's too tired to think straight?"

"My schweschder in *lieb*. I never thought I'd see the day." Mordecai crossed his arms over his broad shoulders, grinning like a hund on the hunt. "He's cranky now. You're seeing him at his worst. If you still get all riled up, then it must be something."

Something, but she couldn't say what. "I'm not riled up. I don't get riled up."

"Sure you do. Remember that time Lilly poured bleach in with the load of dark clothes and washed all the color from your dresses? You were riled up then."

"That was different. She was a silly little girl who hated

doing laundry." Their sister would do almost anything to get out of doing laundry and sewing. The joke was on her. Now she had eight kinner of her own. The piles of laundry must be endless and the treadle sewing machine worn out. "She did it on purpose."

"Nee, she didn't know better." Mordecai always defended Lilly. Who said big brothers didn't play favorites? "Besides, she made up for it later."

Later, when Mudder passed and they were on their own. Then everyone pitched in. "We're going to stand here and argue about something that happened twenty-five years ago?"

"You haven't forgotten."

Good and bad, she remembered it all. The hot, humid afternoons in the kitchen with steaming pots of boiling water to bathe jars for canning. The rows of canned tomatoes, green beans, and pickles. "I don't forget."

"That's for sure."

"What's that supposed to mean?"

Mordecai snapped his suspenders, his eyes brilliant. "I just mean it's about time you let go of your role as caregiver for others and have your own family."

"Gott's will."

"Exactly. Don't stand in His way."

"I'm not. I would never."

"We'll see. It takes courage to step out in faith, especially when it comes to people like Levi."

"What do you mean like Levi?"

Emotions warred in Mordecai's face. The pinched, dark look she remembered from his days as a new widower caring for a son with devastating injuries slid across his face like a cloud filtering the light of a brilliant moon. "I see a lot of myself in him. Me, before Abigail came along."

"I do too." Susan schooled her voice to keep the pain she felt for him at bay. "Gott is gut. He gave you a second chance at lieb."

"You could be Levi's second chance."

"That's really up to him. I haven't seen any indication."

Mordecai cocked his head, his eyes squinted as if against the sun. "He showed you his bad side. That's a good indication."

As far as she could tell, the man didn't have a bad side. He looked good from every angle. "His bad side?"

"Hurting, cranky, the real him."

As far as Susan was concerned, no one could hold anything against a man who'd been stomped by a horse. Something warm and soft quivered inside her. Did Mordecai see something she didn't? She couldn't bear to be disappointed. Such a chance, such an opportunity came along so rarely in the life of a woman such as herself. Older, a teacher, someone who lived surrounded by loving family but with too few new acquaintances to even begin to hope for such a chance.

"Take it from me, it's a good thing."

She would take it from Mordecai. He of all people knew of such things. "Now what?"

"Now it's up to him."

It was always up to the man. She should know that. She sighed. "So I wait?"

"There's a lot of waiting involved when it comes to love and second chances." Mordecai patted her shoulder. "The person has to be ready to take that chance. He's waited six years."

"You waited twelve."

"For your sake, I hope he's on a faster track than I was for that second chance." He stomped ahead into the kitchen. "If you don't start on those dumplings soon, we'll be eating after dark."

Susan didn't move. She was too busy contemplating second chances.

TWENTY-EIGHT

Rebekah brushed a wisp of hair from her forehead for the third time and concentrated on ignoring the throb in her ankle. The evening sun held no less heat at the horizon than it did at midafternoon. The singing would be at the bishop's house tonight. One reason Mudder hadn't frowned when Susan insisted Rebekah don her cleanest dress, her Sunday shoes, and a fresh kapp and go. She said she was tired of Rebekah moping around. Either Susan wanted Martha to have moral support, or she really thought this singing might be the one where a boy forgot all about Leila's defection and asked Rebekah to take a ride.

She glanced at Martha. The girl had been quiet on the long walk. She didn't seem to mind the slow pace necessitated by Rebekah's hobbled walk. The swelling had gone done after the first day, but the pain persisted despite aspirin. The pain in her ankle and the pain in her heart.

They had handled it all wrong. She should've gone to talk to Lupe first. She knew how much Lupe feared men she didn't know. Now every step reminded her of Diego and Lupe. Gone without a trace from their lives. Had they made it to San Antonio? Did they find their father? Were they safe from the men looking for them? The questions tormented Rebekah all day long and most of the night.

Right alongside the questions about Tobias. Two weeks had passed since the thunderstorm and those few moments in the shed. Still, it seemed she'd been holding her breath the entire time. Waiting. They would find the path together. He'd said that. She hadn't imagined the words or dreamed them.

So when would he come? When his daed was better. That's what he'd said. Gott was teaching her patience.

She didn't like it. Not one bit.

All these questions swirling around made the singing seem supremely unimportant. Not that thing for which she'd once pined. Once thought the only path to happiness. Rebekah wanted to yell. Instead she continued to plod along to a singing where the man she longed to see would not be.

Tobias wouldn't be there. He was busy taking care of his family, working the farm, and making saddles. She stumbled, stubbed her toe, and righted herself. The throb in her ankle reached a crescendo.

"Are you all right?" Martha put one hand on Rebekah's arm. "Do you need to rest a minute?"

"Nee. Does Tobias ever go to singings?" She bent over and rubbed her ankle, hoping Martha wouldn't see her expression. Just making conversation. "I mean, did he go in Ohio?"

The flush on Martha's damp cheeks deepened. "Nee, not much, not really. I mean, not toward the end."

She sounded flustered. It seemed a simple question. "He didn't have a special friend in Ohio?"

"Nee."

Rebekah waited for Martha to elaborate. She didn't. "I guess he had a lot of work to do. Not much time to think about courting. Like you."

"Jah." Martha sidestepped a cow patty in the middle of the dirt road. She cocked her head. "Why are you asking?"

"Just wondered." Rebekah pushed open the gate that led to Jeremiah's front yard. She picked up her pace so Martha couldn't see her face. A short row of buggies, wagons, and worn two-seaters filled the space in front of the squat, ugly house that had taken weeks for the men to build after a fire had destroyed the first house on that spot. "Looks like everyone is here."

Martha stopped in the middle of the worn path that led to the steps and the porch. Her hands went to her stomach. "I don't feel very good. Maybe something I ate for supper didn't set right." She stumbled back two steps. "Maybe I should head back home."

"Nee. It's only butterflies." Rebekah slipped back down the steps and went to stand next to her. "It'll be fun. I promise. We sing. We have snacks. The boys act silly and the girls laugh even when it's not funny. That's all there is to it."

And then some girls got asked to take buggy rides. And some didn't.

Martha sighed and marched up the steps. Rebekah followed, even though the butterflies in Martha's stomach seemed to have taken flight and landed in her own stomach. *Just get through it.*

The evening went exactly as she had imagined it. Elijah Hostetler led the singing with a voice he surely inherited from his daed, Jeremiah. The bishop's sonorous voice kept them all on track during church services. The songs, however, were faster and more fun to sing than the ones in the *Ausbund*. After six or seven, snacks were served. Then more singing. More jokes, more laughing.

And then that moment Rebekah dreaded. Two by two, they

drifted away. There went Milo Byler with Vesta Hostetler. Simon Glick, sweet, simple Simon summoned the courage to ask Susie Hostetler to take a walk with him. She smiled and said yes.

Even Martha, the new girl, seemed to have attracted someone's attention. Jacob King. Mordecai would be pleased. Jacob had been interested in Isabella Shrock, and even though he would never admit it, he'd been disappointed when she chose Will instead. Rebekah forced a smile and a quick wave when Martha trotted by, following Jacob out the door.

That left her and Elijah Hostetler. He tipped his hat as he walked by. And kept right on walking.

She blew out a breath she didn't even know she'd been holding. It was for the best. Elijah was a boy compared to Tobias. A nice boy, but still. She took her time opening the door and closing it behind her. The sun had disappeared and the dark night promised cooler air. Despite her ankle, she would enjoy the walk home.

"Hey."

Startled, she missed a step, stumbled, and grabbed the railing just in time to keep from landing on her behind. The throb in her ankle did triple time. "Tobias! You scared me."

His two-seater was parked in the empty space left by those who had gone before. "Sorry." He didn't look sorry. He smiled. "I figured it was time I made good on that talk we had in the shed. Besides, with your hurt ankle, it doesn't seem right for you to walk home."

About time indeed. "I thought maybe you forgot."

He didn't answer. Instead he hopped from the two-seater and strode around to the other side. "Go for a ride with me." He held out his hand. "It's a full moon. We'll be able to see to drive down by the pond."

"There's no water in the pond."

"Jah, there is. It filled up with the rain the other day." He wiggled his fingers. "You want to argue about the water in the pond, or do you want to go for a ride with me?"

She sniffed and took his hand. It felt warm and calloused. His touch rippled down to the tips of her toes. "Ride." She managed to stumble over that one simple syllable. She cleared her throat and tried again. "Ride with you."

"Perfect. Because I want to ride with you."

He let go of her hand, grabbed her around the waist, and lifted her into the two-seater.

"Hey!"

"Hush." He strode back and around and hopped in beside her. "Try not to talk. You only make it worse."

"Make what worse?"

He put his finger to his lips. "Do you hear that?"

"Hear what?"

"The sound of us being alone."

She closed her mouth and cocked her head. A lazy, humid breeze rustled sparse leaves on the mesquite trees that lined the road. Lovely silence.

She settled back in the seat and let the *clip-clop* of the horse's hooves beat a rhythm like music only folks who lived in the country could appreciate. Tobias took a shortcut across Jeremiah's property and let the horse have full rein until they turned onto the rutted road that led to the pond where the kinner liked to fish, catch minnows and tadpoles, and look for night crawlers when it rained.

The smell of mud mixed with the scent of wet, rotting leaves. "Whoa, whoa." Tobias brought the two-seater to a halt. "I believe I see water."

"Not much."

"I didn't say it was a lot."

"Nee, you didn't."

He wrapped the reins around the handle and leaned back, hands relaxed on his thighs. "What did you think of the singing?"

"I thought it stank."

"It stank?" He chuckled. "Is that any way to talk?"

"It stank."

"Because no one asked you to take a ride?"

"Someone did ask me."

"What about Martha, did someone ask her?"

Was this about him spying on his sister? Irritation welled in Rebekah. She had enough of her own family watching her every move. She wouldn't be party to doing that to Martha. "Take me home." She hopped from the wagon. "Better yet, I'll walk."

"Hey, hey, where are you going?"

"I told you home."

"Because I asked about Martha?" He jumped down and stalked after her, his long legs overtaking her in two strides. "I just want her to have a good time."

Rebekah slammed to a halt. "Oh."

"Oh is right."

"I thought—"

"I was using you to spy on my sister." He shook his head, his eyes bright with laughter. "I don't need you to do that. I have spies everywhere."

"Now you sound like Mordecai."

"I could do worse."

"He is a good man." That Tobias recognized that fact warmed Rebekah. She started walking again. "I like the smell of mud."

"Me too. It smells clean, as strange as that sounds."

"It smells like spring."

"Even in summer."

The conversation made perfect sense. Rebekah smiled.

"You have the best smile." Tobias caught her hand and pulled her around so she faced him. "Anyone ever tell you that?"

"Not one person. Not once."

"I'm happy to be the first." His hands came to her shoulders and held her there. His gaze roved over her face from her eyes to her mouth and back. "Would it be all right if I kissed you?"

Rebekah had no idea how to answer that question. Her whole body said yes so loudly she couldn't hear anything else. If her mind thought it was a bad idea, she would never know. She swallowed and managed to whisper, "Jah."

The one-syllable word barely escaped before Tobias's mouth covered hers. Whatever she'd imagined kissing would be like, however she and Franny and her sisters had speculated, they'd had no idea. Better than the best day of the year. Better than homemade ice cream and strawberry-rhubarb pie. Better than a pile of presents, family gathered around to watch them being opened. Better than sleeping late or lying on a blanket and counting stars under a spring sky. He tasted like a promise kept.

She breathed in his scent and memorized the way his hands felt around her waist. How they tightened as the kiss deepened. Just when she thought she might simply float away, he let go. But he didn't go far. His head inclined over hers, his dark gaze probing. Rebekah saw something there that she couldn't explain. She didn't see birthday and Christmas presents wrapped up in hand-colored paper. She saw fear and pain. Uncertainty.

"Tobias?" she breathed. "What is it?"

He shook his head and kissed her again. Hard and sure. Like a period at the end of a sentence. Not a question mark, a period.

He backed away. "I'm sorry. I feel like we're getting ahead of ourselves."

A shiver ran through her despite the July heat. "I think we've been ahead of ourselves since that first day." She wrapped her arms around her middle and stared at the moonlit water. A turtle popped his head above water, disappeared again. "You make me feel . . . off balance. You don't seem sure you want to be here."

"I didn't seem sure just now?"

Heat flamed across her cheeks. "Kisses are one thing."

"Feelings another."

"Jah."

"It worries me."

"This?" She allowed herself to touch his arm, one quick touch, then withdrew. "I worry you."

"Not you specifically." He kicked a rock across the bank and into the water. "It's hard to explain."

"Try hard." Rebekah needed to know. She would never kiss another man like she'd kissed Tobias, of that she was certain. Surely he felt the same.

"Since my mudder passed, it's been hard for me to put my faith in Gott's plan."

The tremor in his voice told her this was the very root of his problem. To admit it to another person, to admit it to her, was huge for a man like Tobias. He admitted to a chink in his armor of faith. He admitted to fearing loss and pain.

"My daed died when I was thirteen." She sidled closer to him. His hand closed over hers. Their fingers entwined. "One day he was there. The next he was gone. No good-bye. No last words. Mudder said his days on earth were over. He went home."

"But you couldn't understand it."

They had this in common. "Not any more than you can understand why your mudder died while giving birth to sweet little Liam."

His hand tightened around hers. The silence stretched, but the bittersweet music of shared sorrow filled it, the notes finding their way up and down the scale in the night air.

"But you found peace eventually."

"Coming to Bee County helped. At first I thought this place was horrible. Then Deborah found Phineas and she was happy. Mudder found Mordecai and they both started over. They had a second chance at happiness, even at their age."

"Because they're so old." Tobias chuckled.

"You know what I mean."

"I do."

More silence. The croak of frogs ebbed and flowed with the slap of water against the banks of the pond.

"So you don't mind that I find myself a little worried."

Rebekah tugged free of his hand and slid her arm around his waist, her mind boggled by her own audacity. "I'll understand it for now. But not for always."

"Nee." He turned to face her. "Not for always."

This time when his head inclined toward her, she waited to close her eyes. So did he. She saw no fear. No uncertainty. Only wonder. Awesome wonder.

TWENTY-NINE

The glee on Caleb's face said it all. Rebekah hid her smile as she watched her brother lovingly finger the display of fireworks that included firecrackers, bottle rockets, and smoke balls. Mudder had looked grim when Mordecai broached the topic of taking Rebekah along. He seemed determined to keep her busy. The fireworks stand set up in a tent outside the Walmart surely held no group of Englisch boys looking for Amish girls to corrupt. If only they knew. Kisses under a full moon had sealed her fate. She would never look beyond her tiny community for that special someone. Tobias still had wounds that needed healing, but his touch said he yearned to find peace. With her. In time he would. She prayed he would.

She breathed and worked to find herself in the here and now. In a fireworks tent that might be more of a danger to Caleb. Her brother would be a pyromaniac, given half a chance. All the boys would.

Sweat beaded on her forehead. She patted it with her sleeve and hobbled farther under the tent to escape the fierce July sun. Her ankle throbbed less and less every day, which only reminded her of the passage of time since Lupe and Diego's disappearance. It was July Fourth already and they hadn't heard anything about them. They were gone. For good. Time to accept that and move on.

Diego would love the firecrackers, she was sure of it. Lupe would like the Roman candles the way Rebekah did.

"Do you think we can afford bottle rockets and Roman candles?" Caleb tried to mask his eagerness. Lately Rebekah had noticed he was trying to act more mature, leaving little-boy ways behind. She would miss the little boy. "How much do we have?"

He'd asked that question four times on the ride into town. Mordecai, who stood perusing the smoke balls and fountains, smiled at Caleb and shook his head. "Pick one, suh."

The money from one day of baked-good sales in town had been set aside for their Fourth of July celebration. "Get some snakes, some poppers, and some bang snaps for the little ones." She picked up a box of punks. "We'll need these too."

"Those are all for babies." Caleb snorted and held up a package of firecrackers as long as his arm. "Look at this, one thousand firecrackers. We could light the fuse and let them all go at once. The horses would bolt."

"So would the little kinner." Rebekah chuckled. "You don't want to waste them all at once. The idea is to make them last."

"Nee, the idea is to make a lot of noise and light up the sky."

"Still, we need to get something for the kinner."

A woman strode into the tent, backlit by the sun. At first Rebekah couldn't see her face in the shadows, but she recognized the high-pitched East Texas twang going on and on, something about a fireworks display sponsored by the Lions Club. Bobbie McGregor.

Bobbie swung her long braid over her shoulder. Her black cowboy hat teetered back on her head. "We need bottle rockets, lots of bottle rockets. I wonder if they have M-80s."

Her gaze met Rebekah's. Her fair skin darkened under a deep tan. "Hey, what's up, Rebekah."

David Byler stopped behind her. He didn't have time to tug his hand from Bobbie's before Rebekah saw how their fingers were entwined. He ducked his head, his face as red as radishes.

"Not much." Rebekah sidestepped toward Mordecai. He would know how to handle this. She didn't have a clue. David was new to their community, but holding hands with an Englisch girl didn't likely find acceptance in his former district either. "Just getting a few things for Friday's picnic."

Mordecai turned to stare at the two. His expression didn't change. He handed Rebekah a package of snakes. "The little ones will like these. You keep a running total of our picks so we don't go over our budget." He turned to Bobbie. "How is the horse? Cracker Jack is his name, right?"

"Tobias is training him, little by little. He's a patient man. I think he'll find a way to tame him." If she squirmed any more, she'd squirm out of her skin. "David was just filling me in on his daddy's condition. I'm so glad he's home in time for the holiday. David and I ran into each other in the parking lot."

Running on at the mouth was a clear sign of lying. Besides, how did David get to the parking lot? He hadn't arrived with them. In fact, Rebekah clearly remembered discussion at the supper table last night about the Byler men helping to pour a new concrete floor for another milk house today. After which Tobias had to work on the saddle he was making for Bobbie.

"Is that right, David?"

The glint of amusement in Mordecai's eyes was a dangerous thing. That and his tone drew Rebekah grudgingly from her thoughts of Tobias. Mordecai might be the kindest, most gregarious man around, but he did not take lightly the transgressions of folks in his district. As deacon he had to investigate and assist with meting out punishment, something he did with a fair and even hand. "You met up with Miss Bobbie just now in the parking lot?"

"Nee, Bobbie was nice enough to give me a ride into town." David apparently hadn't been paying attention to the discussion after church Sunday about the Kings coming in to buy fireworks for everyone for the Fourth of July picnic. If he had, he wouldn't be in this predicament. "I thought I'd buy a few things for our kinner. They've been down since Lupe and Diego left."

Using Diego and Lupe as an excuse. Nee. "We're taking care of that." Rebekah let her irritation bleed into the words as she held up the snakes and the poppers. "Liam and Hazel will have plenty of fun with these."

Mordecai gave her the look. The Look. She closed her mouth and slid closer to the counter where the cashier entertained himself with a magazine about automatic weapons.

"We'd be happy to give you a ride back to the farm." Mordecai's tone indicated it wasn't an offer David would be smart to refuse. "We need to finish the ramps at your house. It'll be easier for your daed to get in and out if he doesn't have to use the steps on the front porch."

"He's so ornery, he doesn't want us doing anything special." The space between David and Bobbie grew. "He says he can manage fine. He's been mighty cantankerous since he got home."

"A man used to working hard doesn't like the idea of sitting around." Mordecai picked up a package of sparklers and held them out. "Liam will like these."

A reminder that David had kinner who looked up to him. Rebekah admired Mordecai's simple ways of getting to the truth of the matter. Where she tended to go in like a bull in a too-small stall, he knew how to get under a person's skin without raising his voice. "He'll like these too." She held up a package of worms. "Hazel still giggles over them and she's six too."

"I better get going." Bobbie sidled toward the tent opening with its flaps knocking in the humid breeze. "I need to practice for the barrel racing at the county fair."

Suddenly she had practicing to do. She should practice keeping her mitts off a susceptible young Plain man whose world had been turned upside down by a move to a new community and a daed with severe injuries. "Y'all should come watch me ride. It's fun. You'll like it."

"That would be—"

Mordecai shook his head. David closed his mouth. "We appreciate the invitation. We have much work to do this summer."

Her cheeks rosy with heat—or embarrassment—Bobbie nodded and slipped away. Mordecai turned his back on David and approached Rebekah. "We better get going. Supper will be on the table and you know how your mudder hates to keep it waiting."

Rebekah scooped up Caleb's growing pile and marched over to the counter. "Jah, we better get out of here before someone gets burned."

"There's nothing going on."

David's tone held a note of belligerence. Mordecai's smile had died. His frown etched lines around his eyes and mouth. Her stepfather could look fierce indeed. "Your rumspringa is yours and yours alone." He pulled a wad of bills from the band inside his straw hat and handed it to Rebekah. "But holding hands with an Englisch girl in public is not nothing. You'll get more than burned. You'll lose everything."

"Like you said, that's the point of rumspringa." David didn't seem at all fazed by the fierce Mordecai look. "To make your own choice."

Mordecai turned his back on David. "Pay up so we can go."

Rebekah signaled to Caleb, who groaned and marched across the tent, his arms full of a pile of fireworks, surely more than they could afford.

No one would leave the fireworks tent happy this day.

THIRTY

This had been a mistake. Tobias sideswiped a glance at Jesse. The man seemed perfectly at ease cruising the streets in his minivan, a Plain man alongside him in the front seat. The tepid air radiating from the van's AC did nothing to cool Tobias's face. When he'd asked Mr. Cramer to give him a ride into town to Jesse's church, he'd been buoyed with the hope that they would find Lupe and Diego at a bus stop or on the steps of the church itself. Then they'd have even more reason to celebrate the holiday.

Maybe they were in one of the humanitarian refugee centers he'd read about in the *Beeville Times-Picayune*. He couldn't bear the sad faces at the supper table the last two weeks. Or the way Rebekah stared at her hands during church service, her thoughts written all over her pretty face. If he found them, she would smile again.

In only a few months these two little ones had earned themselves a place in the hearts of his community. In his heart. Even if they couldn't stay forever, he wanted to make sure they were all right, that they weren't victims of the evil that permeated the world, dead on the side of the road. Uncomfortable with his thoughts, he shifted in his seat, the belt tight against his broad chest.

Jesse glanced his way. "They're fine."

"How can you know that?"

"I have faith."

No doubt he did, but Jesse had been all too ready to jump in and try to find the kinner. He, too, knew that a person didn't stand aside and wait for God to do what he should do himself. "I have faith, too, but I also know what a dangerous place this world is."

"This world of mine?"

"I didn't say that."

"It's written all over your face." Jesse turned on the blinker and made a left in front of a taco house behind a line of traffic headed out to the county's Fourth of July celebration. He chuckled. "I know you think they're safer with you, but they navigated a much more dangerous world back home. And they survived the coyotes in Mexico that would've taken advantage of them."

"Coyotes?"

"The human smugglers."

"Barely. Lupe is afraid of any man who comes near her. What will scars like that do to her when she's older and ready to become a fraa and a mudder?"

Wanting to put a damper on his anger at the thought, Tobias swiveled to look out the passenger window, searching the nooks and crannies made by the doorways and awnings of the stores that lined the street. He didn't see any children who should be at home, getting ready to shoot fireworks and eat hot dogs before taking baths and going to bed in nice, clean sheets. Like the bath he'd given Diego on that first night. Tobias had ended up as wet as Diego. And how was Pedro the ratoncito? Still hiding in the backpack? Tobias wanted to know. He snorted.

"What?"

"I find myself wondering how a mouse is doing. What has the world come to?"

"Diego cares about the mouse. So you care. It says something about you."

Tobias adjusted the vents so the cool air blew on his warm face. "Hogwash."

"It's the truth. I know you want to help them, but I suspect you're also concerned with how Rebekah is taking this." Jesse honked at a gaggle of giggling teenage girls who stopped in the middle of the crosswalk, apparently intent on taking pictures of themselves with an overabundance of cell phones. "She's tougher than she looks. She's like Leila, only mouthier."

Not a topic Tobias intended to discuss with anyone, least of all a Plain-turned-Englisch man. "I'm concerned with Diego and Lupe getting safely to their final destination."

Jesse snorted. "I saw the way you looked at her."

"That's a private matter."

"She feels the same way."

Despite himself, Tobias glanced at Jesse. He stared at the road, but he was grinning. Pleased with himself as if he'd done something grand. If he only knew about the ride down by the pond after the singing, he wouldn't be so pleased with himself. "What do you know about it?"

"She has an open face, just like Leila. I know Leila's moods and all her thoughts because they pass across her sweet face. Rebekah is the same way."

"Rebekah is worried about these kinner the same as I am. I want to find them."

"I think we just did."

Tobias followed the finger Jesse pointed toward the window.

Lupe stood with her back to them. She had Diego on her shoulders, boosting him over the side of a Dumpster outside a Dairy Queen restaurant. The little boy scaled the wall like a monkey and disappeared over the side. Jesse pulled up to the curb and turned off the engine. Lupe looked back, her hair a tangled mess in her eyes. Her mouth opened, but Tobias couldn't hear her words. He shoved open the door. "Lupe, are you all right?"

"Diego!"

A string of Spanish words followed the boy's name. His face reappeared over the top of the Dumpster wall. He waved a fast-food wrapper in one hand. *"¡Hamburguesa!"*

Panic on her face, the girl waved at him. *"¡Vamos!"*

"Don't run, please don't run. Rebekah misses you." Tobias hurled himself from the van and ran across the littered parking lot. "Liam and Hazel miss you."

Lupe planted herself in front of her brother, her arms behind her as if shielding him from danger. "We go."

"Stay. Let us help you. Jesse can help you."

She shook her head. "We go."

"You haven't yet." Jesse stopped next to Tobias. "Because you don't know how to go north on the road to San Antonio without getting caught. Let us help you."

"Como?"

"There's a place called the Humanitarian Respite Center." Jesse edged closer, both hands out as if offering her something tangible. "They take refugees and help them find places to stay until their immigration hearings."

Jesse spoke as if Lupe would understand these Englisch words. Tobias held out his hand, praying Lupe would trust him enough to take it. Trust him more than Jesse, whom she had never met. "Let them come see Rebekah first. She can talk to them."

Jesse nodded. "We can do that."

"Come with us. To Rebekah and Liam and Ida and Hazel." Tobias cocked his head toward the van. "It's Fourth of July. We're having hot dogs and ice cream."

"Ice cream." Apparently this was a word Diego understood. He still had the half-eaten hamburger from the Dumpster in one dirty hand. "Hot dog."

Tobias fought the urge to grab the greasy wrapper and toss it back in the trash. "Let us help you."

Diego scaled the Dumpster and balanced himself on the edge, one dirty leg dangling over it. The knees of his pants were torn. He had skinned his knees at some point. Scabs showed through. He tossed the hamburger to Lupe, who caught it without taking her gaze from Jesse. Diego dropped to the ground, dodged his sister, and trotted toward Tobias. "Liam?"

"Liam and the others are waiting to shoot their fireworks with you."

"He no like." Lupe slid the hamburger into her knapsack. "Sound like gun, bang-bang."

"But he's safe with us."

"No safe anywhere."

Such a world-weary voice for such a young girl. Tobias's heart wrenched. "Not true. We can keep you safe. Diego, where's Pedro?"

Diego's face crumpled. He wiped at his dirty face with a dirtier hand. "He gone."

"Gone?"

"Run away."

Diego buried his head in Tobias's leg. He smelled of sweat, garbage, and dirt, just as he had that first night. "It's fine . . . you're fine." He rubbed the boy's thin shoulders and matted hair. "We'll take you home, give you a bath, and feed you."

Food that didn't come from a Dumpster.

A siren whooped and screamed, cutting the thick, humid air. Red and blue lights whirled, reflected against the restaurant glass in a wild, dizzying pattern. Lupe's mouth dropped open and her eyes widened. "La migra!"

She shot toward the street. Tobias unfurled his other arm and grabbed her as she passed him. She struggled like a scrappy alley cat, fierce and angry, but she didn't have the strength to break free. "No, no."

Her teeth bit into his wrist. Pain shot up his arm. "Hey, hey." He managed to hang on. "Don't do that!"

"Me go, me go."

"Stay." Diego's weak, barefooted kicks banged against his shins. "It's okay, it's okay, I promise."

"Let me have him." Jesse knelt next to Tobias and laid a hand on the boy. "Tobias is right. We'll help you. We won't abandon you."

"No, no!" Lupe shrieked. "They take us!"

A man so rotund his uniform buttons looked as if they were in danger of shooting across the parking lot shoved open his door and hoisted himself from the sheriff's car with an audible grunt. He had a face as smooth and white as a baby's bottom. When he finally unfolded himself, he stood well above Tobias and Jesse. A mammoth man with all manner of armaments on his heavy black belt—a gun, a baton, a stun gun of some sort, and a radio that cackled with static, the microphone attached to a strap on his shoulder. Just the sort to scare young children who had an understandable fear of uniforms.

"What's going on here?" His meaty hand rested on the butt of his revolver. "A little Dumpster diving?"

"Wally?"

"Pastor?"

"You know you're not supposed to call me that!" Jesse stood. He picked up Diego and settled him on his hip as if the boy weighed nothing. "I just give the message when Pastor Dan can't. This here is Diego, and that's my friend Tobias and Diego's sister, Lupe."

Wally's head seemed to bob from person to person as he took in the introductions. His hat looked too tight and his wrinkled forehead suggested it hurt. "You do a fine job behind the pulpit."

Still stuck back on how he knew Jesse. The man took his time digesting situations, apparently.

Lupe tried to wiggle free of his grasp. Tobias hugged her against his chest. "It's okay. He's a friend of Jesse's."

"Policía."

"Yes, but police aren't bad." Not most of the time. Not in America. "We'll explain and he'll understand."

Tobias had almost no experience with police. He hoped he wasn't telling the girl a tall tale.

"So are these *chiquitos* runaways?" Wally leaned against the bumper of his car. It groaned and sank under his weight.

Tobias let Jesse give the man an abbreviated version of the events that had led them to this moment outside a Dumpster in a fast-food restaurant parking lot. When Jesse paused for breath, Tobias jumped in. "My family's willing to care for them until their hearing. We want to get something set up so we can get it resolved, so they're not running around alone out on the street."

He stopped and waited. The sheriff's deputy frowned and chewed on his thumbnail. He studied his boots and shifted his weight. The car's suspension sounded as if it were crying. Lupe fidgeted. Tobias patted her arm, aware of the throbbing where her bite had left marks on his wrist.

"I don't know, Pastor Jesse. We have strict orders to turn any illegals over to ICE posthaste." He shifted. The car groaned again. "They pay us overtime. Operation Border Star from the feds. We get money to do this. You're not supposed to help these kids. You're supposed to turn them in. Don't you read the paper? Sheriff says they could be terrorists."

"These are children. And they're alone and they're hungry and tired and they don't have a place to lay their heads at night." Jesse patted Diego's dirty hair. "Does this look like the face of a terrorist? I reckon he's about the age of your Matthew, don't you think?"

"Maybe. But Sheriff says we have to take care of ourselves. He says these kids coming across the border are a way to clog things up in the US." Wally fidgeted in much the same way as Lupe. He wrinkled his nose and studied the ground some more. "We had a meeting with folks here in town the other day, and they was real concerned because their barns are getting broken into and stuff stolen. Fences broken."

"We no steal." Lupe drew herself up tall, her face fierce. "We no steal from no one."

"No offense." Wally held up a hand. "But the sheriff tells the folks here to take care of themselves. That's the number-one priority."

"Is that what Jesus would say?" Jesse's tone was kind. He settled onto the edge of the car next to the deputy and tucked Diego on his lap. "Look at this little boy and then tell me what Jesus would do."

Wally's expression was troubled. He lifted his hat and scratched his forehead. His bald head shone in the setting sun. "Oh man, Pastor, you got to lay that one on me?"

"We don't learn Scripture in the church in Sunday school and then leave it there, do we?"

Wally ducked his head and plucked at a thread on his pant leg. "No, sir, we don't."

"Don't sir me. You know better. Just like you know the story about when the disciples wanted to take the children away and Jesus said, 'Let the little children come to me.' You know that story, Wally."

"I do, I do."

"Well then?"

Wally sighed, a mournful sigh. Tobias had to hand it to Jesse Glick. He knew his stuff and he knew people. Wally hoisted himself up and slapped his hat back on his head. "What did you have in mind?"

"Take us out to Tobias's place. Let the kinner stay there for a day or two. Tomorrow I'll try to get through to the Office of Refugee Resettlement in the Valley. I'll take it from there, I promise."

The big man sighed.

"After you get off shift tonight, you should come by the house. Leila made her famous lemon meringue pie today. The crust melts in your mouth."

"Are you trying to bribe a law enforcement official, Pastor Jesse?" Wally patted his potbelly, which hung over his belt to an alarming degree. "I'm surprised you didn't offer a dozen donuts."

"I know you like my wife's pie better."

"How about a compromise?"

Jesse glanced at Tobias. Tobias shrugged. The sheriff's deputy held all the cards. They'd only just now found the kinner. They couldn't lose them again that quickly. Could they?

"What did you have in mind?"

"No offense to you, sir, but I don't know you from Adam." Wally nodded at Tobias, then slapped his meaty hand on his chest with a thump that would've knocked a lesser man to the ground. "What do you say we take these kiddos out to the farm to see your family and enjoy the holiday? Then they come on back to town to stay with Pastor Jesse and his wife until we get this all straightened out. What do you say to that?"

Lupe shrank against Tobias's chest. Now she saw him as an ally. He rubbed his wrist, thankful she hadn't broken the skin. "We'd rather have them stay with us. They'd rather stay with us. If it's the best you can do, then we'll take it."

Jesse slapped Wally's arm. "Thanks, pal. We'll take care of them. We won't let them out of sight."

"You've got a deal." Wally opened his car door. "But just so you know, don't you kids try any funny stuff. I'm giving you a special pass here. I expect you to honor that and not try to run away."

"We no run." Lupe crowded against Tobias. She smelled like her brother. They both would get baths tonight before slipping into Leila's clean sheets. "You no use gun."

"No guns." Wally smiled at her. "My daughter Kara will tell you my bark is worse than my bite."

Unfortunately, Lupe—who could deliver a severe bite of her own when she felt threatened—had other experiences in her short life. Ones Wally's daughter would never have to know. Tobias waited until the deputy got in and shut his door to lead Lupe to the van. "Put your seat belt on. Jesse is a crazy driver. It comes from starting out as Plain folk."

He had no idea if she understood. Her perplexed expression said no. "Sorry I bite."

She did look properly downcast. "It's okay. I'm tough. In fact, I hope you don't come down with something. Biting me can be a dangerous proposition."

Again the perplexed expression. "Let's go get you a hot dog."

And a way to stay in America.

THIRTY-ONE

Butch's howling did nothing to drown out the sporadic *rat-a-tat-tat* of the firecrackers. Caleb and the other boys were going crazy with their stash of fireworks. They would be shot up before dark. Susan opened the kitchen screen door and let the poor hund inside. Abigail would frown on it, but she was busy cranking the ice cream maker on the front porch. Fourth of July festivities were in full swing. Plain folks had much for which to be thankful when it came to the freedoms their ancestors had not been afforded in their previous homelands before escaping the persecution by coming to the New World. It was good to be reminded.

It also reminded Susan of Lupe and Diego. Had the kinner found safe haven in another place? She shuddered to think what they must be going through out there in their new world all alone. Barely speaking the language. She picked up the washcloth and put it down. Butch whined. She swiped a ham bone left over from supper the previous evening and deposited it on an old platter. She set it on the floor next to the back door. Butch grinned. She was sure of it.

"You're a spoiled old hund, you know that, right?"

"Talking to the hund now, are you?" Martha trotted through the doorway that led from the front room, a pot of baked beans in her oven-mitt-clad hands. "Someone will think you've lost your marbles."

"And they would be right. Let me take that."

"I splattered the juice on my apron. Daed insisted on driving the wagon." Martha handed over the pot. "We were all over the place. I think he hit every rut in the road. Of course, he wouldn't admit how much it hurt his legs and his hip."

"He's here, then?" The words were out before Susan could reel them in. Of course Levi was here. On crutches, bruised, and battered, but able to stand upright. "I mean, how is he?"

"Hurting, but too bullheaded to admit it." Martha grabbed a washrag and dabbed at the splotches on her apron, an action that only served to make a bigger mess. "I heard him stumbling around in the dark last night. I got up to help him and he nearly bit my head off."

"That's just like a man."

"The doctor wanted him to use a wheelchair and he refused. Said it cost too much." Martha sounded aggrieved. "If he falls and has to go back into the hospital, it'll cost a lot more than a wheelchair, but you can't tell him that."

"Men are terrible patients." Susan didn't really feel the need to say anything. She'd been in Martha's shoes. The younger woman simply needed to vent to someone who would understand. "Just ignore his crankiness and do what needs to be done."

"Men are what?" Jacob strode through the back door, one hand held high.

"Not the brightest."

"Hogwash." Jacob held out his hand. "Burned my fingers lighting a sparkler for Hazel."

"It's too light still for sparklers." Susan studied the hand. What wasn't dirty was red. She grinned at Martha. "See what I mean?"

Martha's gaze didn't connect with Susan's and she didn't seem to hear her speak. Her natural peaches-and-cream complexion had gone rosy. She ducked her head, dropped the washrag, bent to pick it up, and kept her head down as if trying to hide her face.

"Water is the best I can do." Susan bustled to the tub sitting on the counter. "They bought ice to make the ice cream, but it's already in use."

"That's okay." Jacob's tone was distracted, his gaze on the back of Martha's head. "I don't know why I came in. It doesn't hurt at all."

He tugged his hand from her grasp, whirled, and stalked toward the door. At the last moment he stopped and looked back. "We're planning to play volleyball in a while. You should play."

"You talking to me?" Susan looked from him to Martha and back. "My back has been hurting lately—"

"Not you. Martha." Jacob's face turned another shade deeper into a red that reminded Martha of Beeville's volunteer fire engine. "I mean you can play, too, but—"

"I have to help out with my daed." Martha still didn't look at Jacob. Susan wanted to grab her by the kapp and force her to make eye contact. But she didn't. Meddling in courtship was not considered a nice thing to do. "He's still lame, you know?"

"He'll be fine. I'll take care of him." Heat scorched Susan's face. "What I mean is, I'll make sure he gets fed and has a comfortable place to sit."

"Nee, really I should—"

"Really you should play volleyball." Susan snagged the washrag from Martha's hand. "Go on, now."

"The game hasn't started yet."

"Go. Show Hazel how to use the sparklers. Obviously this oaf can't handle it."

"Hey, who are you calling an oaf?"

"Go on, get out of my kitchen. I have food to cook."

Martha scurried past Jacob, who made a show of backing away so as to give her room to get through the door. His hang-dog expression made him look an awful lot like Butch with his ham bone.

A lot like Mordecai the first time he set eyes on Abigail Lantz.

Romance was in the air. Susan sighed. It was lovely to see in young folks.

It would be nice to see it in older folks too.

When had she become so dissatisfied with her life? She'd been perfectly happy to be a teacher. Well, almost. When had the longing become so strong?

When Levi Byler drove up to her school with his load of kinner, that's when.

Hogwash and balderdash.

She whirled and picked up a wooden spoon to stir a fresh batch of lemonade. Ice would be nice. Being content with Gott's plan would be nice.

"Mighty hot today."

She stirred so hard the lemonade sloshed over the side of the glass pitcher and ran down her hands. *Breathe.* She turned, the spoon still in her hand. "July in South Texas."

Levi clomped into the kitchen, leaning heavily on gray metal crutches. He paused but continued to sway. A small Band-Aid over his left eye seemed to be the only outward indication of the other wounds he'd received from Bobbie McGregor's horse.

"I heard there might be some lemonade in here."

"Indeed there is." She snagged a plastic tumbler from the shelf, turning her back to him so he couldn't see the rosy heat that surely meant red blotches crawled across her neck and cheeks. "Have a seat on the porch and I'll bring you a glass. They took all the ice for the ice cream maker."

"I think the girls are making more of a mess than they are ice cream." She heard no *clump, clump* of his crutches. He still stood there. "I reckon I can carry my own glass of lemonade. No need for coddling."

"Which hand were you planning to carry the glass in?" She let her gaze fix on his crutches. "It's not coddling. It's neighborly."

He opened his mouth, then closed it.

She managed to pour the lemonade without spilling a drop. She almost chortled at the thought. *Lord, take this silliness from me.* "I'll carry it to the porch. You first."

"Nee, you first."

A standoff. The man was stubborn.

She tromped past him and through the doorway without looking back. Butch followed her, making a wide berth around the stranger on crutches. On the porch she settled Levi's glass on the bushel basket turned upside down between two haggard-looking lawn chairs so used that the seats hung low in memory of the many users' behinds that had sat in them in days past.

Butch headed directly to the ice cream maker. The hund had a fondness for ice cubes. The girls shooed him away, but not before Hazel tossed him a cube he caught neatly in his wide mouth.

Abigail had disappeared to unknown parts, leaving Nyla, Ida, and Hazel to take turns cranking the ice cream maker. They seemed to be arguing over whose turn it was. Susan could remember what it was like to consider it a badge of honor to crank the ice cream. Now her shoulders and arms were thankful to let someone else wear the badge.

"Have a seat. Do you want some cookies to hold you over until the barbecue?" She swished at the seat with her apron, dispersing a cloud of mosquitoes that buzzed her ears as they departed in an angry huff. "I have peanut butter and sugar."

"Nee. Keep me company for a bit."

For a second it seemed the mosquitoes still buzzed her ears, making it hard to understand. "What?"

Levi eased into the chair, his face creased with pain. "Keep a man company. I could use some adult conversation. All Martha ever says to me is *Rest, rest, rest,* and *How's the pain, how's the pain, did you take your pill? Why didn't you take your pill?*"

His mimic of his daughter's high-pitched, anxious voice was nearly perfect.

"She's concerned for your well-being because she loves you."

"I know that." He sniffed. "The boys are too busy to talk. Between the shop and the farm, I barely see them at the supper table and then they fall into bed, tuckered out from carrying the load that is heavy on their shoulders."

"They all have broad shoulders, just like you do."

Had she just commented on his broad shoulders? The earlier heat returned, this time in scalding measure. "I mean—"

"Sit down. You're giving me a crick in my neck."

Susan sat. Silence ensued, broken only by the girls' giggles at the other end of the porch. The late-afternoon heat bore down on her. Sweat trickled down her temples. She took a surreptitious swipe at it. A horsefly buzzed her nose. She swatted it away. "Did you know Bee County wasn't named for bees?"

Levi's woolly gray eyebrows danced over his dark-emerald eyes, causing the bandage to buckle and smooth. "Don't reckon I did."

"Nee, it was named for Bernard E. Bee Sr., who served as secretary of state and secretary of war for the Republic of Texas."

"The Republic of Texas?"

"Jah, Texas was a country. More than once I think. I can't keep the Texas history all straight the way Mordecai does."

"So this tidbit of information came from Mordecai. Figures."

"What do you mean?"

"He does love a good piece of trivia, your brother does."

"He does."

They both chuckled. The silence that followed didn't seem as uncomfortable.

Topics of conversation were as scarce as rain in the summer in South Texas during the long drought that seemed to perhaps have passed this year. Kinner. A person could never go wrong with the weather and kinner. "I think your concern for Martha that you mentioned at the school picnic is no longer a concern."

"How so?"

"What do you think of my nephew Jacob?"

"Seems like a decent young man."

"He is."

"And?"

"They might be playing volleyball together about now."

Levi tapped his boot on the wood slats under his feet. "I always liked a good game of volleyball." His tone was wistful.

"You'll play again. Before you know it."

"My horse-training days are over, though."

Susan certainly hoped so. "Leave it to the younger folks."

"Are you saying I'm old?"

"I'm saying neither one of us is as young as we used to be." Too old for courting, it seemed. "That can be a good thing."

"How so?"

"An older person knows what he wants and has enough experience to recognize if what he wants is something he should have."

"I know I have enough kinner."

Maybe Mordecai was right. Maybe Levi's thoughts had run parallel to her own. To the heart of the matter. How could he know this was so important to her? Or was it a shot in the dark? "Every one of them is a gift from Gott, don't you think?"

"He gives and He takes away."

"Because He knows what is best."

Levi grunted, whether from pain or agreement Susan couldn't say. "I think a person should keep his heart open to the possibility that he hasn't seen all that Gott can do with a situation. Gott's plan is enormous, mammoth, and so incredibly vast that we have no idea how great and gracious it truly is."

"Now I know where Mordecai gets it."

"What? His faith?"

"His gift of words."

"All our gifts come from Gott, including kinner. He decides when enough is enough."

The silence settled again. Susan let the cooing of mourning doves settle the tremor in her chest. She had overstepped her bounds. How did she know when enough was enough? Levi had his nine kinner. She had none. Would being mudder to a brood that large fill the void in her heart where her own kinner surely should be?

"I expected to see Lupe and Diego running around here when I came home." His gaze dropped to his hands in his lap. He bent his head as if studying something. He had something silver, a tool, in his hand. He turned it round and round. "Surprising how a person can get attached to strays."

That was the truth, whether the stray was a hund with a black patch around one eye that gave him the rakish look of a pirate, or kinner who taught her that a hund was called a *perro* in their language. "I keep thinking they'll show up again. Jesse is searching for them at the detention center. He goes up once a week to take donations."

"More likely one of those Border Patrol agents has caught up with them and carted them back to the border."

Or they made it to San Antonio and found a way to start a new life. The life their grandmother sent them here to find. Susan and her family might never know the truth, but it was nicer to think of the fine possibilities rather than the dark and painful ones. A person had to have hope. For a better future. For herself and for others.

She fought the urge to squirm in her chair. His squeaked as if he'd given in to the desire. "Don't get me wrong."

"Wrong about what?"

"I understand wanting children. Catherine and I wanted them, all of them." Pain painted the words a white-hot color. "Until the last one. Gott forgive me."

Susan forced herself to look at his face. His raw pain etched lines around his eyes and mouth. His gritted teeth made the pulse jump in his jaw. His Adam's apple bobbed. He cleared his throat but said nothing more.

A mockingbird trilled and chirped its lament in the mesquite tree that offered a poor excuse for shade over the buggy parked in front of the house. Susan breathed in and out, in and out. "Gott does forgive you. He knows what it's like to lose a loved one."

"He does, I know. But it perplexes me that I should have so little faith that I can't get past this one thing. Our days are numbered on this earth. We pass through. My fraa is in the arms of her loving Savior. Why do I give it a second thought?"

"You wish to avoid such pain in the future, I imagine." Every inch of her fingers ached with the desire to squeeze his hand. She focused on the mockingbird's tune. "It can't be done. With every opportunity for love and happiness comes the chance that we might instead encounter pain and loneliness and despair."

"How did you get so wise?"

"Following Mordecai around?"

"I doubt that. More likely it was the other way around."

"I read a lot."

"Figured as much."

"Why do you say that?"

"The way you talk. It's not like most Plain women."

"I suppose it isn't." She wouldn't apologize for a voracious appetite for words. It held her in good stead in her job of teaching. "But Gott gave me a brain. I see no shame in using His gift."

"Nor I."

She swallowed an inexplicable lump in her throat. "What is that in your hand?"

His gaze lifted to hers. "What?"

"In your hand, what do you have?"

He glanced down as if only then realizing he held something. "It's a basket stamp."

"What's it for?"

"I use it to carve a pattern on the saddles. The fancier ones, anyway."

He missed his work. "It must take a certain kind of person to hand carve a leather saddle. How long have you been doing it?"

"I apprenticed with two different saddle makers as a teenager. Back home." His gaze went to the horizon as if he sought to see that far, to Ohio and his youth. "I like doing the carving. Some find it tedious, but I like being alone with my work and concentrating on it and nothing else."

"How long does it take you to make a saddle?"

He turned the basket stamp over and over, weaving it through his fingers, over his knuckles, and back. "It takes about two weeks to make the basic saddle, but I need another week to do the carving. If everyone leaves me alone."

"You want to be left alone?"

Her question seemed to hover in the air, heavy and soaked with a meaning she hadn't contemplated before uttering it. His Adam's apple bobbed. His hands stilled. "Nee, not necessarily." His gaze wandered to her face and back to the horizon. "Sometimes."

"But not always."

"Nee, not always."

"Aenti, aenti, it's ready, it's ready." Hazel bounded across the porch, a blue plastic bowl in one hand. In it she'd heaped a small scoop of strawberry ice cream. The girls had managed to get only a small bit of rock salt in the creamy concoction. "Try it, come on, try it."

Her delighted impatience broke the thick tension that permeated the air only a second before. Susan smiled at the little girl. How could life be anything but good when a person had a stepniece like Hazel and fresh, homemade strawberry ice cream? When she sat in a lawn chair on the porch on the Fourth of July with a man who might be starting to look ahead rather than behind? She took the scarred spoon from Hazel's plump hand and held it out to Levi. "You first."

"Nee." He looked sorely tempted but held his hand up like a stop sign. "Women first."

"You don't have to tell me twice." She loaded the spoon and lifted it to her mouth. She couldn't help herself. She hummed with delight. "Yum. You girls did a fine job. It's delicious. Those fresh strawberries really hit the spot."

"It's gut. It's gut." Hazel jumped up and down. "Now you, Levi, now you."

Levi didn't take the spoon. His gaze met Susan's. Something there made her cheeks warm despite the cool residue of ice cream in her mouth. His gaze locked on hers, his green eyes wide and seeking. Susan fought to take a breath. "Go on, try it. I don't have cooties."

He took the spoon. His fingers, hard and calloused, brushed hers. His face reddened. To Susan's everlasting relief, his gaze dropped. "I'm not afraid of your germs."

"You're not afraid of much." Except more pain and loss. Fear could keep a person from joy and love too. "Which is gut because there's nothing to fear here."

His head came up. His gaze sought hers as he spooned the ice cream into his mouth. His eyes closed and he smiled. "That is gut."

She couldn't be sure if he meant the ice cream or her statement. Until he winked at her.

THIRTY-TWO

Reds, blues, and whites glittered overhead, giving the dark sky a patriotic air. Rebekah leaned back on her propped-up arms on the tattered gray blanket crackly with dead grass and cockleburs. It smelled like the mesquite wood fire they'd lit to cook the hot dogs. She stared up at the short-lived yet beautiful sight. Life was like that. Short and sometimes beautiful. She loved the Fourth of July.

Now that the sun had gone down, the heat had begun to dissipate. The mosquitoes and flies were out in full force, however. She batted away one and then the other, slapping at her neck and her arms. Butch curled up on the blanket next to her, his occasional deep-throated whine reminding her that he truly did not approve of all this sound and fury.

Her tummy was full of hot dogs, chips, pickles, and homemade ice cream complete with chunks of fresh strawberries. Even her ankle had stopped throbbing. If Diego and Lupe were here, she might even consider herself content. But no sign of the two wayward runaways. Wherever they were, she hoped they weren't frightened by the pop and crackle that could sound very much like the gunfire they experienced in their own country.

She let her mind wander to the ride down by the pond after the singing. And the way it had ended. Heat rushed to her face. She turned the memory over in her mind like a prism that caught the sunlight, creating a new, beautiful pattern each time. The pressure of Tobias's hand on her back, the softness of his lips on hers, the warmth of his breath on her cheek. Every moment had been precious. Now she would have to spoil it by telling him about David. David and Bobbie. She didn't want to be the one to tell him his brother was meandering off the path onto the tracks of an oncoming freight train loaded with hurt and pain for everyone.

She sighed. So much for enjoying the evening. Being content. Her thoughts seemed to flit back and forth like the birds in the trees, from branch to branch.

"Such a sad sigh. What are you thinking about?"

Tobias. A low growl rumbled in Butch's throat. He raised his head, eyed Tobias, and let it drop. Acutely aware of being sprawled out on a blanket, she struggled to a sitting position. "It's nothing." She'd been thinking of him and here he was. She'd have to tell him. "I mean, it's a lot of things."

"A lot on your mind then?"

"There's something I need to tell you. Do you want to sit?"

He shook his head. "Me first. I have a surprise for you."

"A surprise?" The wave of pleasure overwhelmed her apprehension for a few fleeting seconds. She looked around. "Where? Here? What is it?"

"Come on. Hurry. You'll like it. A lot."

"Tobias! Come quick. They're back!" Rueben raced across the straggly grass, puffs of dirt pluming in the air behind his bare feet. "It's Diego and Lupe. They arrested them!"

"Nee, they didn't arrest them." Tobias held out his hand. She took it without hesitation and he pulled her to her feet. "I brought them home. For you."

His eyes glinted with some emotion she couldn't quite understand, but it didn't matter. Lupe and Diego were home. "They're home? You found them? They're really home?"

As home as two kinner from a foreign country could be in a tiny Amish district in South Texas. She flung herself at Tobias, her arms slapped around his waist in a no-holds-barred hug. "Danki. Danki."

Tobias's arms slid around her, pressing her against his chest. "It's for them too." He stepped back and peeled her arms from around his waist. His fingers brushed her cheek, warm and solid against her skin. "I wish they could stay, but they're here now. Come see them."

They couldn't stay. Rebekah shoved the thought aside and embraced the joy that they were alive. They weren't dead by the road. They weren't sold into slavery by evil men. They had survived.

His hand tight around hers, Tobias strode across the yard. Rebekah hopped and skipped to keep up, thankful she felt no pain in her ankle. A Bee County sheriff's car, covered with dust, was parked on the dirt road, headlights casting a long, filmy light on the mesquite and live oak trees that dotted the space between the house and the barn. The engine rumbled. Behind it sat a blue minivan. Jesse? Leila? What were they doing here?

A dark figure stood in the beam from the headlights. Rebekah struggled to make him out. Jesse. It was Jesse talking to a man in a uniform wearing a white cowboy hat. They both turned as Tobias approached. Rebekah kept going, drawn to the two small figures huddled in the backseat of the minivan. The windows were propped open. Lupe had her arm around Diego. The boy's dirty face had tracks where tears had slid down his cheeks. Dark circles like bruises ringed Lupe's eyes. She looked every bit as scared and feral as she had that first day at the schoolhouse.

"Lupe, Diego, I'm so glad to see you." She tugged on the door. "Are you all right? Where have you been? We've missed you."

Lupe shrugged. Diego opened his mouth. A forlorn hiccup of a sob escaped. Lupe's arm tightened around her brother. "Está bien, hermano, está bien."

"Bang, bang, lots of bang, bang." Another sob.

"They're fireworks. For fun. Not bang-bang of guns." Rebekah slid onto the seat. The van smelled of French fries, greasy hamburgers, little-boy sweat, and unwashed bodies. The remnants of a fast-food meal littered the seat on the other side. Diego clutched a sweating soda cup in one hand. He'd bitten the straw until it was bent and collapsed. Rebekah tugged it from his hands and set it on the floor mat. "We'll take care of you, I promise."

"Nee, don't make promises." Jesse slid into the front seat and turned around so he faced her. "Wally has agreed to let me take them home to stay until their hearing, but it doesn't help that they ran away the first time."

"Your house? I want them to stay here."

"I know you do, but Wally has strict orders to turn over any illegal aliens to ICE. Letting them stay with us is a huge concession on his part. One that can get him in a lot of trouble."

Rebekah slipped her arm around Diego and hugged hard. "Where did you find them?"

"We found them Dumpster diving outside the Dairy Queen. Then Wally found us. He's a member of our church. He's a good guy, so he's trying to give us a break."

"Dumpster diving?"

"Looking for food." Jesse sighed. "Wally agreed to bring them out here so they could see you and you could tell them it's okay for them to stay with Leila and me. We'll take care of them. He thought they would enjoy the fireworks, but it doesn't look like they are much in favor of things that go bang-bang."

Rebekah snaked her arm behind Lupe's shoulders so she could tug both of them closer. "I want them here."

"Stay with Bekah." Lupe shook her head in a vigorous nod. "No run. Stay with Bekah."

"We have to follow the law. It's the only chance we have of getting custody in the long run."

"Is there really a chance of that?" Rebekah tightened her hug. She wanted them to stay. She wanted to scrub Diego's face and wash his hands. She wanted to strip off those dirty clothes and help him into something clean so he could get a good night's sleep next to Caleb. "You're not family."

"It depends on whether they find the father. If they can't, we might have a chance. But it's about what's best for them. To be with their blood relative. Or with us."

"They wouldn't know their dad if they saw him on the street."

"It's the best we can do. To be honest, I don't know how long it'll be before they have the hearing, and Leila and I will be moving—"

"I know. To Dallas." Rebekah couldn't keep the accusation from her voice. Jesse had taken her sister away once. Now he would take her even farther from her family and the life she should be living. "What happens if you leave and they haven't had their hearing?"

"It will make it harder for them to stay. They need a sponsor."

"Then you have to stay."

"It's not that simple. The congregation has helped raise the money for my tuition and our living expenses. I'm enrolled. I can't let them down."

"But you can let these little ones down?" That wasn't fair, but life wasn't fair. "Look at this face and tell me you can't wait until the next semester to start your new life?"

Jesse groaned and faced the front. He didn't want to think about it, but he would. He was that kind of man. A good man. "We'll play it by ear for as long as we can. God will provide. He has a plan for these children."

"He brought them into our lives for a reason. Maybe it was to show you that your calling is here, not in Dallas."

"Don't twist things to suit your wants and needs." Jesse swiveled to stare at her, his glare hard. "You want Leila to stay here because us moving to Dallas is like losing her all over again. But we have to go where God calls us."

"How do you know where that is?"

"You listen for His voice and you watch for signs."

Rebekah pointed at the top of Diego's head with one finger. "What do you call this?"

"We have to go." Jesse leaned out the window and waved at Wally, who stood talking to Tobias in front of the car. "Back to town, I mean."

"They're counting on you." Rebekah gave Lupe one last hug. The girl's sob reverberated in her ear. "I'm counting on you."

"I won't let you down."

He already had and he knew it.

Wally leaned into the front window. "Ready to go? You coming with us, ma'am?"

"Nee." She found it almost impossible to release her grip

from Lupe's arm. She hugged her one more time. Lupe's thin arms held on tight. Rebekah forced herself to slide across the seat. "I'll see you soon. Very soon. Jesse is good. He'll take good care of you. I promise."

Jesse started the engine. "I promise too."

Only the presence of Mordecai, Mudder, and the other adults on the porch, watching, kept Rebekah from burying her head in Tobias's chest. Instead she stood within inches of him, aware with an almost-unbearable intensity of his comforting presence, watching until the taillights of both cars disappeared into the darkness.

"I'm sorry."

"Don't be." She turned to face him, her back to Mudder's stare. "You found them. That's gut. Very gut."

His hand came up, then dropped to his side. "They'll be back. We'll bring them back."

Rebekah sidled closer. "I need to talk to you. About David."

THIRTY-THREE

Silence could be the best blessing of all. Tobias let the brush ride along Butterscotch's long, graceful back. Slow, even strokes that matched his heartbeat. The sound of hay crunching in the mare's mouth crackled in the quiet. The smells of horse, manure, and hay blended in a memory that went back to his childhood. All things simple and peaceful and certain were tied to those early memories of mucking out the stalls and feeding the animals. He longed for that peacefulness again. It seemed so far away, what with his daed's injuries and the situation with Lupe and Diego. And now this thing with David.

Rebekah hadn't wanted to tell him, that was obvious. Her voice had quivered with the knowledge that it would hurt him. He had taken it well. He hadn't yelled at the messenger or showed his emotion. There would be time for that later. When he confronted David about where he'd gone after Mordecai dropped him at the house. David hadn't been at the fireworks. Hadn't eaten ice cream with the kinner.

Daisy was missing from the stall. Which was why Tobias stood here brushing Butterscotch and waiting when he'd rather be in his bed sleeping.

He tightened his own grip on the brush and kept at his job. Butterscotch tossed her head and nickered as if enjoying the rubdown. When all else failed, a person had to keep doing what he knew how to do. Tobias had experienced what David felt for Bobbie. He knew how it felt to want something so badly and know it would only cause heartache for the ones he loved. He'd made the right choice. His feelings for Rebekah proved that.

He would talk to David. He would make him understand.

He snorted. Butterscotch whinnied as if in response. As if she knew what Tobias knew. His daed had moved the family across the country to get him away from Serena. From temptation. Only to find it in a new person with another son.

A cheery whistling sound reverberated in the silence he'd cherished only seconds earlier. He swiveled, brush in the air, his other hand still on Butterscotch's back. David strode through the open barn door, leading Daisy behind him. He murmured under his breath. Was he singing? The words didn't sound familiar.

"What did you say?"

"Ach, you're out here. You should be in bed asleep by now." David turned his back, one hand on Daisy's neck. The smell of a woman permeated the air. The smell of roses. The smell of Bobbie McGregor. "I figured everybody would be in bed by now."

"That's obvious."

"Did a cocklebur get under your saddle?"

"Where have you been? You missed the barbecue and the fireworks. Rebekah said you came back with her and Mordecai."

"Little tattletale. She told you, didn't she?"

"She's worried about you."

"I'm fine." David grinned. "I had barbecue. It just wasn't hot dogs cooked on sticks over a trash can."

"You went back and spent the evening with Bobbie McGregor after Mordecai spoke to you."

"I thought you of all people would understand. You would be with Serena right now if it weren't for Daed. You know you would."

Heat washed over Tobias. His plan to simply talk to his brother had gone awry already. He swallowed his anger and worked to corral emotions that galloped in all directions. "How do you know what I would or wouldn't do?"

"I heard you and Daed arguing. Those walls were mighty thin in the old house."

"Daed doesn't argue."

"He says his piece and calls it a day."

"Right now he doesn't need the aggravation. He's still trying to heal. He's trying to do too much too soon. You're not helping."

"You told him about Bobbie."

And cause the man more anguish? "Nee. I was hoping you'd come to your senses so I wouldn't have to do it."

"You don't have to do anything."

"So you're thinking of leaving the district?"

David's shoulders heaved in a mammoth shrug. He was so barrel chested it was a wonder his shirt didn't rip. The bravado of a few seconds earlier disappeared. "I don't know what to do."

Tobias understood the despair that permeated those words. "Back away while you still can."

"That's the thing." David wrapped his stubby fingers in Daisy's mane. His expression was hidden in the barn's shadowy darkness. "I don't know if I still can."

"You can. Stay away from her."

"Every night I pray and I confess my sins and I promise to do better." He raised his head, letting Tobias see his red eyes. "Every morning I wake up and the first thing I think of is her and when I can see her again."

Tobias's heart lurched in his chest. He remembered that feeling, that awful aching sensation, that void that simply had to be filled and could only be filled by one person. "I felt that way about Serena."

"How did you stop?"

"Just like a person who has an addiction. Cold turkey. I simply refused to give in to the desire."

"I'm not that strong." David rested his forehead on the horse's neck. "I'm not sure I want to be that strong."

"You are."

He lifted his head and gazed at Tobias head-on. "I think I love her."

"You hardly know her. Besides, it doesn't matter."

"How can you say love doesn't matter? It's everything."

"Loving a woman isn't as important as being right with Gott."

"Gott made us to love women. And them us." David led Daisy into her stall and slammed the gate shut. "I'm going to bed."

"Gott expects us to exercise good judgment and avoid temptation."

"How do you know what Gott expects?"

"I listen on Sunday morning."

"I listen too." David brushed straw from his shirt and stomped toward the door. "I listen to my heart and my head. Life is short. Look at how we lost Mudder. Look what it did to Daed. He's still broken after six years. A person should take the love that drops in his lap while he can."

"It might be better to do without an earthly love than to give up the heavenly one."

"You really believe if I leave the district, I'm defying Gott?" David paused at the door and swiveled. "How do I know He didn't send Bobbie to me?"

Tobias couldn't answer that question. He'd asked it himself about Serena. "All I know is I wasn't willing to give up my family and my faith for an Englisch woman. Are you?"

Emotion etched David's face, making him look older than his years. "I'm still trying to figure that out, Bruder. Give me time. Don't tell Daed."

Tobias dropped the brush and strode to his brother. He put one hand on his shoulder. "I'm asking you." He stopped, forced to swallow the emotion that threatened to burst in his throat. "Don't do this to him. His heart has only just begun to mend."

"I'm not doing this to hurt him." David's Adam's apple bobbed. His gaze broke from Tobias's and landed on the night sky over his shoulder. "If I could do anything different, I would. I can promise you that."

He broke away from Tobias's grip, whirled, and fled.

Tobias watched him go for a few seconds. Then he turned back to the barn. The chances of sleep coming anytime soon were slim to none.

THIRTY-FOUR

Susan padded barefoot through the front room headed to the kitchen. She'd spent too much time on her letters to Lilly and Thomas. She tried to write them at least two or three times a month. Lilly returned the favor with great regularity. Thomas, less so. Her youngest bruder did not like pen and paper. Or talking. He was the opposite of Mordecai. Just as Lilly was bony to Susan's rounded figure.

The patter of rain on the roof and the low hum of conversation between Phineas and Mordecai as they jarred honey harvested before the rains came had lulled her. She'd forgotten all about the time. Time to start supper. Rebekah was helping Martha with house cleaning and laundry. She was spending a great deal of time at the Byler farm this summer. Abigail had gone to deliver a baby. Susan slipped into the kitchen, contemplating whether she had celery and carrots to add to the leftover chicken to make chicken noodle casserole.

Phineas glanced up from handing a bowl of honey to Mordecai, who began pouring it into the jars. "Good first harvest."

"Gut. I noticed the shelf was empty when I was in the store yesterday. Sales have been gut." She opened the door to the propane-operated refrigerator and snagged a plastic container of chicken she'd deboned and chopped into cubes earlier in the day. "Are you staying for supper?"

Her nephew picked up a pen and wrote on a label. "Nee, Deborah is expecting me."

"I'm making chicken noodle casserole." A dish Phineas normally couldn't resist, but married life had changed him. He rarely strayed far from his fraa and son. "You could fetch Deborah. She might like a rest from cooking."

"She had enchiladas in the oven the last time I stopped by."

"Then maybe we should go to your house and I should rest from cooking."

She laughed and Phineas joined her. Mordecai's gruff belly laugh did not mingle with theirs. She glanced his way. He had that look of a man deep in thought. Phineas shrugged and stood. He slapped his hat on his head. "I better head that way. I have a sow about to deliver and I haven't seen the kinner since morning."

A mann and a daed who could barely stand to be away from his small family. Rebekah hardly recognized her nephew as the silent, morose young man who'd been so sure the scars on his face would keep him from finding love in his life. A reminder that Gott had answered her prayers on many occasions.

Mordecai still didn't speak.

Phineas elbowed him on his way out the door. "Wake up there, Daed."

His father grunted and dumped dirty utensils in a tub of soapy water. "Tomorrow then."

"Tomorrow."

Susan waited until Phineas disappeared through the door. "What are you so deep in thought about?"

"I'm not."

"You are." As his sister she knew Mordecai better than anyone—even Abigail. "You're like an old man half asleep on a bench outside the dawdy haus."

He ladled honey onto a slab of bread and handed it to her. It didn't matter how close it was to suppertime; room always existed for fresh honey. "You and Rebekah have been spending a lot of time at the Bylers'."

She wiped at honey that dribbled down her chin with a finger she then licked clean. "Jah."

"How are things going with . . . all that?"

"All what?" She uncovered the plate filled with homemade noodles ready to be cooked.

"What we talked about before."

"Nothing to talk about."

"Susan."

"Mordecai."

"I know it's none of my business—"

"Then?"

"You're as crabby as Mudder used to be when Daed went to Missouri and was gone a week."

"Why did you bring this up?"

Mordecai patted the chair across from his. "Sit, Schweschder."

"I have supper to make."

"It'll wait." His tone brooked no argument. It was his deacon voice, not his bruder voice. "Now."

She sat.

"I spent some time with Levi at the hospital and now, since he came home."

"Jah."

"He's a good man with a good heart."

"Yet there sounds like there's a *but* in there somewhere."

Mordecai eased into the chair across the table, his knees cracking and popping like the old man she'd accused him of being only minutes earlier. He splayed calloused, sun-beaten hands across the pine boards that separated them. "There are scars on that heart."

"I know about the scars. They're an awful lot like yours."

"Mine have disappeared in recent years."

"His could as well."

He cleared his throat. For once her bruder looked uncertain, even embarrassed, a rare moment in the many years they had known and cared for each other.

"What is it, Bruder?"

He shook his head. "You sacrificed for us, for me. As a young girl and later, when I . . . when we needed you after the accident."

"It was no sacrifice. I did what family does."

"You gave up much and I want you to know, I mean, I never said it, I should've said it. I value your sacrifice."

Susan stood and bustled to the counter. "This casserole won't make itself."

"Schweschder, I want you to have what I have, if that's your heart's desire."

She pulled a paring knife from the drawer and swiped a large carrot from the pile she'd cleaned earlier. "Gott's will be done."

"Jah. Levi hasn't married all these years for a reason."

"Twelve years passed before you found the fraa for whom you waited."

"Gott blessed me, and I pray He does the same for you."

"What makes you think Levi is not that man?"

"He hasn't come to grips with his loss."

The image of Levi sitting in the chair next to her on the Fourth of July floated before her. The pain in his voice reverberated around her. "It's time he looked forward rather than backward."

"Sometimes it's easier said than done. He lost his fraa in childbirth. A moment of great joy confounded by terrible loss. Such a confusing, terrible confluence would change a man."

She slapped the carrot on the cutting board and chopped in a rhythmic motion born of years of experience. "You think he might not want to take a chance on such a thing happening again?"

"I think you have sacrificed much for others in your life and now it's time to consider how much more you're willing to give up." The *clomp, clomp* of his boots and scent of sweat told her he'd risen and stood close by. "You're still young. Young enough to be a mudder if you think that's something you want."

"He might not want it, I know. He's said as much, in that garbled way men do."

"It's in the way he looks at Liam. Such pain and joy in one dreadful bundle. It hurts a heart to see a man so torn over the blessing of a son."

Her throat ached with the desire to let go a floodgate of emotion. She breathed and picked up another carrot. "Love can heal anything."

"I hope you're right." He paused in the doorway. "I hope you plan to make an extra-big casserole."

She could stretch a casserole with extra noodles with the best of the fraas out there. "Why is that?"

"I invited Levi and his kinner for supper."

Susan turned, paring knife in midair. After a second she remembered to close her mouth. Her brother had already fled.

THIRTY-FIVE

Susan scraped the food from her plate onto the saucer she kept on the back porch for Butch. The hund was getting a delicacy tonight. The chicken had turned to sawdust in her mouth the minute she peeked across to the men's table and saw Levi looking at her. He'd looked away right quick and so had she. Still, he'd seen her looking at him. She hadn't been able to swallow more than two bites of her supper after that. *Silly woman.* She scraped harder.

Butch raced around the corner and came to a screeching halt in front of her, his nails making a *tickety-tackity* sound on the wooden porch. "Go on, you old hund, eat my supper. You'll like it better than I did."

She turned and found Levi standing in the doorway, propped up on his crutches. "Do you always have to sneak up on a person?"

"I didn't sneak." He waved a crutch. "Hard for a man to do on these things."

"Did you get enough supper?" She waited for him to move so she could get past him and back to her dirty dishes. "There's more dump cake if you're interested. Kaffi too."

"Nee." He didn't move. "I was thinking I'd like to get a look at a couple of things at the shop. Tobias is working on a saddle for a ranch hand over by Victoria. I usually do the fancy work, but he's not wanting to take me to work. Says it's too soon."

He stopped, his breathing hard as if he'd sprinted around the bases in a game of kickball. Why was he telling her this? "I figure I'm a grown man. If I decide to go to my shop, I go."

"So what's keeping you from going?"

"Nothing, I reckon."

This was the strangest conversation yet. His face with its skin the pallor of a man fresh out of the hospital turned a deep red. Susan wanted to take pity on him, but she couldn't for the life of her figure out what to say.

"So you want to see the shop?"

Bells dinged in her head. She was denser than the densest stone. He was asking her to take a ride with him. "Are you sure you're up to it?"

His mouth, with its full lips, turned down. He positively glowered at her. "Not you too?"

"Sorry, sorry!" She put her hand on his. Without thinking. When she did think, heat exploded in her head. She snatched her hand back quicker than if he were a rattlesnake curled up on her front step. "I mean, jah, I can go. If you want me to."

"If you want to."

"I want to."

"Your bruder is loaning me a buggy." He slung himself backward on the crutches, leaving a space just wide enough for her to squeeze through. "I'll leave the wagon for Tobias to take the kinner home once he's worn them out."

Susan took the opportunity and swiped past him, inhaling his scent of wood and sweat and soap. "I should finish the dishes."

"We're doing them." Abigail stood at the counter, both arms plunged into the tub of soapy water, a grin plastered across her smug face. "You did all the cooking. Let Martha and the girls and me take care of the cleaning."

She cast a knowing glance at Levi, who clomped past, his gaze on his boots, as if he hadn't just asked her to take a ride with him.

"Go on, take a load off." Abigail cocked her head toward him. "Go find something to do."

She knew. She surely did.

Martha should do the same. And Rebekah. Where was Rebekah? She should be out with Tobias. Because they were young, they would go later. They needed less sleep. Muttering to herself, Susan marched through the front room with a quick, surreptitious glance at Mordecai. He sprawled in the rocking chair, the newspaper in his lap. He pretended to read it, but she was fairly certain he was actually dozing. Had he known when Levi asked to borrow the buggy that he intended to ask Susan along for the ride? Mr. Matchmaker.

She slipped out front and found Levi waiting in the buggy. "Quick, before the kinner catch on and want to go along."

Or realized Levi had asked Teacher to take a ride with him. What would his kinner think? Were they ready for their daed to court? Was this courting?

Susan hopped into the buggy and slid onto the seat, careful to keep a decent amount of space between them. Heat shimmered in the air. She patted her face with her sleeve. "Hot tonight."

The weather. Always the fallback position. Levi nodded but said nothing.

The ride was quiet, but not uncomfortably so. Something

about Levi seemed different. Away from the house. Away from his kinner. He seemed to simply be. He was in control of the buggy, maybe not of his life, but he seemed content to be in this moment.

She settled back and waited. Twenty minutes later they pulled into the new saddle shop. Levi manhandled his crutches, easing himself to the ground. He came around to her side as if to help her down. She smiled at his rueful expression. "It's okay. I've been getting out of buggies all my life."

She waited while he unlocked the door and opened it. "You first."

It was warm and dank in the shop. Levi set aside a crutch and began opening windows with one hand. She helped even though his expression said he could handle it on his own. A half-finished saddle sat on a saddletree in front of the line of windows on the east. "Tobias likes the morning sun when he works." Levi eased onto a stool near the tree and let the crutch rest on his outstretched leg. His hand smoothed the light cream-colored cowhide. "He has a nice touch."

"He learned from you, I imagine."

"Have you ever seen how a saddle is made?"

"Nee."

"You start with a whole cow and a sheep."

Susan didn't know whether to laugh or simply nod. "A whole cow."

"The hide. You get two long pieces of cowhide, basically both sides of the cow. And you need all the wool of a sheep for the underside that's closest to the horse."

"I see."

He seemed to warm to his subject. "I take a big oval piece of leather and get it soaking wet and throw it over the tree and start banging on it, getting some shape to it. Then I trim away a part and shape it some more and trim it some more, shaping it and shaping it."

Susan nodded, more interested in the way he moved his hands as he explained it to her. In his head he was making that saddle. "Not much gets wasted then?"

"Nee, not much. Some of it has to be sewn to the cantle. I take about a sixteen-inch piece of leather lace and take this awl and make holes through about an inch of leather and use two needles to sew it down by hand. I can do one in an hour if everyone leaves me alone, but it wears you out."

"Are you worn out, then, from all these years of making saddles?"

"Nee."

There was a point to this. Some reason he wanted to tell her this. Wanted her to see this. "Not any more than Gott is tired of working on you, then?"

His gaze lifted and he smiled for the first time. She felt like a student receiving a good grade. "I think we're like that leather in Gott's hands. He keeps shaping us and shaping us, smoothing away the rough edges and cutting away the excesses. He has a pile of shavings around His feet and He keeps smoothing and shaping, thinking eventually He'll see that honed character, that person He expects each of us to be."

"I reckon you're right." Susan eased onto a footstool a full yard away from Levi. She cupped her hands in her lap, unable to take her gaze from his chiseled face. "Sooner or later, He'd like to look up and say, 'It is good.'"

Levi nodded. He stood, his weight swaying against the crutches. "Exactly what I think. Would you like to try carving something?"

"I would." Her hands were trembling. He would see and he would know this was the first time in years she'd been alone with a man. The quiver in her voice surely had given her away. "I don't know if I'll be any good at it."

"The fun is in the trying. Come here."

She followed him to the counter made of bare plywood. Rows of small boxes held a cornucopia of tools. Above them, he and Tobias had hammered horseshoes onto the wall so leather laces could be hung from them. The air was ripe with humidity and dust and the smell of wood shavings and leather.

Levi handed her the basket stamp he'd held that night on the porch on the Fourth of July. He laid a square patch of leather in front of her, leaning so close she could see the beads of sweat on his neck. He leaned the crutches against the counter and balanced his weight against it. "Hold it like this."

His fingers wrapped around hers, calloused, strong, yet gentle. Her breathing sounded loud in her own ears. "I don't know if I—"

"Like this." His hand guided hers and the pattern began to appear, each notch laid against the next, neat and delicate. "Would you like to make a leaf?"

"I . . . jah . . ."

He leaned closer. All she had to do was meet him halfway. Those missed opportunities of years past would fade away and she might find what she'd been looking for all these years. "Levi."

"I know." He slipped back a step and held out another tool.

"This is the camouflage tool. It hides things. You use it to finish out lines and corners of other designs."

The man spoke in riddles. She held out her hand. Instead of giving her the new tool, he took her hand and pulled her toward him. "Levi."

"I know." The crutches fell to the floor. He leaned down until his head hovered above her face. His eyes held a torment she knew must be a reflection of her own. His pulse jumped in his jaw. "Gott help me."

He kissed her. Or maybe she kissed him. Susan couldn't be sure who moved first, but his lips touched hers and it didn't matter. She found herself on her tiptoes, trying to reach more of him. His hands were on her shoulders and then cupping her cheeks. His arms wrapped around her waist and lifted her so she could slide her own around his neck. His lips moved from hers and left small, delicate kisses on her cheeks, her forehead, and then her neck. "What is it about you?" he whispered. "All this time I didn't think of another woman, until you."

"I'm not known to be irresistible." She tried to make a joke about it, but heat scurried across her neck and burned her cheeks. Truth be told, she didn't care. She wanted him to kiss her again. Soon. "Is it that I'm your kinner's teacher?"

His chuckle tickled her ear. "It doesn't seem likely."

Her feet still dangled in the air. He should put her down. She shouldn't rest on his chest this way. She found herself hoping he wouldn't. Ever. "What are we doing?"

"Are you so old you don't remember courting?"

"I'm not old—"

A high-pitched laugh mingled with a lower, rumbling one.

The door opened. In tumbled David and Bobbie McGregor. Levi's son had his arm around Bobbie's shoulders. "Daed, what are you doing here with her?"

Susan found herself unceremoniously deposited on her feet. "What are you doing here?" Levi's growl left no doubt as to his understanding of the answer to that question. "With her."

THIRTY-SIX

Rebekah flung herself in the air, smacked the ball with all her strength, and flopped to the ground. The volleyball zipped over the net and thudded against the hard, sun-dried ground between Tobias and Caleb. "Score! We win. Girls win!"

Tobias planted his hands on his hips, his belly laugh belying the frown on his face. Whooping, Caleb scampered after the ball. "No way, no way. One more game."

"Nee. No more games. It's too dark." Tobias started toward the porch. "I can't see the ball anymore. That's the problem."

"Maybe you need glasses." Rebekah scrambled to her feet, slapping dried leaves and dirt from the back of her skirt. "It's not that dark."

"It's time to start moseying home." Tobias kicked at the stubbled grass with a dirty boot, his head bent. "Chores to do."

"I'm hungry." Caleb slapped the ball from one hand to the other. "I reckon Mudder has cookies in the kitchen."

Hazel took off after her brother. The other kinner followed. "Me too, me too."

"I guess you'll have to wait a minute or two." Rebekah eased onto the porch step. "That's about how long it will take for them to inhale every cookie in the kitchen."

Tobias settled next to her. She fought the urge to scoot closer. He tapped the ground with his boot. "We could sneak away for a quick ride."

"Sneak away?"

"Jah. It'd have to be in the wagon."

"You don't think they'd notice?"

"I think they will eat your mudder out of house and home and then go outside and look for night crawlers and then sneak into the barn to see the baby kittens and then play hide-and-seek in the hay stanchions until we drag them kicking and screaming into the wagon."

He knew kinner. She fanned herself with her hands, not sure if the sudden heat was from the vigorous game of volleyball or the thought of taking another ride with Tobias Byler. She'd been living for this moment since the last time they took a ride together. Waiting for another ride to end the way the first one did. A flush burned its way up her neck and across her cheeks. "Mordecai will notice."

"He was nodding off under the *Budget* the last time I passed through the front room."

"But Mudder—"

"If you don't want to go, then just say so." His smile seeped away, replaced by a frown that caused grooves around his mouth. "Maybe you didn't have as much fun on the last ride as I did."

"It's not that." She'd had more than fun. She'd been overwhelmed with feelings hard to sort out. Careful delight. Fettered happiness. Joy wrapped up with a bow of uncertainty. She couldn't put her finger on it. Did he feel the same way? What ran through him when their lips touched? The feeling that he'd come home? Or fear of the unknown? Fear of falling head over heels into the deep well of emotion like that which flooded her whenever she slipped too close to this man.

All the same, she wanted that welter of emotion again. She craved it. Craved the feeling of being crushed against his chest. No getting around it. Rebekah stood and dusted off her apron. "Let's go."

"Fine." He stood. "After you."

"Fine." She stalked ahead to the spot where the horse nibbled at sparse grass next to the barbed-wire fence that served as a corral of sorts. The wagon was nearby. She climbed in before he could start hitching the horse. He glanced back and grinned. "Now you're in a hurry to spend time with me."

"Nee, I'm not." She sputtered and stopped. "You just like to give me a hard time."

"I do."

"Why?"

"Because you make it so easy." He harnessed Butterscotch to the wagon and patted her rump. "And because your face gets all pink and pretty when you're mad."

"It does not. And I'm not mad."

"Okay, you're not mad. You're flustered."

"You don't fluster me."

"Fine."

"Fine."

He hauled himself into the seat, landing too close for her liking. She scooted over. He frowned. "What's going on with you? You act like you're suddenly afraid of me."

"I'm not scared of anything."

"Except sitting too close to me. I don't have cooties."

"I'm not a little kid."

"Gut. Let's go, then." He tugged at the reins and clucked. Butterscotch ambled in a half circle and headed for the road. Lights flickered, came closer, blinding them.

Rebekah shielded her eyes. "Who is it?"

"Looks like . . . it's my daed, I think. I didn't know he'd left the house." Tobias sounded like the disapproving father. "He should be resting. Last time I saw him he was in the front room, talking to Jacob—checking him out, I think. Jacob has taken a shine to Martha—and vice versa."

"He's a grown man. If he wants to go for a buggy ride, he should."

"He's still healing." Tobias pulled up on the reins and brought the buggy to an abrupt halt. "Doctor said he should take it easy."

"Hard for a man like him to do."

Tobias didn't answer. His gaze seemed riveted on the buggy. Rebekah followed suit. Susan sat in the front seat with Levi. Rebekah clamped her mouth shut to keep from squealing in a most ungrown-up way. Good for her. Susan deserved her moment. She deserved to find love. Still, it must be hard for Tobias to see his father with another woman, even after six years. "I'm sorry—"

"Who is that in the back?"

Rebekah peered past the headlights, trying to make out faces in the dark. "Is that your bruder?"

David sat in the backseat, arms crossed over his chest, face hidden by his hat.

"This isn't gut."

If Levi and Susan had gone for a ride, how had David ended up with them? Not exactly conducive to courting, if they were indeed courting. Levi pulled his buggy even with the wagon. His expression was hidden in the darkness. "Did you know?"

The words were delivered with a biting curtness.

The memory of David with Bobbie McGregor in the fireworks tent surfaced. Rebekah opened her mouth, then shut it. Levi was talking to Tobias, not her. Thank the good Lord for that.

"I knew, but I thought I—"

"After everything you went through, how could you let this happen?"

What had Tobias been through? Rebekah opened her mouth again. Susan shook her head. Rebekah sighed and closed her mouth.

"I didn't let it happen. I talked to him. I said all the things you said to me. He's a grown man." Tobias jerked his head toward the backseat. "What happened?"

"Nothing happened." David straightened and shoved his hat back on his head. "Ask him what he was doing at the shop with—"

"You'd do well to hush." Levi didn't look back, but if eyes could shoot bullets, his would've. "He and Bobbie McGregor came into the shop all cuddled up together."

What had Levi and Susan been doing at the shop after dark? From the pink spreading across Susan's face, there had been more than one couple cuddling. Did people their age cuddle?

Levi popped the reins and the buggy jerked forward. He swiveled his head as the buggy passed them. "It's time to go home. Gather up the kinner."

Disappointment curled around Rebekah's heart and squeezed, making it hard to breathe. She would have to wait for Tobias's touch. As much as she enjoyed giving him a hard time, she also enjoyed that touch. That kiss. *Gott, forgive me.* She shouldn't be thinking of herself at a time like this. Especially about hugs and kisses. Love was more than that. Much more. Still, she couldn't deny how Tobias made her feel, no matter how hard she tried. She slapped away the thought. Tobias's family needed him. His daed needed him. She would do the same thing for her own bruder or schweschder. "It's okay, Tobias, another time."

He maneuvered the wagon back toward the house. "I'm sorry."

"Don't be. As you know, we have our share of misadventures when it comes to the Lantz family."

"Jesse and Leila left because they wanted to worship in a different way, not because they wanted to fraternize with Englischers."

It was good of him to see the difference. Many Amish—including some in her own district—would not make that distinction. Even Mudder had difficulty doing it. "Either way, it hurts to lose them."

"I'll not lose David."

The steely determination in his voice told Rebekah he wasn't a man easily deterred when he made up his mind about something. Had he made up his mind about her? His touch said he had. *Thank You, Gott.* "What did your daed mean about 'after all you've been through'?"

Tobias parked the wagon next to the fence with a soft, "Whoa." They sat without talking for a minute or two. He wound the reins around his left hand and then unwound them. "It pains me to tell you this, but it might be you have a right to know. If things go the way I hope they will."

"Know what?" More importantly, what things and what way did he want them to go?

"Up north, I got tangled up with an Englisch girl."

"Was it serious?"

"I loved her."

A pain as sharp as the crunch of a bone crushed under a two-ton horse sliced through Rebekah's chest. He'd loved another. His heart had been taken. She heaved a breath. Past tense. He loved her in the past. Not now. Not anymore. Rebekah took another breath and interlocked her fingers in her lap to keep them still. Her throat hurt from swallowing inexplicable tears. He had loved another. She was no one's first. "What happened?"

"I realized it was a mistake. That's why we moved down here." He cleared his throat. "I chose my district, my family, my faith over Serena."

Serena. What a nice name. Rebekah could imagine her. Long black hair, dark eyes, lipstick and eye makeup. Jeans and blouses that left nothing to the imagination. How did a Plain woman compete with that? Nee, she didn't have to compete. Tobias chose long before he met her. "But still, you loved her."

"Ripped my heart in two, but I know it was the right thing. I am Plain. However I felt about Serena, I did not have those feelings for her way of life."

"But she felt the same about you?"

"She said she did. I believe she did. She'll never forgive me, I reckon."

"And now you're over her?"

"I regret causing her hurt. I regret letting it go as far as I did. For not showing better judgment and restraint." Tobias swiveled on the seat so he faced her. "Serena was—is—a good person, a good woman. Smart and kind. I hurt her and what I did was wrong. I asked her to forgive me and she said she did, but I know she didn't understand. She couldn't."

For a man like Tobias to like, even love her, Serena would have to be that kind of woman. Someone who could hold her own with him. Questions bombarded Rebekah like tiny, razor-sharp knives that pricked and wounded. Would he feel that way about her, given time? Did she have the qualities that would make him want to be with her and no one else? Keeping her gaze on the corral fence, she cleared her throat. "Your love sound strong."

"It was. It had to be in order to drive me from all that I know and believe in."

"How do you know you won't ever do that again?"

"You mean how do *you* know I won't do it again?"

"I'm only a Plain woman."

Tobias's chuckle sounded weak. His fingers traveled across the small space between them and tucked themselves around hers. "You have your own ways. You are Plain in faith, but not so in looks nor heart. I close my eyes at night and I see you smiling at me with those dimples. I can hear your voice and the way you say my name."

Heat washed over Rebekah in scalding waves. She saw similar images of Tobias when she closed her eyes at night. Now she would see him with another. She tugged her hand free and scooted to the far end of the seat. It didn't seem far enough. "This isn't about looks. It's about a way of life and a way of thinking." She hopped from the wagon, seeking solid ground beneath her feet. She turned and looked up at him. "I don't want to be anyone's second choice."

With her last ounce of willpower, she pivoted and plodded toward the house without looking back.

THIRTY-SEVEN

Saying the wrong thing to women seemed to be Tobias's strong suit. His arms as heavy with fatigue as his mind, he pulled the wagon into the barn and tugged on the reins to bring it to a halt. On the workbench along one wall, Daed had left a lit kerosene lantern, its flame flickering in the humid night air. It wasn't like him. The potential for a fire that would destroy their most important work tools—their horses—loomed too great. Still contemplating how telling the truth could cause a man such grief, Tobias hopped from the wagon and began to unhitch Butterscotch.

A disgusted grunt stopped him in midstep. He whirled and peered into the closest stall. David sprawled in the hay, head propped on a bale. That explained the lantern. Tobias turned his back on his brother and went back to his task.

"Sorry we messed up your ride with Rebekah."

"Why are you out here?"

"Daed said I should sleep here. He said I shouldn't be around the kinner. It's like he's practicing *meidung* when I'm still on my rumspringa. I haven't made any choices. Isn't that the point of all this?"

"You went to the shop with Bobbie."

"To talk. To tell her I'm not sure."

"Not sure of what?"

"Of anything."

A flicker of hope sprang up in Tobias's chest. He breathed and fanned the flame as he led Butterscotch into her stall and picked up a brush. "When we talked before, you made it sound like you had made up your mind."

"When I'm with Bobbie I feel like a different person." David hauled himself to his feet and walked to the stall gate, dusting off his hands as he went. "But when I come home, I see the kinner playing and Martha in the kitchen and life is exactly the way it should be."

"Like you're being split in two."

"Jah. Ripped in two."

"I remember that feeling." Tobias rested his head against Butterscotch's warm flank for a second and closed his eyes. It was easier to talk about this with his back to his brother. "Like I told you the last time, I've been where you are. I know how it feels."

"I know you do and I know how it ended. I know I have to make this decision for myself, but I look at you and wonder how long it will take to get over someone as beautiful inside and out as Bobbie. You still moon around over Serena."

"Not anymore."

"You think Rebekah will make you forget her, finally."

"I don't know." He raised his head and turned to face David. "She seemed pretty upset to find that I had feelings for another woman."

"You told her."

"Nee, Dad did. Because of you."

David's face reddened. "Sorry."

"She had to know sooner or later." Tobias led Butterscotch into her stall, then shut the gate. He turned back to David. "Talk to Daed. If that doesn't work, try Mordecai. He's a wise man."

"Or talk to me."

Tobias looked beyond his brother to the barn door. Bobbie stood in the opening. She moved forward until her face was backlit by the light of the lantern. She'd been crying. Her eyes were red. She sniffed and swiped at her face with a tissue. "Do you mind, Tobias? I need a word with your brother."

"You shouldn't be here."

"If David is going to break it off with me, I'd rather know now." Her voice cracked. "A clean break heals more quickly."

"If Daed sees you two here—"

"Go on, give us a minute." David slapped his hat on his head and pushed open the stall gate. "I'll be up to the house in a minute."

The now-or-never moment. Tobias trudged past Bobbie, trying not to inhale that rose scent.

"My dad wants you to keep Cracker Jack. Or sell him. Whatever you want to do with him. He's yours."

"What?" He looked back. "We can't just keep him."

"He says he's a problem horse. He won't ever be a ranch horse. If you can train him, he's yours."

"We'll talk later."

Maybe. If David decided to stay. If he went, there would be no talking. And the horse would go back if Daed had to deliver him personally.

Tobias forced himself to keep walking. Whatever happened now was between David and Bobbie.

THIRTY-EIGHT

Don't think, simply work. Easier said than done. Rebekah straightened, hand on her aching back. Her fingers stuck to the damp fabric of her dress. Picking tomatoes in the July heat was not her idea of fun, but the canning frolic later in the week would make up for it. All those jars of stewed tomatoes and tomato sauce lined up on the shelves in the cellar would hold them in good stead come winter. Too bad it didn't keep her mind off her heart and the audacity of Tobias to have loved another before her.

Her mind skittered away from the pain that thought brought. *Don't think. Don't think. Don't think.*

The screech of a horn mingled with the chatter of birds perched on the mesquite tree that offered her no shade. Startled, she whirled to peer toward the road. They had Englisch visitors. The interruption would be welcome. Any excuse to get out of the sun for a few minutes. She shaded her eyes with sweaty fingers. A green Volkswagen puttered along the dirt road, a steady stream of dust billowing behind it.

Leila. Not the visitor she wanted. Another source of pain. "What's she doing here?" Rebekah directed the question to Butch, who lay sprawled in the sparse grass in the shade of a live oak, head resting on his paws, eyes closed. He didn't even raise his head to look. "Some watchdog you are."

The dull ache of disappointment and discontent her sister's name tended to produce seemed fainter today. Leila took care of Lupe and Diego. Jesse was trying to find their dad. He would try to find a way for them to stay. Rebekah thanked Gott for that.

Forgiveness seemed within reach. If only Gott would forgive her for being so stiff-necked, hard-hearted, and mulish.

Maybe Leila had brought Lupe and Diego for a visit. Maybe she had news on their father. Maybe they had a hearing date. Rebekah laid a huge, almost-ripe tomato in the basket and wiped her hands on her apron. She picked her way through the rows of tomatoes, cucumbers, green peppers, and lettuce to find out. Butch yawned and stretched, then followed her.

By the time they reached the road in front of the house, Leila had her door open. She slid from her seat, her face shiny with sweat, her belly preceding her.

"What are you doing here? Is there news? Did you find the kinner's daed?"

"It's good to see you too. I'm fine, how are you?" Leila swiped at her face with a red bandanna. Her smile belied the irk in her words. "Diego and Lupe keep asking for you. I figured it was time to bring them for a visit. Jesse went to Karnes County, so we have the whole day to ourselves."

Before Rebekah could ask what was in Karnes County, the back door opened with a protesting squeak. Diego spilled out, followed by Lupe. "Bekah, Bekah!" He threw himself at Rebekah, his face immediately lost in the folds of her skirt and apron. "Where Caleb? Liam?"

The last few words were nearly unintelligible between his accent and the way all that material muffled them. Still, Rebekah understood his excited little-boy talk.

"Caleb is in the field with Mordecai, harvesting honey. Liam is at his house, I reckon." With Tobias. She refused to think about that. Tobias with his special friend named Serena. Rebekah peeled the boy's hands from her apron. Perfect little brown handprints remained. It looked like chocolate. "What's this?"

Diego raised his head. A ring of chocolate had dried around his mouth, along with a streak across one thin cheek. Rebekah glanced at Lupe who stood behind her brother, a similar dirty grin stretched across her face. "What have you two been eating?"

"I had a hankering for a PayDay and a soda, so I stopped on my way out of town." Leila rubbed her belly, her shiny face contorted. "Ouch. I have a fierce case of indigestion this morning. I thought the salt from the peanuts mixed with the carbonation of the soda would help. Anyway, the kiddos chose Baby Ruths. Not a bad second choice. They have quite the sweet tooth. Like my husband. They fit right in."

Fit right in. They fit right in here on the farm with their Plain family too.

Rebekah took a breath. Leila hadn't come here to argue. She'd done something nice by bringing them out to see everyone. Maybe they could stay for supper. Spend the night. Nothing said they couldn't have a sleepover.

"You two go on in the house and wash your hands and faces. Susan and Mudder are in there doing laundry." She flapped her hands. "Go on. Watch out, they might throw you in the washer and run you through the wringer to get you cleaned up."

Shrieking with laughter, the two dashed up the steps and disappeared into the house.

Leila leaned into the window of the car. "Gracie slept all the way out here. I don't want to wake her up getting her out of the car. She's teething so she's up half the night. Neither of us is getting enough sleep." She backed away and knelt to give Butch a scratch behind the ears. The dog's tongue lolled from one side of his mouth, an ecstatic look on his face. He loved Leila, bearer of table scraps and good scratches behind the ears. But those days were gone. "Diego sleeps good. Every time I get up with Gracie I find Lupe huddled on the couch practicing English words in a notebook she takes everywhere."

"Tobias said she did that at his house too. It's like she's keeping watch."

"She's afraid all the time."

"That's no way for kinner to live."

"She thinks the bad men are still after her." Leila grunted and stood. Both hands went to her belly. "I need some of that baking soda mix Mudder made for indigestion. Do you think she has some around?"

Mudder had all sorts of home remedies stored in the kitchen at the ready for what ailed her family. She would be excited to see her grandbaby. "Are you sure it's just indigestion?"

"I'm not due for three more weeks." Leila's hand went to her back. "I'm uncomfortable morning, noon, and night, but I was with Gracie toward the end too. Especially when it's so hot. I can't ever cool off."

"Then get Gracie out of the car and come on in. I want to know what's going on with the immigration people and finding Lupe and Diego's daed."

"That's what I wanted to tell you. Jesse found a legal-aid lawyer who thinks she knows where their dad is." Leila's hand shot out. She braced herself against the car's hood, her breathing loud and shallow. "Ach, oh my, oh my."

Rebekah wanted to know the whole story. Where was their father? Could they talk to him? Would Lupe and Diego get to see him? Would they stay with him? In America? The look on her sister's face turned the torrent of questions into one of concern. "What is it?"

"Can you get Gracie? I need to sit down."

Rebekah hurried to unbuckle the car seat, her fingers all thumbs in her rush. Gracie's eyelids fluttered open. Her rosebud lips turned down in a frown. She stuck her thumb in her mouth. "It's me. Your aenti Rebekah. It's okay." She lifted the baby into her arms, amazed at how heavy she seemed for such a small bundle. "Let's go inside. Can you make it?"

"I can't go inside. I'll just rest a minute on the steps." Leila heaved a deep breath, hobbled toward the house, and started up the steps. She leaned over, one hand on her back, the other on her knee. "This baby is making quite the ruckus in there."

"He's coming, then?"

"It feels that way. He or she."

"Can you call Jesse? How fast can he get here?"

"Karnes County is only about forty—"

The screen door opened. Mudder stuck her head out. "There you are. The kinner said you were out here. Where's my bopli?"

Rebekah handed Gracie over to her groosmammi. "Leila is in labor."

Leila moaned. "It can't be time. Jesse's not here. He has to be here."

Silence for a split second. Mudder opened the door wider. "Well, don't just stand there, then. Get in here."

One step, two steps, three. They were in the house. Rebekah had never expected to share these walls with Leila again. Mudder's expression said she thought the same. Her hand soothed Gracie's brow. She turned to Leila. "How are you doing, Dochder?"

Leila grunted. Her breathing was harsh. "If you consider being in labor three weeks early and no mann in sight fine, then I guess I'm fine."

"Don't you have one of those cell phones?" Mudder put her arm around Leila. "Just call him."

"The church gave him a phone, but we couldn't afford one for me." She began to cry.

"Nee, nee, nee, hush. No crying." Mudder put her arm around Leila. "We'll send one of the men to the store to call him. He'll be here in no time. Let's get you settled. We're having a baby."

Mudder would deliver her grandbaby. No Ordnung or bishop could change that. Rebekah hid her smile. She should be horrified, but she could only imagine the joy it would give Mudder to bring this grandchild into the world. It wouldn't make up for all the days that would follow when she wouldn't get to see him take his first step or utter his first word or smile or laugh or sing, but it would be something.

"Get my bag, Rebekah, don't just stand there." Mudder propelled Leila up the stairs. "We'll need towels. Get Susan from the kitchen. Tell Hazel to keep an eye on Gracie. Put a blanket down on the floor in the front room. She can play with her there. There's work to be done."

Jerked from her reverie, Rebekah did as she was ordered. She raced into the kitchen where she found Susan pulling bread from the woodstove oven. Diego and Lupe sat at the table, Hazel between them, eating cookies. As if candy bars hadn't been enough. She handed Gracie to Lupe. "You play with the baby. All three of you." She turned to Susan. "We have a bopli to deliver."

"What, what?" Susan slammed the loaf pan to the counter. "Whose bopli?"

Rebekah explained the situation. Susan's frown grew as the story unfolded. "Bopli don't come that fast. We have time. I'll go find Mordecai. He needs to send Jacob to tell Jeremiah that Leila is here and having a baby here. Phineas is with him. He can go to the store to call Jesse. Be sure to get the number from Leila."

Susan was right. This would be an obvious exception to the rule when it came to keeping apart from the world. Boplin trumped everything. "Deborah will want to be here too. Ask Mordecai to send Caleb for her."

The delivery of their schweschder Leila's baby would be shared by all the sisters, even little Hazel babysitting Gracie. Rebekah didn't want to miss a moment of the time they would spend with this little one. She raced about gathering supplies. By the time she whipped into the room that had once been Esther's, Leila was screaming.

"Ach, Schweschder, I'm so sorry." She smoothed Leila's sweat-drenched hair. "I'm sorry it's so hard."

"It's not as bad as last time." Leila panted. "It's moving faster, which means it'll be over sooner."

"That's a gut thing." Mudder wiped Leila's face with a damp washrag. "You know how to do this. You're doing fine."

Leila grabbed Mudder's hand and clasped it to her heaving chest. "I'm so glad you're here with me now. I missed you the first time. I needed you, but I knew you couldn't be there. It was my fault."

"No sense in pointing the finger of blame." Mudder patted Leila's face with her free hand. "I wanted to be there, too, but that wasn't Gott's plan. I don't understand, but I know He has a plan for both of us."

Leila nodded, her face fastened on Mudder's. Tears tipped the corners of her eyes and streaked into her hair. Mudder's eyes were red to match the tip of her nose.

Rebekah teetered on the edge of a private circle. She tore herself away. Her time might come someday, but it wasn't today. Her heart ached with a pain worse than any she'd ever experienced. Mudder snatched her hand. "What is Jesse's number? We're sending Phineas to the store to call him."

It took only a few moments to convey this information to Susan, who trotted away to hitch up the wagon, her face determined. She would want to be back in time for the birth too. They would all want to share in this special moment, made even more special by being so unexpected. A special gift from Gott.

Leila's scream reverberated in the hallway as Rebekah pushed through the door into the bedroom.

Please, Lord, don't let Leila suffer for too long, but let Jesse get here. Please. Let this bopli be strong and healthy. Let me be strong for him and for Leila.

It was all the prayer she could muster. An hour passed. Then another. It might be faster than the first time, but not all that fast in Rebekah's way of thinking. Mudder's concerned expression seemed to agree. "Is something wrong?"

"Nee, not a thing. The labor is slowing down. That happens sometimes."

As if Gott knew Jesse needed time to get there.

And Deborah. Breathless and flushed, she slipped into the

room. "I'm not too late, am I? Caleb told me what's going on. We rushed right over. I thought we'd never get here. I had to wait for Esther. She's downstairs watching all the babies. I'm here, Leila, I'm here."

"No, you're not too late. This baby is never going to come." Leila grunted and gasped. "Never."

Deborah knelt next to the bed. "It only seems that way. I remember how it feels. Just think of holding that bopli in your arms. Soon now, it'll be soon."

Leila grabbed Deborah's hand, then Rebekah's. "Schweschders. You both know I had to do what I did."

She wanted to talk about this now. Rebekah squeezed her damp fingers. "I know, it doesn't matter, it's done."

"I didn't want to cause Mudder pain."

"She knows that."

"I love Jesse. I love God. How can that be bad? I had to do it."

"I know. We understand."

"You don't."

Leila was right. If nothing else, Rebekah's encounter with Tobias had taught her that. She didn't understand the desire to leave this place and this faith. Tobias had been in the same place as Leila, but he'd chosen his faith over love. Rebekah would do the same, given a choice. Plain Rebekah. Not like Serena. Never like Serena. Tobias's first choice. Maybe he learned something from that first choice. Maybe he deserved a second chance. Mudder had a second chance. So did Mordecai. It looked as if Levi would too.

Who was she to judge?

Or to be so selfish as to deny Tobias joy when he had chosen his faith and family over love. He'd done the right thing and she was punishing him for it.

"Now, now. I have to push now."

Leila's scream blotted out the rest of Rebekah's thought. Her sister grabbed her hand and squeezed. The bones in her fingers crunched. She was sure they would break. Mudder muttered soft nothings, words of encouragement meant for Leila, but soothing to Rebekah just the same. She fastened her gaze on Mudder's face. She smiled, her expression rapt.

"He's coming, he's coming, Leila, I can see the top of his head." Mudder chuckled. "He has hair. Lots of it. Must take after his daed. You were bald as an old man when you were born."

Leila's laugh sounded more like a sob. "I didn't know that. When did I get hair?"

"Not until you were almost a year old. You were late getting your teeth too. You took your sweet time doing everything."

Leila shrieked again. "This bopli is tearing me apart."

"He's a big one. You were tiny, like the runt of the litter."

"How can you remember after so long?"

"I remember everything about each one of my boplin. Deborah took twenty hours to get here and then she fell asleep in your daed's arms the second she arrived. Didn't even bother to eat. Rebekah had a full head of hair and she came in only two hours, screaming at the top of her lungs. She was a big talker even then, and she came into the world in a hurry." Mudder smiled at Rebekah. "She's still in a hurry. She hasn't learned to stay still and wait upon the Lord. To be still and know He has a plan for her."

Rebekah's throat ached. She swallowed back tears. "Impatience is my biggest sin then."

"We're all impatient because we think it's about us when it's usually not. My sin is worry. For all of you." Mudder squeezed Leila's knee. "Come on, Leila, one last big push."

"I can't. I'm too tired."

"Don't you want to see this bopli?" Deborah held on to the other knee. "I want to know if Gracie has a little brother or sister. Don't you?"

"I do, I do."

"Then push."

Leila screamed. Her grip on Rebekah's hand tightened until she wanted to scream too. She bit her lip and tasted salty blood. "Gut, Schweschder, you're doing gut. Keep going. Keep going."

The door opened. Jesse stuck his head in. "I'm here. I'm here, Leila. Am I too late?"

"Nee, just in time." Mudder held up Jesse's new son, a red, wrinkled, squalling bundle of bones wrapped in a faded old towel. Gracie had a little brother. "Your suh has ten fingers and ten toes and his daed's hair."

Rebekah would never forget the look of awe on Jesse's face. "Go on. Come back in a few minutes. We still have business to take care of. Your fraa will take care of your son."

Still looking stunned, Jesse backed from the room. "I love you, Leila, love you."

The door closed.

Mudder laughed as she laid the baby in Leila's arms. "You are blessed by such a loving mann."

"I am." Leila sobbed as she clutched her son to her chest. "He's beautiful. He looks just like his daed. He's sweet, sweet, sweet."

"That he is."

Mudder's words were muddled. Rebekah tore her gaze from her handsome new nephew to glance at her. She ducked her head, intent on her work, as if she didn't know an abundance of tears streamed down her smiling face.

"Mudder, are you all right?"

"I'm wunderbarr." Mudder sniffed and wiped at her face with her sleeve, scissors dangling from her fingers. "It'll be your turn one day. I hope I'll be able to deliver more boplin."

This would be the only child of Leila and Jesse delivered by a Plain woman. Gott gave them this special moment to savor, to make memories, to hold on to when the days of separation came. As they surely would. "Can I hold him?"

Leila nodded and handed him over. "His name is Emmanuel. Jesse and I decided on that name when we had Grace."

"Gott is with us. As He is today." Rebekah cooed at her nephew, touching his cherubic cheeks and smoothing his matted hair. He did look like Jesse, but he had Leila's wide, full mouth. It remained to be seen what color his eyes would be. "He needs a bath."

Emmanuel opened his mouth and let out a cross cry. "I'll take him to Jesse, if that's all right."

"For a moment and then have Jesse bring him back to me. Mudder will stay with me."

Mute, Mudder nodded. She'd stopped crying, but her eyes were red rimmed and her nose as bright as a fresh cherry.

"Gut, I want to hear more stories about how I was as a baby." Leila patted the pillow next to her. "You should rest a minute; you look tuckered out."

Rebekah left them, three heads bent close, their chatter low and content. The Lantz women doing what they did best. Holding the family together no matter what happened.

With Gott, all things were indeed possible, even when they didn't seem probable.

Gott found a way.

THIRTY-NINE

Nothing smelled better than leather, to Tobias's way of thinking. He inhaled and bent over the saddletree, a swivel knife in one hand and a sponge in the other. The pull-down strap was cinched plenty tight, giving him assurance the swell wouldn't move on the tree as he began to tool the design he'd laid out with a light scratch earlier. The oak leaves and acorns were symmetrical, giving him a certain sense of satisfaction when nothing else in his life seemed as orderly. Rebekah was mad about Serena. David was mad about Bobbie. Daed was mad about David. Just about everyone was mad about something. So he would do what he knew how to do. Make saddles.

He had a roping saddle started in the corner, the saddle jockey done and the padded seat that went underneath ready. But first he wanted to do the design work on this saddle while the afternoon light was good. The leather had begun to dry a bit. He applied the sponge to dampen it again and began to tool the design, delighting in the way it appeared under his fingers.

"May I come in?"

The peace of the moment dissipated like fog after a morning

rain that ended with sun bursting from behind drifting clouds. He lifted his swivel knife, careful not to take his displeasure out on the leather. After a breath or two he turned. "Morning."

"Morning." Bobbie moved away from the door's shadow and into the light. She looked as if she hadn't slept in a while. Her braid needed work, her plaid shirt was wrinkled, and her eyes were red rimmed. "You're hard at work."

"David's not here."

"I know. I came to see you."

Tobias dropped the knife on the table. He couldn't do intricate work when his mind was occupied by difficult situations. He would make a mistake, and leather was expensive. "Why?"

She stepped closer. "I like that design."

"That's gut. It's your saddle."

"You're making my saddle?"

"I said I would."

"After everything, you don't blame me?"

"My bruder has a mind of his own."

She touched the saddle horn with two thin fingers. She had a Winnie the Pooh bandage over one knuckle. Something about that fact made Tobias sad. She withdrew her hand. "I came to tell you David and I talked. I told him to go on home to his family."

The knot between Tobias's shoulders loosened. He picked up the swivel knife. It felt warm and familiar in his hand. "Why did you do that?"

"I love your brother."

"So you sent him away."

"I love him and I know him. He will never be happy without

his family." She waved her hand toward the counters and the tools and the saddletrees. "He won't be happy without this. Without you."

"What about you?"

"I've decided to go to A&M in the fall to study agronomics. I was going to do community college first, but my grades are good and I was accepted so I figure it's time to explore new horizons."

"That was a hard decision, I reckon." He knew exactly how hard. "I know firsthand."

"One of the hardest I've ever made." Her voice quivered ever so slightly. "My mama ran off on my daddy when I was in grade school. It's just been me and him for a lot of years. I see your big family and how happy y'all are. I can't take that away from David. It wouldn't be right."

"I'm sorry."

He truly was sorry. He knew her hurt like he knew his own bruders and schweschders. How it took a person's breath and didn't give it back for days at a time. He knew how it ached in the middle of the night. How it was the first thing a person felt in the morning and the last every night. He also knew that with time, it faded until it became a dim memory and a person could start to breathe again. To feel again. To fall in love again.

"David told me about your Serena."

Tobias flinched. The sound of her name spoken aloud was like a punch in the face. "He shouldn't have done that. And she wasn't my Serena."

"She might beg to differ."

"She was a kind, smart person who might have done what you did, had I given her the chance." Instead he'd flung his decision at her and walked away. Still, she'd written him a letter only a week later, forgiving him and wishing him well. "You're a better person than I am."

"Men take longer to grow up, that's all." She smiled, a wan effort, but still a smile. "You'll get there."

"I already did."

"You found someone new? Someone of your kind?"

"I did." Even if Rebekah was mad at him. She would get over it. Or be mad a long time. "She's smart and kind too. You'll find someone right for you. Probably someone at that university."

"Maybe." She smoothed her fingers over the leather. "How long until you finish?"

"A couple of weeks."

"I'll ask Daddy to come out, pay you, and pick it up." Her eyes were bright with unshed tears. "It's better I don't come here again."

"And Cracker Jack?"

"I told you. Daddy wants you to have him. He'll bring the paperwork when he picks up the saddle."

He opened his mouth to protest, but she held up her hand and shook her finger at him. "Have a good life, Tobias Byler."

She swiveled on her snakeskin boots and walked out of his life. And more importantly, out of David's life.

Tobias went to the door. She climbed into her huge pickup truck and drove away, dust billowing, engine rumbling, and the smell of diesel acrid on the breeze. David would hurt, no doubt about it, but Bobbie McGregor had given him a special gift. A love so great she did what was best for him and not what felt best for her.

That was true love indeed. Tobias would make her the best possible saddle. The woman who loved his brother deserved that.

The dust began to settle. A buggy passed Bobbie's truck coming toward the shop. Jacob King had the reins. He jumped down as Tobias strode out to meet him. "What's going on? Is something wrong?"

Jacob gasped as if he'd run all the way from his family farm to the shop. "You should come."

Someone was hurt. Rebekah? "Why? What is it?"

"Everything." Jacob had all Mordecai's flair for the dramatic. "Leila had a baby at our house and Lupe and Diego are there and Jesse came. I went to your house and Levi is on his way but he said to come tell you because you would want to visit the kinner—"

"Whoa, whoa!" Lupe and Diego were at Mordecai's. With Rebekah. His chance to make amends and see the kinner. He would convince Rebekah she wasn't a second choice. She was the only choice. "Why don't you give me a ride and tell me all about it on the way."

FORTY

Finally, her turn had come. Susan settled into the oak rocking chair, Emmanuel cuddled in her arms. Leila was taking a much-needed nap. Susan touched the baby's soft cheek. He looked like his daddy. The events of the past week faded away as she gazed into Emmanuel's round face with his misshapen nose, scrunched-up forehead, and blotchy skin. He was beautiful. Gott did good work. The baby's tiny fists flailed, even as he slept.

She leaned back and rocked, humming the same lullaby she'd sung to Mordecai's children when they were boplin. The same song she sang to Phineas and Deborah's little ones. And Esther's. She sighed, choking back tears. Tears of happiness for Leila. Tears of regret for herself. *Gott, take this regret from me. Let me be content with the life with which I've been blessed.*

"That was an awful big sigh."

Susan opened her eyes. She'd managed to avoid Levi until now. Their paths hadn't crossed since the night in the saddle shop so unceremoniously interrupted by the grand entrance of Bobbie and David. A stab of sympathy chased away her embarrassment. Levi's pain over his son's inability to make the right choice—or any choice at all—must be nearly as great as Abigail's over Leila's or Leroy's over Jesse's final choices. The possibility of raising kinner to lose them to a world so incomprehensible and so often far from Gott would twist a soul into agonizing knots. "Just contemplating the ways of the world."

"A person tends to do that with a new life in her arms." Levi leaned on his crutches and clomped to the straight-back chair that sat opposite Susan's rocker. Grimacing, he settled in and let the crutches slide to the floor with a clatter. Typical man with no thought to a sleeping baby. Pain etched his features, along with exhaustion and a certain sadness. "We haven't talked since . . . the other night."

"Nee. There's nothing to talk about."

"Nothing?" His thick eyebrows tented. "I don't know about you, but it wasn't something I tend to do often."

She smoothed the blanket around Emmanuel, rearranging the folds. "How's David?"

"I thought I'd weathered that particular storm with Tobias." He rubbed at a white stain that looked like paint on his pants, his expression absent. "David is a good boy—good man. I've spoken my piece. As has Tobias. And Mordecai. Now it's up to David. And Gott. Hard as it is to leave it in Gott's hands. I thought I could outrun the devil. As if temptations don't exist everywhere in this world."

"Still, I'm glad you came here." The words were out before Susan could corral them. She was happy he'd come. Why not say it? "All of you. The district needs more families to sustain itself."

"But that's not why you're glad I'm here." He met her gaze. "Is it?"

"No need to get too big for your britches about it."

Levi leaned forward, elbows on his knees, the chair creaking under him. "You look so motherly with that baby in your arms."

"Once again, you sound surprised."

"Nee. I'm trying to move past things."

"What things?"

"You know what things."

"You have to accept that the awful thing that happened to you can happen again or not. But you can't stop living or taking the chance to love again. And I'm not talking about me." Although that would be more than nice. "Babies are lovely gifts from Gott, every single one of them."

"I agree." He sighed, a gusty, lonesome sound so like the one Susan had made earlier. "They shouldn't come with a price."

"They come with all the burdens, heartbreaks, joys, and happiness that we can possibly imagine. We can raise them up, only to have them turn their backs on us and we lose them anyway." Susan reminded herself that she held a sleeping baby. She inhaled his sweet scent and schooled her voice in a whisper. "All the same, they give us hope for the future. They give us responsibility and a stake in what happens in this world. We can never stop fighting for them."

She stopped, unable to smooth the quiver in her voice.

"You are a wise woman."

Susan looked everywhere but at Levi. What did he know?

His chair squeaked. The *clomp, clomp* of his boots told her he approached. She forced her gaze upward. He loomed over her, his face filled with a strange surprise. "Can I hold him?"

"You want to hold him?" She swallowed and breathed. "Of course you can hold him. Sit in this chair."

She rocked forward and stood.

"Ouch, ouch!" He stumbled back, crutches askew. "That was my foot."

"Ach, I'm so sorry. I rocked on your foot? I'm so *doplisch*."

"It's all right. No harm done." He righted himself and sank into the chair. "I reckon it's a minor pinch compared to being stomped on by a horse."

So true, but still. Her cheeks burning, Susan laid baby Emmanuel in Levi's arms and took a step back. Levi's big, calloused hand came out. His fingers wrapped around her wrist and drew her toward him. "Wait."

His touch sent a tremor radiating through her body, head to toes. His fingers were strong, his skin tough. She couldn't move. "What made you want to hold the bopli?"

"This thing with David and the Englisch girl is hard. It was hard with Tobias when he was so sure he wanted a life with his Englisch girl. It's hard to know how to do the right thing with Martha. And there's still Milo, Rueben, Micah, and Nyla and Ida and Liam. I've never known a harder thing than being a parent." He studied the baby in his arms, but his thumb began to rub circles on the skin stretched across the back side of her wrist, sending prickles racing up her arm. "Nothing harder, but also nothing fills up my heart like my kinner. I don't know if I'm doing it right. I only know Gott blessed me when He let me keep Liam even when He took my fraa home."

"You could see yourself accepting more blessings of that variety?"

"I could."

Susan closed her eyes for a second, the sheer joy of it of such a magnitude she feared it would topple her. She wanted to hug him. She wanted to kiss him. She backed away.

He didn't let go. Instead he tugged harder. She had no choice but to bend. He stretched toward her. His lips brushed hers. They were exactly as she remembered them. Warm and soft and perfect. He drew back and smiled. "I just wanted to make sure I didn't dream the whole thing."

"I thought it might have been a dream as well."

"Nee. It happened. It is happening."

Susan leaned toward him. The second kiss lasted longer, reached deeper into her heart, and took up residence there. They kissed with baby Emmanuel slumbering between them. The thought warmed her as much as the kiss. Levi could start again. She could start for the first time.

"Aenti Susan, what are you doing?"

Susan stumbled back and whirled.

Horror mingled with surprise in Hazel's voice. The little girl stood at the door, hands on her hips. "Are you and Levi in lieb?"

Levi chuckled. "Do you want to answer that, or shall I?"

Susan shook her head. "Little girls should be seen and not heard. Go play."

Hazel ducked her head and grinned. "Teacher has a special friend." She sang the line over and over as she skipped away. "Teacher has a special friend."

From the mouths of babes.

FORTY-ONE

A son should never see his daed kissing a woman, any woman other than his mudder. Still, Tobias managed a smile as he backed onto the front porch, letting Hazel scramble past him, still giggling. If he were younger, he might giggle too. Daed didn't need to know his oldest son had seen him smooching the schoolteacher in broad daylight. His daed had found the thing he needed in a woman who'd never been married, seemed almost as opinionated as her brother, and had the same penchant for using a lot of words. Opposites did attract. Like Rebekah and him. He'd come here to see the kinner. And Rebekah. She had to come to grips with his past. She would see that he'd made the right choice. His choice had brought him here to her.

She would see that. Someday, David would see it, too, when he found the right Plain woman for him. Tobias would pray that it wouldn't be in the too-distant future. For either of them.

Until then Tobias would see Rebekah every time he closed his eyes. He would see how she looked that first time he leaned down and kissed her, like a startled doe, with skin so soft and blue eyes so clear. He shook his head as if that would allow him to think more clearly. "Stop mooning around. Find Lupe and Diego."

"Talking to yourself?" Jesse pushed through the door and closed it behind him. Despite red-rimmed eyes and a dark five-o'clock shadow, he looked as happy as any man Tobias had ever seen. With his faded blue jeans, white T-shirt, and black sneakers, he also looked as Englisch as they came. "That's a bad sign when a man prefers himself as company for a conversation."

"Nee, it's just been a long day."

Jesse plopped down on the top step as if his legs would no longer hold him. Butch rose from his spot on the corner of the porch, sauntered over, and nosed the man's arm. Jesse scratched between the old hund's ears. His tail thumped in time on the wood. "The sun's still up. The day's not over yet."

"How are Leila and the bopli?"

"Fine. Sleeping." Jesse rubbed his face with his free hand. "Emmanuel has a mighty good set of lungs for a little boy who arrived almost a month early. I reckon we'll be hearing from him plenty often. No sleeping through that caterwauling."

"You're spending the night here, then?"

Bright red spots pinched Jesse's cheeks. He shoved his hand through already-tousled hair. "That would be too much to ask. I'll go home for the night and come back tomorrow to pick her and the baby up. Abigail isn't letting go of Gracie anytime soon, so she'll stay here too."

"Then let Diego and Lupe spend the night at our house." Tobias eased onto the step next to Jesse, careful not to sit on Butch's still-wagging tail. "Liam and the girls would like that a lot, and I reckon Diego and Lupe feel the same."

As would he. It was hard to protect the two kinner when they were out of his sight all the time.

"I came looking for you to talk about all that."

Something in his tone tipped Tobias off. His stomach tensed. He swallowed and waited.

"I've been talking to people I know from this organization called the Interfaith Welcome Coalition. They're at the bus stations in San Antonio when ICE dumps off the immigrants who've been released after they pass their credible fear interview and make their request for asylum. They give them cell phones and money and help them figure out the bus schedules so they can get to other parts of the country to their families. They have some houses where they can spend the night if it's too late to head out."

He didn't know what most of that meant, but Tobias nodded, still waiting.

"I showed the photo of Lupe and Diego's dad to a bunch of the volunteers. One of them is a lawyer who does pro bono work for an organization called Refugee and Immigrant Center for Education and Legal Services. RAICES. That means 'roots' in Spanish. She thinks she saw him at the shelter in San Antonio."

Too much information came at Tobias all at once. Jesse might as well be speaking Greek. Tobias latched onto the thing he understood. The photo. "That photo is old. How can she be sure?"

"She wasn't at first, but then she looked at the photo of the kids he held in his hands." Jesse smiled, deep dimples appearing. "She said the man was sitting on the floor at the bus station when she approached him. They mostly deal with women and children, but they try to help the men who come in from the Pearsall Detention Center too. She stopped to talk to him because he looked troubled. He had the exact same photo in his hand that Lupe has. I had been showing both photos around to everyone, asking if they'd seen him. She remembered it. He was staring at it."

"The photo of the kinner with their groossmammi."

"Yep. It was Carlos Martinez."

"It's been years since they heard from him. Where's he been all this time? He's not a new illegal."

"That's the thing. He might have been in the States for a while, but if he was working on the border and got caught up in a raid, he would've been treated like he was part of this latest wave. He was probably sent to the detention center in Pearsall and got bonded out. That's what they're doing with them now. Either bonding them out or granting asylum-hearing requests."

"How long ago was this?"

"Last week."

"Would he still be there?"

"Could be. Karen says he was released by ICE with an electronic ankle monitor. They're doing that now to make sure they show up for their hearing with the immigration judges. His is in San Antonio, but not until next year. That's how backed up they are."

Tobias contemplated the horizon. The sun dipped behind Mordecai's barn. Crickets chirped in a song far too cheerful for the topic at hand. A mosquito buzzed his ear. He swatted it away. "Looks like we need to go to San Antonio."

"Yep."

"Did you tell Lupe?"

"Nope."

Good move. No sense in getting her hopes up. "What if we don't find him?"

"Karen says if we turn the kinner over to the Office of Refugees, we'll never get access to them. Once the federal government gets them, no volunteer organization gets near the kids."

"So they stay here illegally?"

Jesse stood and dusted off his hands on his jeans. "One step at a time. I'll call Karen and ask her to drive into San Antonio with us tomorrow to the shelter where folks are staying." He glanced at his watch. "It's a two-hour drive. We'll want to go early. Talk to Mordecai. See if he and Abigail will let Rebekah go with us."

Tobias stood. He towered over Jesse, but the man had a presence about him that made him seem taller than he was. Bigger. Two hours in a car with Rebekah. With Jesse as a chaperone. "Why do you want her to go?"

"She speaks the most Spanish."

"He's been here awhile. Surely he speaks the language."

"Some immigrants never learn English, especially if they are illegal. They don't mix with the general population for fear of being caught." Jesse stretched and yawned. "Don't you want her to go?"

"Jah, I do." The words came out too quickly. No way to walk them back now. "I mean—"

"That's what I thought. Don't worry about it. It's a long trip there and back. Plenty of time." Jesse chuckled and slapped Tobias on the back and strode away. "But just so you know, I imagine Mordecai will go, too, so no shenanigans."

Shenanigans. Plain folks didn't go in for shenanigans.

What were shenanigans exactly? Tobias found himself wanting to answer that question firsthand. Instead he stomped around to the back of the house in hopes he could see Lupe and Diego in the kitchen without coming upon his daed kissing Susan.

Now that must be what Jesse meant by shenanigans.

FORTY-TWO

Refrigerated air felt a lot like winter. Rebekah shivered and tucked her cold hands under her arms. The car, which Karen Little called an SUV, had all the bells and whistles according to Jesse, who seemed to know all about cars. He and this lady lawyer had gone on and on about it as if Plain folks cared about four-wheel drive and backup cameras and folding mirrors. It had three rows of seats so Karen could take whole immigrant families from the bus station to the houses where they could spend the night until they moved on. Now that was important.

Karen seemed like a person who would know what was important. With her gray pantsuit that looked like men's clothes and her dark-rimmed glasses perched on the end of a thin nose, she looked like Rebekah imagined a lawyer would look. Only she was a woman. A woman who wore no jewelry or makeup like most Englisch women did.

Rebekah was glad Karen drove and not Jesse. As much experience as he had, it couldn't be as much as an Englisch lady. Traffic into San Antonio was thicker than flies on garbage. The closer they came to the city, the more it thickened. Honking, squealing brakes, eighteen wheelers, Greyhound buses, pickup trucks. Rebekah marveled at how so many people could live so close together, just as she did every time they came to the zoo or the botanical garden or the Alamo in what Mordecai called the tenth largest city in the US of A.

He always said it just like that. US of A. Only his insistence had convinced Mudder to allow Rebekah to come to the big city this time. Only because Mordecai would be with her the entire time. Only because Lupe and Diego's lives depended on it. Their existence in the US of A depended on it. She shivered again, this time with apprehension. What if they didn't find Carlos Martinez?

"Are you cold?" Tobias reached past her and adjusted a knob on a small console in front of her. The space between them closed for a few seconds, then reopened as big as the pasture where Mordecai tended his bees. "Just say so. Don't sit there shivering."

"I'm not. I'm fine."

Tobias had been quiet for the better part of the trip, his gaze fixed on the road whizzing by in a blur that made Rebekah dizzy. She glanced at the front seat. Jesse had his head back. She couldn't see if his eyes were open. Karen fiddled with the knob on the stereo. The music, already soft and hypnotic, quieted.

A snore trumpeted from the backseat. Rebekah jumped and shrieked. Tobias laughed. "You sure are jumpy."

She wasn't jumpy, just not used to traveling in such close quarters with a man who had kissed her the way Tobias had. Did he think about it? She did. Morning, noon, and night.

"What was that noise?" Jesse swiveled. "Was that Mordecai?"

"Jah." Tobias laughed harder. "How does anyone in your house sleep, Rebekah?"

She squirmed. It wasn't that loud and she really didn't think it was a good idea for them to talk about sleeping arrangements in front of Jesse and an Englisch woman. She studied her hands. To sit so close to Tobias and yet feel so far from him was more than hard. It was excruciating.

"What's the matter?" His voice was barely a whisper. She glanced up. His hand slipped over the leather expanse between them, fingers outstretched. "Are you worried?"

She shook her head and glanced toward the front. No one was looking. Another snore told her Mordecai still slept. "Lupe knew something was up. She came to the bedroom door when I was slipping out this morning. She wanted to know where we were going."

"You didn't tell her, did you?"

"I told her we were going to see a lawyer about what to do for them. She wanted to come."

"She couldn't come."

"Nee."

"Is something else wrong? You seem so far away."

"I don't know what to think." She glanced at the front seat. Jesse was wide awake now. "About anything."

Or feel. This wasn't the time or place for discussion of a private nature. She leaned away from Tobias. "How is David?"

Word had spread about the split between David and Bobbie. Even though the Byler family had lived in the community only a short time, a collective sigh of relief had been heard from one corner to the other. "Moping around like he just lost the love of his life."

"You sound as if you're judging." He, of all people, had no right to judge. He had loved another, too, an Englisch woman with the nerve to have such a lovely name—Serena. "It takes time to get over a thing like that, as you well know."

"Nee, I'm not judging. I do know how he feels."

"Don't rub it in." Heat burned her cheeks. "I don't need to be reminded."

"I wasn't trying to rub it—"

"Karen, how did you get started helping these people from other countries?" Rebekah turned toward the front seat and lifted her voice to be heard over the noisy rush of AC air. "Do you drive all the way to San Antonio all the time to work with them?"

"A few times a week, usually. My base is in Karnes County, though." Karen's face framed by tight, dark curls appeared in the rearview mirror for a fleeting second. "My parents are Mennonites. The home we're visiting is run by Mennonites."

Mennonites. They were a lot like Amish, only different. That's what Mordecai said. With her suit and her SUV, she didn't look anything like Amish. "You're Mennonite?"

"Born and raised. I still go to services when I get back home to Bastrop."

"What does that have to do with the . . ." Tobias seemed to be searching for a word. "Immigrants like Lupe and Diego's father?"

"The Interfaith Welcome Coalition includes people from different churches like Methodist, Catholic, Presbyterians, Quakers, and Mennonites." She smiled in the mirror. "Different faiths banded together to help."

"How did Carlos seem to you?" Rebekah leaned forward to hear over Mordecai's snores. "You said he seemed troubled. Did he tell you what was on his mind?"

"He didn't say much. I gave him a food voucher and a prepaid disposable cell phone. And some printed materials in

Spanish—information on legal options. That's what we do for all of them."

"You didn't ask him who those people were in the photo?"

"It was obvious from the look on his face. People important to him. Family. He missed them."

A *tick, tick* sound told Rebekah that Karen had put on the turn signal. They were exiting the highway. Rebekah pressed her face to the window and watched as the scenery turned from high-rise buildings and stores to houses. It didn't seem to take too long before they turned into the driveway of an older two-story house painted a soft yellow color faded with age. "We're here." Karen put the SUV in park and snapped off her seat belt. "Luz, one of the volunteers, said she saw Carlos a couple of times last week. He's been coming by now and then to visit with a mom from El Salvador who's staying here with her three kids. Men can't stay in this house overnight. It is only for women and children. He seems to be living on the street."

Living on the street. What a strange way to put it. Lupe and Diego's father had no house to sleep in, no money, no job. Where did people like him who were hiding from immigration go? "So he might come here today to visit her?"

"If he does, it will be in the evening. She thinks he hires out with the other day laborers downtown when he can get work."

Karen led the way into the house. Rebekah hung back, letting the men go first. Mordecai smiled and patted her shoulder. "A lot to take in, isn't it?"

"I can't believe we might meet Lupe and Diego's father."

"Are you happy or sad about that?"

Mordecai had a way of getting to the core of problems. "Both, I guess."

"Understandable."

Was it? Or selfish? Lupe and Diego had managed to worm their way into her heart. She would miss them if they left with their daed, but it was best for them. Wasn't it? Would they live on the street too? Or would they be allowed to stay in this Mennonite house until they had a place to go? Would they be sent back to their country with their father after he had his hearing? The questions pressed on her, heavy with uncertainty. Her neck ached.

The house was crowded with furniture and toys. The walls were painted a pale blue that made it seem happy somehow. Kinner played with blocks in one corner. A baby cried in a playpen. The mouthwatering aroma of food cooking—beans, maybe, with bell peppers and onions and garlic—floated in the air. Rebekah tried not to stare at the women who sat at a table filling out forms and talking softly in that same singsong Spanish Lupe and Diego used when they were jabbering, just the two of them.

"Here she is. This is Angelica Sanchez." Karen pointed to the arm of a thin woman with dark hair pulled back in a long ponytail. She stood at the kitchen table chopping tomatoes. Karen pronounced her name with a soft *g*. "She knows Carlos Martinez."

The woman nodded but didn't stop chopping. Nor did she smile. In fact, her eyes filled with tears. Karen spoke to her in Spanish. The woman responded with a torrent of Spanish that was too much, too fast for Rebekah to comprehend. Karen's smile faded. She glanced at them and then away.

"What is it? What is she saying?" Jesse's expression said he saw the same thing she did. "Can you translate?"

"It's too fast. I'm not getting it."

Rebekah squeezed between Tobias and Karen, trying to get closer to hear better. It didn't help. The woman's distress was obvious, though. Anguish bled through every word. She dropped the knife. Her hands flailed, punctuating her words. Karen stopped her a few times, interjecting questions, her expression perturbed at first and then horrified.

"What is it? What's she saying?"

Karen patted the woman's arm and thanked her. *"Lo siento. Lo siento mucho."*

I'm sorry. I'm very sorry.

Karen put an arm around Rebekah and drew her away as the woman picked up the knife and went back to chopping tomatoes, her face once again stoic.

"What happened?"

"In the other room."

They followed her into the living room where Karen sank into a couch and drew Rebekah down next to her. A woman feeding a bottle to her baby eyed them with curiosity, then rose and padded away on bare feet. Karen shoved her glasses up her nose and sighed. "I'm afraid the news isn't good."

"We gathered that much." Mordecai dropped into a rocking chair and clasped his hands in front of him. "Something happened to him?"

"He's dead."

The words seemed foreign. It took seconds for them to sink in. It couldn't be. Not after they'd come all this way. After he'd come all this way. And Lupe and Diego. They had no parents now. Only the grandma who'd sent them here for a better life.

Swallowing against the lump in her throat, Rebekah pushed aside the pillow next to her and the smell of wet diaper that emanated from it. "How can that be? How does she know?"

"Carlos hadn't been around for a few days. He was supposed

to come see Angelica. She tried calling him on the cell phone we gave him. No answer. She was worried, but there was nothing she could do. No way to find him. She thought he'd lost interest."

"He was interested in her?"

"They were trying to find a way to stay together."

Lupe and Diego's father had found love—or the beginning of love—in America and the hope of a new life. The lump grew. Rebekah breathed through the ache that spread through her chest. She would not cry in front of everyone. "What happened?"

"A homicide detective from the police department showed up yesterday." Her gaze downcast, Karen smoothed a wrinkle in her gray slacks. "Carlos had paperwork on his . . . person with the address here on it. The detective showed around a photo of him and wanted to know who knew him. Being afraid of law enforcement, as they all are, Angelica denied it at first. She's so afraid of being deported—"

"What happened?" This time Jesse interjected with the question. "Homicide. He was murdered?"

Karen nodded. "I'm so sorry. They found him near a highway overpass where a lot of the homeless people sleep at night. He'd been beaten and bashed in the head with a tire iron or something like that."

Bile rose in the back of Rebekah's throat. Her stomach heaved. She put her hands against it, willing her breakfast to stay down. Tobias sank onto the couch next to her. He didn't touch her, but she felt his presence like a warm, sure hug.

He sighed. "Why?"

"Why? Who knows? He had something someone wanted. A pack of cigarettes. A soda. He wouldn't give it up. It doesn't take much when people are desperate."

No one spoke for several seconds. The sound of children giggling mingled with voices speaking in Spanish on a TV in the corner that no one seemed to be watching. A woman called to another. Something about lunch being ready in a few minutes. Normal, everyday sounds.

"They'll try to find who did this?" Mordecai posed the question. "It seems a person should be punished for it."

"They'll try, but folks who live on the street are the see-nothing, hear-nothing, know-nothing kind. It's safer not to know anything."

"What will happen to his . . . to him?" Rebekah managed to get the question out without a quiver in her voice. "He has no one to bury him."

"The county will take care of it."

"A pauper's burial." Jesse's jaw worked. He clasped his hands so tightly, his knuckles turned white. "No one to mourn."

Karen didn't answer, but her face spoke volumes.

"We should go home." Mordecai stood. "There's nothing we can do here."

"I have a couple of things to take care of first, if you don't mind waiting a few minutes." Karen rubbed red eyes. "It's lunchtime. You could stay and eat with the families. There's always plenty."

Rebekah's stomach roiled. "I'm really not hungry."

"I don't think any of us wants to eat right now." Tobias eased from the couch. "I could use a breath of fresh air while you take care of your business."

Rebekah wanted that fresh air too. With Tobias. "Can I go outside too?" She directed the question to Mordecai, feeling as if she were nine years old.

His gaze went to Tobias, but he nodded. "Don't go too far. I'm anxious to be away from here and get back to the country."

Rebekah joined him in that desire. She followed Tobias through the living room. Something made her stop at the screen door to look back. Jesse was engaged in a deep conversation with a woman who held a sleeping baby in her arms. He knelt at her feet, his expression earnest, his voice soft. The woman gestured at her child and then at the ceiling.

"Are you coming?" Tobias paused on the other side of the screen, his features obscured by the netting.

"Jah."

She joined him on the porch swing. The yard was tiny, but someone had spent a great deal of time planting yellow, orange, and red flowers. They were sun lovers that arched toward the sky as if seeking summer. Flowers that embraced the South Texas heat. A nice view to take a person's mind from her troubles.

"I'm sorry."

"Why are you sorry?" She glanced at Tobias. Sadness etched lines around his mouth and eyes. "It's not your fault."

"I know how you wanted this to end with a happily ever after."

"I'm not a silly girl. I know better than to expect happily ever after." She also knew what it was like to lose a parent. Lupe was even younger than she'd been when her daed left the earth. "It's just that they've been through so much."

"They have. Too much for kinner so young."

"It makes me wonder what Gott's plan is for them."

"But not to question that He has one."

She rubbed at a stain on her apron. "I believe, if that's what you're asking me."

"So do I, even when it seems impossible to see the gut in

something so heinous." His hand slipped over hers. His fingers, warm and strong, squeezed. "I do see the gut in you. So much gut. A gut heart. You will be a gut mudder."

His praise melted the hard knot of anger and fear of the future that had been barricaded in her heart since Leila ran away with Jesse, leaving her alone and lonely. All her hopes and dreams seemed within reach again. "I'm happy you think so."

"I know so. I can see you running after the kinner, shaking a rolling pin at them and warning them to be on their best behavior when groosmammi and groosdaaddi come for supper."

She smiled at the image. "Are you in this picture too?"

The question came out with no thought to how it would sound.

"I am if you'll let me be, if you'll forgive me for losing my way for a while. If I had known you were waiting, I would've come sooner."

His fingers squeezed again. She sniffed against tears that couldn't be allowed to fall. "I was thinking that if you hadn't been . . . in love with the Englisch girl, you wouldn't have come here and we never would've met."

"Gott's plan then?"

"Maybe. It helps to think of it that way. What else do you see in that picture you're imagining?"

"I see Lupe and Diego in the picture."

She closed her eyes. She saw them too. Diego playing kickball with Hazel. Lupe helping Hazel make her favorite snickerdoodle cookies. "Me too."

"Whatever it takes."

She wasn't sure what that meant.

"We'll do what it takes to keep them here. In America."

"I agree."

"Even if it means breaking the law?"

Rebekah studied the beautiful yellow flowers shaped like horns. "I don't want to break the law. We've already done that by keeping them in our homes this long. I think we should have Karen help us do it the right way. But no matter what, they stay with us."

"Agreed."

Tobias leaned in and kissed her cheek as if to seal the promise. She turned her head until their lips met.

The sound of a throat clearing was like a shot fired. She jumped. Tobias's hand jerked away. The images of their shared future fluttered away on the breeze.

Jesse stood on the porch, frowning. He slapped both hands on his hips, looking the spitting image of his father, Leroy. "You may be away from home, but the same standards apply."

He might as well have said Gott was watching, the way Mudder would've.

"We're just—"

"I know what you were doing."

"Did you want something?" Tobias didn't seem nearly as shaken as Rebekah felt. He eased back onto the swing. "Or is it time to go?"

"I came out here to tell Rebekah something."

She clasped shaking hands in her lap. They still felt the warm pressure of Tobias's fingers. "What is it?"

"You were right. I'm not going to Dallas to college. Not yet anyway."

"You're not? I mean, that is good news, if it's what you want. Seminary was your dream."

"It still is, but you were right. There is work to be done. A lot of people who need my help now. Not later when I'm through studying."

He looked so sure of himself, so happy at the thought. A silver lining in this trip and the terrible news it brought. Leila and the babies would stay close to home. Rebekah would find a way to watch them grow up, even if it wasn't at the house down the road. Tobias's scent of leather wafted over her.

One of the silver linings.

FORTY-THREE

How did a person tell children their father was dead? Now Rebekah knew how Mudder had felt six years ago when she had to tell not two but five kinner that Daed was gone. She peeked into the kitchen. Lupe sat at the table with Hazel and Diego. They were drawing with crayons. Hazel and Diego chattered and giggled as if something had happened too funny for words. Lupe might feel too old for such an activity, but it didn't show. She had great patience, it seemed, for the younger children, praising Diego's tree and helping Hazel with her kitty cat.

"You want me to tell them?" Tobias removed his hat and ran his hand through his hair. "I've had some experience with this."

"I have more Spanish." She inched into his space, longing for a touch that would soothe the pain she felt at being the bearer of this bad news. "I'll start with Lupe. Diego is too young to remember his daed. It won't mean much to him. Lupe remembers."

"And she had hope of having a parent here, family, in this new country."

"Now she'll have no one."

"She'll have us."

The promise in those words made her smile. "No sense in putting it off."

"I'll wait outside. Come find me when you're done." His gaze warmed her more than any fireplace blaze. "I have something to ask you."

Again, a promise in the words.

"Until then." With a quickly breathed prayer, she marched into the room. "Time for bed. Hazel, you and Diego run upstairs and get ready for prayers. I have to talk to Lupe."

Lupe began to stack the papers. "See pretty pictures we make?"

"They're very pretty."

Lupe looked up, one hand suspended in air. "You have something to tell me."

A perceptive child. "I do."

"You find out something in San Antonio?"

"We did."

"We have to go jail."

"Nee, nee." Rebekah slid into a chair across the table from her. "It's about your daed."

Lupe ducked her head and slipped the crayons into the box one by one. "You find him?"

"Jah."

Lupe's gaze darted around the room. "He didn't come for us? He didn't want to see us? Why you not tell Diego? I go get Diego."

She popped from her chair. Rebekah grabbed her arm before she could slip by. A tear slid down Lupe's cheek and teetered on her upper lip. "He not come."

"He's dead, Lupe. He's gone."

Lupe sank against Rebekah's chest and buried her head in her shoulder. "No, no, he not dead. He here waiting for us. He take us to California. We live by ocean. We eat *pescado* and pick up shells."

"Did he tell you that in a letter?"

"No, Abuela tell me that. She said find him and we go to California. We eat fish from the ocean. That's what she said."

The tears soaked Rebekah's dress. She tightened her arms around Lupe and began to rock. "It's okay. It's okay. You'll stay with us and we'll eat fish from Choke Canyon Lake and go swimming in the Gulf of Mexico. We'll find shells there and glue them on wood in pretty patterns. We'll eat deep-fried shrimp and fried pickles. You'll see. You'll like it."

The tears subsided into an occasional hiccupping sob. Lupe raised her head. "What happened to Papa? He sick?"

If telling Lupe that her daed was dead had been hard, this was even harder. He risked everything to come to this land of opportunity, this land of plenty, only to suffer a terrible, painful death at the hands of criminals, the likes of which there were plenty back home. "They said some men where he was staying robbed him and beat him up. He died."

"Bad men."

"Jah, bad men, not the bad men you know, but bad men."

Lupe grabbed a dish towel from the table and wiped her face. She sniffed. "We bury him?"

Another piece of information that would be like a knife in this young girl's heart. "He's already buried." She didn't need the details. Buried in a pauper's grave because no one claimed the body. "You don't have to worry about that."

"I tell Abuela. I write letter." Her face solemn, Lupe picked up a piece of paper and pushed away from Rebekah. "She should know her son dead."

Yes, her son. "You want me to help you?"

Lupe shook her head. "I write. You read then."

"I'll make you some tea."

As if tea could ease the aching heart of a child who now had no mother and no father. A child far from home and from the one family member on whom she'd always depended. Rebekah made the tea and sat with Lupe while she wrote, slowly, carefully, the tip of her tongue peeking from the corner of her mouth, her cheeks wet with tears she didn't pause to wipe away. Time passed but she didn't stop and Rebekah didn't dare interrupt. Mordecai came to the door. She shook her head and he slipped away.

The clock read after ten when Lupe finally looked up, dropped the pen on the table, and shoved the paper toward Rebekah. "You read."

"Are you sure? It's private."

Lupe cocked her head, her expression puzzled. "You family."

"I'll read and then I'll put it in an envelope for you. Come here." She hugged Lupe hard, patted her back, and let her hand slide down the child's soft hair. "You and Diego will be fine. I promise." She whispered the words into her ear. "We'll tell him tomorrow, okay?"

Lupe leaned back so Rebekah could see her face. "We fine with you. We stay with you and Tobias."

Rebekah nodded and said a silent prayer that Gott would help her keep that promise. "Get ready for bed. I'll be up in a minute and we'll say prayers."

"I pray to stay with you and Tobias. Tobias is hombre bueno."

"He is hombre bueno. That's a good prayer."

There were so many bad men in the world, it seemed. To cling to one of the good ones was a special blessing. Looking much older than her twelve years, Lupe patted Rebekah's face. *"Buenas noches. Díos te bendiga."*

Good night and God bless you.

Rebekah waited until Lupe left the kitchen, shuffling her feet like an old lady, to pick up the letter. It was written in such simple Spanish, she was able to understand most of it. Tear splotches ran some of the ink, making it hard to decipher in a few places. She picked up the towel Lupe had used so she wouldn't add to the mess.

Dear Abuela,

Here we are in America. We are safe with a family that is Amish. They take care of us. They try to help us. They try to find Papa. I'm sad to tell you that Papa is dead. I know this makes you sad and I'm sorry I am not there to give you a hug and cry with you. I think he is in heaven. Bad men killed him. They will not go to heaven, I think. He is buried in a nice place with pretty flowers and shade trees. Please don't be sad for me and Diego. We will be good here with Rebekah and Tobias. They will take care of us. They won't let the bad men get us. They let us make pupusas and curtido. Rebekah teaches me to bake bread and plant tomatoes. We will learn English and go to school. Diego had a mouse named Pedro for a pet but he ran away. Now he has a turtle named Tomas. Turtles can't run away. Little boys need pets. I don't need a pet. I wish for us to be together, but I know we can't. Don't worry. We will make our way here like you wanted us to do. We will have the good life you wanted us to have. I will write again when I have better news.

Besos y abrazos,

Guadalupe

Kisses and hugs. Lupe had embellished her father's burial place with flowers and shade trees, but Rebekah didn't begrudge her this. Or her grandmother. She folded the letter in thirds with shaking fingers and slid it into the envelope. Tomorrow Lupe could address it and together they would go to the post office and mail it.

Then Lupe and Diego would start their new life. Whatever it took, Rebekah would make sure they had that. She and Tobias together would make it possible.

Time to go see what Tobias wanted to ask her. Time to see about her own new life.

FORTY-FOUR

A star-filled night sky. The scent of fresh-mowed grass wafting in the air. A soft breeze that felt cool on Tobias's face after the heat of an August day. Karen had given Jesse a ride home. Everyone here had gone to bed. A man couldn't ask for a better place or time to ask such an important question. Gott had led him here, to this moment. All the way from Ohio. He'd given Tobias his second chance at love. The right love.

He inhaled, wiggled in the rickety lawn chair, and tried to ignore the whirlybird gymnastics of the butterflies in his stomach. A grown man didn't get butterflies in his stomach. The screen door creaked. The butterflies soared and dive-bombed his stomach. He squinted in the semidark. Rebekah padded barefoot across the wooden porch floor. She looked tired and sad and all the same, beautiful.

"You're still here. I was afraid it was so late you'd have left."

"Nee."

Now that she was here, he found himself wordless. To take this step meant to give up all his fears, to step out in faith no matter what the future brought. Agonizing joy or beautiful pain.

He could keep his mouth shut and lose nothing. Or ask for everything and have everything to lose.

She settled into the lawn chair on the other side of an upside-down bushel basket that served as a table of sorts. It held a Ball quart jar that someone had used as a tea glass and a pile of buttons sorted by color and size. Why, Tobias couldn't imagine.

"You said you wanted to ask me something."

He cleared his throat. "How did it go with Lupe?"

"That's what you wanted to ask me?" Her tone was irritable. "She was sad. She wrote a letter to her groossmammi to tell her of her daed's death. That's a hard thing for a little girl to do."

"For anyone to do. What did you tell her about the future?"

"I told her not to worry. She said she wanted to stay with us. She said you're a hombre bueno."

"Did you agree—about the hombre bueno part?"

He slaughtered the pronunciation of the Spanish words, but she nodded, her dimples appearing and disappearing.

He swallowed and cleared his throat again. She leaned back in the chair and crossed her arms, her gaze on the yard.

He had not lost his nerve. He would not flinch in the face of a future that included this woman and those children. He stood and lifted the bushel basket to the other side of his chair. Then he shoved his chair over so the arm touched hers.

"What are you doing?"

"What's it look like?"

"Like you've lost your mind."

He settled into the chair and tugged her hand from her lap. "I reckon I have." Her skin was warm and soft. He ran his fingers along hers. She sighed. He lifted her hand to his lips and kissed each finger. "I know I have."

"Tobias."

"We haven't known each other that long." He settled her hand back on her side of the chair's arm. "We haven't courted the way most folks do. Not really."

"It's been a strange summer." She sounded as if she'd been running. "The kinner from another country. Leila and Jesse. David and Bobbie. You."

All combined for getting to know each other in a way that wouldn't have been possible otherwise. Gott's plan? "Before Karen left, I talked to her. While you were with Lupe."

"About what?"

"About representing those kinner. Finding a way to make them legal and keep them here."

"Can she do that?"

"She said she'd try. I told her we wanted them. You and me. She said she understood. She said a married couple would have better chances. Like Jesse and Leila. Or Mordecai and your mother. I told her not to worry about that."

Rebekah's eyebrows popped up. "You told her not to worry. What did you mean by that?"

He was playing ring-around-the-rosy with the words. Instead of coming right out and asking her. There was a right way and a wrong way to do this. He stood again and tugged on her hand. "Stand up."

She stood. The top of her head barely reached his shoulder. He took her hand again. "Will you be my fraa?"

"Finally."

"Finally? That's what you want to say right now?" It wasn't a yes, but it wasn't a no, either. "We've only known each other since April."

"I mean tonight. You hemmed and hawed around long enough." She smiled, the dimples appearing and staying this time. "I was beginning to think you would lose your courage."

"At least you recognize it takes courage for a man to say those words."

She leaned into him, her weight slight against him. She closed her eyes and bowed her forehead against his chest. "You haven't even said you love me. Do you love me?"

"Do you think I'd ask—?"

"Tobias Byler! Answer the question."

"I do love you."

She raised her head, her eyes bright in the starlight. "I love you too. I will marry you, if you'll have me."

"Finally!" He lifted her off her feet and kissed her long and hard.

Everything about the day and the week and the summer fell away. Nothing else mattered. Whatever the future brought, it would be worth it. If they had two years or ten, it would be better than the alternative. They would make a home, they would make babies, and they would have a life together. And live the days Gott gave them on this earth to their fullest. When those days ended, he would go a happy, content man.

He set her on her feet. She swayed and slapped her hand on his arm to steady herself. He chuckled.

"Don't laugh."

"I reckon I swept you off your feet."

"I reckon you did." She stood on her tiptoes and put her hands on his cheeks. "My turn."

Tobias leaned down and embraced her, letting his lips cover hers. What she lacked in experience she made up for with wonder and a curiosity born of having waited for this moment with the man with whom she would spend the rest of her life. Every kiss was sweeter than the last. Tobias prayed that would never change.

EPILOGUE

Spring smelled so clean. Rebekah gripped the kitchen counter and breathed in the scent of fresh-cut grass that wafted through the open window on a breeze that rustled the curtain. Their curtain in their kitchen in their house built by Tobias and the other men. From her vantage point she could see the corral across the road and the saddle shop beyond it. Close enough that Tobias, David, and Levi could walk over for the noon meal most days.

Tobias had Diego on Cracker Jack again. He'd grown so much in the last year, his long, skinny legs hung down the horse's flanks. Cracker Jack had turned into a perfect ride for a boy who knew no fear and loved all animals. He'd spend every day in the saddle if Tobias let him.

A pain that radiated from her lower back into her stomach made her lean forward and close her eyes. She rubbed her belly, breathing in and out, in and out. The baby was almost two weeks late. Maybe today would be the day.

"What's the matter?" Susan waddled across the room, a bowl of bread dough in one hand. Her belly was only slightly smaller than Rebekah's. She wasn't due until May, but Vesta Hostetler had taken over the classroom not long after Susan had realized a baby was on the way. "Did the enchilada casserole disagree with you?"

"Nee, I reckon this baby is finally set on making an entrance."

Susan dropped the bowl on the counter. "And you're just getting around to mentioning it?"

"I reckon there's no hurry. You're here. Tobias is here. Mudder is just down the road." Another pain rocketed across her belly. This one might rip her in two. She leaned on the counter and panted through it. "Maybe you could walk out there and tell Tobias to come on in. He can send David to get Mudder."

Susan headed toward the back door. "Lupe, Lupe, get in here," she shouted as she let the screen door slam. "We're having a baby."

Lupe shot through the door seconds later, her face lit up with a smile that Rebekah had been delighted to see more and more often in the year since the kinner had settled in with them. Her face and hands were dirty from working in the garden, the knees of the pants she insisted on wearing muddy. "Baby is coming."

"I sure hope so. Otherwise this is an awful case of indigestion."

Lupe scrunched up her face the way she always did when an English word befuddled her. "What is indigestion?"

"Never mind. Help me into the bedroom."

Tobias wasted no time in appearing by her bedside. He sent Lupe to bring a glass of water and a wet washcloth. "This is it, then?" He slid his straw hat from his head and began to knead it between his big hands. "Soon?"

"Soon you will hold your son or daughter in your arms. Today for sure." She rolled on her side to face him and tugged the hat from his hands. "You'll ruin it, you keep that up."

He knelt at her side. "Promise me you'll stay. You won't go anywhere."

"It's in Gott's hands. If your daed can face his fears and have a new bopli with Susan, we can get through it too."

"I know. I know." His Adam's apple bobbed. "It's bound to bring back memories, though, for them and for me."

"I was thinking, if it's a boy, we should name him Carl."

After a minute, understanding flashed in his eyes. "For Carlos, for Lupe and Diego's daed."

"Jah."

"That would be nice. They'll like that. You are such a gut person to think of that. More than I deserve." He caught her fingers in his and bowed his head. "I'm so thankful."

The silence that followed was replete with a prayer Rebekah had inscribed on her own heart. A prayer for her own unborn child, for her family, for her mann, for the blessings she'd received and didn't deserve.

"Amen," he whispered without raising his head. "Amen."

"We take each day on faith." She slid her hand through his thick hair. "Thankful for the time we've had together. What comes tomorrow, comes."

He lifted his head, grabbed her hand, and pressed her palm to his lips in a warm, sweet kiss. "I'm thankful that Lupe and Diego are allowed to stay with us. I'm thankful for Karen and the other legal-aid folks working so hard to help us keep them. I'm thankful Daed and Susan are as happy as we are. I'm thankful we'll soon have a bopli to love and protect and so will they. I'm thankful you make the best apple pie this side of the Mississippi. I'm thankful David stayed. I'm thankful Bobbie went. I'm thankful David seems to be spending a lot of time with Vesta these days. I'm thankful Martha and Jacob will marry. I'm so thankful . . ."

The litany of blessings went on and on for so long Rebekah barely noticed the labor pains anymore. She closed her eyes and leaned into her husband's hug. She couldn't wait for this baby to arrive so they could watch Gott's plan unfold before their eyes. So many things remained to be seen and to be done. They would take each step with Lupe and Diego in faith. And with this new bopli. Gott hadn't let them down yet and He never would.

— DISCUSSION QUESTIONS —

1. The Amish believe in *meidnung,* or "shunning," as a form of tough love designed to help their wayward members recognize the error of their ways and follow the rules of their district. It also is intended to shield the other members and keep them from falling into the same temptations. Jesse and Leila weren't baptized so they aren't shunned. Still, Rebekah isn't supposed to spend time with them because she may be swayed to follow in their footsteps. How would you feel about not being able to see or talk to a family member because they choose a different lifestyle or way of worshipping? Could you do it? Would you think it was the right thing to do?
2. Rebekah sees Diego and Lupe as two small children in need of food and shelter. She doesn't care where they came from or how they arrived at the shed next to the school. Would you feel the same way? Would you take in two children who showed up on your doorstep from another country illegally? Why or why not?
3. Has there ever been a time in your life when you thought

you had to break a law in order to do the right thing? How did you reconcile your actions?

4. Levi lost his first wife in childbirth and is raising nine children on his own, including Liam, the child born when his mother died. Levi can't figure out how to celebrate his child while mourning the loss of his wife. How can he be happy and sad at the same time? How can he not look at Liam and see his wife's death? What would you say to a husband in this situation? What words of wisdom or comfort would you be able to impart? Does God cause these things to happen? Is the return of his wife to her Maker cause for celebration? Would you celebrate the death of a loved one as God's plan for that husband, father, or brother? Why or why not?
5. Susan has spent most of her life caring for other people's children. She loves children. She has come to the realization that she wants her own. Do we always get what we want when we pray? Could there be a reason that God has a different plan for Susan? What value does her work with other people's children have in God's eyes? In yours? Could it be more important than giving her the answer to her prayers?
6. Levi doesn't want to risk having another child for fear of suffering the same terrible loss again. Susan is in love with him, but she wants to have children of her own. Is Levi's fear a lack of faith? Should Susan be willing to risk not having children of her own for her love of Levi? If not, what does that say about her love for Levi?
7. Does God intend for every woman to marry and have children, or are there people in this world for whom

He has other, equally important and fulfilling plans? Have you ever been told by family members to "hurry up" and get married or it will be "too late"? How did you respond? Have you been made to feel "lesser than" because you haven't married or are married and have chosen not to have children? How do you deal with that?

8. How do we reconcile our hopes and dreams and wants with the unknown timeline set by God for our lives? What do we pray for when time seems to stand still and our hopes seem to be going unfulfilled?
9. Lupe and Diego entered the country illegally, sent to the United States by a family member who loved them and wanted a better life for them. Are Rebekah and Susan and the other members of the community right to help them, or should they turn them over to the authorities? What would you do? What do you think Jesus would say about it?
10. What does Scripture say about following the laws of the land and our rulers? What does it say about helping those who are less fortunate than us? What does it say about Jesus and the children who came to see Him? Are these scriptures in conflict? How do we know what is right and best?

ACKNOWLEDGMENTS

First, thanks to saddle maker Tom Kline, owner of Kline Saddlery in Fredericksberg, Texas, who kindly allowed me to poke around in his shop and explained the craft to me. Any mistakes are all mine.

The writing of *The Saddle Maker's Son* presented many challenges, both on the page and off. I am forever grateful to my editor, Becky Monds, for her ability to see the story in the mess and show me how to fix it. In this case, she had her work cut out for her. Her patience is epic. I'm also thankful to Zondervan and HarperCollins Christian Publishing for not shying away from the story. It is not my intent to stir the political pot. This is a story about who we are as Christians and how we are called to respond to those around us who are in need. *The Saddle Maker's Son* encourages readers to ask themselves what they would do in this situation. What does Christ call them to do? What are we all called to do? Ultimately, it's a love story, both romantic love and agape love. I'm blessed to work with a publishing team who makes room for me to tell the stories that are laid on my heart.

As always, I must thank my agent, Mary Sue Seymour, for

her support and friendship. Her guidance, encouragement, and unfailing kindness keep me on course.

None of this would be possible without the support of my husband, Tim, and my children—now amazingly all grown up—Erin and Nicholas. I love you guys.

Last, but by no means least, I send my deepest appreciation and respect to the readers who buy books and read stories. Your support makes it possible for writers to do what we do. Your feedback and encouragement bless me beyond measure. You give me the encouragement I need to continue writing. Thank you and God bless.

LUPE'S FAVORITE SALVADORAN RECIPES

Pupusas

Ingredients:

2 cups masa harina
1 cup warm water
1 cup filling (suggestions below)

In a large bowl, mix together the masa harina and water and knead well. Work in more water, 1 tablespoon at a time—if needed—to make a moist yet firm dough. A ball of the masa should not crack at the edges when you press down on it. Cover the masa and set aside for 5 to 10 minutes.

On a clean, smooth surface, roll the dough into a log and cut into 8 equal portions. Roll each portion into a ball.

Press an indentation in each ball with your thumb. Put about 1 tablespoon of desired filling into each indentation and fold the dough over to completely enclose it. Press the ball with your palms to form a disc, taking care that the filling doesn't spill out.

Line a tortilla press with plastic and press out each ball to about 5 or 6 inches wide and about ¼ inch thick. If you don't have a tortilla press, place the dough between two pieces of plastic wrap or waxed paper and roll it out with a rolling pin.

Heat a well-greased skillet over medium-high heat. Cook each pupusa for about 1 to 2 minutes on each side until slightly browned and blistered. Remove to a plate and keep warm until all pupusas are done. Serve with curtido and salsa roja.

Filling Suggestions:

- Fill the pupusa with grated cheese. Use grated quesillo, queso fresco, farmer cheese, mozzarella, Swiss cheese, or a combination of two or more. Add some minced green chili.
- Fill with chopped sausage and a little tomato sauce.
- Fill with refried beans.
- Fill with a mixture of sausage, cheese, and refried beans for Lupe's favorite pupusas *revueltas* or mixed pupusas.

Curtido (Salvadoran Cabbage Salad)

Ingredients:

1/2 head cabbage
1 carrot, peeled and grated
4 cups boiling water
3 scallions, minced
1/2 cup white vinegar
1/2 cup water
1 jalapeño or serrano pepper, minced
1/2 teaspoon salt

Place cabbage and carrots in a large heatproof bowl and add boiling water to cover cabbage. Set aside for 5 minutes. Drain in colander, pressing out as much of the liquid as possible. Return to bowl and toss with remaining ingredients. Let sit at room temperature for a couple of hours or overnight. Then chill and serve.

Salsa Roja (Red Sauce)

Ingredients:

3 tablespoons olive oil
1/4 cup chopped onion
1 garlic clove, chopped
1 serrano or jalapeño pepper, chopped
2 cups tomatoes, peeled, seeded, and chopped
2 teaspoons dried oregano
Salt and pepper
1/4 cup chopped cilantro (optional)

Heat oil in saucepan over medium heat. Add onion, garlic, and chopped pepper. Sauté for 2 to 3 minutes or until onion is translucent. Stir in tomatoes and oregano and simmer for about 10 minutes. Remove from heat and cool. Puree the sauce in a blender (or by hand as the Amish would do it!), adding water if needed. Add salt and pepper to taste and cilantro if you like it.

ABOUT THE AUTHOR

Kelly Irvin is the author of several Amish series including the Bliss Creek Amish series, the New Hope Amish series, and the Amish of Bee County series. She has also penned two romantic suspense novels, *A Deadly Wilderness* and *No Child of Mine*. The Kansas native is a graduate of the University of Kansas School of Journalism. She has been writing nonfiction professionally for more than thirty years, including ten years as a newspaper reporter, mostly in Texas-Mexico border towns. A retired public relations professional, Kelly has been married to photographer Tim Irvin for twenty-nine years. They have two children, two grandchildren, and two cats. In her spare time, she likes to write short stories and read books by her favorite authors.

Twitter: @Kelly_S_Irvin
Facebook: Kelly.Irvin.Author

Enjoy the first two books in Kelly Irvin's

AMISH OF BEE COUNTY SERIES!

AVAILABLE IN PRINT AND E-BOOK.

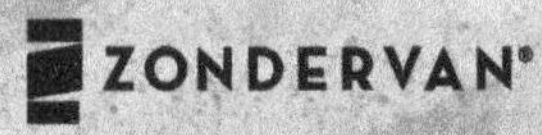

9780310339861-A